WINGS

OF

LIES

BOOK ONE

M.S. Quinn

Wings of Lies

Cover Design by Jaqueline Kropmanns

Editing by Jessica Kendell

Map Illustration by M.S. Quinn

ISBN: 978-1-965304-01-3

AUTHOR'S NOTE

Wings of Lies is a fantasy romance novel that explores potentially triggering and dark themes. It is intended for an adult audience. A list of content warnings can be found in the back of the book.

For the dreamers who never give up.

MAP OF ELORA

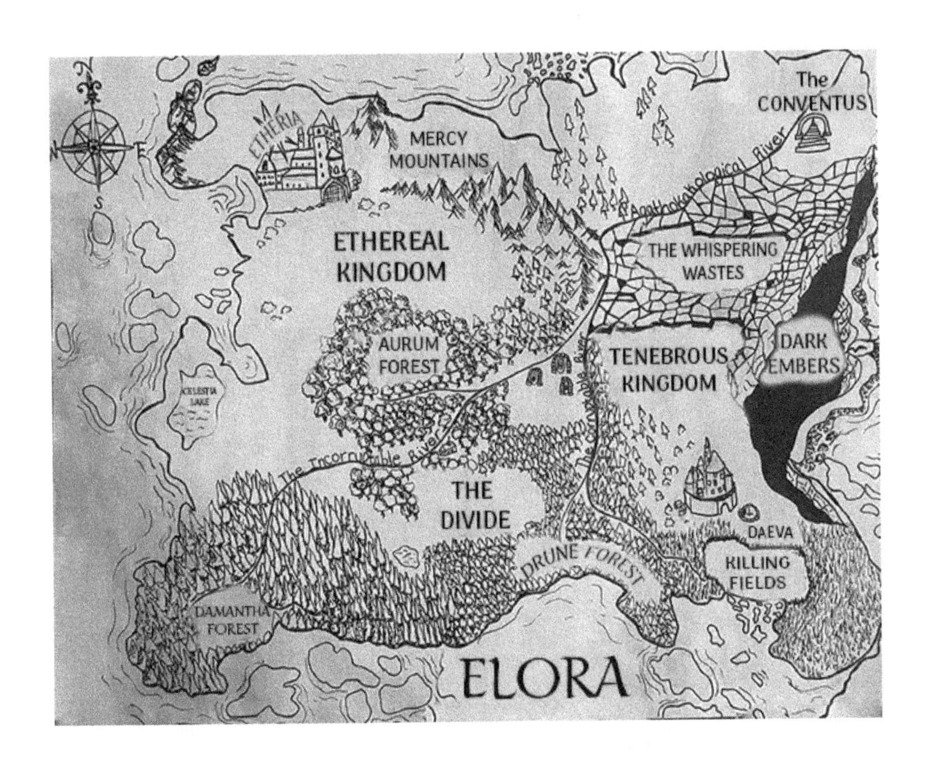
ETHERIA
MERCY MOUNTAINS
The CONVENTUS
ETHEREAL KINGDOM
THE WHISPERING WASTES
AURUM FOREST
TENEBROUS KINGDOM
DARK EMBERS
The Incorruptible River
THE DIVIDE
DAEVA
DRUNE FOREST
KILLING FIELDS
DAMANTHA FOREST
ELORA

CHAPTER ONE

They captured and poisoned me.

I struggled to remember why, how, who—whether it was one person or more—but the memory slithered away into the endless sea of inky black, much like everything else. There may have been a time when I remembered, before the burning sensation seared into my blood, gradually eroding parts of me, but that time has passed. At first, I fought. Whether it spanned weeks, months, or years, I fought the black cage I called The Void until... I gave up.

I let The Void claim a couple of memories. I no longer wanted them. They were as tainted as this imagined place. But the moment I surrendered one, The Void hungered for more—especially memories of *her.* Only a cluster of illuminated strands remained, entwining and pulsating with the remnants of my thoughts.

It was like someone locked me in a cage with my brain, granting me a front-row seat to its gradual destruction.

My mind faded as I watched the pulsing ball. *Who was the* she *I forgot?*

The thought ignited the disjointed, chaotic mess in my mind with a steady light, transporting me to a girly bedroom filled with the clamor of a panicked voice—a memory.

"Lucy, run! Run!"

No, it couldn't be. But my mom had only used that tone—the one that brokered no questions, that held a thick layering of protectiveness—three other times. Each time, saving our lives. He was here. On my nineteenth birthday, no less.

I dropped my mom's book. Fear raced down my spine, and, for a fleeting moment, I yearned for my amulet or her soothing touch. Both quelled the turmoil within. But I told myself I'd fight if this day ever came. For her.

The burst of light dimmed, and the memory faded, leaving me with the odd silver mass and a lingering sense of longing—a bitter, unyielding ache. *For what?* I couldn't remember anymore.

But I was okay with not knowing.

Another section flared, brighter than the last, pulling me into another memory.

I was wrong. It wasn't him.

My mom stood in the center of a quaint living room, surrounded by uniformed figures. Long ebony strands curtained her face and fell over her stiff shoulders. Chin raised, she faced them while I cowered around the corner, forcing my trembling knees to steady.

They outnumbered us. Or... her. But my mom couldn't do this alone. I could catch them by surprise with all their attention focused on her. For once, I wanted to protect her more than I wanted to be soothed by her touch. The moment I moved to join her, she gave the tiniest jerk of her chin, and her eyes erupted in violet fire.

No. Wait! No!

The stubborn urge to stay and fight dwindled, replaced by a surge of urgency forcing my feet into a run. Once within the safety of the lush pines, the urgency yielded to calmness. She'd be okay. Everything would be okay.

The towering evergreens faded, and confusion returned. The Void's slime attached to the bundle of strands, slowly consuming the white glow and reducing the knotted mess to a solitary strand of light—a mere speck in the surrounding umbra. My thoughts faltered, relinquishing thoughts of her. I felt something in the darkness for the first time—a deep sense of dread.

It sparked another image.

A blurred figure of red and black loomed among the trees.

"What's happening?" I asked, my heart pounding in time with my growing uncertainty, disrupting the forced calm. "Why are you doing this?"

"You know why," the figure said, blowing a black cloud of dust into my face.

The walls of darkness thickened around me, urging the poisonous black slime up the thread. Before The Void consumed the whole thing, a ball of brilliant, explosive light fractured my dark, numb world. A cloud of billowing shadows flew toward the silver speck, their wispy tendrils wrapping around the slime and halting its ascent.

Waves of heat blasted into The Void as two figures materialized—one composed of shadows and the other emanating pure, white light.

"Wake up, Lucille!"

I winced from the reverberations of her voice.

"You need to wake up, Lucille!" she yelled again.

I recoiled, needing to clutch my ears, but I didn't have a body, did I?

Am I Lucille?

"Yes."

The answer to my thoughts didn't come from the body of light but from the shroud of shadows behind her. From a pained male voice.

He heard my thoughts.

From the ache that strangled his word, I sensed he knew me. They both did, but I didn't know who they were.

A question teetered on the edge of my thoughts. *What did I want to ask?* I glanced back at the glowing speck of light. The thick slime pressed against the wispy shadows while the encroaching walls of black closed in on the white radiance.

Are you here to save me?

Her light flickered.

The Void darkened.

"Hang on!" she yelled, her voice wavering.

She walked closer, her strobing light doing little to stop the thick sludge.

"Lucy, I need you to open your eyes. The poison won't destroy you if you open your eyes."

My eyes were open.

"Your actual eyes! Wake up!"

Her blaring tone echoed as I tried to understand. She made sense. But I forgot why. The Void had stolen that answer a while ago.

The shadowed man stepped toward her and her weakening light. The inky sludge followed him, its malevolent presence repelled only by the faint wisps of gray and black emanating from his silhouette and the feeble glow she wielded.

"We can't keep this up for much longer," she whispered.

Why didn't that scare me?

It should. I knew it should. But it didn't.

The slime attacked, and she blipped out of existence.

The speck of light in the middle of The Void flickered, surrounded by a swarm of shadows that whirled protectively around it. However, the speck was no match for The Void, which loomed like a leviathan of darkness. I closed my eyes and waited.

"Damnit, Lucille! You don't get to give up! Fight it!" the man bellowed.

Shadows and flames of purple and white attacked, their ungodly heat searing into The Void. I screamed as they burned away the cage around my mind.

Something eased inside me, and I opened a pair of heavy eyelids, expecting to see light, but I was only met with more darkness.

I tensed. But this was... different. My chest rose and fell, and a throbbing pulsed in my ears. I twitched my fingers against the cool press of metal beneath my skin. I scrunched my nose. *What the hell was that smell?*

Urine? Sulfur?

Who cared? This felt... real.

My eyes adjusted to a tiny crack of light seeping through the border of a door. The yellow glow slashed across my arms and chest, illuminating my dim surroundings.

Walls of damp concrete boxed me in, pressing against my naked feet and bending my neck at an awkward angle. I didn't fit. On the table or in this... closet? *Was I in a freaking closet?*

I tried to plug my nose from the wretched scent, but something tugged on my heavy arm. I reached my other arm out to investigate, only to feel another tug in that one, too. My eyes traced from my shadowed shoulder to the tiny strip of light near my elbow.

And finally, I saw them. IVs.

They pinched my arms, legs, and groin. I reached for the hard plastic jutting from behind my knee and followed it to a rattling tube. My eyes shot up, looking for what they connected to. The dim closet made it difficult to see, but three bags of black fluid and one clear bag—hopefully filled with hydrating fluids—flowed into my body. Based on the uncomfortable tube inserted into my groin, I'd probably find a bag of my own urine somewhere below the table. That explained the ammonia smell. But nothing else.

My eyes jumped from the tubes to the bags to the sliver of light, my heart rate ratcheting with every jump, and breaths dying at the back of my throat. Sweat slicked my hands and forehead. I tried to dive back into my memory to find any explanation.

But my memories... they were... gone. At least all the ones that mattered—the ones about who I was and how I got here.

Who cared that I craved chocolate like a madwoman? Who cared that I loved the smell of winter and campfires? Who cared that armed with only bobby pins, I could pick locks like a pro?

The Void let me keep superficial facts about myself while the voices in my head reminded me of my name, and I knew my age from...

My body locked up, ears ringing. Something snaked around my heart, squeezing until tears pooled in my eyes.

Oh hell. Oh, heavenly hell. What was wrong with me? What was this feeling?

I couldn't breathe as the memory tore into me. *She* should be with me now. She should be calming me, so I didn't have to feel this... this... whatever the hell this was!

"Mom!" My voice cracked. "Mom!" I cried, clutching my sternum as if it could force air into my spasming lungs.

"What happened to us?"

A sharp pain sliced into my mind, and an unbearable itching consumed my skin. I cried out and tried to clutch my head but was stopped by the short tubes of the IVs.

Fuzzy purple images jolted into my mind.

I snuggled in a loveseat in a small cream-colored living room, my toes curling into the soft fuzz of the gray rug. A fire crackled behind a chicken-themed grate, filling the space with warmth and the smell of burnt oak. I took a sip of my hot chocolate, relishing its sugary taste, and took a break from the cracked yellowing pages of a book I'd stolen from my mom's locked room. Its unique symbols made my head throb almost as much as the low jazz music playing in the background did. It wasn't my kind of music, but I suffered through it often and through every monotonous day in this isolated mountain home for *her.*

Tears trailed down my cheeks. I squeeze my lids tighter, screaming at my brain to give me something more. I tried again and again, picking, poking, tearing apart my muddled mind to figure out how I got here and where she went. But there was nothing else.

"Shit!" I yelled.

The ringing in my ears increased. My spine begged to move from the unyielding surface, but all I could do was fling my weakened arm out toward what I assumed was a door. I hissed as the tape holding my IV wrenched against my skin.

"To hell with this!" Gritting my teeth, I took hold of the tape and plastic and yanked it from my skin. Blood dribbled down my arm, and I applied pressure, holding my hand against the wound for a moment before yanking the rest of my IVs free. No longer tethered to the tubes, I combed the door's surface in search of the handle. Pins and needles swallowed my arm, forcing my hand lower and knocking it into the doorknob. Relieved, I took a moment to rest my useless limb, and then I twisted.

Locked.

I twisted harder. My sweaty palm shook, sliding against the metal. Metal that didn't budge an inch.

No. No. No!

Needles prickled beneath my skin.

I heaved my other arm over and twisted with both hands.

Tears rolled off my cheeks. I jiggled the knob until my sobs were wet gasps of air.

"No!" A wild energy shot through me. Shaking, I forced myself up and toward the door. But even with the added strength of my upper body, my fingers could no longer twist.

"Let me out! Someone please! Let me out of here! Help me!" I screamed.

Dots invaded my vision, and sand weighed down my arms. Thump after pitiful thump, I pushed past my weakness and continued to bang on the door. I couldn't stop. But the stabbing pain rose. The pressure pressed against every inch of my skin like something vicious begged to escape.

"Please!" I cried. "Help me!"

My screams tore through my throat, raw, guttural sounds. Darkness crept at the edges of my vision until a pulse vibrated the air.

Light lit up the tiny, damp room. I grabbed for the door in a frenzy. But the knob didn't give.

I blinked the tears out of my eyes and gasped.

White flames covered both of my hands.

You always end up in cages, don't you, Lucille? Except, this one's your own doing.

That voice... It couldn't be her, could it? But it sounded like her, only more bitter. The same voice from that dark hellhole I woke from. If it was her, maybe she could actually help me this time.

Stop freaking out and use the power on your hands to get out.

"Why are my hands flaming?"

Because you have powers.

"How?"

She didn't respond.

"Hello? How is this possible?" I asked, waiting. "Why won't you answer me?"

I can't.

"Then why are you in my head? I need help!"

If you want answers, grow up and get out. I'm not allowed to explain.

She sounded so... angry and different from before.

"Answers? Like about my mom?" I asked.

Among others.

"Do you know where she is?"

Silence.

"Please, if you won't tell me anything else, at least tell me that."

Elora

"Where's Elora? Where am I?"

Not Elora.

"Helpful."

I don't want to help you. But I don't have much choice. You'll find your answers once you get out of your cage. Escape and remember the names Oliver and Magda. Ask Oliver about Elora, then— She paused. *Magda everything else,* she rushed out.

"And I'll find my mom that way?"

You'll find your answers. But Magda's answers come at a price. Her voice was fading.

If she knew where my mom was, I'd pay any price.

"Wait, but who's Oliver? And how am I supposed to escape? The room is locked!" I yelled.

Use your powe...

"Wait!" I yelled, but she never returned.

I looked down at my hands, bringing them closer to my body. They flickered with white flames but weren't hot. How in the world were they going to help me?

"Can you manifest keys?" I asked. Dammit, I was losing it.

For the sake of trying everything, I put my hand on the doorknob and said, "Unlock."

It didn't unlock. So, she was lying. Or, yet again, I was crazy.

"Open," I said, trying again.

The flames danced around my hand and the cool knob, achieving nothing. No surprise there. *Was this even real, or was I hallucinating?*

Suddenly, metallic fumes filled the small space, stinging my eyes. I blinked as the doorknob melted into a pool of molten metal, then disintegrated into particles of glowing ash.

I sat there, trembling as the flames sank back into my skin.

This couldn't be happening.

But I didn't have time to understand. The door was unlocked. I could escape and find my mom. Once I found her, everything would be back to normal. It'd be okay.

I shifted, letting my legs dangle over the table, and felt a tug in my groin. Dammit, the catheter. Tensing, I grabbed the tube and slowly dragged it out of my body. I clenched my teeth. Black specks clouded my vision as it popped out, and the sensation worsened when I attempted to stand. Numbness shot up my limbs, and I collapsed against the table, blacking out.

CHAPTER TWO

There were three things increasingly odd about this dream: a purple hue tinted my vision, I invaded the body of a younger version of myself, and the dream seemed familiar.

I wanted to scream. I wanted to slam my door in her rigid face. The urge tore at my insides, burning and lashing out, growing more destructive as it gained momentum. I punched the wall. The pain cleared my head enough to resort to smashing my face into my stupid frilly pillow and screeching.

How could she?

All I wanted to do was to go into town and see what all the fuss was about. But no! I wasn't allowed to go anywhere alone, and I couldn't go with her because she didn't trust people around me! Or she didn't trust *me*. So, I remained stuck here, stuck in this damned house.

Was she punishing me? Was this still all because of him, and what happened?

The first three years, I understood. We were on the run, jumping from town to town. I followed her lead as she protected me. The blocking rune locked away my powers, reduced me to a human, and helped to keep me hidden. But we had no stability and no way of contacting anyone. So, the lack of friends or the friends I left behind when he found out I went to public school hadn't bothered me.

But now, after months of being in the same place, still blocked and safe, she continued to isolate me.

I couldn't even use our phone to call my old school friends. It was for emergencies when she had to go into town and left me at the house. She suffocated me, keeping me captive, surrounded by fields and livestock. My only entertainment included movies, books, and animals that didn't talk back. There was no one else. Public school was now forbidden. She always said, "It wouldn't be safe," "We can't, Lucy," "What if the rune or amulet stopped working and you had an incident and he found us?"

Fine. Her logic made sense. Kind of. But not even allowing me to go into town with her? I was to be sequestered, never to see anyone else ever again?

Would this forever be my life?

The thought put pressure behind my eyes.

This wasn't living!

I slammed my face into the pillow. My head and skin throbbed. Tumultuous emotions tore into my soul, sending a painful pressure and an itch from the top of my head to my toes. That should've concerned me, but I was so overcome by the foreign feelings I didn't think about it.

I squished my face harder into the pillow, nails ripping at the chiffon fabric, and let out another screech. This time, it helped. The release eased some pressure on my muscles.

"Lucy!"

My head whipped up at her voice, eyes widening, unable to fully comprehend the situation as I gazed around.

I glanced at my wrist. The black rune had faded to white, resembling a scrawling scar. I had felt the pressure and itch, but I assumed the release and the lessening of my anger had come from the amulet against my chest, which should've been the color of the elderberries surrounding our house. Instead, my release came from the white and purple flames engulfing my body and bed.

Her worst fears come to life.

Never, not since I'd grown into my powers, had it covered me so fully. And never had the white mixed with such a deep purple.

Everything throbbed—my head, my skin, the crushing pressure on my chest. I fixed my wide, blurry eyes on my mom, needing her help. Her eyes flashed purple, and I waited for the calm. She tried again, and as the pinks of her cheeks paled, I knew she couldn't penetrate my flames.

"Let it go," she whispered.

My powers consumed my clothing, bedding, and headboard. Then it jumped to the wall behind me. The wood and fabric burned swiftly, but so did the brick.

Shock pierced my power and quenched the flames on my skin, but not the flames burning our house. I scurried off my bed. The moment my power left me, my mom touched my bare shoulder, sending a seed of calm into my pounding chest.

Things happened fast after that. She wrapped me in my night robe and hurried me from my room, steering me toward the kitchen.

"I'll be right back," she said, running to her room. Then she returned from the smokey hall, coughing and carrying two duffle bags.

It was déjà vu all over again.

"Let's go. Hurry." She herded me to our front door.

"I don't understand." My voice wobbled.

It took us three years to find this home, to stop bouncing from place to place. And it took five months for my built-up restlessness to ruin it—all because I wanted to go into town, all because of my anger over things I didn't have and wanted.

I should've known when I felt my anger that the amulet was depleted. This was all my fault.

My mom touched me again. The same calm tenderly softened the sharp bitterness of my mind.

We rushed out of our small, burning farmhouse and jumped into the stolen, beat-up, green VW Bug.

She held out her hand. "Give me it."

I unclasped the amulet and placed it in her outstretched palm. A lovely purple light surrounded the circular crystal and its intricate swirls of silver, changing the lavender back to the deep elderberry purple.

I glanced back. Our bushes burned, white smoke billowing into chemical gray. It almost looked like a normal house fire if you ignored the color of the consuming flames and how quickly they ate away at the structure. Half of the house was completely gone, and the other half caved in on itself.

The rising smoke was a beacon in the sky.

I stared into my palms, searching for my power and the stupid emotions that did this. A power I could no longer feel as the shock overwhelmed the weakening calm of her gift. Which she remedied by placing the amulet in my palms.

"Put it on, Lucy."

I stared at it, knowing what would happen when I put it on. I desired it and, for the first time, questioned it.

"Do you ever think it'd be better if I didn't wear it? If you stopped calming me?" She tamed me when my lows took me too deep, preventing me from experiencing the full spectrum and force of my emotions, like I did today. She calmed my rebellious desires.

Her forehead creased. "We don't have the luxury of training you." And by training, she meant my powers because every day for the past five months, we had trained physically, which was why, as a thirteen-year-old girl, I was unusually toned. Although my strength wasn't even close to her caliber. "The rune he forced on you was the worst and best thing that could've happened to us. It helped keep us off his radar. But now..." She peered at the rear-view mirror. "This can't happen again, Lucille Chiara." I flinched at the use of my full name. The soothing of her power did nothing to temper my guilt. "We only have the amulet now to keep your emotions on lockdown and your powers at bay whenever I'm not around. We need to be extra careful."

My mom was right, and I didn't want to give up the calm. It was so much easier than feeling all the horror he branded me with.

"Especially now that your power has grown," she said, shooting me a meaningful look before returning to the winding road. "In more ways than one." It was a soft mutter, not meant for me. More secrets. But I didn't care to press.

My mom would take care of everything. She always did.

Fiddling with the chain, I placed it around my neck, letting the calm take over. My body relaxed. It was better this way—safer, peaceful. As my adrenaline seeped away, the drain came. After so long without using my powers, I had forgotten about the consequences. In retribution, my eyelids weakened, and heaviness filled me.

BLINKING, I AWOKE TO a point of blinding light and a dull throb in my head. I pressed a palm to my temple as my other hand frantically searched my neck for my necklace. I didn't remember what it looked like, who gave it to me, or why I needed it, only that I did.

The bitter smell of iron nagged me from my hunt. Shielding my eyes from the light, I sat up, facing the door and the melted handle I had forgotten I destroyed. Dizzy, I cast a wary gaze at my flameless hands.

I shook my head. It was time to leave.

I tensed, then pushed the door open. My shoulders sagged. The larger cement room was doorless and empty, except for the eerie lights that buzzed above, interrupting the ringing in my ears.

Inhaling, I pushed myself off the table—and crumpled to the floor.

My forearms caught me before my face hit.

I glared at my traitorous legs. Black shorts barely covered my pelvis, and a white t-shirt hung loosely around my frame, leaving bone starved of muscle and dotted with blood. I looked like a three-year-old's stick figure drawing.

With the help of the doorframe, I pulled myself up and took a tentative step. Each step faltered, my insides flinching in discomfort.

But when I reached the next doorway and rested my sweaty forehead against the cool cement, I didn't care.

I peered around the corner into a long, dimly lit hallway. One side led to a dead end, and the other led to a turn. Everything was solid cement, unadorned, and smooth.

No wonder no one heard me when I screamed. They held me in a cement room within a cement room within—based on the lack of windows—a basement.

At the corner of the turn, something tightened in my chest.

Why did it do that?

Along with the pressurized ache, the stabbing needle sensation was back, too.

I peered around the safety of the wall, and my stomach sank.

Stairs. *Great.*

Using the wall for support, I climbed. Sweat beaded on my forehead and underarms. My breaths came out in soft pants that I prayed no one heard. At the last step, I placed my hand against the brass doorknob and pleaded to whoever was listening that it wasn't locked.

The knob turned.

As I pushed the door open, I entered an unlit hallway flanked by closed rooms, stretching towards an entryway and the front door. Beyond the glass, trees swayed, urging me to sprint toward them and escape.

Instead, I crept.

The bottoms of my clammy feet stuck to the polished wood floor. I tensed with each suctioned step, moving down the sterile white hallway. I was one step away from entering the foyer when I heard a snore. My hand flew up to muffle my nose and mouth as I shrank back against the wall. Pressure surged inside my body alongside the stabbing needles.

I knew I shouldn't. I knew I should retreat. But I snuck one look.

A man in a cream cowboy hat slept in a recliner with most of his face covered. I panned between the door and the man. Twelve feet separated me from escape. I lifted my foot, cringing as my ankle popped, and stepped back.

Uncertain whether the door was unlocked and wary of the noise it'd make, I couldn't afford to take the risk. I crept back down the hallway toward a room at the end and scurried inside.

Two floor-length windows faced a vast evergreen forest.

I stumbled over to one, relieved by the sliding tracks and easy locks. I grabbed the lip of the sill and pulled.

It didn't budge.

My fingers grazed the top of the frame, flipping the locks, and I tried again. When nothing happened, I tried the other window with the same results. *Why wouldn't these damn windows open?*

I sat down on the sill, taking stock of the furnished bedroom. There had to be something that could help me pry them open. *Maybe something in the closet.*

I slid open the closet doors and rifled through musty clothes. Hangers scraped against the metal pole, making me cringe. I dropped to the shoes, poking around for something useful. But unless I wanted to chuck high heels and sneakers at the glass until it shattered, I was screwed.

Although... I sat, found a pair of sneakers, and tied them as tight as I could. I didn't want to run barefoot through a forest.

The warmth of the sunlight hit my face as I turned back to the windows. *Why wouldn't they open?* Then something occurred to me.

It was me. I didn't have the strength. My useless, bony arms couldn't pull open the window.

I dug my nails into my palms, pacing in front of the pane of glass. If I didn't escape, he'd lock me away again. I'd never find my mom. She'd never be able to tell me who I was or fix the agonizing pressure trying to take over.

I needed out. I had to find her!

The stabbing pressure surged against my skin, sending me to my knees. I hunched into myself, clawing at my chest.

"What's happening to me?" I cried.

Hysterical, I slammed my fists repeatedly into the window, overcome with the stabbing pressure. "Make it stop. Make it stop," I whimpered.

After the third pound, a white flame burst from my hands. They plunged through the glass, melting a hole through the window faster than they melted the doorknob.

Globs of glowing red slid off my shaking fingers and plopped to the sill, burning holes into the wood. As I pulled back, the rest of the glass shattered.

I jolted. If he wasn't up before, he was now. Ignoring the shards of glass, I dove through the window, hissing and dropping to the ground. My flaming hands scorched the grass. I jerked them back and shook them as if that was their off button. They mocked me, flickering higher instead of fading back into my skin.

Something banged inside the house.

Shit, was that a door?

I forced my unsteady legs up, keeping my hands away from my body, and through sheer willpower, I ran into the forest.

It wasn't pretty. It wasn't graceful. It was hardly even running.

CHAPTER THREE

I stumbled my way through the forest like a newborn fawn for what seemed like hours. My traitorous hands flickered in front of me like a neon sign, turning everything I touched to ash. I was leaving a path to follow without meaning to. But no amount of shaking, blowing, or rubbing them on the dirt put them out. No, they just flamed in front of me—unresponsive and useless. Plus, they drained my energy.

On my fifth fall, I peed myself. My body was failing me. I couldn't keep this up. But resting intensified the squeezing pressure on my chest and heightened my flames. While running didn't cure the feeling, it helped to lessen it.

After so many falls, my legs refused to stand. Sunlight waned behind the canopy of trees, turning my hands into even more of a beacon.

I heaved in and out, looking left and right for a cream cowboy hat. But before my quick breaths could suffocate me, my flames sank in time with my eyelids.

STARTLED AWAKE BY A snap, I found myself in a moonlit forest. I tensed, listening intently as someone moved in the distance. They took a few steps, then paused as if uncertain of their destination, or they were searching for someone. I scooted closer to the thick brush and only relaxed when the noise faded.

My forehead dropped, and I held back a groan as my entire body throbbed. Luckily, they didn't catch me while I slept, but I couldn't hide here.

With a little more energy, I stood, grabbing onto a small branch to help support my measly weight, grateful my stupid flames were put away. It bent, but it held as much as my wobbly limbs did. I stepped, wincing at the crunch of leaves resonating in the quiet, and wandered through the shadowed trees with my arms wrapped around my body.

If only I knew where I was and what the heavenly hell had happened to my memories and my—Footsteps crunched in the distance.

I darted behind a tree trunk. The damned crushing pressure sensation took over as they approached. I stifled my quick breaths, cramming against the rough bark, and they passed me.

Oblivious.

The tall guy didn't know I was there. He walked through the forest without a care in the world.

It couldn't be a coincidence that he was here, could it? He wasn't wearing cowboy attire, but who's to say he wasn't working with the other guy?

I didn't know. But I also didn't have the luxury to let him go. With his casual confidence, he clearly knew his way around these woods, and without water or food, I wouldn't survive trying to find a way out alone. But I also wasn't stupid enough to give myself up.

I let him walk ahead before creeping after him.

After passing a few trees, black dots shimmered before my eyes, making me sway. I shot out a foot to steady myself, caught a root, and tumbled to the ground.

My head jerked up, and our gazes met.

"You can see me?" he asked, shocked.

I nodded and sat up, not bothering to brush myself off. Dirt and grime covered me, along with blood, urine, and sweat. A little more dirt didn't matter.

"Am I not supposed to?" I eyed his jeans and the green sweater that swallowed his skinny frame.

If he were one of my captors, he wouldn't look so surprised, right?

He tilted his head to the side. "Are—" He snapped his head up, breaking off his sentence.

Soft voices sounded in the distance. The stranger's face paled. "Get up, skinny girl!" he said, gesturing to me.

I wanted to, but like a disconnected fuse, my legs only twitched. My muscles refused to lift my helpless sacks of bones.

"Get up!" He waved his hands frantically.

I wanted to. I wanted to stand as badly as I wanted to breathe. But I'd given my everything and had nothing left.

"I can't," I said, eyes a silent plea to the stranger.

He looked between the noise in the distance and me, then crouched and grabbed my arm.

"What—"

He pulled me across his shoulders like a scarf. "Sorry, kind of. But this isn't going to be comfortable for you. Just hold on."

I only nodded as he took off away from the voices.

Either I weighed nothing, or this guy had more muscles than I realized as he sprinted through the trees. Also, he possibly had night vision as he avoided stumbling in the darkness, weaving through the forest, and running faster than I thought possible.

"Where are we going?" My voice bobbed up and down. His shoulder pressed into my lungs with each push off the ground.

"So far straight. Maybe a turn here or there. Then straight again to get far away and keep our pretty little heads."

I snorted.

"I'm glad you think this is funny. Currently, my kidney thinks otherwise as you repeatedly beat it with your knee," he said, barely winded. Which was odd, considering he ran at breakneck speed while carrying me.

"I don't. It's just the way you said it."

He nodded. "Glad I could help. Now, mind telling me why a young girl dressed for summer wanders through this forest during fall, all alone, and looking half dead?" The ease at which that sentence came out of his mouth gave me pause. *Was this situation normal in these woods, or was he trying to keep the mood light for my benefit?*

The nippy night made more sense now. At least his body heat seeped through his sweater, chasing away most of the goosebumps covering my exposed limbs.

Choosing not to answer his question, I asked my own, using the same tone. "Mind telling me why a young guy like yourself wanders through this forest during fall, all alone, and acting like he's supposed to be invisible?"

It was his turn to snort as he leaped over a log, not breaking his stride. "Touché."

My eyes narrowed, panning between the back of his head and the forest behind us. I couldn't tell if our pursuers were there. But I took the lack of noise as a good sign.

"Are you going to answer me? Or better yet, tell me how you knew we were in danger?" It might've been some other danger I didn't know about, but I suspected it wasn't, and he somehow sensed it.

His back vibrated with laughter. "Naw. So, interesting young girl who wanders through forests not dressed for the weather, where's that leave us?"

Why did he keep calling me a young girl? I was definitely not as young as his tone implied. "How about with names? So, you can quit acting like I'm twelve."

He jumped over a small trickle of water, and the landing jostled me lower. Heaving me back into place, he resumed the sprint with labored breaths.

"But you're pretty small. I mean, I can feel all your bony limbs. There's hardly any weight to you. Maybe thirteen, then?"

I glared at the back of his head, regretting that he couldn't see it. The bouncing up and down, completely at his mercy, also didn't help. But that didn't stop my snappy reply. "So are you." My body currently looked twelve years old because starvation and the inability to move for weeks, months, or years on end would do that. But I wasn't about to enlighten him on those facts.

By his silence, I suspected my words hit a nerve. He may be tall, but he lacked definition. Whatever muscle he had was just enough to carry my starved body.

"Oliver," he said, tone sobered.

I jolted, staring with wide eyes at the back of his head.

Oliver? Like the person I needed to find? Was this some trick?

"Lucille," I said, keeping my voice steady.

The harsh air pushing out of his lungs filled the quiet. Glancing back, I strained my ears for any other noise, hearing nothing but Oliver. "I think we lost them."

He laughed. "*I* lost them. You're lucky you weigh like twenty pounds, or else the ending of this story would've been more tragic."

Slowing to a jog, then a walk, the trees dispersed, opening to the twinkling lights of a town across a grassy field. My throat closed at the sight.

Oliver eased me to the ground and plopped himself next to me. We both took this moment to rest, staring at the lights ahead. My chest and sternum thanked me for it. Although no longer forced against his body heat, the damp grass pulled goosebumps from the backs of my thighs.

I glared at them. Would they even be able to carry me to the lights, or would Oliver have to help again? I shifted my attention to him.

With the strength of the full moon, a black streak in his bangs stood out against the mop of blonde hair. They flowed into his light eyelashes that bordered emerald eyes. The color matched the sweater that swallowed his slim build. As long as the sweater was, it still barely skimmed the top of his jeans. It couldn't quite fit his height, which made sense as he towered over me while I sat beside him.

"You know, staring at strangers is slightly rude. Is there a reason you're looking at my body?"

My eyes shot to his, cheeks warming. "You're tall."

He scanned me up and down. "I'm tall? You practically analyzed every inch of me, and that's all you say? I'm tall? No compliments, no questions, just a two-word statement?"

I nodded, frowning at his blubbering.

"Have you looked at you? Are you sure you're not just short?"

I raised my eyebrows. My brain might've been working slower than usual and lost most of its memory, but that didn't make me stupid.

He smirked. "I'm 6'6". So yeah, I'd say I'm tall. But you're still short. And I'm still not positive you're not twelve."

I sighed and followed his gaze to my bony legs. Brown and blue covered almost every inch of my limbs. Somewhere in the grime, blood and urine hid, like they hid in my black shorts. I didn't let myself think about how I smelled. My hair—I reached an arm up to finger the frizzy dark ends. I plucked a leaf out of the waves, knowing there was most likely more.

A breeze carried the leaf, tumbling across the grass. I tucked my knees to my chest and wrapped my arms around them, curling into a tiny ball—a twelve-year-old child indeed.

"Here." A swath of green fabric landed across my knees.

I turned my head toward Oliver. "I—"

He cut off my objections. "I think your goosebumps have goosebumps. Not to mention, you look like a starved, abused animal. At least with the sweater, you'll only scare half the people in town." The side of his lips quirked in a crooked smile. "Plus, I have this"—he plucked at his white, long sleeve—"muscle on my bones and a cheery personality to keep me warm."

Right. And boatloads of energy.

Conceding, I shoved the sweater over my head, smelling spring rain. Heavenly heat soothed my spiky skin. Extra fabric bunched at my hips and wrists. Once I stood, it'd cover me mid-thigh, making me look more childlike. But if it could conceal the dirt and bruises, plus keep me comfortable, I didn't care.

"So, does this mean you're following me to town?" I hoped I didn't sound too eager.

A mischievous glint lit his face. "I don't know. Maybe. I guess that depends on whether you can stand."

I didn't know if I wanted to laugh or stab him in the eye.

He chuckled at my glare and pushed off the ground. "But really, can you? We might've got a head start, but I don't want to test how long it takes them to find us. Which they won't. If we move."

In the distance, lights enticed me with the promise of food and water, possibly safety, and, if I was lucky, a warm bed.

"You got this, Lucille," I whispered under my breath, pushing back into a crouch. My flimsy muscles strained to keep me stable. It took almost all their strength to hold the position. I bit my cheeks in frustration.

A tanned hand fell into my line of sight, showing off an interesting tattoo on the corner of his wrist. "As much as I enjoy watching your determination in action, we don't have the time."

Flicking my eyes from his wrist to his face, I knew he was right.

"Cool tattoo," I muttered, clasping his hand. He lifted me, placing a supportive arm around my waist as my legs steadied.

"That's better than I expected. I for sure thought I'd have to fireman carry you again. And if your swamp water appearance didn't draw attention, that sure would've. Too bad we can't do something about the bruises underneath your eyes or..." Oliver licked his thumb, eyeing my cheek.

"Don't you dare." All kinds of different substances were on and in me. The last thing I needed was Oliver's saliva spread across my cheek, even if it did make my face look cleaner.

Sheepish, Oliver dropped his hand.

He supported me as we walked, filling the silence with his chatter. Either Oliver liked to talk or hated awkward silences with strangers.

"Okay. So, once we cross the rest of this field, I figured we could find you some food. You truly look starved. And my conscience would take a beating if I left a starved child out to rot."

Again, I wasn't a child. But if that's what he needed to believe to help and stay with me, then fine. I nodded, too tired to do anything else.

My thoughts strayed to the voice that invaded my mind. If this was the Oliver she had talked about, I was one step closer to finding my mom.

CHAPTER FOUR

After ten minutes of jumbled walking, we reached a little town called Greenwick. Wrought iron lanterns lined the cobblestone streets, illuminating scattered golden leaves on the sidewalk. Voices and music spilled out from restaurants and cafes. People were everywhere.

I death gripped Oliver's side as strangers shot us glances and whispered into friends' ears. After the first two strangers asked if I was alright, Oliver picked me up, not caring about my weak objections. It didn't stop their eyes. It didn't stop my cheeks from prickling or my hands from clutching Oliver's shirt, but it prevented anyone else from approaching.

Oliver walked us into The Grind, a café with fewer people. Cradled against his chest like a child, I squirmed, wanting down. Being held in the arms of a 6'6" giant inside an establishment didn't help the stares.

But he refused to let go.

"Oliver!"

He ignored my protests and waited silently for the host, disproving my earlier assumption that he couldn't keep his mouth shut.

"Oliver, you're making it worse. Let me down."

Stubborn, he stared straight ahead.

Once the hostess turned our way and noticed the tall guy standing with a scrawny, dirty girl in his arms, she rushed over. Her blue eyeshadow, soft face, and blonde ringlets screamed young.

"O—" She opened her mouth to speak, staring at the dirt on my legs.

Oliver interrupted. "My friend here had a little tumble with her wheelchair. Seeing as she's paraplegic, I couldn't let her drag herself to find food. So, if you could stop staring at her legs and find us a table, that'd be wonderful."

My blush traveled from my hairline down to my clammy hands. I officially wanted to leave.

"Do you—did you want to call someone?" she stammered.

"She's fine. Just a place to sit, please?" Oliver said with a smile. It was like I wasn't even there.

"Of course! Follow me," she squeaked, leading us to a dim corner near the back. We gained a new pair of lingering eyes with every table we passed.

She placed down two menus. "Here you go," she said, then hurried away.

Oliver set me in my chair, knocking my knees against the wood. He mumbled an apology, which I ignored, and sat across from me.

"Your listening skills are astounding. You didn't have to lie to her," I chastised him, overheating and fidgeting in my seat.

He shrugged. "Better than answering questions I don't have the answers to. Or questions that would give us more trouble than they're worth. What's a little lie here and there to ease into situations? It's no biggie."

By trouble, I assumed he meant the authorities.

"Maybe we should get the police involved," I said. They could help me figure out why someone stashed me away in a basement. A hospital may help, too.

Oliver snorted. "Don't be stupid."

I narrowed my eyes, not liking his tone. Despite the skin-crawling feeling of seeking out help, he had a point. The moment I explained my situation or my unusual memories was the moment I'd be declared insane. No way in hell they'd believe me. I hardly believed me.

We stared at each other. An emotion flickered in his face. One I couldn't place.

Before I could ask, a server came over with two glasses of water. "Hi, I'm Max, I'll be—" My hands grabbed at a glass before he set them down. "Oh, ah..." Max trailed off, shocked, as I gulped down the water. The cool liquid filled my empty stomach. He looked at Oliver in question, but Oliver's eyebrows were as high as his.

"She's very thirsty," Oliver said, pushing over his water glass as I emptied my own. My fingers twitched, wanting to finish his as fast as I did mine. I almost did, too, only choosing not to because of Max's reaction.

"I'll bring over a pitcher," Max said, failing to reel in his surprise. "Are you ready to order?"

"Yes, I'll go first, handsome." Oliver winked. "And it's on one check." He dropped a nod to my menu, giving me time to look while he smiled and talked to Max.

My stomach screamed at me to order every item on the menu. After all, Oliver was paying. But I couldn't. Not because the table wasn't big enough or the fact that my stomach was most likely the size of a pea, but because I was already drawing more attention.

"Are you ready, miss?" Max asked, looking uncomfortable and cutting off Oliver.

"I'll have a BLT with a double order of fries, a fruit bowl, and a chocolate milkshake, please."

He scribbled down my order. "Coming right up." Then he left.

I shifted my attention to Oliver. The pity lurked in his furrowed brow. He knew. Oliver finally understood why I ordered so much food.

I grabbed his water. He watched me attempt to drink slower. I waited for the questions I knew would come.

"Your eyes." He pointed. I reached up and rubbed, thinking he meant something was on them. Dirt fell to the table. *Gross.* "Are they fake or real?"

My mouth opened and closed like a fish. Out of all the questions I thought he might ask, I wasn't prepared for that. "Ahh, they're real. Why?"

He leaned back in his chair, arms crossing. "Just making sure."

I didn't believe him. But they were just eyes. I couldn't for the life of me remember what color they were, but eyes were eyes.

"Do you know who was behind us?" I asked, cutting to more important questions.

"Are you going to tell me why you were in those woods?"

Before I could answer, Max and another server brought a pitcher of water and our food. I snatched my steaming sandwich and chomped into it, ignoring how it burned my mouth. The buttery bread and salty bacon made me moan. I took two more quick bites, filling my cheeks. It only got better when I took a sip of my chocolate milkshake.

Nothing, absolutely nothing, could bring me as much joy as chocolate. That much was confirmed in the memory of that cozy loveseat.

"If you don't stop now, I promise you, your head will be in the toilet, and all that smiling will turn into wincing and gagging," Oliver warned. His fork hovered with a piece of lettuce inches from his face.

Mid bite, I took out the handful of fries I had half shoved in my mouth. I considered Oliver's words, glancing between the leftover food and my half-finished milkshake.

"I wouldn't..." Oliver sang, watching me fiddle with my straw.

My hand plunked onto the table, defeated.

"Well, now that I know I won't have to hold your hair while you puke chunks of your food up, why don't you answer my question, and I'll answer yours?"

Gross.

"I escaped from my cage and ran. Other than that, I have no answers."

He set his fork in his salad bowl and pushed it aside. "What do you mean?"

"I mean, they caged me in a cement closet and starved me, which was why I woke up looking like a twelve-year-old girl. I had IVs coming out of my limbs, flaming hands melting doorknobs and glass, and voices speaking to me about strange powers and places to go." My voice continued to rise as I explained the past horrible hours of my existence. I left out the part about his name and my mom, not yet ready to dive into that conversation.

Oliver blinked. "I'm sorry. Can we unpack that a bit? They had you caged in a cement closet? Where? Who is they? How'd you get out? For how long?"

"Like I said, I don't know." Touching the tender area near my elbow, I felt not only the small lump from the IV but my bones, too. If I had any muscles, they were gone now. "Long enough to make my nineteen-year-old body look like it's twelve, I guess."

He gaped at me. "You're nineteen?"

Did I really look that young to him? I haven't been in the presence of a mirror yet, but it couldn't be that bad.

The conversation stopped as Max walked over, dropped off the check, and scurried away.

"I think so, but it depends on how long I was there."

All I had to go on were a few memories. The most important one left me with a twisting ache in my stomach. Like a masochist, I replayed it, remembering her demanding tone, the need to fight, and the dread begging me to run into her arms. *But who were they?* Every time I tried to picture the figures surrounding my mom, their uniforms flickered between white and blood-red, between brilliant metal and leather.

"When's your birthday or creation day?" Oliver asked.

Creation day...? Was he trying to be inclusive in some weird way?

"I don't know."

"When did they capture you?"

"I don't know."

"Do you know who captured you?" The tone of his voice lifted.

A blurry form of black and red popped into my mind. "No. But I'm assuming it was the same people chasing us."

Oliver drummed his fingers against his lip, unsurprised. He knew something.

I leaned forward. "Who are they? Do you know the guy who wears a cream cowboy hat?"

His nostrils flared as he nodded.

How did he know them? And why did he find me at the perfect time?

A niggling suspicion lingered. "Are you working for them?"

His hand shot out, gripping my wrist against the table. Shocked, I jerked back, squirming in his hold. But my nonexistent muscles against his lanky strength were no match. About to scream for help, he yanked me forward.

"If I were one of them, you'd already be back in that closet. This"—he pulled down the V of his shirt, exposing his chest. An angry, discolored scar puckered and indented the once flat expanse—"This is what happens when you have a run-in with *them*," he spat, then released my wrist and crossed his arms.

"How?" I asked, horrified. The collar of his shirt covered most of the scar, but I could still see three puffy pink rectangles peeking out.

"Fire."

They burned his chest in the shape of a handprint? "Why?"

"As much as I'd love to relive those moments and bask in their beautiful misery, now's not the time." He gave a fake smile.

If they could do that to him, what were they doing to me?

"—before they got—"

"Who are they?" I asked, interrupting whatever question he was asking.

"Marcus," he spat. "That's the name of the cowboy-hatted scum."

The name didn't ring a bell. "And the rest?"

He shrugged. "Scum that works for him, I suppose."

"Why does he want me?"

"I was going to ask you that. What were you doing before they got you?"

"I..."

Memories stirred. My mom stood in a cute rooster t-shirt with pants to match, clenching her fists as they surrounded her. And I just hid around a corner, working up the courage to fight, only to be shoved out by... *What exactly? The jerk of her hand? Some unseen force?*

"Lucille?"

"I don't know."

Oliver squinted. "What do you mean?"

"Most of my memories...are gone."

"Your memories?" he asked, voice higher and louder than I liked. I peered around at the oblivious patrons, thankful for their noise. "But—" he sputtered. "Then—how do you know your name? Or age?"

Dammit, Lucille. You don't get to give up. Fight it! The man's voice from my nightmare echoed in my head. A bellow that shook the foundation of my mind, vibrating the cells of my body, waking me up from certain death. His words were angry. Desperate.

Why?

"Some I still have, and there were voices... in my mind when I was in a coma."

He opened and closed his mouth two times before deciding to nod his head. By the wrinkles creasing his brows, he didn't look like he believed me, but at least he didn't outright call me crazy.

My skin crawled, voice dropped. "It wasn't even the small room or IVs that were horrific. It was waking up to that and not knowing how long I was there. Not knowing why. Not knowing..." An ache built in my throat. I swallowed. "I have a sense of who I am, little superficial facts. Likes, dislikes, my age, my name, but anything important, most of the useful information about myself is gone. It was like someone deliberately tried to steal all my memories and only had time to steal the most valuable ones. Then another voice helped me escape by telling me to melt the doorknob." *Yeah, I'd just tack that onto the end.*

Oliver bobbed his head, mouth opening, "I—"

"Excuse me, but we're closing." The young host returned.

"Yep, we're going." Oliver scribbled something on the receipt and stood. I mirrored him.

The hostess's eyebrows shot into her hairline. "How—"

"Spontaneous remission," he blurted, scooping me up. Surprised stares followed us out the door.

Shit, his lie. I forgot.

"I think my miraculous standing was less of a scene than you running us out."

"I'm impulsive at best." He shrugged. He jogged us to the end of the block, found a wooden bench under a twinkling tree, and sat us in it. Uncomfortable sitting in his lap, I slid beside him.

"What are you at your worst?" I asked.

"Fear." The way he said it turned my head. The speckling of goosebumps graced the back of my neck.

With Oliver's simple acceptance and help, it was easy to forget we had met hours ago. I knew nothing about him, yet, on the off chance the voice in my head was a reliable source, this was who I needed. Because what the hell were the chances there was a second Oliver out in those woods?

"I don't know where to start. No memories, a melted doorknob, voices in your head, escaping without getting caught..."

I slumped back into the wooden bench, head tilting to the dots of silver in between the branches and twinkling yellow lights. The beauty of it all was lost on me as my skin itched and my body throbbed. Food and water could only do so much. "I'll tell you everything I know if you can find me a bath and a place to sleep."

He snorted. "Easy."

CHAPTER FIVE

"Welcome to Greenwick's one and only bed-and-breakfast. Greenwick's Bed and Breakfast!" exclaimed a cheery young man at the front desk. He had warm brown eyes, a mop of brown hair, and a big smile. "I'm Zade," he said, giving all his attention to Oliver.

Oliver practically skipped to the front desk and rested both arms on the countertop. "Hey Zade, I'm single and need a room."

Wow. Oliver came on strong.

Zade's smile widened. "A room for just you... or?"

"I mean, certain company would be—"

I cleared my throat. We didn't need any extra company.

Zade peered over Oliver's shoulder, raising a brow. "Is she with you?"

"Yeah. She's my... little sister."

We looked nothing alike, but sure.

"Is she okay?"

"She's fine. Enjoys playing in the dirt a little too much," Oliver said behind his hand like they were sharing a secret.

Irritated, I glanced at the stairs—all four of them. My legs withstood the trek here—albeit stumbling and batting away Oliver's hovering hands—but it counted.

"Does she need extra shampoo and soap?" Zade asked. "Maybe a brush?"

My teeth dug into my cheeks, and I glared. He was lucky I was focused on the stairs and not their faces. I contemplated turning around and doing something about my anger when hundreds of bugs skittered up my arms.

What the hell?

I peeled up the sleeve of Oliver's sweater, searching for the reason behind the incessant itch, when it stopped. Dirty pink skin greeted me, bugless. I sighed. *Stupid dirt.* Little granules rained down on the tile of Zade's lobby as I rubbed my skin, speckling the lovely white floors. I smiled, satisfied. I left Oliver to grab extra supplies after he finished *flirting* and continued to the stairs.

I lifted my shoe off the ground, believing if I could scale twenty stairs, run through a forest, and walk here, I could climb up four steps. My foot hit the wooden lip. I stubbed my toe and cracked my knees against the carpeted edge.

"Are you sure she's okay?" Zade asked. His high-pitched tone grated on my ears.

Oliver walked over, wrapping an arm around my waist, and helped me up the last three steps.

"She's just clumsy," he called over his shoulder. "See you later?"

"You know where to find me."

I rolled my eyes and glared at my arms as they erupted in that annoying itch. I needed a damn bath, like now. A weird pressure pushed behind my eyes, reminding me a bath wasn't the only thing I needed. My impatience could attest to that. But before I sank my head into a soft pillow, Oliver and I had to hobble our way to our room.

Oliver unlocked the door and plopped me in the desk chair near the bathroom. "You want to shower first, or should I?"

Sweat, blood, and urine soaked my clothing, creating an acid-sweet smell that wafted off me in the most unpleasant of ways. Grime made my skin unbearably itchy, especially in the last few minutes. Add all that to the throbbing exhaustion peeling away at my senses, and I wanted to throttle Oliver.

"What?" I said, and the pressure behind my eyes increased.

He flinched, hands raising, backing up. "It was a joke! Just a joke. Bath, maybe? Yeah? You know, with your standing difficulty and all. Should I run you a bath?"

I trailed him with my glare as he retreated into the bathroom, turning on the faucet. My eyes glazed over as I waited for the tub to fill.

A hand interrupted me from my daze. "Your bath awaits you, milady. Would you desire help?"

"Are you always this energetic?"

He shrugged, smirking. "Depends on where my mood carries me. And tonight is a wondrous night."

Not one ounce of my mind, body, or soul agreed with him.

Blankly, I stared. Taking the hint, his smile dropped. He picked me up, carrying me to the edge of the tub.

"Sorry. My mouth gets me into trouble sometimes," he sighed, grabbing the plastic bag filled with supplies.

I snorted, not surprised.

"Here," he handed me shampoo, conditioner, and soap. "Figured you might want that, little sister," he winked. I barely refrained from shaking my head. As he crouched on his way out of the bathroom to avoid hitting his head on the frame, he sang, "*impulse control.*"

The voice crack at the end eased my annoyance. Once the door latched, I peeled off my clothing and dipped my toes into the warmth. A small moan escaped my cracked lips as I slid in. The water turned a murky yellow from the layers of mud loosening off my skin. *So gross.* But the heat soothed the aches and pains, relaxing my limbs.

I lathered and rinsed every inch of my skin twice. Then, I did it for a third time after I drained the chocolate milk looking water and refilled it. After washing my hair, I was ready to come out.

My lips pursed, and my legs trembled while I dried off. I slipped on Oliver's sweater. Luckily, it was long enough and not see-through, even if he did prefer men.

Curious, now that the mud monster had been washed away, I stopped by the mirror above the sink. Built-up moisture blurred my upper torso. Steam curled around my fingers as I reached forward, hesitating before wiping away the film.

My black hair fell in choppy, wet waves down to my shoulders. Sharp angles and hollow cheeks made up my face—attractive but woefully malnourished. At least my skin was unblemished, although the dark bags under my eyes and the pale skin made me look like a vampire. Lifting my gaze from the bruised pillows under my lashes, I met my eyes and froze.

They *were* unnatural.

Two rings, one white and one purple, hugged my pupil. The barely perceptible purple blended with the black dot while the white sat on top. Outside the rings, a smokey gray colored the background, with white and lighter purple flecks scattered throughout. They clustered near my rings and dispersed like an exploding star as they moved from the center.

Now I understood why Oliver asked if they were fake or real. But that still didn't explain the knowing gleam I saw on his face or why my eyes looked like they belonged in a different world.

Or why I had flaming hands.

Walking out of the bathroom, I found Oliver sprawled on the second bed, mouth open and eyes closed. I huffed, picked up a pillow, and threw it at his face. It was the least I could do.

He jerked awake, blinking at me a few times. "Wow, you *are* older than twelve *and* can walk."

I smiled, in a better temperament for his humor, and scanned him up and down. "Are you going to shower?" Dried mud speckled his jeans, his hair looked like he had rubbed it with a balloon, and drool crusted the corners of his mouth.

He shrugged. "Eh, probably wait till there's more hot water. So..." Vivid eyes stared at me expectantly.

"What do you want to know?"

"Everything. But first, the voices. Who were they?"

I shook my head and sat on the edge of the other bed. "They didn't say. There was a woman and a man the first time. They forced me awake. The second time, it was only the woman talking to me like you are now, but I couldn't see her." I fiddled with the fraying end of Oliver's sweater, unwilling to look up. Self-conscious and contemplating brain damage, I didn't want to see judgment reinforced in his gaze.

"What did she tell you?" he asked, with not an ounce of disbelief in his tone, as if my tale was that easy to swallow. Would he continue this accepting curiosity when I mentioned the next part?

My thumb and pointer twirled the green strand. A scar exposed itself as I turned my wrist toward the light. It looked like writing but sharper and unreadable. I grazed my finger over the puckered skin. *Where did I get this?* Something about it tickled my mind. Something I needed to remember.

"Hello, earth to Lucille?"

I tore my attention away from the odd scar. "What?"

"The female? What did she say?"

"She mentioned a place and two people."

"Where and who?"

Something about his tone made me peer up. He wore the same knowing gleam as he did in The Grind.

"In the café, what did you mean about my eyes?"

Edging toward the end of the bed, he clasped his hands between his knees. "How'd you melt the doorknob to escape?"

My face scrunched. "How does that—"

"Bear with me, would you? I'm getting to that part." The sass had me itching my arm. "How'd you do it?"

"I have pow..." It sounded insane. "Powers."

Not surprised, he nodded, smirking. "Which is why Marcus took you, and you have that ring around your eyes." His smirk grew into a full-blown smile.

"What do you mean?" I didn't like the glee in his expression. It meant whatever he said was about to turn my world upside down. Again.

His smile held despite my irritation. "Do you see the purple ring around my pupil?"

I leaned off the bed as he leaned forward, staring into the unnaturally bright green hue. Around his pupil circled a dark purple ring.

The same purple ring that graced my unusual starry depths.

"Yes," he said, noticing my surprise. "What if I were to tell you it signified the blood of a specific species?"

"What other species is there besides humans?"

Something sputtered inside me. A tickle fluttered around in the gaping hole of my mind, wanting to connect to Oliver's words. I knew at one point what he was talking about, but the answer hovered out of reach. Although, the importance didn't. This answer could help me and my mom; I knew it. He just had to say it. I needed him to say it.

Oliver's grin turned mischievous. I curled in my eager fingers, silently berating myself for the thoughts of violence.

"Many, Lucy. Oh, that's what I'm going to call you from now on. Lucille is too long."

Spoken, they were the same length.

Breathe.

But how the hell could I breathe when it felt like hundreds of tiny feet scurried along my skin? Not to mention the rising pressure pushing behind my eyes and underneath the incessant itch. It felt like what I'd imagine a snake wrapped in plastic would feel like—tormented by the need to shed its skin, only to be suffocated with it instead.

"Unless you have just woken from a long coma-induced slumber, were locked in a cage with needles sending god knows what into your blood"—my voice, the itch, and the pressure all rose—"and then ran for your life on pure adrenaline and willpower, exhausted, scared, and out of your mind, I'd refrain from the theatrics and tell me what the hell I want to know!" I snapped into his face, happily watching his smile drop. He was playing with a grenade whose safety pin had been pulled hours ago. He had my answers. I needed those answers.

I stood and felt a snap. The pressure and itch eased while my tumultuous emotions rode me. Barely towering over Oliver, looking down into his wide eyes, color washed from his face. Unsatisfied by his sickly pallor and lack of words, I stepped closer. A song whispered in my ear, coercing me to listen to its addictive melody of anger. Of violence.

My hand lifted. The seductive tune coming from the untouched depths of my soul consumed my mercy. Yet, my hand, inches away from wrapping around his throat, stilled. But not from the terror I witnessed on his face, from the change that occurred on my skin.

I sank to the floor in front of Oliver's muddy shoes. The flashing colors disappeared from his wide, glassy eyes.

This time, it wasn't just white. Dark purple intertwined and danced among the lighter flames. When the two colors heightened, specs of black manifested, deepening the already dark purple flame.

Stunned that I wanted to murder Oliver, the musical whispers disappeared, releasing me from their grip. The twining colors sank beneath my skin, removing the lingering itch and pressure. My lids fluttered, my head lolling to the side.

"Lucy!" Oliver yelled.

Groggy, I blinked up at him. He sat in the center of his bed—away from me.

He was scared of me. I was scared of me.

"I don't understand what's going on," I whispered.

Horror squeezed my stomach, pushing bile up my throat and slapping a bitter taste on the back of my tongue. I couldn't believe I wanted to hurt him. But it consumed me. A sweet little tune puppeteered my actions.

"I'm unsure of your power. But I can tell you it has something to do with being an..." he hesitated.

"A what?" I whispered, wanting him to continue.

"An angel."

CHAPTER SIX

Stunned, I stared at Oliver. "We're angels?"

He moved his head from side to side. "Ehhh, sorta."

"Explain." *Please, please give me something to explain what I almost did.*

"The purple ring signifies angel blood. But that doesn't mean you're a pure angel. Most of the time, at least around here, if you see someone with a purple ring, they aren't full-blooded, or they're Fallen."

I blinked. Besides the continuous flutter tickling my mind, none of this sounded familiar. And yet, probably because I was locked in a cage and most likely half-insane, I believed him. Although, glowing hands and Oliver's bluntness helped.

"Which are you?"

"I'm a Nephilim. Half angel, half human."

"And what am I? Am I a Nephilim like you?" The thought eased the tension in my shoulders, especially since he didn't say anything to set my guilty conscience of murder at ease. But if I was like him, he could explain what was happening to me.

"I don't know. It's hard to tell a Nephilim and an angel apart," he said. "But you have two rings. I've never seen any Nephilim with two rings. I've never even heard of it. And I've heard of a lot."

"Have you heard of angels with them?"

He sighed, scrubbing at his head. "No."

"Okay, what about a Fallen? Am I one of those?"

Oliver scooted back to the edge of the bed and slid to the carpet, brave enough to be near me again. He rested his arms on his knees. "A Fallen is a fallen angel. They did something bad, disobeyed angelic law, were cast out of whatever place they came from, and had their wings ripped out of their back." He raised his arms and twirled his finger. "Turn around and lift your shirt."

"Why?"

"Fallen have scars on their backs."

I turned, grabbed the edge of his sweater, then paused. I wasn't wearing any underwear.

"Here." He handed me the comforter off the bed.

I wrapped it around my waist and pulled his sweater up to my shoulders. "Well?"

He was silent.

"Oliver?" I flinched as his icy finger traced a line along my back.

"You're not Fallen," he whispered. "But you do have scars. It looks like someone carved five tally marks across your lower spine." His somber tone hinted at the meaning behind his words.

"You think someone tortured me?"

"Yes."

"Marcus?"

Oliver pulled his hand back. "I wouldn't put it past him. But your scars aren't fresh. If he did torture you, it was a while ago."

I sighed, sliding his sweater down, and turned back around. I'm glad I didn't remember my torture, but I wished I knew who did it and why.

"Is there *any way* to tell a Nephilim and an angel apart?" I asked.

He rubbed his thumb over the black tattoo on his wrist, sinking further into the side of the bed with each pass.

"Angels usually have more power, seeing as Nephilim are half-human and inherit a lower dose of power from their fathers."

"What about their mothers? Do they give their children power?"

"Female angels can't be mothers. It's not possible for them to have kids with humans or their species. It's against creation, or so I was told. Whatever that means."

Did that make me a Nephilim? But from the memory of my mother's eyes flashing purple and power forcing me outside of our house, I didn't think she was human. *So what did that mean?*

"What's your power?" I asked, curious about what he could do.

We sat in silence as he bit his lip. "Let's just say my deadbeat dad didn't give me anything pleasant. Although"—he perked up a bit—"I don't mind the lusceler or what we call super speed, fast healing, or immortality. Guess that makes up for whatever relationship we never had."

"You're immortal?" I gaped. "How old are you?"

His smile turned wicked.

"I turned one hundred a few months back."

"No, you're not one hundred."

"Oh, but I am."

"No—you look—"

He interrupted. "We get to choose when to stop aging. I chose 27. Anyone with angel blood has the ability. Well, except the Fallen. They lose it when their wings are ripped out. But that's neither here nor there."

"Anyone with angel blood?" I squeaked.

Excitement twinkled in his emeralds, accompanying the sly tilt of his lip. "Yes. Which does, in fact, include you."

"What?" *What else was I forgetting?*

Oliver blabbed about immortality and all its amazing perks, but I wasn't listening. Because as important as all this information was, there was something I needed to know above anything else. "Where's Elora?" I interrupted.

He fell silent.

"That's the place. Where she told me I needed to go. Where is it?"

His head fell back against the bed. He heaved a sigh, staring at the ceiling.

"Is it close?"

"Yes and no."

"Explain," I demanded again, impatient.

With pursed lips, he considered me. "It's a world. In a parallel dimension."

My eyes widened. I thought Elora was a place here on... "Are we on Earth?" I asked, horrified that he'd say no and rock my already teetering mind.

He nodded. "Yes, and I can see your wheels turning. But before I say anything else, I'm taking a shower, and you're going to bed before you pass out—"

I opened my mouth to protest.

"Or kill me."

"Fine," I said, cheeks flushing.

Standing, Oliver held out a hand to help me up. I double-checked mine before taking his. He smirked, noticing my paranoia, then walked to the bathroom.

I cuddled under the covers and closed my eyes, hoping I'd be one step closer to finding my mom tomorrow.

WAKE UP, LUCILLE.

"Do you know where she is?"

Wake up, Lucille.

You'll find your answers once you get out of your cage.

Wake up, Lucille.

We're bonded.

Wake up, Lucille.

She sobbed as I fell. The never-ending sound tore open the carefully crafted calm.

Wake up, Lucille!

I'm your guardian.

Touch him. Now.

Wake up, LUCILLE!

I SCREAMED, SPRINGING UP from my bed, drenched in sweat.

"You okay?"

I jerked to my right.

Oliver.

He sat on the other bed, tying his shoelaces. Yesterday came flooding back. Besides his messy hair and wrinkled clothing, he looked well-rested. The same couldn't be said for me. My muscles and joints throbbed in revolt.

"Yeah, fine. Just a bad dream..." I couldn't remember, but that's what I assumed. Finally, calm, I broached the topic he skillfully avoided last night. "So..."

"So..." He raised an eyebrow like he didn't know what I meant.

"Elora? Where is it?"

"It's near."

"And?"

"And," he drew out. "It's not an easy place to get to by yourself. You'd never be able to find it."

I swung my legs off the bed and sat across from him. "So, show me the way."

"No." He stood.

"No?" I swiveled, watching him walk toward the door. Needles shot across my skin as my chest squeezed. I was this close to finding more answers about my mom, and he was going to leave me. Pressure throbbed in my hands. "Wait! You can't go!" I said, flinging out my arm as if I could stop him. A pulse of pure-white light shot from my hand, flying straight for Oliver's head.

He ducked in time, panning wide-eyed from my hand to the charred hotel door.

"I'm just going pee. I figured you wouldn't want to join. But if my head is on the line, you can watch and make sure I don't escape down the toilet pipes," he said slowly, palms raised as if to placate my outburst.

I looked between my dimming flames and the black spot still smoking behind Oliver's head. "Yeah, no, sorry," I gulped. "Go—go pee."

I stared aghast at my hands, no longer lit by white light. That was the second time I almost hurt him or worse.

When the toilet flushed, I peered up, at a loss for words. Guilt lodged itself in my throat. Did I beg for forgiveness and hope he'd take pity on me and take me to Elora or did I—no. I had no other option.

I had no place to go but Elora. I needed him.

"I can't take you."

The same tormenting energy sliced up my arms. As hard as I could, I bit into my fleshy cheeks, hoping the sharp sting would keep the crazy flames away.

"But Oliver! You said I wouldn't be able to get there on my own. What do you expect me to do?"

"Not go? Just because some voice in your head said you should, doesn't mean you should. I mean, not unless you have some contract or something," he muttered, shrugging his shoulders like this conversation meant nothing.

"You're here. You have angel blood and can take me where I need to go. My only other option is to go gazing into people's eyes to see if they maybe have the purple ring and ask them to take me to Elora." That didn't sound like the worst idea. I was desperate enough.

His face scrunched as he gazed into the distance, running his hands through his hair. "No, scratch that. That's probably not the best idea unless you want to go to a psych ward or have a knife to the throat. Elora is a tightly kept secret among our kind. If you don't know about it, you won't."

"Then what? You can't honestly think I'm going to drop this and go about my—my whatever the hell this is! I mean, they locked me in a room and tortured me, then I get dropped into your lap after I'm told to go to Elora?" I lifted my hands, shaking them. "That's a pretty damn big coincidence, don't you think?"

He let loose a heavy breath. "Yeah, fates a fickle bitch, isn't she?" Sinking back down on the bed, he stared at me. Pain flashed across his face. "The thing is, I promised myself I wouldn't return until I found a way to reach... someone."

That stirred up a lot of questions and an idea. "What if..." I wasn't sure how, but I had to try everything. "What if I could help you? In exchange for taking me to Elora, I'll help you find a way to this person?"

After I found Magda, another person the voice in my head told me to find—who had my answers—then my mom. But I'd tell him that part later.

He considered me for a second. "You want to go that bad? You don't even know anything about my situation. Or Elora."

Yes, I wanted to go that bad, and I would do whatever it took to get to her. Nothing was about to stop me. I needed my mom, and she needed me.

The bubble of laughter that erupted from him confused me. He shook his head. "Maybe this is part of it, the vague bastard," he muttered.

"What?" I asked.

Abruptly, he stood. "Fine. Deal. You'll help me find a way to her, and I'll take you to Elora. We can talk specifics on the way."

Relief washed through me. I didn't think it'd be that easy. But thank whoever for small mercies.

"I guess she was right about you," I said, relieved.

He squinted at me before understanding loosened his brows. "It was me. The person the female in your head spoke of was me." It wasn't a question. And by the weary surprise pinching his lips, I regretted saying anything. "I'm really starting to hate voices in heads," he sighed, shaking his head. "Let's go."

I held back my eager smile, hurrying to put my shoes on. "So, how far is it?"

"Oh, probably about two days," Oliver stated, glancing toward the daylight streaking through the window of our room.

"That's what you call near?" I scoffed.

He shrugged. "Near enough." Then he started clapping. "Now get that booty up! We got to go shopping. We have supplies to get."

"Clothes and food," I agreed, tying my shoes like I'd chugged four cups of coffee. My muscles ached when I stood but held strong with their renewed strength. It may be straight adrenaline, too.

Up and down, he surveyed my steady legs. "Among other things," he muttered, raising a brow. "Seems sleep and the angelic healing is working. I wasn't sure what the cowboy-hatted scum was pumping into you." Oliver rubbed at the burn mark on his chest.

I stared at the scarred skin peeking out from his white shirt. At first, I thought it might've been some metal branding tool that made it. But after almost incinerating Oliver's neck with my flaming hand, I didn't think that's how he got it.

"What is he?"

Oliver sank back down to the corner of the mattress like the mere thought of the man stole his energy. "Marcus is a highly praised lackey in the Tenebrous Kingdom and a powerful Syric."

I blinked. "A Syric?"

Another weird angel term?

"Yeah, Syric." He shook his head, gazing at the charred mark I made on the door. "A dangerous asshole with the ability to melt off your face with his glowy red runes." He slapped his legs in emphasis and stood again. "So, keep that in mind the next time you see his half-covered psychotic smile."

"And the Tenebrous Kingdom?"

Oliver snorted. "Oh, this beautiful place in Elora. You'd absolutely love it. Gorgeous waterfalls, luscious green grass, unique wildlife you've never seen before. It's great."

"Really?" I asked.

"No. Let's go."

We walked out of our room and back to the front lobby. Oliver smiled at each stair I confidently stepped down without his help.

"I'm so glad I don't have to fireman carry you all the way to Elora."

I snorted. "What do you mean carry?"

His smile turned sly. "How do you think we're getting there?"

My brows furrowed. "A car?"

He chuckled.

CHAPTER SEVEN

Oliver and I left the hotel with a complimentary muffin. Per usual, he filled the silence with his chatter until we found a store that fit Oliver's needs. When I interrupted him and asked how we were traveling to Elora, he said the last thing I wanted to hear. Camping.

Last night, I slept on a soft, warm mattress with a thick, cozy comforter. Now, we'd have to suffer with the hard ground. The metal table was enough. Not to mention, my legs weren't in hiking shape. They were twigs awaiting a gentle breeze to snap them in two.

My glare followed him to a superstore called Everything You Could Want & More.

"Think they'd have your memories?" Oliver laughed as we walked through the sliding doors.

Tiny feet skittered up and down my arms, begging me to scratch as I fused my drilling gaze to Oliver's cheek. Oblivious, he took a cart and led me to the area labeled hiking clothes. "Go grab something..."

He grimaced, scanning me up and down. "I'll get the rest of our supplies."

"Fantastic," I mumbled.

I perused racks of tops and bottoms, letting my fingers glide over the fabrics until a dark floral pattern caught my attention. The joggers were thick but stretchy, promising warmth without restricting movement. With the joggers, a green long-sleeve, and a black coat in hand, I headed to the dressing room, snagging a pair of hiking boots on the way. After changing and yanking the tags off, I went to find Oliver. He changed into navy khaki pants and a green quarter-zip sweater.

Oliver surveyed my new outfit. "I like it." He paused. "You're definitely aging before my eyes."

"Thanks for the kind sentiment," I said dryly, handing him the tags to my clothes.

He winked. "Anytime."

At the one and only cashier, Oliver paid the outrageous amount and packed our stuff.

"Let's buckle up and make some mischief!" He handed me a backpack and shrugged on his own, leading the way out of the store.

Within five minutes of our walk, Oliver paused in front of the café from last night. The gall he had for bringing us back here. We didn't do anything crazy, but I'm sure our faces weren't long from their memory. No way was I going in.

"Do you want some food? Those blueberry muffins did nothing for me," he said, rubbing his flat belly with his other hand on the door.

"Is this the only café?" I huffed.

Oliver laughed at my discomfort. "Probably. Not coming in?"

I shook my head. "Nope."

"Fine, I'll buy you something. Not my fault if you don't like it," he sang back.

Rolling my eyes, I removed my pack from my already sore shoulders and leaned back against the brick face. For how late it was in the morning, I was surprised not as many people were out and about. A few elderly couples strolled by, walking hand-in-hand, smiling and laughing. They were oblivious to anyone around them, happy to give all their attention to each other.

"Here."

I jumped. Oliver slapped a warm, wrapped sandwich into my chest, taking me out of my thoughts. Melted cheese and meat wafted into my nose.

"Thanks."

"Yeah." Oliver turned and strode away.

"Wait!" I heaved my backpack back on and rushed after him. "Where's the fire?"

Oliver barreled on, ignoring me. I jogged, trying to keep up with his long legs. As much as I wanted to hurry to Elora, I didn't have the stamina to sprint the whole way.

"Oliver." I grabbed his bicep. "Slow down. What's the rush?"

He shrugged off my hand. "Nothing."

I frowned. "Did I do something wrong?"

He went into the café smiling and came out almost... bitter.

"No, but if we want to get to Elora, we can't dilly-dally."

True, but his words lacked their usual pizazz, and it was his fourth sentence within ten minutes. On the way to the superstore, a short walk, Oliver practically recited an entire book. But he had a habit of not talking when I wanted him to.

Did I pry more? With one look at his sour expression, I decided against it.

"Okay. But slow down. I'm half your size and was just in a coma."

He considered that and continued.

Oliver couldn't keep a slow pace to save his life. When he did slow down, it lasted a couple of minutes before he sped back up. Then, once he noticed I lingered too far behind, he'd slow. This process went back and forth. Regardless, my pace never changed. He couldn't leave me behind, and I was in no shape to sprint for two days.

At least I could walk with weight. But Oliver had mentioned quicker healing abilities.

When he plowed into the clearing from yesterday bordering the forest we ran out of, I lowered the last bite of my sandwich and hesitated on the sidewalk.

"Is it safe to go back in there?" Nerves danced in my stomach, keeping my feet planted.

"I could say yes to help your fears, but it'd be a lie. Remember, we made a deal," he called back, noticing my lack of movement. Bitterness tainted his helpful reminder.

What was his problem?

But damn, he was right. I needed to get to Elora. If going through the forest Marcus recently chased us out of was the only way, then I had to. My prickling fingers and squeezing lungs utterly disagreed. *Did I want to do this?*

"It's for mom," I whispered to myself.

It helped—only a little.

I dropped the last bite of my sandwich onto the ground, no longer hungry, and jogged after him. "Fine. But actually, slow down this time! I can't keep up."

"We'll fix that in a second," he said, striding forward with his long legs. I scratched my arms and followed yards behind.

Ass.

I almost teared up once we walked a bit into the thick trees, and the landscape changed to a more uphill terrain.

Uneven pants forced their way out of my mouth. My stamina, though better than yesterday, wasn't enough. The speedy angel healing wasn't some fairy godmother granting me muscle in all the places I lacked.

"I suppose we are far enough in now," Oliver said, returning to where I stopped. "It's time you use some of that power of yours."

My brows caved in. "What?"

"You have angel blood. Which means you have speed, or what we call lusceler, and we already know you have some burn-metal-door-knobs power." He rolled his eyes. "So, let's go. Stop acting like a baby."

"I don't know how." A pout threatened to form, but I reined it in.

"No worries. I'm going to give you a crash course."

The invisible irritants were back. I scratched my arm and narrowed my eyes at his stupid, playful smirk.

"You need to find your need. When you wanted to fry off my neck, or when you flung a ball of flames at my head, why? What caused it? Jealousy?" He winked. I scratched. "Joy? Anger? Fear? You need to tap into a small part of that power and use it differently."

Oliver blurred as he moved from one side to the other instantaneously. "Why do you think we got out of those woods so fast? We covered miles, Lucy. That's why they didn't find us." He laughed, blurring in circles around me.

Streaks of vibrant green appeared randomly in the circuit he ran, but every time I reached to poke him, my finger brushed air. My eyes couldn't keep up.

"I know, pretty cool, right? I told you there were perks to being an angel. Or part." His eyebrows danced.

"So, all angels have this lusceler?"

"As long as they have enough angel blood in them. Try it."

I figured the best way to start was to choose a spot to run to. Near the hill stood a gnarled tree, dark and broken like lightning hit it. It was a short distance away and a good stopping spot to attempt this angel speed.

"So, just have a need to go fast and run?" I cast a glance at Oliver, seeking confirmation.

He shrugged, jutting out his bottom lip. "Sure."

What a wonderful teacher.

Focused on the burnt tree, I pushed my shoulders back and sighed. *I can do this.*

Oliver interrupted my internal pep talk. "Any day now."

I shot him a glare, scratching my hands, and ran.

But that was all I did.

The trees didn't blur. My hair didn't fly back from my face or look like a hot mess like Oliver's did. Nope. My feet thumped against the ground like any ordinary human.

Oliver blurred to my side. "Can I ask what you were thinking?"

I glared at the laughter in his voice. "I don't know. Run?" Breathless, I flung the backpack off my shoulders. I should've taken it off before running.

"Did you feel the need to go?" he asked.

"I wanted to go."

Oliver hung his head as if *I* was the impossible one to deal with. "That's not good enough, Luce," he said, shortening my name further. "Wanting something doesn't do shit. Focus your mind on the need to move, on the need to go faster. Almost like if you don't, you'll die. You need to hunger for it."

I huffed. *Fine.*

What I needed was for my skin to stop itching. My jacket covered my arms, so I knew I hadn't encountered any plants that caused irritation. No bumps or scrapes peppered my skin.

Ignoring my inner complaining, I eyed the rotten stump I just left. "Need it," I whispered. "Need, need, need. What did I need?" To stop itching. *Shut up, brain!*

What was my need?

My mom.

I had no idea where she was or what was happening to her. If I didn't move, I'd never get to Elora. I'd never find Magda. I'd never find my mom.

I couldn't let that happen. I couldn't deal with the consequences if I didn't find my mom.

Like this morning, when I thought Oliver would leave me, something squeezed my chest, making me wild. It kicked the hidden beast awake, shoving at my skin, causing a stabbing throb and an itch.

A live wire sparked beneath the surface. I ran, and my hands burst with colorful flames.

Shit.

Oliver frowned. "You pulled too hard at your power."

The sensations faded, leaking out of me like someone had pulled the plug. Dizziness replaced the itching and the stabbing pressure as my flames sank back into my hands.

"I felt it." I sighed, taking a seat.

"You felt too much. Did you want to try again?"

I rested my head in my hands, needing a moment. "Not unless you want me to pass out."

He walked over to me, boots crunching in the leaves. "Your body is still healing you, on top of keeping you upright with the little muscle you have. Which means we'll stick with the good ole human pace that brings me so much joy," he said dryly.

The annoyance in his emerald eyes rekindled a slight itch on my skin. At this rate, I wanted to claw it all off.

"Try to keep up, and if you can't, I may need to carry you again." He turned away from me and started toward the steep hill.

Could he carry me and two backpacks?

I followed. Despite the energy drain and dizziness from the run, I kept up with Oliver fairly well. Or more likely, he finally slowed down for me. The backpack thumped against my sweat-soaked back.

A friend accompanied the pout that had yet to leave my face. Oliver's sour expression and silent treatment were back. Whatever happened at the café still bothered him.

I let him stew. If he wanted to talk about it, he would. Or not.

Hours passed, and my legs held. The terrain grew steeper, and Oliver's mood grew worse. He bulldozed through bushes, acting like he weighed three hundred pounds, swatting and kicking branches and sounding like a herd of angry bison. Not that I'd ever seen a herd of angry bison—or, at least, I had no memory of it. When a branch almost smacked me in the face, I couldn't stand it anymore.

I rushed in front of him, surprising myself as the trees blurred for half a second, covering the few yards between us. I luscelered. But I couldn't even be happy about it because of Oliver's tantrum.

"What the hell is wrong with you?" I demanded. He was going to attract all the attention in the world with his noise.

His emerald eyes flashed. "Nothing."

"Bullshit! You were just fine before the café. Then afterward, you became this tantrum-throwing child, taking out your frustration on the bushes and rocks, almost whipping me in the face with a branch."

He stepped closer. "I don't have to tell you anything."

A pressure pushed behind my eyes. "You do if you want my help." That same itch returned to my skin. Glancing down, I narrowed my eyes at my arms.

There were no flames, and my jacket sleeves remained intact. Yet, the itch relentlessly assaulted my skin, and my anger was the common denominator in each instance.

My head tilted back up to meet his sharp eyes. We stared at each other in a battle of wills. If he didn't back up soon, I feared this itchy anger would shift to itchy fingers. Already, I tensed my arms to keep them by my sides. His face paled.

"What?" The satisfaction of making him fear me crept into my voice. Even my lips couldn't contain the tilt of my smirk.

"Your—"

A branch snapped behind us.

"We're not alone."

CHAPTER EIGHT

I stilled. Ominous clouds billowed in, obscuring the blue sky. The air crackled with charged energy, thick with the acrid scent of burnt ozone, silencing the chirping birds. We both searched between the trees.

A gust of wind barreled through the trees and knocked into us. Stumbling, I latched onto Oliver's arm. Leaves and dirt whipped around in a chaotic storm, stinging my face with the force of the wind.

"What's going on?" I asked as he righted me.

"Elementals." Oliver's hair was in disarray, more so than usual. His black streak moved and blended with his blonde strands.

"What do you mean?"

Thunder boomed nearby.

Oliver grabbed my shoulders. "I mean, we need to get the hell out of here! Can you run like you did before?" The urgency of his voice told me he didn't mean regular running. We needed to go fast. Unnaturally fast.

"I can try."

A pressure built underneath my skin, similar to the sensations from my first attempt at lusceler, yet this time without the accompanying itch. The pressure edged toward agony as if a million needles fought to break free from my body.

Lightning flashed, hitting a tree in the distance and sending a jolt through me straight to the millions of needles. They stabbed through my hands, and brilliant white fire erupted.

I stared at them in dread. "Again? That's not—"

Another boom echoed through the air, even closer. The white flames on my hands spiked.

"Lucy! Can you do it, or should I carry you?" Oliver grabbed my shoulders, shaking me.

I whipped my flaming hands out to the sides.

Oliver shook me again. "Lucy! Do I need to carry you?" He yelled over the forceful wind.

"No! I can do this!"

Lightning continued to flash, hitting trees and coming closer.

Shit! I shrugged off his touch and waved my hands around, begging them to go out. "Come on!"

"Lucy! They're almost on us!"

I bent over my knees, heaving, keeping my flaming hands in front of me. "Something's wrong. I can't breathe."

"It's called panicking. Calm down, take control, and breathe!"

"I am breathing!"

My white flames shuddered. Purple intertwined with the white.

"Dammit, Lucy, that's not even close to what I said!"

"What you said *sucked*! Fix this! Make it stop!" I yelled, staring at my traitorous powers, unable to rub at the pressure pushing down on my chest.

"Keep those away from me, okay?" Oliver scooped me in his arms and luscelered away.

We blurred through the forest. I held my hands as far away from our hair and bodies as possible.

Lightning hit a tree to our left. I yelped, jerking my head into Oliver's chest and shielding my face from the exploding shards.

"Marriage-carrying you is slowing us down! They'll catch up to us if you can't figure out how to put out that crazy heat and channel that power into running." With my ear to his lungs, he wasn't lying. I could hear the toll this took.

"I don't know how."

"You need to need it."

Oh, my heavenly hell. I wanted to shake him. *Need it. Need it.* How much more could I possibly need it? The answers to my past and my mom were in Elora, and these elementals, whatever they were, stood in our way. Of course, I wanted to move. Of course, I needed—

Oliver flinched, and I fell.

I slammed into the ground, tumbling across roots and pine needles. A trunk the size of my wrist caught the last of my momentum, snapping into my back. I gasped.

"Lucy! Are you okay?" Oliver blurred to my side, kneeling beside me, hands hovering in the air. "I'm sorry! So sorry. I didn't mean to drop you, but your skin was blazing. I didn't know if you were seconds from erupting or something. You scorched my hands through your clothing."

Groaning, I rolled off the miniature tree I broke with my back. "I tried to need it. But I think I only made the squeezing pressure worse."

"You panicked?"

"Sure."

Oliver reached for me, thought better of it, and stood. "At least your flames are put away." He nodded down to my grimy, lightless hands.

Yay, no more suffocating, needle-poking pressure, only shock and pain shooting into my back from being thrown into a tree.

"Think you can try luscelering again?" he asked, peering around at the ominous sky. The wind blew on a gentle breeze, no longer an angry tempest.

I stood, poking at the base of my spine, flinching. "I'll try."

Oliver held out his hand. "When you're ready."

As I was about to place my hand in his and dive into my power, my hair stood erect. Thunder roared with deafening force as lightning flashed, crashing down on us.

I don't know how I did it, but I moved out of the way—fast.

Oliver grinned like a fool, despite the fact we almost became charred flesh, and grabbed my hand. "That was need. Now you're going to do it again. I'm not letting go. So, either it's run with me, or I rip your arm out of its socket while I drag you."

Wonderful.

The squeezing pressure came back, along with the needles. Luckily there were no flames. Yet. But with no other option, I *begged* myself to find the live wire beneath it all.

"Ready?"

I nodded, squeezing my free hand into a tight fist.

He took a step.

We luscelered.

In the deepening shadows of the forest, we sprinted faster than the human eye, driven by the urgency to avoid lightning strikes. Oliver released me once he realized I could keep pace.

Pressurized energy filled every cell in my body, moving my feet in impossible ways. I glanced down to make sure my feet touched the ground, wanting to laugh at the thrill of it but stopped by the needle-like stabs of my power and a powerful gust of wind pushing against our speed.

"Faster! We need to outrun them." The rushing wind weakened Oliver's voice.

"Who are they?" I jumped over a fallen log with no conscious effort.

"They're called Powers, elemental—" A boom of thunder covered his voice.

"What?" I screamed.

"Elemental angels!"

My steps faltered. "Why are we running from angels?" *Weren't we on the same side? What was I even thinking? Were there sides?*

"Well, I don't think they want to talk. Watch out!" Oliver grabbed my arm, yanking me to the side and out of the path of another incoming lightning bolt.

Blood rushed from my face. The pressure under my skin increased, pushing my legs faster. Not once did my legs falter or slow down. But I knew the foreboding drain was coming. It was just a matter of when.

We covered miles and miles of terrain. They never showed themselves, but their powers over the turbulent weather never ceased.

Moisture thickened the air as the clouds overhead turned black.

That couldn't be good.

Drops of rain fell, pelting our bodies. Oliver cursed up a storm. My legs trembled, longing to collapse under the relentless assault. I had no doubt we'd both find welts once we stopped.

"Keep going, Lucy! Don't stop!" Oliver yelled, noticing my slowing pace.

It was smart on their part. The lightning bolts we dodged. But with a downpour, we couldn't.

I put on a burst of speed, ducking my head. The faster we moved, the lighter the drops became—a good sign. But the numbness that crept into my feet wasn't.

I glanced at Oliver, and we shared a smile. He even gave a cocky wink. We were losing them. Then the ground shook, and trees groaned. Oliver's smug expression dropped as he lost his footing and collided headfirst into a nearby trunk.

I stumbled over the rippling earth to his sprawled body. "Oliver!" I used all my body weight to turn him over, feet slipping in the mud. He groaned. Blood dripped down from a gash on his forehead. "Are you okay?"

The earth steadied, the whooshing of leaves settled, and my quick breaths filled the eerie quiet. I looked around, searching between trunks for movement.

"There's no way we lost them," I whispered, looking down at Oliver. His eyes were closed. "Oliver," I said. "Oliver!" I shook his shoulder. "Shit."

He was still breathing but unresponsive. I whipped off my pack, searching for something to hold against his head. Toilet paper would work.

Water seeped into my joggers as I kneeled next to him, putting pressure on his wound. I panned between his rising chest and the quiet forest. The stillness poked at my nerves. I didn't see anyone. I didn't hear anyone. But it would be foolish to think we lost them.

A couple of yards away, thick bushes jutted from the mud. If I managed to drag Oliver over there, we could hide ourselves behind them.

A strange sensation crawled up my legs when I grabbed his arm. The throbbing of my welts dulled, and sand replaced my blood, weighing me down. *Not now.* I squeezed my eyelids shut, holding back tears of frustration. The energy I used was exacting its toll.

Oliver groaned. I snapped my eyes open.

"Hide," he whispered.

"What about you?" I couldn't leave him like this. But I barely had the energy to move myself, let alone a concussed Oliver. My hand weakened the longer it held the wadded toilet paper.

"Now, Lucy," Oliver said more forcefully, blinking at my face.

Pressure pushed into my chest, shoving harder with each second I took to decide what to do. The hair along my arms rose underneath my wet jacket.

I couldn't leave him, could I?

But I didn't stand a chance against them. Maybe that's why my mom sent me away when I wanted to fight with her.

Burnt ozone overwhelmed my nose. I glanced at the bushes.

Oliver would be okay.

I dropped to my hands and knees, crawling towards the bushes. But before I entirely abandoned Oliver, my hair prickled with electricity, and lightning flashed.

An explosion of pain ripped into my back right before oblivion.

CHAPTER NINE

I walked down a dim hallway lined with pictures of a woman and a little girl. Vertigo blurred my vision, and my stomach attempted to revolt. I stumbled into the wall and knocked a picture down.

Groaning, I steadied myself and picked it up. Two faces stared back at me. I scrunched my brows at the image of the woman.

No way.

Underneath thick eyelashes, staring at me, were my mom's eyes, and around the picture rimmed a purple halo. Or... I moved my head. No, around my vision. A translucent purple screen crowded the edges of my sight. I shook my head back and forth, blinked a few times, then immediately regretted it. The purple tint stayed, like my last dream.

The one where I exploded with flames and burned down our house.

A rush of tingles sank into my gut, heavy and cold. I pressed my right wrist into my side, trembling. I squeezed my eyes shut, wishing they'd fuse together. My left hand clutched at my neck, searching for the calm, hoping to shove away these feelings with my amulet. But I couldn't hide from the truth.

My amulet, which I no longer had, was real. Which meant—I lifted my wrist—the scrolling white scar wasn't a scar but a powerless blocking rune. The inactive rune served as a permanent reminder of how dangerous I was. It also underscored the risk that, without control, my powers could lead him to me. But I didn't know who *he* was anymore. My last memory didn't give me those specifics. *I bet my mom would have an idea.*

So if my last purple dream was a memory I relived, then this one was too. But as I brushed the yellowing bruise peeking from the sleeve of the green shirt Oliver had bought me, I knew this purple dream was different from my last.

I didn't invade a past version of myself, puking was a strong possibility, and I seemed to be able to roam freely instead of being a part of the events unfolding. Plus, I had an odd sense of being in two places at once, which explained the vertigo.

I analyzed my mom and the little girl beside her. It was *me*, around two years old, wearing a sparkly red and brown dress—no, a red chocolate-smeared dress. With my lighter hair color and chubby cheeks, I hardly recognized myself at first, but my eyes gave me away. My mom's dimples betrayed her restrained laughter, matching my toothy chocolate grin.

An ache built in my chest as I placed the frame back on its hook and continued down the hall. Picture after picture lined the walls of only me and my mom. One with me covered by a basket on a picnic blanket, looking like a little turtle trying to crawl away. Another with me cuddled against my mom, sitting next to a Christmas tree. She smiled down at me like I was the only star to matter in the heavens. On and on they went until I found *one* that included a man.

He stared into the camera straight-faced while my mom angled her face away, smiling without her dimples. The only one flashing their pearly whites was the little polka-dotted toddler in the middle. I snorted, embarrassed for myself. At least chocolate didn't smear my face. But that dress. Someone decided to puke rainbow ruffles, sparkles, and unicorns all over me.

I stared a little longer at the man. Unsure of who he was. If I was some type of angel, he couldn't be my father, nor could my mother be my mother. *But if I was a Nephilim, why did my mom have powers? What did that make her? An angel, Fallen, or Nephilim? Or something else entirely?*

I turned from the picture and looked at the last of the captured memories I couldn't remember. Every time I gained a year, my mom took a picture of me next to a chocolate birthday cake. But they stopped when I reached five. So, either my mom no longer continued the tradition, or this memory took place when I was about five.

Shouting startled me out of my musings. I pressed against the wall. Recognizing my mom's voice, I crept toward the soft glow at the end of the hall and peered around the corner.

The man from the picture and my mom were in a screaming match.

They stood between the living room's opening and a chicken-themed kitchen. The kitchen looked rather comical. Thinking back to my few memories, I think my mom had a chicken obsession. It would've made me laugh if not for the tears streaming down the pale skin of my mom's face.

"You're lying to me," he said, crossing his thick arms over his chest. His spotless white long-sleeve bunched at his waist, showing a belt with a dagger and a feather.

The dagger was odd enough, but a feather?

"We've been over this!" she cried. "You drilled me and drilled me the moment I brought her home. I told you the truth. You know I told you the truth. She's just—" My mom glanced back at the hallway, and I ducked behind the wall. I wasn't sure why. It was a memory. It wasn't like it mattered if she saw me. But maybe since I felt like I was eavesdropping, it was instinct. "A miracle," she finished.

He grimaced, looking like he wanted to throttle her. "Then explain to me what I felt today. What I saw."

Her black hair stuck to the tears on her cheeks. "She's just growing into her power. We've never experienced someone like her. That's probably why your senses were heightened today. That's all," she said with wide jade eyes, begging him to believe her.

"My senses are only heightened when I feel—"

She grabbed his arm, pleading. "I know. But you know I'm telling the truth."

"Or you think you are. She should be sent to the council."

My mom's arms fell away as she stepped back. "So, you're going to turn in your family?" she spat, her eyes flashing purple.

He pursed his lips and raised a blonde brow. "Is that how you speak to me now?"

"Is that what you want for your daughter?" she countered.

He jerked as if she slapped him. "Quiet." The veins in his arms popped as he made a fist. She flinched, closing her mouth, but continued to stare at him with a heat of a hundred flames. "*I* am willingly breaking the laws for you. *I* am allowing this on the grounds that it's unheard of. But if you cannot manage your part, *I* will turn her in and leave you here to live out your punishment. Alone," he snapped back.

How could he talk to her like that?

A fierce flush hit her cheeks. She stood, lifting her chin in defiance. "Is that what you truly want? For us? For Lucille?" Her head shook like she couldn't even comprehend the suggestion.

I almost stumbled out from my corner like a dimwit, not believing my ears. *He* was my father?

"They will always come first. Right?" she scoffed. "Or maybe turning us in would put you in their good graces so you could finally rule with your own law. Is that it?"

I admired how she held her shoulders back, acting like she had a foot on him when he stood two heads taller. Her fists clenched, almost like she wanted to hit him. The smoldering anger in her expression made me question why she didn't, but I also noticed something broken and fragile holding her back.

He lifted his arm, and she flinched. "If that were true," he smoothed down a piece of her inky hair, leaning forward so his bared teeth almost touched her ear. "She would already be there."

She jerked away from his touch. He didn't look so happy about that.

A new round of tears streamed down her face. "I won't let you take her to them," she said, stepping out of reach. "And if that's the only reason you came, then maybe this visit should be your last."

"Don't say things you'll regret, my love."

The endearment sounded almost sweet if I ignored his foreboding tone and the tension in my mom's shoulders.

"I want you to leave," she said, turning her back on him to grab a washcloth and scrub the cleaned counters. So she never saw the flash of regret that interrupted the steel in his eyes or the split second of sadness as he glanced toward the hall, where I watched them.

His eyes narrowed before turning back to her. "Since I cannot sense any lies, we will keep our arrangement."

My mom laughed humorlessly, staring at the ceiling, pausing her cleaning. "To continue to check if your precious wife and daughter haven't become something you despise?"

"Wife?" he said with disbelief. And *disgust?*

I clenched my fist as the purple film hugging the edges of my vision covered the rest. My view of my father's pristine white clothing was now a girly lavender. What a perfect color for the tiny man. My mom's clothing remained black.

"That term and any term like it is not allowed to grace your beautiful lips."

She said nothing in response, turning to the stove and wiping the rag across the shiny surface.

He took another step, lifting both his arms, then stopped, dropping them to his sides.

"You better train her and keep her pure. I'll see you next year," he commanded, then turned to me, sending me a suspicious glare.

Oh shit.

The funny feeling of being in two places at once increased. My stomach contents hit the back of my throat. I gagged them back down.

He shouldn't be able to see me. This was a memory.

Or maybe this was a well-crafted dream, and the purple tint was just a coincidence. I'd wake up to find I didn't burn down my house, there wasn't a rune on my wrist, and my mind was playing severely deranged games with me.

He stepped away from her scrubbing and toward the hall. Jerking his head to the side, he motioned for me to follow him.

The fluttering of butterflies and hovering wasps kept my tongue stuck to the roof of my mouth as I followed him outside the house. We walked off the front porch and into the shadows of the night. Once we were far enough away from the house, he stopped and turned.

His eyes panned up and down my body, lingering on my face. "Who are you? What time did you come from?"

What time did I come from? What did he mean? "I—"

A pulse resonated in my ears. My gaze shot to the white flame covering his hands. It looked like mine.

The immense heat shriveled the hairs on my fingers and made me sweat, soaking into my shirt.

I tried again, about to give him my name. "I—"

"Spit it out before I send you back to the hell you came from. I may not be able to kill you. But burning alive in this time will damage your powers enough to prevent you from jumping to another dream."

My mouth closed. I didn't understand what he meant about jumping to another dream, nor did I care.

He wanted to burn me alive.

I stared into his cold, merciless eyes and heard it—the musical destruction of ice. His hateful words and the disgust curling his lip strummed the cord of pelting sleet. It didn't matter if this purple-tinted dream was real or imagined. He awoke the icy vibrations deep within my core and enticed the melody of rage. With the nameless tune surfaced an incessant itch.

A slight purple shimmer flickered to the surface of my fingers, cooling the searing waves of heat that threatened to blister them. It thickened the purple haze. "You don't recognize me?" I said, tilting my head to the side.

He huffed, flames heightening. "The only thing keeping you alive on this dream-walk is the fact I don't know your name or maker. The council will need it to find and eradicate you and your makers."

I lifted my lips in a fake smile. *Maker? Would it matter to him that he threatened his potential daughter and himself? Does it matter to me?*

The unusual, addictive melody said no. My heart? Well, I couldn't currently feel it.

"This is my memory. I control it," I declared.

His wrath changed to a strange, considering look. "No. It's *my* memory you dream-walked into and gave power to. Invade the body, you relive the experience. Invade the memory, you give it and anyone in it the power to alter the memory. A poor mistake on your part." He smirked, then charged me, swiping at my legs and sending me to the ground.

I coughed as the wind knocked out of me, surprised by his speed. I stared at the man who was supposed to be my father in this wretched memory-dream, hoping it was a lie. Hoping all of this was a lie.

A ball of flames bounced in his hands as he stared down at me. "Tell me your name, your maker, and the time you came from."

I sank further into the jarring noise. The itch scurried from the tips of my fingers up to my shoulders. "Go to hell, Fa—"

Searing heat flew toward my chest. I screamed, flinging up my arms and meeting his flames, *burning alive.*

I woke up gasping, my eyes darting to my arms, and slumped. They were a little muddy and damp from the dirty sleeves sticking to my wrists, but they didn't hurt, and I wasn't burning alive.

"It was just a dre—" I stopped, twisting my wrist to inspect the blocking rune. It wasn't a dream. I had dream-walked into his memory. At least, that was what he claimed. I lowered my head into my hands. The memory of the dream-walk had begun to fade, leaving me with my inactive rune, fragmented recollections of our conversation, and the unsettling knowledge someone was after me.

"Shit!" I lifted my head, eager to ask Oliver about dream-walks. Glancing around, I realized I sat in the tent he bought. I turned to my left, searching for him, and inhaled sharply.

The movement shot a line of pain from my shoulder down to my lower spine.

What the heavenly hell?

Confused and most likely a masochist, I reached back. My fingers sank into a hole in my shirt and brushed a bandaged area. I yelped, pulling back. *What happened?*

The last thing I remembered was Oliver lying concussed next to a tree. He could barely move. But he had to have put up this shelter.

Where was he?

I cringed as I stood. The half-zipped doors flapped in a breeze. I unzipped the rest, opening my mouth to call out for Oliver when I heard a soft snore.

He rested inches to my left, against the closest tree, covered in mud. Crusted drool lined the corner of his half-open mouth. The wheezing snores combined with his haphazard appearance eased the tension in my shoulders. Tension I didn't know I was holding.

But we were both alive—dirty, exhausted, and not entirely whole, but alive.

"Oliver." I nudged his boot. His body wobbled. "Oliver," I said louder, nudging harder—still nothing. Worry crept in, thinking about his concussion.

I sank to the ground and grabbed his shoulders, wincing at my sudden movements. "Oliver!"

"What?" he groaned.

I sat back on my heels. "You sleep like the dead."

He opened his eyes, head still resting against his shoulder. "That's because I feel dead."

"What happened?"

He nodded at my injury. "You got hit by lightning."

"How?" *How was I alive? How'd we escape?*

"How'd you get hit by lightning? You never actually hid. How'd we get here? I scared them away and lugged your dead weight to this beautiful clearing. Hence the mud," Oliver supplied.

I frowned. Dried blood surrounded the gash on his forehead. There was no way he scared them away. He couldn't even stand.

"How am I not dead?"

"You're not human, Lucy. Or at least not fully human. Like most of us with angel blood, you heal fast and have tougher flesh." He stretched out his body unconcerned, then scowled. "But carrying your limp body all the way here with two backpacks full of gear is something I never want to do again. So please refrain from getting knocked out next time. Or at least have someone else with you when you refuse to listen to instructions."

I rolled my eyes. I'd try my best. But his story still didn't make sense.

"How'd you do it?" They had us.

A MISCHIEVOUS GRIN LIT his face as he waggled his eyebrows. "You're not the only one with unique powers."

"What are they?" Now, I was beyond curious.

He shrugged and stood. "Maybe you'll find out one day."

"Do you feel murdery when you use them?"

"Uh..." He looked at me strangely. "Sometimes afterwards."

Okay, so maybe I was a Nephilim.

"What can you do?"

"Nope. Not telling." Then, very maturely, he zipped up his lips and threw away the key.

"Why not? Come on!"

"Like I said, maybe you'll find out one day. But today isn't it. Give me a break, would you? I carried your ass through mud and hills, bandaged you, and laid you in the tent," he said. "Possibly falling and dropping you a couple of times, but that's neither here nor there."

"Sorry, you're right. Thanks for saving me."

He shrugged, looking guilty. I didn't know why. He had done everything possible, and I was putting Oliver in danger.

"Oliver, have you ever heard of dream-walking?"

He frowned, brushing the mud out of his dirty hair. "No. Why?"

I glanced away. *How much should I tell him?* He had just risked his life to save me from elemental angels. If he knew someone was after me and that he might have to face more danger, would he still want to take me to Elora? I didn't know, and I couldn't risk it. But next time I could be prepared.

"Do you know what this is?" I showed him my wrist.

He grabbed it. "Yeah. It's a faded Blocking Rune created by an Archangel's feather. Those runes are nasty little shits. Who carved this onto you?"

"I don't know. I barely remember it. But I think I've had it for years."

Surprised, Oliver dropped my arm and stared at me. "Years? Your powers have been suppressed for years? Do you have any idea how unhealthy that is?"

"No. Memory issues, remember?"

He shook his head. "Blocking Runes are supposed to be used for a year max. They suppress anything supernatural. They're for children who grow into their power too early and have control issues. It doesn't happen often, so they're not used often. I guess I've also heard of angels carving them into prisoners of war to weaken them. But they're supposed to be temporary. You're saying you think your rune was active for years?"

I nodded. "It'd make sense. I'm terrible at controlling my powers."

Oliver huffed. "That's a fact."

"So, can you help me learn how to control them?"

He grimaced. "I'm a terrible teacher."

"Do you really think I could get worse?"

"Well, when you put it like that." He stood, walking toward the tree line a few yards away. "Sure, I'll help you after I hunt our dinner."

My brows furrowed. "But it's getting dark!"

"Exactly, we need a fire and food before the sun sets. Find some small sticks, would you?" he called over his shoulder, fading into the landscape of birch trees.

He was just going to leave me here alone?

I scanned the shadows between the endless white trees. Oliver said he scared off the Powers. They should be gone or, hopefully, dead. He wouldn't leave me if they were still looking for us. I kept telling myself that as I picked up kindling, and the itching and stabbing pressure crept along my arms.

They were signs of my power. It was the only explanation. Every time I spiraled into my fear, the stabbing needles tore across my skin, and white flames erupted. As for the ceaseless annoying itch, it only came when I was angry. The purple flames came after, and sometimes music. What they did, besides enraging me to the point of attempted murder, I didn't know. But I needed to find out, if only to help my mom.

It didn't take long for me to have a pile of kindling in my arms. I set it near our tent, wondering what to do next. Oliver still wasn't back. Although, if he was off finding food, it may be a while.

I walked to the edge of the birch trees. Their leaves rustled in a soft breeze, sending out a sharp wintergreen scent. It soothed my lingering itch but did nothing to the hovering pressure.

My toe edged the line between sun and shade, between looking for Oliver or sitting and thinking about who was after me. Neither one brought me comfort. Both choices provoked the pressure beneath my hands. I squeezed them into fists and lengthened them, hoping to relieve the pain. But my power only listened to my emotions.

About to step into the darkening forest, a black shadow flashed in the distance. A black shadow that seemed far too large. Something tickled the back of my mind, almost like the shadow was familiar, but fear pushed the thought away. My punishing power attacked me instead. White flames erupted from my skin, curling around my fingers. I took a step back, holding them away from my clothes. Then I took another until my boots hit our tent.

Where the hell was Oliver?

CHAPTER TEN

A shuffling noise startled me, and the flames on my hands heightened.

"Oliver?"

The shuffling continued, followed by a pause. The setting sun darkened the forest's shadows, hiding everything within. But my eyes never strayed, searching for any movement, every sense on high alert. A soft pressure pulsed behind my eyes at the slight chance it wasn't Oliver. But it had to be.

"Oliver, come on. We've been through hell. Stop joking around." My voice carried through the chirping crickets.

Then all noise quieted.

"I'm safe. I'm not a wimp. I'm safe," I whispered to myself. "It's just Oliver."

But the silence of the forest reminded me of the Powers. *What if they found us?* Oliver's story was wishy-washy to begin with. He had a concussion, and they knocked me out with a lightning bolt. There was no way he got us away that easily while injured.

What if they only let us get away to give us a sense of security?

My bright flames flickered around my hands, nearing my sleeve. "Oliver, come out."

Minutes passed as I stood with every muscle tense, waiting for the air to change, for Oliver to pop out, but not even the breeze crinkled the tops of the trees.

Why was he hiding?

A few seconds more, and nothing.

I huffed, dropping my shoulders. "Lucy, you're such a damn scaredy cat," I muttered to myself. The pounding of my heart quieted with my easing muscles. The needles returned to their horror house beneath my skin, releasing me from my white flames. I took a hesitant step, my head turning back and forth. Still, nothing moved. Before I bent over to search Oliver's backpack for matches, an ear-piercing wail wrenched through the stillness.

My horror house of needles surged, tearing through my insides to the surface of my skin. I screamed, hunching into myself. White light burst free, overtaking the black spots that attempted to take over my vision. It layered my naked torso in flames.

With my flame illuminating my surroundings, I could see further into the forest, but the thing didn't show itself. Instead, it wailed for a second time. My flames jumped.

The thing shuffled closer to the edge of our campsite.

I backed up a step. It shuffled closer, slower this time, like it was taunting me. My white flames pulsed with more light as the thing in the forest played with my nerves. Its noisy steps edged the line between the shadows and light. I could almost make out the outline of the dark figure as it stood there, watching, waiting.

Frozen, I didn't know what to do. The fire coating my skin remained useless until the thing came closer.

I swallowed down my suffocating breaths, trying to calm myself. But it wasn't working—it never worked. I pawed at my neck, frantically searching for my amulet, and felt my flaming hand hit my chin. I froze. But, of course, I was immune to burning from my power.

The thing wailed again and stepped into the clearing.

I was going to die. After everything I had been through, I was going to be mauled by this creature from hell.

Dark slime dripped down its gangly human limbs as it crouched on all fours. Spikes along its spine shuddered with the movement, readying to charge. I couldn't see its nonexistent face. Inky sludge covered it. No nose. No mouth. No eyes. Just a creature sent straight from my nightmares.

Breathing heavily, I slowly stepped to the side. One more step and the tent would no longer be at my back. Then, I was going to run. On my final step, it flexed its finger-like claws and bolted.

A pulse resonated through the air as I tried to scream. But I couldn't with how hard I panted. White light surged toward the creature about to maul me with its spindly claws. The pressure behind my eyes throbbed. I wanted to squeeze them shut to relieve the pain but couldn't take my eyes away as my flame shot toward the creature. Right before it made contact, the thing disappeared. My dangerous energy hit the tree behind it.

Flames consumed the bark and leaves. The once large tree disintegrated into particles of glowing ash and fell into a small pile of soot. A dark silhouette stood next to it, partially hiding behind another tree.

"Please don't kill me, Lucy."

I froze.

"Oliver?"

"Yeah?" he squeaked, coming into the cast of my light.

One tree—one tree stood in the way of killing Oliver. Whatever power I unleashed was fast. There would have been no way to pull my flame back.

"Are you completely insane?" I screamed, waving my hands around. "What the hell were you doing behind that tree? I almost burned you alive!"

He nodded down to my breasts. "You know you're naked, right?" he said, unfazed.

I whipped my arms up to cover myself, feeling heat spread from my neck to my forehead. "There—" I glanced to my sides. "There was this thing!"

Where did it go? It blipped out of existence and hadn't come back.

Oliver's mouth pressed down into a frown. "About that..." He ran his hand through his hair, laughing nervously. "So... that monster thing. With the drippy mud skin and creepy limbs... yeah, that might've been me."

"You?"

"Yeah, well..." He laughed again. "After I hunted for our food, I thought about how I would teach you, and my first thought was to see how you'd fare against an attacker. To get a baseline of your powers."

I nodded, biting my cheeks. Hard

"Didn't know you'd do that..." he trailed off, sheepish.

I nodded again. That was all I could do was nod. My cheeks were raw with how hard I bit into them. Oliver admitting to scaring the living flame out of me to test me was smart but incredibly asinine! That pile of dark ash beside us could've been him.

"Lucy, are you okay?"

My skin would've been itching if I didn't feel like I was about to fall over or asleep.

Guilt tugged at the creeping smile on his face, and I lost it again.

"You are insane!"

I couldn't believe him. I didn't know what I could do, which may be another reason to test my powers. But not on him! Not on anyone. My powers were too dangerous.

"I'm not trying to make you scream at me for a fourth time, but do you think we can have this fight after you put on a shirt? It's hard to take you seriously when your boobs are out."

Gritting my teeth, I stomped away from him.

I put on my jacket, realizing the back had a large hole. *Dammit.* It was my last piece of clothing, so I had no other options. At least it covered my chest and had a soft inside. Although, a bra would've been nice. Too bad I incinerated it because of Oliver's *thoughtfulness.*

I stomped back to Oliver and the fire he made. His head tilted up from whatever he was working on in his lap.

"I'm sorry, Lucy, for almost killing myself in a crazy plan. I deserve the glare you're giving me." It was hard to tell if his apology was sincere with the half smile that twitched on his face. He picked up a skinned, impaled rabbit, balanced it on two sticks over the fire, and then patted the ground beside him. "I think I figured a couple of things out."

"Tell me and explain the monster thing you did." I crossed my legs, the loose material rustling as I moved. My numb, shaking hands hovered near the fire, warming. Moments ago, the chilly air didn't affect me. Now I was freezing.

"What's the main emotion you feel before your white flames pop out on your skin?" he asked.

"Fear."

"And what about your purple flames?"

"Anger."

"Good. Those are your baselines. They are the emotions that control you and your power, which is normal for a beginner. As kids, Nephilim get a feel for their powers using their baselines. Then they learn real fast that they can't rely on their emotions forever, or they'll hurt themselves or someone else. With the amount of power you just threw at me, you will have to learn fast. Use anger and fear to coax your flames to the surface for now, then as you dive into your well of power, study what happens and break the emotional connection."

Easier said than done.

Oliver noticed my expression. "We'll practice in a second. But first, I think I know what your white flames are."

"What?" I asked, excited.

"I think they're your Glory. An Archangel's Glory, in fact. I've experienced it before. Funny story—"

"No, no funny stories. What are you saying? You think I'm an Archangel?" I knew nothing about them, shocker. But I had hoped the word would spark a familiar nudge. My brain did that sometimes. It nudged at me like it was trying to make me remember something.

"The pure white glow, crazy consuming heat, and the force are exactly the same as their Glory. So yeah..." he said, trailing off at my glare.

"I don't know, Oliver. What if I'm a Nephilim *with* Glory?"

He snorted. "Even if a Nephilim has a father who is an Archangel, they don't pass down their Glory power. That's a specific power to them."

I rubbed at the ache in my chest, almost wishing I would've been left with different memories. Something that didn't pull at my gut every time I saw her face. Something that didn't leave me on the edge of my seat, thinking the worst but hoping for the best.

"But what if I have a mom?" I whispered.

Oliver stared at me, mouth shut, wheels turning in his squinting eyes. "Do you?"

"She's one of the memories I kept," I ran my finger through the dirt, swallowing. "I saw her, surrounded by, I'm not even sure who. It was dim, and they were wearing uniforms. I wanted to help, to protect her, like she always did for me. But the moment I decided to join the fight, something forced me out of the house." I laughed, though none of this was funny. "That's the only memory I have of her."

Equally as quiet, Oliver asked, "But how do you know she's your mother?"

"I just... I felt it," I said, touching my chest.

Oliver scooted closer, giving me a knowing smile. "Family doesn't have to share the same blood. You can still be an angel and have a mom."

"Aren't angels created? Like they blip into the air fully grown or something."

He nodded, taking the rabbit off the fire, cutting it apart, and divvying up on a set of plates. "Yes, they are. I'm not sure about the blipping full-grown part, but I'd assume so. Angels are hundreds of years old. So, who knows?" he said as he handed me one and a wooden fork.

The peppery and herbaceous aroma of the meat made my stomachache. I was more than ready to sink my fork into the sizzling goodness. But before I did, I said, "I think I was born."

He gave me a strange look. "Are you sure you lost your memories? Because it seems you know more than you're letting on."

"No—I—" A fluttering sensation tickled my mind. "I was born. I don't know how I know that or why the thought came to me now. But it's true."

He took a bite of his rabbit, chewing slowly. "It's just... Nephilim don't have Glory. It's unheard of. Although Archangels or any other types of angels don't have your purple flames."

"Other types?" I asked, taking a large bite of my juicy rabbit.

He set his fork and half-finished plate down, sighing. "Okay, let's rehash the whole angel hierarchy."

I couldn't tell if Oliver was being sarcastic or if he was eager to speak on the subject.

"There are six levels of angels with the Seraphims at the top. I haven't seen one and probably never will. Nor do I know anyone who has. The amount of power and rule they have is, well, they're at the top for a reason. The next highest are the Archangels." He motioned to his imaginary ladder. "A warrior-type angel. They are scary. In a, I will enact my justice in a burn-you-to-bits-with-my-Glory kind of way. Like you."

I swallowed, looking down at my food.

"Some have an extra power specific to them, which makes them extra scary. They are also... How would you say it nicely?" He tapped a finger against his lip. "Stuck-up assholes and stone-cold killers. Dominions are under them. They are still ruthless assholes, but they have sick telekinetic powers and keep the other angels under them in line. Then there are the Thrones, which are more of a scholarly type. They like books. A lot of books. We already had a run-in with some Powers—"

"Which you have yet to explain how we got away from."

He rolled his eyes.

Was he purposefully avoiding the subject?

He continued, ignoring my questioning look. "We ran into an earth and sky elemental."

"Sky isn't an element."

"No, but it's a class within the Powers. A sky elemental is someone who has the power over wind, rain, and lightning. I guess you could say thunder, too. Which means she is most likely a colonel," he explained.

She, as in he saw who they were. *Is*, suggesting they still lived. "Colonel?"

"A military ranking. Pretty high up there," he shrugged like it was no big deal that Oliver went up against a Power who had control over three elements and ranked high in their military.

"How'd we survive?" What tale could Oliver even tell that I'd believe?

He ignored me, focus glued on the fire. "Virtues are the last level. They are also part of their military but do more healing than fighting. Not that they can't. I'm pretty sure every level of angel is trained to fight. They are the most level-headed and friendly. Not that that's saying much. For some reason, all pure-blooded angels act like they have a stick shoved up their asses, unlike us, the Nephilim half-breeds who are above the disgraced Fallen and other manner of supernatural creatures. And that wraps up the short overview of the angels."

"How, Oliver?"

"My powers, Lucille."

He hardly ever used my full name. And never in such a severe tone. Whatever he did, whatever powers he used, he didn't want to talk about it. We were safe, and I was pressing too much. I needed to let it go for now.

"*Your* powers have aspects of an Archangels. Even your healing is accelerated. That blast that incinerated the thick tree should've knocked you out after all you've been through. A Nephilim would've passed out or died." He stared at me, fire flickering from the emerald depths of his eyes.

"So, you're convinced I'm potentially a stone-cold killer with a stick shoved up my ass?"

He snorted, breaking his moment of seriousness. "I'm saying your memory isn't reliable; you almost killed me twice now, at times have murdery eyes, have Glory, which only Archangels have, have accelerated healing— more so than a Nephilim—and can potentially have a mother that isn't blood-related. That's what I'm saying."

Was I an Archangel? But I didn't blip into existence. I was born and raised by my mom, not a ruthless Archangel. If that were the case, then I would've been able to protect her. Oliver said angels were all trained in their military. If I were one of them, I would've never cowered behind a corner, hesitating to protect the only person I loved.

Oliver, noticing my internal battle and wrongly assuming my thoughts, said, "Blood doesn't matter when it comes to love."

"I know."

He gave me a weak smile, then stared into the fire. "I had—I *have* a sister who isn't blood-related to me. Not with her inky dark hair and olive skin."

Entranced by learning something personal about him, I listened to his soft words.

"I remember when my mom brought her home. She was so tiny and cried way too much. But sometimes, my mom let me hold her, and she'd stop crying. She'd look up at me with her dark eyes and stare. Only with me, though. She didn't talk to my mom at first, and I was too young to ask why or where she came from. I just remembered liking that I was no longer an only child, and she liked me more." An inner light lit Oliver's face. Not joking, not moody, not the mischievous smirk he frequently wore, but a genuine smile. It was the first one I'd ever seen grace his face.

"What was her name?" I asked.

"Melanie. But I called her Lainy."

"Called?"

His smile dropped as he rubbed his scar. "Marcus took her a long time ago."

"Why? Where'd he take her?" But I had a sneaking suspicion that I knew where. "You think she's in Elora, in the Tenebrous Kingdom?"

I knew nothing of Elora, but Oliver associated Marcus with that kingdom. A lackey, he said, meaning someone worse was above Marcus pulling the strings. But if Marcus kidnapped angels for his sovereign, why was I caged on Earth and Oliver's sister taken to Marcus's kingdom? Unless kidnapping, and drugging to the point of uselessness was the first step before he handed me over to his sovereign in Elora.

"You're sure she's there?"

"I know she is." He kicked at the fire again, then abruptly chucked his plate and barely eaten food into it.

I swallowed. "How?"

He glanced at me—his expression filled with guilt, anger, and glassy pain. "My mom kept us sheltered on Earth. She never liked to talk about my father, only telling us the bare minimum of what we were. Maybe she would've explained more when we were older, but she never got the chance." He turned away, not elaborating. "I grew up in foster care, such a joyful experience. Instead of picking fights like any normal, abandoned kid would, I dove headfirst into research about angels and Elora. They thought I was crazy. When I was old enough, I figured out how to travel to this *different* world, but I still never found her. It wasn't until I became desperate enough that I made an associate." He dropped his head, rubbing his wrist. "After *years* of me floundering, they helped locate her," he said, voice cracking. "*Years,* only to learn that my sister was being kept in an impenetrable kingdom."

I poked at my bones and the little bits of meat I no longer had the stomach for. "Do you think he took my mom there?"

Oliver jerked to look at me. "That's why you want to go to Elora. Not just for answers, but for your mom."

I nodded. We acknowledged each other, connecting on a shared understanding of want and pain. Then, something flashed in his eyes as he turned away.

Compassion? Guilt? I couldn't tell.

"It's possible. He had you. But not knowing what or who your mom is, I don't know why he'd take her."

"Why'd he take Melanie?"

Oliver quieted. Bringing up her name did a number on him. "Power," he finally said. "My mom had an angel friend who was a seer. She saw that my sister would grow into another powerful seer. Somehow, the Tenebrous Kingdom must've found out."

"So, my mom might be an angel they kidnapped for her power?"

In my memory, her eyes flashed purple, and something forced me outside the house. So Oliver could be right. Maybe my mind was so muddled that I thought I was born, when, in reality, I was an angel, and my mom wasn't my biological mom. The thought did nothing to temper my love for her, but it did increase my guilt for my ineptitude.

Oliver nodded. "Maybe. Or she's in the Ethereal Kingdom."

"Why would they kidnap her? Are they better or worse than the Tenebrous Kingdom?"

"Depends on who you ask. In my opinion, both kingdoms could burn in hell. The Ethereal Kingdom is filled with all those purebloods with sticks in their asses. If your mom happened to piss off the wrong high-ranking angel, they could've taken her as easily as Marcus could've."

I dropped my head into my hands. "That's helpful."

"Do you remember anything else?"

"The uniformed soldiers kept flashing between white armor and blood-red leather. Does that mean anything?"

Oliver snorted. "Yeah."

I perked up.

"White or light blue armor is what the Ethereal military wears. Red is what the Tenebrous Kingdom wears."

Dammit. "That sure narrows it down."

"When we get to Elora, what kingdom will we be in?"

"Neither. We'll be in The Divide."

I laughed. It wasn't a humorous one. Not when exhaustion and a throbbing pain pummeled my head, back, and feet. "Which is?"

"A place between the two kingdoms. Neutral territory."

I shook my pounding head. I was about to ask if he knew who Magda was, but my eyes fluttered, and I didn't think I could retain anything else.

"You're drained. Go to bed before you topple over into the fire. I don't feel like seeing if you're fire-proof tonight. We can practice your power tomorrow."

I sighed, standing on wobbly legs. "Yeah. There's just so much I don't know."

When I started toward the tent, I heard a soft. "There sure is."

The moment I saw my sleeping bag, I flopped and fell asleep.

CHAPTER ELEVEN

Her gentle voice whispered to me, humming horrifying words.

There once was a daughter of seven circles, hidden, protected, avoiding the hurdles.

There once was a palace of crystalized ice awaiting the daughter to sacrifice. Unbalanced and sorrowful. Hopeless with no tomorrow.

I didn't want to hear it. "Stop."

There once was a world concealed from her, vibrant in color, awaiting a shudder.

"Be quiet! Stop!"

When the ice whispers. Be prepared for the fissures.

"I said STOP!"

"LUCY, WAKE UP!" OLIVER shouted. "Wake up!"

I lurched awake, finding the tent covered in frost. The frigid air froze the moisture in my nose and the breath puffing out of my lungs. White clusters speckled my sleeping bag, and a purple flame twined with black. The colorful flames slowly dissolved the end of the silky fabric once covering my toes. It crept along, eating holes like a picky eater, and suddenly changed tactics and dissolved a giant chunk.

I jerked my feet up and scrambled out, head throbbing. "What's it doing?"

"I was going to ask you the same question," he accused, squatting outside the tent.

Once the purple flame reached halfway up the sleeping bag, it dimmed and left, leaving Oliver and me gaping at the melting frost and the snacked-on material.

"Her voice... I had a dream. But the words... I can't remember them all. Something about a daughter, ice, and sacrifice?" I shuddered.

"Your mom's voice?"

"Maybe. You said I was yelling. Do you know what I said?"

He ran his hand through his hair. "You kept saying stop and be quiet. After that, I was a little more concerned with not getting eaten by whatever the hell that was."

I glanced at my hands, shoulders dropping.

At this rate, I'd be naked by the time we arrived in Elora. From wrist to shoulder, my jacket sleeves were gone. Numerous holes in varying sizes peppered the rest. I looked...

"I think the style you are working toward is homeless chic or Swiss cheese couture," Oliver supplied, guessing my thoughts.

I laughed—something I hadn't done in some time.

"Cute! I'm glad after all my random blabbering, I could finally make you laugh." He ruffled through his backpack. "Here. Less Swiss cheese like." Oliver handed me a black shirt outlined with purple flowers—the same pattern on my joggers.

I eyed him and the lightweight material. "Thanks," I said, taking the shirt.

"No problem, Luce, just don't kill me in my sleep, okay?"

Sheepish, I sent him a weak smile. I wished it was that easy. After all of Oliver's near-death experiences, I seriously wondered why he didn't leave me.

I glanced at my discarded jacket and sleeping bag. *So that was what my purple flame was? Slow-devouring ice?*

Oliver gave my sleeping bag a wide berth and packed our gear. "Let's get going. We have half a day left, and on the way, you'll practice." Oliver flung the backpack onto his shoulders, ducking under the tent's opening.

After changing, I gingerly put on my backpack and climbed out. My lightning wound felt better, but the added weight made me cringe.

The moment I left, Oliver blurred around me, taking down and packing the tent faster than he put it up.

He was always in a rush, not that I was complaining. I wanted out of this forest.

"Here's breakfast." He handed me a granola bar, then took off at a jog.

"Not jogging," I groaned.

I took off after him. He bounded through the grove of birch trees, jumping over stumps and swerving around bushes, never missing a beat. Then there was me, tripping over pebbles, catching on thorn bushes, wincing every time my backpack chafed against my lightning scar.

"Why are we jogging?" I yelled out to him as a branch so kindly whipped me in the face. Each downed log we ran by pleaded to be sat on.

"It's a warmup," he exclaimed, sounding at ease as his legs pounded into the ground, unlike my labored pants.

"A warmup for what? Are you trying to kill me?"

He didn't answer for the longest time, then said, "No, I'm really not. I want you to survive, Lucy. So let's practice." He stopped, allowing me to catch up. "Lusceler is the first thing we're taught to understand how to tap into our power. It won't drain you if you use it in small bursts. So, catch me." He winked and blurred away.

"Oliver!" I screamed. Energy and the needle-like pain of my Glory shot across my skin. I chased after him, catching up to his blurring form. He smiled and stopped when he saw me. Unamused, I whipped out a hand to smack him in the chest and missed when he stumbled back, falling on his ass.

"Fuck-a-duck, Lucy! This is why you need practice."

Horrified, my flickering white flames sank back into my skin.

Oliver stood. "You need to believe in yourself. You've luscelered before. I knew you could do it again and only ran away to prompt you into action instead of thinking about it. And you did, but your panic and fear took over, and I almost got a Lucy-sized handprint."

"I'm sorry," I said, biting my lip.

"We're going to try again. But *when* you lusceler, feel your power. Get a sense of how it moves through your body. It should be a trickle of energy, not a river."

"Okay," I said, unsure.

"You got this. On a count of three," he said. "One... two... three!"

Oliver luscelered, and I was right beside him. As we ran, I tried to focus on the energy. It prickled and tickled like a gentler combination of sensations I received from my Glory and my purple flames. But the more I focused on the exhilarating sensation, begging it to stay a trickle, the more the prickles became stabs.

No, no, no.

We hit a rocky incline, and my hands blazed with Glory. Oliver stopped us, noticing my white flames.

"Well, you almost had it."

Defeated and tired, I sank onto a rock and waited until my stupid flames disappeared. "Why is this so hard?"

"Because you're a grown adult now learning about your power. Not sure how often that happens."

I sighed.

Oliver stared up the hill, where the pine trees opened to boulders, looking uncertain. The sun beat down on their white flesh while we paused in the shade. "We're almost there." He ran two hands through his hair, squeezing his head.

"Are you worried? Because I have an idea of who can help us find our answers." I wasn't sure why I didn't mention it earlier, probably because my powers continued to shock me with their attempts at ruining my life and killing Oliver. "I believe she's in Elora," I mumbled to myself. Gosh, she had to be. But there was no way that woman would tell me about the name Magda if she wasn't in Elora. Especially after telling me my mom was there.

"No." Oliver dropped his head, refusing to look at me. "I have a plan. We just need to get to The Divide."

I stared at him as birds chirped and squirrels skittered across the bark of the trees. This was hard on him. He had been avoiding Elora for so long, and now he would have to break his promise to himself—because of me.

The scent of pine sap calmed my guilt with its earthy freshness. "We'll find her, Oliver. We'll find them both."

He sighed, giving me a half smile that didn't meet his guilty emeralds. "Yeah. We'll see."

Standing, I grabbed his hand and gave a hopefully reassuring smile. "We will."

He snatched his hand back like I'd burned him. "We have a few hours left climbing rocks. Practice feeling your power. It could help you."

I glanced down to make sure I didn't accidentally burn him. "Right. Okay."

Stepping on the loose dirt, I latched onto trees to help pull my weight up. Oliver followed me, dodging all the dirt and small rocks I kicked up.

Once we passed the tree line, the terrain became steeper. I had no time to practice my power when I was too focused on crawling over boulders. We gripped their jagged, warm edges and pulled our bodies up. Sweat slicked my palms. A couple of times, we lost our grip on the rocks, sliding down until we caught ourselves or each other. My heart crawled up my throat as I gazed at the potential rocky death behind me, happy to have Oliver and his help.

He stood on a boulder up ahead, tilting his head to the ledge a few meters away, rubbing the tattoo on his wrist. Three irritating rocks separated us. I sat, giving myself a break before climbing them and the five others to get to the ledge.

"I'm sorry, Oliver."

One second. Ten seconds. After thirty seconds of stewing in my guilt, he turned, and I wanted to apologize again. His eyes were moist, and his lips were pressed into a fake smile. I think it was supposed to be reassuring, but it came off as painful.

"Don't apologize. The deals have been made."

The weight of our gloomy mood was reflected in the darkening clouds of the sky. Rain decided to let loose on us the moment we reached the top.

"We're here?"

Snow and evergreens dotted an open expanse of rock. It had four ledges. Off of three of them were sheer drops to your death. With the wind whipping at my joggers, threatening to knock over my wobbling toothpicks, I wasn't about to get near them.

"This way," Oliver ushered me from the ledge toward a rock that jutted from the earth. Coming around it, I could see it wasn't a random tall rock but an arch.

"This is the entry to Elora. Once we step through the archway, we won't be on Earth anymore. Are you ready?"

Nope. But this wasn't for me.

"Are you?" I asked.

He stared at the archway like it was the end of something good and sighed heavily. "Let's get this over with." His words twisted the knife.

"We'll find them, Oliver."

He didn't respond.

The archway blended in with the rocks surrounding it. I walked closer, and pinpricks of iridescent light shimmered. The blues, yellows, and reds mixed with a background of white, changing its hue with each tilt of my head. "Do you see it too?"

"All supernatural creatures can. To humans, it's just an archway off the side of a cliff."

His long fingers lightly traced over the top portion of the arch. As they passed, words glowed a soft white. They curled at odd angles and connected in weird formations—writing in a different language.

"What does it mean?" I asked.

"It's angelic. It speaks of light, darkness, night, and blood. Each word is a representation of a supernatural creature. You must have the blood of one to enter. If not, you will likely fall off the cliff and meet a pleasant end on some rocks."

There was the humor that was missing, albeit a little off. "Well, doesn't that sound nice?"

Silver flashed as he took a knife out of his pocket. I eyed it warily. "Blood opens it," he explained, cutting his thumb and rubbing it against the writing.

A blue light flashed. It lit up the space around us and settled in the center of the arch, glimmering like a wobbly mirror. Giving me one last look, Oliver took my hand. Heart pumping with anticipation, I took a deep breath and walked through the arch.

I didn't feel the rush of air like I would if I was falling to my death. Instead, my ears popped, and my body pulled in odd directions. Light twisted in unusual formations and colors, at times blinding me. Goosebumps rose on my skin as particles tickled and kissed my exposed flesh. Within seconds, it was over, my hands and knees hitting solid ground.

My fingers flexed in the soft moonlit grass as I blinked the portal light away. Slowly, I adjusted to the night sky and the oddness of having come from daylight. I glanced on either side of me, wondering where Oliver was, then looked up to a horde of figures.

CHAPTER TWELVE

BLOODHOUND AND RUNE

Rune watched from a distance, blending in with the shadows of the trees and giving me a clear view of the scene through her eyes. The Nephilim listened. Good, *he'd* be pleased to hear.

The female knelt frozen on all fours before Marcus and his soldiers. Her eyes widened in horror and surprise as she stared at them.

"Well, well, well. You actually did it." The female flinched at Marcus's sickly satisfied words. "Over the phone, you sounded almost unsure. I'm shocked."

The confusion in the female's eyes revealed that she hadn't yet grasped that the Nephilim had betrayed her. We told him to call Marcus and arrange this deal. Despite his vehement protests, the Nephilim didn't have a choice. Although, I thought he might find a way around our demands. Good thing he didn't.

"My mom, Oliver!" the female cried, turning to face the guilty Nephilim standing in front of the Earth portal. "How could you do this to me?"

Marcus laughed as the female clutched her neck, heaving. The Nephilim took a giant step toward her.

"Lucy—I—"

"How could you hand me back to *them*?" she interrupted him, tears streaming down her face.

"Lucy, you don't understand," The Nephilim urged.

"Don't call me that! You're one sick bastard, using a story about your sister to garner sympathy and hide your guilt about stabbing me in the back!" she screamed, and Rune growled.

Quiet, Rune. They can't know you're there.

"Lucille, please. I had no choice!"

The Nephilim better keep our deal to himself.

"Well, this has been splendid, but the time for pleasantries is over. Leave while you still can, boy," Marcus drawled and snapped his fingers down, "Emile, Jemihal, seize her."

"Show me proof of my sister, bastard!" The Nephilim screamed in Marcus's face, distracting him enough for the female to scramble up and lusceler.

Marcus's soldiers slammed her into the ground before she could breach their circle. Rune's anger shot through our mind link.

Don't you dare, I snapped at her.

She dug her claws into the ground, forcing herself to stay, sending me a feeling akin to a glare. As young as she was, I wasn't surprised by her attitude. But it made it difficult to control her, especially when I wasn't with her and only had our connection to stop her defiant temperament.

"Let go of me!" The female squirmed and kicked beneath Marcus's soldiers until purple flames burst from her skin and attacked. Ice devoured the two holding her, crawling down their throats and freezing them solid.

"She just killed them," Marcus's soldiers yelled.

Was that why he wanted her?

By the astonishment in her expression, she hadn't meant to. She stood, ready to escape again, and swayed.

"Get the cuffs on her!" Marcus called out. "It shouldn't be hard now. She's drained."

"Did you hear what I said, scumbag?" The Nephilim seethed.

"When are you ever going to learn? Your sister is dead. There's no getting her back," Marcus said—blunt, disinterested, straight to the point.

"The hell she is!" he yelled.

A couple more soldiers strode from the formation with a pair of cuffs and knocked the swaying female down.

"No," she shrieked, flailing about to escape their hold.

Rune stepped out from behind the trees.

Rune! Do not engage.

Rune paused, but not because of my command. The queen's pet had portaled in with the Searcher and two Cambion Demons.

"I killed the female myself. She screamed in agony as her flesh bubbled and fluids burst. Her blue beauties popped with all the heat," Marcus laughed with manic glee.

The Nephilim screamed, and his eyes flashed green as he swung at Marcus. I didn't know what power he had, but regardless, Marcus dodged his swing and kneed the Nephilim in the groin and then the face, knocking him out cold.

Marcus laughed, unaware of the onlookers. "He never learns." He moved to the squirming female. "Knock her out if you can't get a damned pair of cuffs on a weak, useless female."

One of his soldiers took out an axe and bashed the blunt end into her head. She stilled, Rune growled, and the pet bellowed. "Marcus!"

Marcus jerked his attention to the Tenebrous portal. "Prince— wh— what are you doing here?"

"The queen sent me." He strode forward, blue eyes enflamed.

"Why?" Marcus asked.

"She sensed someone coming through the portal."

"Sensed?" Marcus asked, taking a few steps closer to the Earth portal.

The pet took in Marcus's retreating steps, the female cuffed on the ground, and the circle of soldiers that gave the queen's pet a wide berth. Blue flames erupted on the pet's hands, and Marcus took another step back.

"Yes, sensed. She spelled the portal. So she was surprised to sense her second-in-command come through the Earth portal when he was supposed to be in Deava. You defied a direct order from your queen. Care to explain?" The blue flames in the pet's hands formed into balls, and he bounced them as he waited for an answer.

Marcus turned and fled, sprinting to the Earth portal.

Blue flames shot from the pet's hands, reducing the soldiers to ash and raging toward Marcus. They destroyed the Tenebrous portal along the way and missed Marcus's feet by inches.

Why'd the pet do that? That was the way back to their kingdom.

The Searcher and Cambion demons were cuffing the female's arms and didn't notice what happened.

The pet approached them, extinguishing his flames, and took the female from the Searcher.

"My flames destroyed our way home in attempts to kill the traitor. We'll have to go the long way," he said. The Searcher glanced at the portal, and then they walked into the woods together.

Follow Rune, and don't get caught. I'll check back in later. If anything happens to the female or they're not headed in the right direction, signal to me. Do not intervene.

CHAPTER THIRTEEN

It was yet another purple-ringed dream but without the vertigo. This time, I invaded the body of a recent version of myself. I couldn't tell how old I was, only that I stood taller, and my chest pushed at my shirt.

I sprinted outside into the last light of day and headed toward the woods behind our house. Dark clouds drenched me with their rain and pelted me in the face as I pushed myself into lusceler.

"Bring it on!" I yelled to the sky, slamming my soaked slippers into every puddle. Fist clenched, the pressure swelled with each splash. I pushed myself faster, the canopy of green guarding me from the rain.

It was coming.

It started as a touch, nudging me. Then, based on the torrent of emotions, it rose until the pressure intensified and hit my barrier. And when it hit my barrier, stabbing into me beneath my skin, I only had seconds left.

Millions of little needles tore at my body.

I sank to my knees.

My power tried to obliterate my protective layer. Or at least that's what it felt like. When I couldn't hold in my cries any longer, I flung my head back. Wet strands of black hair slapped against my shirt, and I screamed as an explosion of white flame burst free, disintegrating my clothes into a pile of ash.

At release, my screams stopped, hissing rain filling the silence. I wanted to cry, but my body wouldn't allow it in this state. This was her fault because of her stupid confession. But how could she have kept me so in the dark—lied to me for so long?

The thought turned to acid in my stomach. For nine years, my mom lied to me, to my father, about—I stopped myself. That thought still hadn't registered. Or it did, but it was too complicated to wrap my brain around.

She hid so much from me. No wonder she'd always been so hellbent on calming me and keeping me off everyone's radar.

But she couldn't hide it all. The thought was bitter and filled with a sick kind of resentment. It only happened twice. My mom never gave me an explanation either time. The incidents were ignored and avoided in conversation, brushed away with innocent excuses or her power.

I thought back to the plume of smoke from our burning house and the shock of seeing my room explode with white and purple flame. And even further back, to when I touched him. My eyes flickered to the angelic rune on my wrist, now white and useless. A crutch and a perfect tool to hide what my mom didn't want anyone to know. I wondered when my father figured it out. If I ever had the misfortune of seeing him again, I could ask.

The more I replayed her words, the more I understood and felt the unfairness of it all. I wanted her to take it all back. I didn't want any of it to be true.

I laughed. It was humorless and dark, like the coils that curled in my stomach. My nostrils flared, and my laugh turned into a feral scream stemming from my pent-up emotions. Bile invaded the back of my throat as a crashing tune vibrated in my ears, pulling forth an incessant itch.

Pounding the ground, welcoming the pain, I tortured my vocal cords again. My breath turned to fog before my eyes. The white flame flickering along my body changed to a deep purple, and sleet bounced off my face, settling on the ground.

Ice?

The puddle beneath my hands froze around my legs. I stilled, eyes wide, watching the ice spread. It blanketed the forest floor in a frost, freezing any water droplets on the vegetation around me.

Our burned house didn't look like this. The only time the purple flame ever created ice was the first time it ever surfaced on my skin. I never thought that power had come from me. I had always thought it came from the stranger. But no vengeful man whispered in my mind this time.

The purple flame undulated, surrounding a black core, dancing and curling together. I grazed my finger against the shiny, hard puddle. From the brush of my flame, a second layer of ice formed. I touched my arm, but the flames were neither cold nor hot, just a soft hum of energy against my finger.

This was why he carved permanent scars on my back, why my mom and I were in such danger, and why she always did everything she could to hide us and drug me with her touches. It was all because of this purple flame that didn't burn but froze.

The thought snuffed out my power, leaving me numb and empty.

I was left naked and exposed to Earth's stormy clouds. Ice turned back to rain and struck me and the melting puddle. Exhausted, I curled into myself, laying in soppy dirt and leaves. Grit rubbed into my arms, and sticks jabbed my back.

Who cared?

I wasn't sure how long I lay there. My eyes refused to register the world around me or the pain that crept into my naked limbs. At one point, a flash of light sparked in the distance, then vanished. It didn't matter. My empty thoughts were so much better than the turmoil from my mother's words.

A shadow shifted in my peripherals. I ignored that, too. Animals roamed these woods constantly. It was probably the large black wolf I saw sometimes. It wasn't normal, neither the size of the beast, its odd fur, nor how it always returned to the same spot. But it kept its distance, so I was never threatened by the wolf. I never told my mother about the times I saw it. I figured she'd cart us away again if I did. So, I kept one secret from her, nothing compared to what she kept from me.

The forest, a gloomy, dismal place, shifted. Dark boots stopped two feet in front of my face. Unfazed, I stared at them and ignored the fact no one came through these woods. This was my mother's worst nightmare, and yet I couldn't care less. A repeated tinking sounded as rain hit something metallic. Even the tangy scent of apples and pine wasn't enough to lift my head.

The shadow spoke. "Who are you?"

I didn't care to answer. Not after today. Not ever.

"Where're your clothes?"

That was an easy question. "Burned."

"How?"

That was too much to explain, too much thinking.

"Are you cold?"

"Maybe," I said.

But I was. My fingers and feet were numb, trying to keep my organs warm while I lay there, uncaring about the potential of hypothermia.

It was funny I wasn't immune to the elements unless my powers covered me.

The air shifted. Something dark and heavy blanketed me, protecting me from the rain.

"Your lips are blue."

I brought my hand up to my lips, curious. It was my first movement in a while. I smiled after the fact. My hands were frozen. They couldn't feel my lips.

A pulse resonated, and a flash of light sprung from the darkness. The light got brighter as it came closer, and warmth brushed along my skin as a sizzling sound whispered in my ear. I closed my eyes as pain prickled my hands and feet. My teeth clenched to keep from groaning, surprised by the strange warmth.

"Stop," I said, voice tight with unshed tears.

"No. You'll freeze." They snapped, tucking the fabric tighter around me.

Were they angry?

I blinked my heavy lids, wanting to see who was before me. But the endless night and bright light shrouded them.

"What are you?"

My lips twitched. What a funny question. "I'm a girl, if you couldn't tell." I was naked—or had been before they covered me. Even if my arms laid across my breasts, they pushed between my arms, too big to hide.

I couldn't make sense of this. *Why was this stranger so curious about me?*

They sighed, frustrated. "Can you tell me anything about yourself?"

I could tell them lots of things. Could tell *him*, I realized. Things that would get my mother and me killed. Things that she protected me from so that'd never happen. Secrets she kept from everyone—absolutely everyone. For good reason, too.

"My name's Lucille. I hate my father. My mother lied to me. And my life is a ticking time bomb. Here." I ripped off the metal chain still hanging around my neck and gave the stranger my amulet. It no longer held my mother's soothing power. I didn't want it anymore. Who cared if my mother would throw a giant fit once she found out? It was just a reminder of her secrets and a reasonable payment for the warmth and cover this stranger gave.

She said she had it made by some witch. The crystal itself was imbued with a type of magic that allowed it to absorb power to be used later. It could fetch a hefty price, even if the stranger never figured out its magical aspects.

He took it from my hands, continuing to stay silent. *Was he staring at it? Did he pocket it?*

"You need to stay," he said, pausing. "Lucille."

I continued to squint at the light, trying to see his face.

"Did you hear me? You need to stay with your mother." His voice hardened.

"O-kay," I said, confused.

He grabbed my arm. It was hot through the material. "I mean it. Go back home and stay put."

"Okay," I said, wanting my sluggish mind to make sense of this. He wasn't telling me anything I didn't already know. I did need to go home. My mom was probably out of her mind by now. *But stay put?* We'd most likely run again.

The thought had me itching to touch my newfound inky strands of anger coiling in my core. I hated running and hiding and all the isolation. I hated that the one person I trusted most could lie to me and keep my origins secret. I hated that if the amulet still held power, I would've snatched it back.

"Good," he said, satisfied.

The light and heat blipped out of existence. My eyes took a few seconds to adjust to the dark. I lifted my head. There were no footsteps, no movements through the woods, almost like he was never there to begin with—just gone.

Without the heat of the light, my limbs became cold again. Reluctantly, I stood on shaky legs, pulling the heavy cloth around my body. I would've thought I made it all up if it wasn't for the cloak. I searched the forest, hoping to find the stranger, and then figured it was best to get back to the house before my mom came looking.

My mom stood on the threshold of our small house, holding a folded blanket. The glow of our front porch light shined on her silky black hair. She tapped her foot, and I figured I better walk faster. I wished I could just walk around her to the door and not deal with this. But even though my mom was a small woman, she had been training and handling me for nineteen years. If she didn't want me to pass, I wouldn't.

Bitterness hit the back of my tongue again. I waited, knowing what was coming.

"You can't run off like that, Lucy."

"What else am I supposed to do, Mom? Burn down another house?" I snapped, satisfied by her flinch.

She pursed her lips, narrowing her eyes.

"Or maybe I should withhold a key detail of your life and cover it up as some kind of deranged story and see how it messes you up?" The tickling itch responded to my anger and what sounded like cracking ice. It was the same sound I heard before, but the itch was a new sensation. I knew my mom felt it, too, as she lifted her hand.

"Wait," I said, taking a step away from her. Her hand hovered in the air as I stared at it, questioning. Did I want my mother to shove calming emotions down my throat?

I stared at her hand, already knowing the choice I'd make. The choice she was begging me to make within the crinkle of worry on her forehead.

"Okay, but I meant what I said earlier, Mom. I want you to teach me how to control my emotions and powers," I whispered. Then, I walked into her arms and rested my head on her shoulder. A wash of calm seeped into my back from her tender touch.

My mom was the best thing to protect me—protect us from myself and others. And now it made sense why.

"Where'd the cloak come from?" she asked. Her heartbeat jumped a little at the question like she feared the answer.

"I found it on my way back," I lied. She was frantic enough. I didn't want her to know about the stranger. Not yet. Although, no one had ventured through these parts, so I might not be able to get out of this argument.

Surprisingly, my mom wrapped the blanket around my body and let it go. Her hands rubbed my shoulders, warming me with her heat and layers. "Well, let's start you a warm bath, and I'll make some hot chocolate."

I pulled back, "We aren't leaving?"

"I figured you'd want to relax before we do." At my wide eyes, my mother smiled. "We can take the night and leave in the morning. If we're lucky, we can return if there's no activity." The fact that my mother even considered coming back meant she loved this place. We'd been here for four years with no issues. We had both grown attached, so I never mentioned the wolf that showed up six months ago.

"And maybe we can practice your powers and emotions," she conceded.

I smiled and let her lead me into our quaint little home, glancing back, hoping to see the stranger. Instead, I saw what I did daily—the vast forest that surrounded our house. Alone, just the two of us for miles.

And it used to be okay. She was my best friend and my rock. She was always there for me, keeping me calm and safe. The scars on her back proved how much I meant to her. But now, there was a lot I needed to figure out.

CHAPTER FOURTEEN

"Look how tiny the female is," hissed a voice.

"Why would she want someone like her?" hissed another. Each letter 'S' was a drop of water hitting a hot stove.

"We should eat her."

"Eat what? Look at her skinny arms and legs."

The raspy voices slowly pierced through the jumbled dream-walk of the stranger and dull throbbing in my skull. *What did they just say? Something about eating?*

"Idiot! Remember the last time we ate a prisoner?"

"What about just a nibble?"

"No."

Were they talking about eating me? Awareness shot through my drowsiness. It took every ounce of willpower not to open my eyes or scramble away from the voices. Maybe if I continued to act asleep, they'd leave me alone.

"But I'm hungry, Cacus," he whined closer to my ear. Hot, pungent breath hit the side of my face. I tensed, fighting the urge to lean away, and heard a soft chinking. Warm metal slid against my wrists, forcing my arms behind my back—the cuffs.

The throbbing in my head screamed at me through my rising panic.

Breathe. Don't let them know you're awake.

"Oh! Bael, we're almost to Chatoyant Forest!"

"Yant Foxes. My favorite." His spoiled egg breath shifted away.

My neck hovered at an awkward angle, nearly touching my shoulder. Despite my muscles screaming at me to shift, I figured it best to stay this way until I understood what was happening.

My bruised head bounced painfully against a wooden wall. After the fourth bounce, I stiffened my lolling muscles—a small change. One I hoped wasn't too noticeable. But it was worth it as it saved my head from the constant bruising. Unlike my bottom, which absorbed every bump from every nook and cranny we dipped into. *Did they know how to drive?*

A soft clip clop interrupted the hissing voices of Cacus and Bael. They were arguing over how many Yant Foxes they'd eat. *Better than eating me. But what was that clip-clop noise?*

Horses?

I ached to open my eyes and squeezed them tighter as the jostling reached a standstill. *Keep them shut. Don't move. Pretend, Lucy. Pretend.* But the tightness in my neck cramped, shooting a biting pain into my muscles. I jerked my hands, wanting to massage it. Metal clanked against metal. I stiffened, hoping they didn't hear. *Stay still, Lucy. Stay—shit!* Unable to withstand it, I straightened my neck, waiting for the pungent scent and hisses to descend. When they didn't, I risked a peek.

I was in a *carriage.*

The tan, boxy thing, illuminated by one small window, revealed a figure hidden in the corner.

A guy slept wedged between boxes, with his knees bent and head tilted back, which was good. What wasn't good was the familiar uniform hugging his toned frame, only black instead of blood-red and with an azure blue emblem. The colors must be a ranking.

Hissing erupted, making me rethink the idea of opening my eyes. Slowly, I turned to my right, thinking it was too late to return to pretending.

Maybe it wasn't too late. *But how could I possibly close my eyes again, knowing three feet away, hunched two scaly monsters?* My fingers hooked into a plank groove, barely preventing me from scooting away. But I was already moving too much.

They filled the back half of the carriage with their bulbous bodies. Horns jutted from their unnaturally large heads. At first, they both crouched underneath the square window, staring at something. Then, one hissed and shoved his shoulder into the other. Their horns scraped across the top of the wooden ceiling as they fought. A small circle of light flashed through the gaps of their shoving.

A peephole underneath a window?

My eyes widened as one slammed the other into the wall, rocking the carriage and dislodging my weak hold on the wooden plank, sliding me forward. I cringed at the sound of my metal chains dragging. But they took no notice, too occupied with shoving each other.

With small movements, I glanced to the corner, wondering about the male, and met drilling blue eyes.

Shit, a hundred times over.

We stared at each other, neither moving nor blinking. Under his scrutiny, tiny beads of sweat condensed on my forehead. I wanted to drop my eyes, but something predatorial held me. I swallowed. His searing gaze followed the contraction of my muscles, making me inhale my spit. My face flushed as I held back a cough, then hacked, lips failing to muffle the noise.

"Shit!" I squeaked as one of the black creatures yanked me into their arms.

"Bael! She lives, and her eyes! She will be pleased." The creature rasped. Bael turned his head toward me, and my stomach dropped to my toes.

I was going to die.

He laughed with a mouth of sharp, crimson teeth. "Afraid pipsqueak?" he hissed.

Afraid? Was I afraid of the three beady eyes the same color as its razor teeth and the symbols dotting its entire body? Was I afraid of the slits it had in place of a nose or the slimy scales that squeezed against my body, preventing me from moving?

No, I was terrified.

The thing squeezed me harder as it laughed with his buddy. A familiar pressure stabbed at the invisible barrier under my skin.

Bael crowded in. My heart pounded against Cacus's large bicep, compressing my jerking lungs.

"She smells good, brother."

"So, what about that nibble, Cacus?" Bael shifted his weight between his feet, shaking the carriage. "Please, please?"

He was begging to eat me? To take a nibble?

I shook. Bael's red razors glinted in the window light, slick with saliva. A glistening glob trailed down his chin while he widened his lipless mouth. Rotten egg breath heated my face, and I realized Cacus had lowered his mouth to my ear.

"You don't want to eat me. I—I taste bad!" I stuttered out. Black specs seemed to think it was a good time to invade my vision.

I was about to pass out, and they were going to eat me.

Caucus and Bael laughed before they both drew in and sniffed.

"No, you smell delicious."

Bit by bit, the stabbing sensation ripped into my barrier, seeking the outer portion of my skin. *Please surface!* It couldn't be like with Marcus's goons.

Its sticky lips pressed against my neck when it happened—a flash of light, a sharp jolt of pain, hissing, rocking, hands jerking, and a tingle.

One moment, I was about to be snacked on, and the next, my back was pressed against a chest angled away from the hissing things. The scaly creatures bared their teeth, holding their arms to their chests.

"Stupid beasts. She's not a snack! She's our prisoner!" I flinched at the ferocity of the male's voice in my ear.

"But it wouldn't damage her too much. Just her ear?" Bael supplied, hopeful. The thing sounded like a little kid begging for a second cookie after dinner. They were insane! *What were these things?*

The guy behind me snorted with disgust. "*She* is not for *you*. Find a snack in the forest, or next time, I'll take the teeth you cherish."

He jerked me around to face him. But my focus lingered on Cacus's and Bael's hissing. Pointed black tongues came out of their mouths and wrapped around the wounds on their arms. I shuddered.

"You." A calloused hand came up and gripped my chin, forcing me to look at the guy who held me, shocking my skin with pinpricks of electricity.

Full lips pressed into a line, right at my eye level. His grip on my chin tightened, and the pinpricks of electricity increased. I dropped my gaze from his grimace, finding a bright red scrolling scar beneath his chin. I followed his chiseled jawline up his sweeping cheekbones and landed on his pissed-off bright blue eyes.

"Try something like that again, and it'll hurt you more than us. Understand?" He punctuated his question, which wasn't a question, with a shove, pushing me away like he couldn't stand to touch me.

Unbalanced with my restrained arms, I fell into the wooden wall. Stunned, I leaned there, flickering my eyes between the bulky black beasts and the guy with the indifferent expression.

"Did you hear me?"

My fingers dug into my palms. The cords in my center hummed, plucked by his domineering tone.

"Go to hell."

Cacus and Bael snickered to the side of us, shutting up quickly with a jerk of the male's head. I guess my new jailor was an asshole with authority. From the way he not only bruised my chin but shoved me into the side of the carriage, I knew he was as bad as Marcus and Oliver. A wash of betrayal and defeat struck. *How would I ever find Magda and my mom now?*

Oliver gave me up. He was the first person I trusted, and he placed me back into their arms. Now, here I was—cuffed, with two creatures who looked like nightmares and a guy with a penchant for rough handling. I had no clue where Marcus and Oliver were. Maybe this was their hired help.

Was this what she meant when she said to come to Elora? A weight settled on my shoulders and burrowed into my chest. *Was this all one big ploy?*

"Get out. It's time to set up camp," snapped an older man from behind the bulbous bodies of Cacus and Bael.

Graying hair and a long beard peeked through the small gap between the creatures. From the wrinkles on his forehead, he appeared to be in his sixties. A gray cloak flowed behind him over a gray tunic and pants, dull and different from the casual, more modern clothes I wore. Even the full garb the younger man wore was different.

Carriages, old clothing, stiff leather uniforms, strange creatures—*This* was Elora?

The older man stood chest-level with the carriage. One long scar ran from the start of his nose to the middle of his cheek. It moved as he pursed his lips impatiently, watching the younger man grab supplies in the back. The creatures pushed each other, hunched and shambling the few feet to the back opening.

I thought about refusing to leave the carriage, but the empty, enclosed space brought back memories of my cement closet. So, I followed behind the *things*. Weak and unused to the weight of the chains, I tripped out of the carriage. I squeezed my eyes shut and braced for another crack on my skull. But before I could suffer another head injury, a shot of electricity hit my bicep, and my descent stopped.

What the hell was that?

I narrowed my gaze on the tingling hand.

"You know, you squeal like a little female," Blue-eyes remarked.

Did he mean little girl?

The sensation of skittering bugs replaced the odd tingles. "At least my face doesn't look like one," I said, cringing. That was the worst-timed impulsive comeback I'd ever said and a complete lie. I wished he looked like a little girl and not like some male model or handsome storybook prince.

His face turned cold, or colder, and he let go. The electricity and itch disappeared, and I landed in a painful heap on the ground, my left hip taking the brunt of the fall.

"Ouch." Wincing, I lifted my torso, brushing off as much dirt and gravel as possible, which wasn't much with my wrists locked behind my back. Gravel dug into my tricep. *Great, more scrapes and bruises.* I couldn't brush it off, so I left it between my dirty, ripped skin, glaring at the stupid pebbles.

That annoying itch started back up, growing when I glared at my blue-eyed jailor, who had the audacity to smile smugly as he jumped gracefully to the ground. I wanted to grow claws like the beast unpacking our gear and wipe that smile off his perfect face.

I stood, looking around. White trees about two feet wide bordered the clearing, wrapping around us. Their peeling peach flesh and golden leaves were similar to the trees I left on Earth. The only difference was what hid underneath. Instead of another layer of white or tan bark, iridescent scars reflected off the lowering sun.

Strange.

"Where are we?"

When I first got to Elora, it was night, which meant by the light shining through a cloudless sky, I had been knocked out for... I didn't know. Long enough for it to be afternoon again, but that could've been hours, days, a week. Based on the state of my clothes, I assumed it was through the night and the better part of the day.

"Elora," Blue-eyes said.

"Elora is the world. Where exactly in Elora are we?"

"She's smarter than she looks," Blue-eyes mocked, handing over supplies to the snickering monsters.

I gritted my teeth, catching a piece of my torn cheek that I always bit into. "Well?"

"Well, you better get used to disappointment. Your questions aren't worth our answers, prisoner."

Asshole.

I analyzed the five feet separating us and the iridescent birch tree line. It's not like they were paying attention. If this was my only chance at escaping and finding my mom, so be it. I was already cuffed. *What more could they do?* Without a second thought, I ran. Before I sprinted all of three steps, my face slammed into a woolen cloak, and Graybeard shoved me to the ground.

He squatted, looking smug. Unguarded disdain pushed at his bushy eyebrows. "I'd refrain from making that mistake twice. Next time, I won't be so nice," he said, standing and walking back to the others. They carried wood, blankets, pans, and other odds and ends to the center of the clearing.

I yanked at my chains and yanked again. The metal cuffs dug into my bony wrists. *That damned Nephilim!*

Whether Oliver, his name made me sick, found me, or Marcus, I would have still ended up where I was now. The little bit of freedom I had was an illusion. I wrenched at the cuffs until warmth slid down my pinky finger. Then, the itching came. *Great.* I didn't need ice right now. I needed my Glory, which meant I needed fear.

I closed my eyes and pushed my rage away with thoughts about my mom and what could be happening to her. The itching faded, replaced by poking and pressure.

That's it. Come on.

My mom was always there for me. The pieces I remembered from my last dream-walk enforced that notion. And someone took her from me.

The poking turned to stabs.

"Meditating isn't going to help you," Blue-eyes called out.

I ignored him. The moment I melted these off, I would need to lusceler away.

What if someone was hurting her?

My Glory surged. Needles stabbed me, and a powerful shock jolted into my body. I screamed.

"What the fuck are you doing?"

Scared and stubborn, I tried again, pushing past the pain. My Glory tried to erupt, and a larger bolt of electricity slammed into my body, locking up my muscles. I fell forward, about to faceplant into the ground.

Gravel crunched, and Blue-eyes caught my shoulders.

"Stop! The cuffs prevent the use of power through electric shocks."

I stopped. But not because he looked ready to slit my throat if I didn't. The electricity scrambled my thoughts, and I couldn't take the pain.

Would I ever see my mom again?

Once he realized I could hold my torso up, he released me and stood. I vacantly stared at his black leather boots, refusing to test if my legs would hold me until the lingering vibrations left.

"What do you want from me?" I whispered, trying to hide the fact that my throat was tightening. His hand moved in my peripheries, latching onto something near his hip. I lifted my gaze an inch and saw the top of a sword.

Part of me thought it'd put me out of my misery, and another part bristled at my weakness.

"Probably nothing you're thinking about right now," he said, fingers flexing on the hilt.

If I had any energy left, I would've scoffed. He had no idea my thoughts were bringing me to a suffocating place. A place where rage, fear, and hope dug their own graves, hanging on by fraying threads.

I lifted my gaze, forgetting to hide my pain, as I stopped at his dark-lashed eyes.

"Then what?"

He released his hand from the pommel, crossing his arms. "I'm here to ensure you get where you're supposed to go."

"Which is where?"

Why did I have to sound like that? So... pitiful.

He stood there and watched me hunch in on myself, lying in dirt and gravel. Swallowing, I shoved down the tears threatening to spill and welcomed the distraction of a different sort. "I need to pee."

"Brock will take you."

As if signaled, the older man came around the corner of the carriage. Or that's what I thought it was supposed to be. It was more like a dirty, run-down, wooden box on wooden wheels—a thing of the past, much like the clothes they wore.

"Brock," I pushed the harsh syllable out of my mouth, testing it out. "And you are?" I didn't care, but the more logical part of me figured it was best to know.

"Aspen," he stated with something I couldn't pinpoint in his expression. There was no similar inquiry, which was what I expected. I was a prisoner. My name didn't matter.

Scar-faced Brock grabbed my bicep and led me away like the captive I was. We walked into the forest of birch trees that were not birch trees. If I ignored the iridescent scars, they reminded me of the forest I had camped in with—I cut off the thought. I didn't want to remember who caused this. Not while a calloused hand now dug into my bare skin, shoving me on. Each shove and stumble cut away at the little hope I had left.

"Here," Brock pointed to a spot, moving in front of the tree to give me privacy. If you called two feet privacy. Prisoner, I kept reminding myself. I wouldn't get the luxury of freedom or being more than a few feet from these—I still didn't know what they were. If they were in Elora, they couldn't be human. Angels, possibly, but I didn't think to look that closely at their eyes. Those other creatures, Cacus and Bael, weren't angels.

But then, what were they? Monsters? Demons? Some other creature species?

Inch by inch, I tugged down my joggers with my cuffed hands. Luckily, they were loose and untied, or I would've had to ask for help or wet myself. At one point, Brock glanced back to see what had been taking so long, and I shot him with my fiercest glare. He sneered in reply.

The surrounding area had no chirping or skittering animals to interrupt the silence. Instead, we were left with the noise of my dribble and the crunching taps of Brock's foot.

Paused in a crouch, I shook myself like a wet dog, deprived of the luxury of toilet paper. Just one more thing to be happy about as I struggled to inch my pants up. Before they reached my upper thighs, a hand latched onto my arm, yanking me away from the tree.

"Let's go." Brock shoved me forward. I tripped on my joggers, exposing more of myself. Mortified, I arched back to grab them, hurrying to pull them up, only to be shoved again. They fell to my hiking boots.

"Come on, put them on already," he taunted.

The smile in his voice as he viewed my exposed privates twisted my stomach. My cheeks heated, and my throat tightened. The tears I tried so hard to hold back fell as I shimmied them up. Once they were in place, he continued his shoving, like I needed another reminder of how helpless I was.

"What do you want?" I cringed at the weak whine of my voice.

"Nothing." Brock changed tactics, latching onto my arm, and dragging me behind him instead of shoving. The tip of my hiking boot caught onto a thin root, unbalancing me as Brock's fingers pinched my skin, forcing me to regain my balance or be dragged.

"Then who does?" He stayed silent. "Who do you work for? Marcus? Are you a part of the Tenebrous Kingdom?"

"Seems you know more than *Marcus*,"—he spat his name—"let on."

"So, you work for Marcus?"

His fingernails dug into my skin, almost piercing through. "Never. Now shut up."

We broke through the trees, and Brock dragged me to Aspen. Who sat on a dead log sharpening his sword. Brock shoved me in front of him, making me stumble, and left. I clamped down on my cheeks, tasting blood, welcoming the physical pain over the emotional one.

I stared down at Aspen, hoping he couldn't see the dried streaks of tears that stuck to my cheeks.

"I see Brock didn't have to carry your limp body back. Wasn't sure after your foolish display from earlier." He continued to move the whetstone across the edge of his curved blade, brown locks hiding most of his face.

I refused to say anything.

"You didn't listen to me."

Listen to him? About what? Being a prisoner without the right to know things?

"Why would I listen to a word you have to say?" I snapped, clenching my teeth as I spoke to hold back more tears.

He finally lifted his head. Coffee locks scattered across his forehead as his eyes narrowed. They roamed my face, glanced on either side of me, and then back to my face. Despising his attention, I dropped my gaze to his neck and the silver chain that partially hid beneath his stiff leather uniform. I imagined choking him with it. The skittering of feet prompted me to imagine more ways I'd kill him to escape. The only good thing about my purple power was the ease at which it shoved every emotion away except my blistering anger.

"Cacus and Bael should be finding our dinner. I'd say make yourself useful, but the cuffs hinder that. I guess go sit somewhere until we eat."

"Oh, and sweetheart?" My gaze jumped back to his at the condescending endearment. "Don't try to wander off. Not only are you powerless, but these ancient forests would swallow you whole and kill you. That is, if I didn't catch you first." His glacial eyes flashed a bright blue before settling back to their normal color. It happened so fast that I was sure I was imagining things.

"Whatever you say, asshole," I said, then turned and left to find a place to *sit.*

Far from them, on the opposite end of camp, seemed like the best choice. My back and wrists rested against one of the peeling white trees, shoulders aching—especially the one hit by lightning. I sat at an angle and faced the thicker part of the woods. They beckoned, whispering of freedom, of answers.

I shot a glance at Aspen, still sharpening his sword. A few feet away from him, Brock stoked a fire. But no one paid attention to me. The temptation to run and find a way to Magda's was there.

I knew they were paying attention. It may not look like it, but they knew exactly where I was and what I was doing. And if by any chance my jailor told the truth, then I wouldn't make it a night out there, not with these cuffs on and not with having no supplies or survival skills. That was what Oliver was for. Now, I had no one.

A heavyweight replaced the anger simmering in my core, removing the itching tickles.

I was helpless and alone. With no answers.

Something flashed in my peripherals. I stared in between the dimming gaps of the white trees, waiting. But the shadow was gone.

A twig snapped on my other side. I jerked.

"Jumpy?"

I squeezed my fists at his voice. Glaring, I tilted my chin up, eyeing two specs of red hidden in his swaying beard. His yellow eyes narrowed into the forest. I swung my neck back, looking again, but there was nothing.

"What's out there?" I asked, regretting that I was talking to him but needing to know if my other jailor told the truth.

Brock grunted. "Anything and everything. From creatures that would burrow into your stomach to eat your intestines to healers that would attempt to save your life for a few coins. We're in The Divide. A place where there are no rules or laws for anyone. It's a free-for-all of sorts. Some live here, and many die here."

The Divide, so we weren't in the Tenebrous Kingdom yet.

"You're actually telling me?" I hadn't expected such a thorough answer.

Weren't his eyes just yellow? Now, they were the color of a fall leaf before it crinkled and fell.

His arms crossed. "Makes my job easier. So, you don't think you can run off like all the rest."

All the rest?

I opened my mouth and forgot what I was about to say as the burnt orange turned green. "Your eyes."

A slow, pretentious smile answered me, covered partially by his thick mustache. "That sliver of hope I still feel in you, it's best you drown it. No one is coming. No one is getting past our group. And running will get you killed. You wouldn't survive out there." He nodded down to my cuffs. "Not even a night. So please, save Prince Aspen and me the inconvenience of having to find your bleeding carcass." With that beautiful description, he turned away and ended our conversation with a "Dinner's ready."

He felt my dimming hope? What hope? I could barely feel it. He must've sensed the particles of dust squashed beneath the boots of betrayal and capture.

Marcus handed me over to a prince. Or maybe handed isn't the right word. Before they knocked me out, Marcus sounded surprised that some prince had shown up. He wasn't expecting him. But they all must be from the Tenebrous Kingdom, so why would it matter to Marcus if he took me to his sovereign or Prince Aspen?

My bottom and back were stiff by the time I decided to stand. As much as I tried to ignore my stomach, its screams were too loud. It didn't help watching the four figures eat Cacus and Bael's catches. *Although, how did they manage to collect food for everyone else and not just eat it all themselves?* Maybe they had their fill of Yant Foxes before they came back.

Nightfall crept in, casting long shadows across the campsite as I made my way over to the sputtering fire. Luckily, my princely jailor was gone. He disappeared into the woods along with the disgusting creatures. Brock was the only one left by the campsite.

"What can I eat?" I asked, keeping a safe distance away. Brock had utterly mortified me, but I was also starving.

Brock peered up from his stump. "Squirrel and rabbit," he stated, holding out a metal plate with two chunks of meat, staring back into the fire as he did.

Was I supposed to grab it with my teeth? Or was this another reminder he was giving me, wanting to break down the last of my hope and rub the dust in my face? He smirked knowingly when I didn't take it.

I bit my lip, feeling the itch, hating him even more.

He set it beside him. "Prince Aspen has your keys."

Great.

I stood and waited for his arrogant bastard to return. While I did, a neon orange bug the size of a piece of rice landed on my arm. Another landed next to it.

"Firewings. Don't let them bite you," Brock said, unconcerned despite his warning.

I looked warily between him and the orange bugs. "Why?" They were cute.

"It burns. And once bitten, it's a beacon to its swarm that they've found a meal."

Wonderful.

"But don't squash them either. It'll end with the same result."

Gritting my teeth, I asked, "What the hell do I do then?"

He shrugged, then said, "They don't like fire."

That was ironic.

I leaned my left side near the fire. The uncomfortable heat pinkened my skin, and the bugs flew into the night sky. I followed their bright bodies, wishing I could escape as easily as them.

The food was cold by the time my arrogant jailor came back. But it didn't matter. I'd eat it. My body needed food.

As he approached, Brock gestured to my plate, then my hands. "She can't eat. And if I fed her, she'd likely bite my fingers off."

He never offered that option. Although, the thought of maiming one of them brought a twinge of happiness. But it wouldn't have made a difference. I'd rather kneel on the ground and shove my face into my plate of food like a stray dog than let those worn, calloused fingers come near me ever again.

Like I had a choice.

My princely jailor walked directly into my path, adorned with a cloak similar to Brock's, only black. He inserted himself in the small space between me and the fire. I wished I could have held my ground and make him back up a few steps, so he'd catch fire. But this was where hopes and wishes died. Instead, I was the one to back up.

"I don't think she has the guts to bite anyone's fingers off. Do you?"

I narrowed my eyes. A trickle of indignation tickled the tips of my fingers. "Wanna find out?"

His cold gaze slowly roved over me, taking in everything from my wavy limp locks to my scrawny ankles. By the muscle pumping in his jaw and the ire warping around his chilling gaze, I could tell he found me lacking.

"No. I want you to eat your food and be quiet," he snapped, walking around me to unlock my cuffs.

The release of my wrists eased the tension in my shoulders, pulling out a blissful sigh from my mouth. Finally, I stepped toward my plate, eager to sink my teeth into the food, not caring it had a rubbery sheen. Inches away from snatching up the plate, my arm jerked back, tethered to something.

What the...

My eyes traveled down my arm, to the metal cuff, to the other metal cuff attached to a thick muscular wrist, and back up to the expressionless mask on my princely jailor's face.

"Seriously?"

"The cuffs don't work unless they're both locked," he stated, glaring at me like I was the one who forced him to cuff himself.

"Uh, you couldn't, I don't know, cuff the same wrist twice? Or lock them in front of my body instead of chaining me to..." I eyed him up and down, giving him a taste of what it felt like, and snorted. "Well, you."

He tensed as his eyes... Glowed? The firelight highlighted his left side, leaving his right in shadow. But both his eyes and something red under his chin were lit.

"Remember she wants her alive, Prince Aspen," Brock said, carving into a chunk of wood. Unphased.

"Eat your damned food!" my jailor yelled, taking one step closer.

"Gladly!" I screamed back but lost my bravado when his eyes erupted in blue flame.

"Scream at me again, and I'll dump you and your food into the fire!"

Frozen, I stared. *What the hell was that?*

"Eat!"

I stepped back from the ferocity of his voice, no longer craving to test him. *What in my right mind made me want to in the first place?* He had flames for eyes. He was corded in muscle and wore a sword and daggers on his hip that couldn't possibly be for show. *And I had what? Ice and flames when I was emotional?* Powers that the cuffs now blocked unless I felt like electrocuting myself.

My shoulders slumped as I turned. His one step closer barely gave me enough slack to touch the plate with my fingertips. After wiggling it into my palm, I stood and gazed at the rubbery thighs. Bits of white fuzz speckled the meat. Despite their gross state, my fingers trembled from holding back. My hunger was a needy, depraved thing.

"Is it drugged?"

"No," he said at the same time Brock said, "Maybe."

Believing the princely jailor, I jerked my chained wrist, latched onto the bony meat, and devoured every morsel. Cooled juices slid down the sides of my cheeks, and I ended up wiping them with my bare arm.

"Cacus and Bael have better manners than you do," Brock said, lip lifting in disgust.

I found that doubtful and flipped him off. "Go to hell."

In less than a second, something swiped at my feet, and I fell onto my back, bones and plate flying from my hand while the other dangled in the air.

"Insult me again, and we can have some fun," Brock said, stepping on my wrist. Without his full weight, it wasn't too bad. Until he put more weight into the step, then pivoted back and forth, grinding my bones together. My gasps turned into whimpers. "Would you like that?"

"No, I wouldn't. I wouldn't," I begged.

"That's enough, Brock."

Brock jerked his head up, shot my princely jailor a scowl, and then glanced down at me disgusted. "Glad we understand each other." He pressed harder, giving me his last punishing pivot. I cried out, and my princely jailor shoved Brock off me.

"I said stop!"

But he couldn't get Brock off me fast enough. Agony slammed into my wrist, and it snapped.

I bit my lips hard, muffling the wail, as Brock stalked off.

Tears trailed silently down my cheeks as I lay on the ground, refusing to move. My dangling arm lowered. The chain jangled, and with a soft chink and snap, my unbroken wrist flopped to the ground, heavier.

"You should have never come through that portal."

I twisted my head to meet his glowing eyes. Rage, unlike any I'd ever seen, twisted his princely face.

And I—weak, alone, broken—agreed.

CHAPTER FIFTEEN

After a terrible night's sleep, icy water jolted me awake, splashing over my face and soaking my shirt. I gasped, coughed on the water that went up my nose and looked wildly around. My princely jailor stood over me with a large bucket in hand as I sat on a pad with soppy blankets.

"What the hell was that for?" I shouted in between coughs, goosebumps growing goosebumps as the morning chill brushed against my skin.

His eyes were alight with satisfaction as he pressed his lips together.

Invisible fingers strummed two cords in my core.

"You wouldn't wake up," he stated.

"What, and you couldn't shake me awake? You had to dump a damn pail of freezing water on me?" My nails bit into my palms. Or no, one palm. My other tweaked with pain and hit the stiff cloth wrapped around my hand and wrist. *Did he splint it?*

"Clearly, you're not dying, and now you don't have to wash off in a stream," he said, pulling my attention back to him. "Now get up."

His cocky words plucked the cords, enticing the itch. The crashing musical ice started. Blood rushed to my cheeks. In seconds, I stood, shoving my hands into his chest, chains jangling, and wrist protesting. A pulse of purple light flashed before the cuffs around my right wrist electrocuted me.

He didn't re-cuff my broken wrist. *Why? To satisfy his conscience?* I doubted he had one. My power vanished, replaced by lingering aftershocks that made my knees wobble.

"I—" I dropped my hands quickly, ignoring the throbbing in my left one, and stared at the white frost coating his chest. *Was it going to dissolve his leathers like the sleeping bag?* Part of me hoped it did; another knew if that happened, I'd be executed. But the ice did nothing.

He stepped forward, and I stumbled back. He took another step forward, and I took another step back until my legs bumped into Brock's tree stump. I tilted my head up, holding my breath. He appraised me with unreadable eyes and intimidated me with his nearness. His hand rose, and I flinched, expecting him to hit me or worse. Last night, I insulted Brock, and he broke my wrist. Today, I accidentally attacked a prince. *Would he break my arm or leg?* I leaned back as far as possible, squeezing my lids shut, and waited. A light flashed, and I opened my eyes, squinting at his raised hand covered in flames the color of his eyes.

The heat painfully licked my skin, and I fell over the stump. I hurried back a foot with my splinted wrist clutched to my chest. His hand moved, but instead of burning me alive, it brushed the leather on his chest, thawing the ice. His threatening irises, wreathed in blue fire, trapped me.

What was he? An angel?

He lowered himself, placing his elbows on the stump. The heat from his flames burned my cheeks, threatening to take out my eyebrows. While he smirked, his power retreated into his interlacing hands, but his eyes were still consumed by fire.

My heart abused my sternum, pushing at the needles beneath my skin.

"Don't. Do that. Again, prisoner." A light flashed beneath his chin, and the blue fire flashed brighter in his eyes before he stood and left.

I let loose a breath, taking in three more. He had flames and, by the looks of it, could control them ten times better than I could.

My wrist throbbed, pumping along with my erratic heart. Chills skittered across my back. I wished it was caused by my soaked shirt, not the guy packing up the janky carriage with the two monsters.

"Huh."

I scrambled back from Brock's voice and stood.

Brock sneered. "Scared?"

Yes. Not that I'd tell him that.

"That's the first time I've seen the prince attacked without getting their head severed or burned off."

Great. I already didn't want to move from my spot. My wet pad laid unrolled in hopes that they'd leave me behind.

"I suppose the need to keep you alive restrained him."

"So, he won't kill me?"

Brock eyed the wrist clutched to my chest, crouching down. "Kill, probably not. She wouldn't be too happy about that. Maim, on the other hand, I'd be surprised if you didn't break a few more bones." His mustache spread with a knowing smile, rolling up my blanket and pad.

I backed out of reach. "She who? Your sovereign?"

He stood with my supplies. "You'll find out."

"Sweetheart," my princely jailer sang. "Time to go. Don't make me chase you down." His eyes pulsed with blue flame.

A flash of irritation overpowered my apprehension. I should've pushed him harder. Dragging my feet to the carriage, each slide and pull stirred a question of whether or not I'd be safer with them or on my own. That was if I could manage to escape.

Right now, I'd be lucky enough to keep my life.

He met me at the back, the monsters already stuffed inside. "Next time, I'll drag you by your feet if you take that long."

"I'd like to see you try," I snapped with false vibrato.

His rosy lips squeezed into a hard line. With two abrupt steps, he backed me into the ledge of the back doors. He leaned down, his mouth brushing my ear. A tingle of a different sort sent a shiver down my spine.

"Don't make me do something you'll regret," he whispered, reaching for my legs.

Was he going to grope me?

My Glory prickled, but before it surged and my cuffs shocked me, he picked me up and threw me in. My bottom hit the exact second he jumped, straddling me with his feet.

"Hands," he demanded, reaching out and caging me in with his boots.

"Why?"

His scar pulsed with a red light.

"I said, give me your damned hands! Now, prisoner!"

The glow in his irises convinced me to lift my hands. He unlocked a cuff from my uninjured wrist, grazing my skin. Tingles surfaced, and his tight hold eased with the light beneath his chin. He widened the cuff and latched it around my splint, loose enough to slide around the thick cloth without pain.

"Does that feel okay?" he asked.

Stunned by his gentle tone and question, I nodded.

Brock shut the doors, dimming the janky box. My princely jailor dropped my wrists and straightened. He stepped over me, and I wiggled to the side, far away from the monsters and the confusing prince. Brock signaled to the horses to move, and we were off. *Yay.*

Bump after bump shot into my boney butt and vibrated up my spine. *Did this dirt road contain nothing but potholes? Or was this another form of torture?*

Fortunately, last time, I was knocked out for most of the ride. This time, I had to listen to Bael and Cacus hiss about food and feel my princely jailor's gaze. I think I'd rather take the agony of my Glory over this.

As time passed, I slept against my better judgment. It was the closest thing to knocking myself out, and I hoped to dream-walk again. The last few dream-walks gave me pieces of my past back and more questions, but it was better than nothing.

Sleep came and went. Flashes of colors to darkness to whispered words I forgot, then to the waking world. The day turned to night, but except for a couple of mortifying stops, we never made camp. Brock and my princely jailor traded out driving multiple times, and we continued like that.

My two meals a day consisted of apples, cheese, and dried squirrel meat chucked at me whenever Brock or the prince felt like it. Sometimes, I only ate one meal, not because they didn't give me food but because any food I couldn't catch was fair game for the monsters.

After the fourth day, my will hung on by threads. I stared at the splint on my pinky finger. It wasn't there yesterday. Brock broke my finger for insulting him a second time after he stared at me like a perv during our bathroom break. He stomped on my hand as punishment. I think he hoped to break all my fingers but only managed one. When we returned to the carriage, my princely jailor grabbed my hand. He panned from my crooked pinky to my tears to Brock's face, and his eyes lit with blue flame. He jerked me from Brock's grasp and helped me into the carriage without a word.

Today, I woke to find it splinted. Brock would've never helped me, and the monsters were too idiotic to know how to splint a bone. They'd probably chomp it off as a solution. So that left my princely jailor as my secretive nurse.

I glanced at the corner where he silently slept. We spoke maybe eight sentences to each other in the last four days, in between his grunts and glares.

His knees were tucked to his chest, arms draped, and head leaning back—the same position I found him in the first time. Except now, instead of a perfect head of silk, it lay flat and glistened. Creases formed at the corner of his eyes.

A bad dream? I sure as hell hoped so.

With that sword attached to his hip, I could only imagine the amount of killing he doled out. All the muscle that swallowed his body and the blue flames that flashed in his eyes didn't exactly say pacifist. I bet monsters haunted his dreams. He deserved every second of the pain that pinched his face.

I looked away, glancing at the quiet monsters. All six beady eyes were closed. Returning my gaze to my princely jailor, the hilt of his sword gleamed in the dim light.

What were the odds I could stab them all and live?

But before I got my desperate ass killed, a jarring impact thrust me forward. My wrist wrenched against their chains, palms splayed to catch myself. I gasped at the impact, my broken bones giving out, face-planting.

The carriage rocked back and forth, then jolted again from another slam, tilting the carriage onto two wheels. I tumbled headfirst into the wall, lying on my back when we banged down, level.

Brock shouted something, and the carriage picked up speed.

"What the hell is it?" I shifted onto my forearms and knees, looking for the prince. He stood, arms spread, bracing himself in the corner with glowing irises.

Cacus and Bael hissed at the next hit, lumbering toward the back doors, nearly crushing my body as I rolled out of the way. Our hasty speed abruptly stopped as the whole carriage skidded to the side. Yips and throaty growls drowned out the horse's whinnies.

"Go! Get out of here!" Brock yelled.

A loud, throaty squeal punctured the increased yips until it stopped, along with my heart.

We were stuck.

They slammed into us again and again, rocking the carriage but unable to tip us with Cacus and Bael distributing their hulking weight. A slam splintered the wood near my princely jailor's face.

Their growls became louder. Almost as if they were excited by the wreckage.

Was no one going to answer me?

"What the hell is attacking us? Wolves?"

The growls quieted for a moment, followed by the clang of metal and grunts. The prince cursed, lunging for me just before the next hit. His arm wrapped around my waist, hauling me to the center, away from the shuddering walls. He pressed my back tightly against his chest, refusing to let me move. The pounding of his heart hammered into my spine, quickening my own.

With his free hand, he reached for the pommel of his sword, unleashing a long blade with scrolling blue symbols lit up with the flame that wreathed his eyes. Heat pulsed off the fiery waves, scalding my exposed skin. I shrank back into the prince, unable to escape his vice-like grip.

"Hellhounds," he finally replied.

Cacus and Bael snickered like they enjoyed that fact. I couldn't say I was surprised. They seemed both dimwitted and gruesome enough to enjoy our possible demise.

The growls and slams died down while the clanking metal increased. He released me, giving my flushed skin sweet relief.

"We need to leave this carriage and help Brock."

"Wait, what?" This carriage was the only thing separating us. "Is that our only option?" Brock could rot in hell for all I cared. I wasn't going out there. I didn't know how to fight. I didn't even have a weapon. Not to mention, my powers were currently out of commission. I'd been zapped so many times I assumed only an immense amount of fear or anger would get them going, and even then, the damned cuffs prevented that!

My jailor scrutinized me, jaw muscles pulsing. "This carriage will be splinters of wood if we don't leave it. They don't eat animal meat. They killed our horses to prevent us from moving."

The wooden carriage abruptly rocked. I fell into him. His fingers dug into the sleeves of my shoulders.

"They feed off fresh angel blood, so they won't stop. And Brock is alone out there."

"I don't care!"

He placed me behind him, turning his pissed-off fiery eyes on the black and red runed backs of Cacus and Bael.

"Take off my cuffs," I demanded, palms sweaty.

He shot me a glare. "No." Then yelled, "Now!"

Cacus and Bael pushed open the splintering doors, jumping out one after the other. Their feet pounded the ground with their weight. The prince landed softly behind them, sword raised and ready. I refused to move from my spot.

"Cacus, go help Brock," he commanded.

One of the black beasts lumbered away toward the sound of a fight at the front of the carriage. And despite wanting nothing to do with the beasts, I wished Cacus would stay.

I crumpled to the planks.

Skeletal hounds surrounded us. Shadows undulated around their bones, like a messed-up kind of fur. Although, that did nothing to soothe the thoughts of death as their chests were at the same level as the ledge of the carriage.

"Get out," he demanded, giving me a quick, narrowed glance before returning his attention to the skeletal death hounds.

"Take off my cuffs," I begged, scooting closer, holding them out. So what if I looked pathetic or weak?

Fleshless bony heads snapped their jaws. They bayed and licked two-inch-long fangs, staring with blood-colored eyes. My bladder threatened to give out at their piercing sounds and did, just a little, as they prowled toward us.

"No."

"Aspen, please!"

He flinched like I'd hit him. I never used his name, never wanted to. It was different with Brock. His name sounded like an insult. But Aspen... Damnit. I liked his name. And I didn't want to like anything about him. But right now, I'd try anything.

"Get the fuck *out* of the carriage!" he seethed.

"No!"

He backpedaled to the ledge, attention on the snarling smokey beasts inching their way nearer, reached back and latched onto my ankle. Stunned by the soft buzz of energy tickling my skin, I didn't fight back as he dragged me. I was about to slam into the ground when, at the last second, he picked me up and set me down.

What was that? Not that odd change of behavior, but the vibrations from his hand? I shot him a look, but he pushed forward to Bael, ignoring me.

I didn't think we stood a chance with only three of us, practically two and a half, against five hulking beasts.

White puffs of steam diffused from the Hellhound's nostrils, clouding the area and infusing the air with a rotten egg smell. Their shadowed fur faded to light gray, indiscernible against the trees.

Scratch that. *They* didn't stand a chance. There was no *we*, as I scrambled underneath the carriage, hands jangling against my pelvis. Millions of needles probed my skin, answering the call of the pressure squeezing my chest.

The prince's attention flickered to my retreat. "If you run, they will kill you."

Exactly why I was hiding, not running.

"Take off my cuffs, Aspen." I inhaled and added, "Please." Hoping he understood how much that cost me. A cordial please to my careless jailor who didn't deserve any civility from me. But my Glory climbed, stabbing me, and in a matter of seconds, I'd be a writhing, debilitated snack—easy eating.

I needed his help. *I really needed to keep breathing.*

He stared me dead in the eye and shook his head. "Stay there." Then he charged into the steam with his sword raised, Bael following with his pounding strides until they were both faint blobs of color.

Defenseless, I squirmed further back. Shadows flashed through the white clouds, snarling and yipping. At times, a blur of blue followed, but only the clang of metal proved the prince had made contact.

I flinched with every sound, with every flash, Glory stealing my strength as I lay belly down between the two wheels of the carriage. It was coming. I only knew that because I could grind into the skin of my cheeks, nearly biting through, and no longer feel it. One minute. Two. I shoved my mouth into the corner of my elbow, and it peaked. I muffled my scream as a jolt of electricity seared into my body, sending me to darkness.

You have no one to blame but yourself.

Don't be a wimp. Come here.

Stay here. Stay safe.

Escape your cage.

Fight it!

I'm sorry, Lucy.

There once was a daughter of—

Hushed clanking woke me from the cacophony of voices. Blinking, I twisted my head, finding a battlefield void of steam with added bodies and chaos.

My eyes latched onto the prince. He arched his flaming sword up and down, slicing, stabbing, and twisting into two Hellhounds. Every slice created a charred line that partially disintegrated bone, deterring them from the sword but not stopping them from attacking. On his other side, Brock swung a flameless sword at a different set of hounds, chipping away at bone with little impact, which had to be why they fought him with more brutality than the ones that hesitated against the prince.

Good. Hopefully, the repulsive man got what was coming to him.

To the side of Brock fought Cacus and Bael. *And they were—Snickering at their Hellhounds? Yes, snickering. Dimwitted beasts.* But the Hellhounds seemed to keep their distance, jetting around them in circles and never engaging. It was almost like Cacus and Bael had some plague. Still didn't stop them from swiping and kicking the Hellhounds, laughing the entire time.

A red light flashed in my periphery. Glancing back at the prince, I scooted farther away from the Hellhounds now spewing red flames from their nostrils. *Wasn't the damned cloud of steam enough?*

They shot at the prince's head. He ducked, swinging up as he stood, and cleaved through the skull of another. The head charred in half, dead. He was on to the next, dancing with death and the hounds of shadows. Transfixed, I watched in horror and awe.

He whirled, twisted, and slashed, never slowing, never hesitating. When he used all his momentum to slide under his last hound, eviscerating its underbelly and rolling to his feet right as it slumped, I couldn't help but be impressed. He sprinted over to Brock. Who struggled with a sword that was equivalent to a dull steak knife.

Brock swung wildly at a hound licking a glistening red off its claws. Based on the blood bleeding into his cloak, it had to come from Brock. Bit by bit, he carved into the Hellhound's neck, and despite the fact he was carving through, the hound only dodged, too fixated on the blood.

My eyes widened as another Hellhound, the largest in the pack, left Cacus and Bael in favor of Brock. Head bowed low, saliva oozing down its canines, it crept up behind him. Six feet, five feet, four feet...

He was about to die, and nothing pleased me more.

Days of his abuse, and I hoped the hound slaughtered him in the most gruesome of ways. But before the hound attacked, the prince intervened with his flaming sword. Two inches away from cutting into its side, the hound twisted, snapping its jaw around the blade, teeth disintegrating. It didn't whine or whimper. No, the Hellhound yanked the blade from the prince's hands, flung the sword to the edge of the trees, and circled him.

Weaponless, reevaluating his position, he fisted his hands before his face.

Was he going to box with the Hellhound?

He'd die, too. For some horrifying, unexplainable reason, that scared me. Like the thought of him dead was inconceivable, it couldn't happen. An hour ago, I thought about stealing his sword and killing him. But now, with death staring him in the face, I didn't want him to die. *Why?*

I glanced at his sword near the tree, thinking foolish things. *No. Just no.* If they died, I could escape, find Magda, and then my mom. They needed to die.

But if the Hellhounds lived, I'd die.

The hound snapped at the prince, going for his legs. He jumped back, hands erupting in blue flames. That seemed to pause the hound briefly before it attacked his legs with renewed vigor, forcing him to back up.

But why go for the prince's legs and expose its neck when it was tall enough for more vital strikes? The Hellhound didn't even make contact. What was it doing?

Movement to the side captured my attention.

"Aspen, watch out!" I yelled.

Dammit! Why was I helping him?

He pivoted at the last second, a claw snagging his elbow as he turned, and the two hounds collided. They fell into a pile of tangled bones and shadows. The prince, not giving them a chance to recover, punched them with his flaming fist, leaving charred marks on their muzzles.

I officially had a new definition of crazy and hated myself for helping him.

I'd never escape.

He boxed with two sharp-toothed, fire-breathing, steam-snorting hounds crafted of sharp bones and wispy shadows, blurring as he pivoted and ducked, smashing his fists into any and every part of their bodies. Aspen luscelered around, which meant he was an angel or at least part and untouchable.

Almost.

One Hellhound sank its teeth into his arm before he dodged it. In turn, he grabbed ahold of the Hellhound's jaw, obliterating it and the rest of its head.

Heavenly shit.

He was lethal. I mean, I assumed. But to see it, to know he was the one holding me captive. My stomach rolled. I needed to escape. With them distracted, this may be my only shot. So what if there was a chance I'd die in the forest? At least I'd have a chance, as minuscule as it was, better odds than staying with them.

With my forearms and some interesting wiggling, I pushed back toward the front of the carriage. No one noticed me or even glanced at me the entire time they fought.

Almost out, I ducked under the front axle at the moment something sharp stabbed into my legs. I screamed, clawing into the dirt as a Hellhound dragged me. Blinding agony shot up my legs, and I scrambled for the harness of the dead horses, latching on. I shrieked and immediately let go, unable to win the game of tug-of-war with it tearing the flesh in my thighs. It continued to drag me.

My Glory prickled.

Gravel and dirt scraped against my palms until we stopped. Pain speared up my spine as the Hellhound released me, swiping at my side to flip me over. Blood seeped into my joggers with each pound of my erratic heart as I met red sentient globes of death.

The Hellhound licked the yellowing bones of its muzzle. I squirmed back, whimpering. It followed with slow, measured movements as if liking the game and knowing I wasn't going anywhere without the ability to stand. Still, I shoved back foot by foot until it took one long stride and stepped onto my rib cage. Pressure compressed my chest, and like it thought I needed more pain, the

Hellhound sank its claws into my sides. Breathless screams ripped from my lungs. Its nails twitched, digging deeper, and blood spread into my flimsy t-shirt. A long, skinny tongue shot out and lapped at all the glistening red.

It moaned in pleasure, lapping quicker. Like a drug addict seeking more drugs, it jerked back on its claws, shredding, digging, and slurping up more of my blood. Agony worked its way up my shredded throat, begging me to scream, only to get lost in my wet, stuttering breaths.

The teasing needles of my Glory hovered, refusing to build further. Even if it did, what good would it do? It'd only knock me out. But if my cuffs didn't knock me out, the lack of blood would.

My feet tingled, not a prickling tingle that hurt, not a buzzing warm tingle from the prince's skin, no, a numbing tingle. The blue sky became fuzzy around the edges.

Time seemed to stop as I squeezed my eyes shut while it drank my blood like a damn vampire. Shame and confusion overwhelmed me as I waited for the end.

I was weak, useless, and a liability.

Just like I was for my mom. I couldn't even protect her. *But how could I if I couldn't even protect myself?*

I thought I was at least good at surviving, that I could eventually escape and survive until I found her. But it seemed I was failing at that, too.

A bubble of laughter surfaced, moving the nails of the Hellhound, and making me choke on the warm blood traveling up my throat. Soon, it'd be diving its big tongue into my mouth to slurp that up. But I couldn't help but find it funny how irrevocably naive I've been and how alone I truly was.

I thought I'd at least have more help or someone to guide me to my mom. First, the voices, but they never came back. Then Oliver, but he betrayed me. There was the dream-walk of the stranger who helped me, but who knew where he was? Now, it was just me and the hope of finding the only other person who cared about me.

My captors may care. In the way one cares about a mess they have to clean up, or maybe another dangerous creature would eat my leftovers. Then they wouldn't have to bother themselves by cleaning up my dead carcass.

As the numbness crept up my calves, it brought me back to the nightmare in Marcus's cement cage, of me struggling to beat the darkness and that unrecognizable male voice demanding I fight.

But what hope did I have of fighting off a beast ripping apart my body and draining me dry? I wasn't strong enough for this. If my mom was still alive, I hoped she'd forgive me.

I let the Hellhound drink from me, waiting for the rest of the numbness as an annoyingly sweet melody whispered in my ears. Second by second, the music gained volume. But it wasn't the normal clashing ice or a haunting melody. No, this was... jazz music.

It filled my chest with warmth and comfort, bringing to mind a steaming cup of hot chocolate and ending with a soft, off-tune hum.

My mom's voice.

A treat before death.

Bittersweet tears trailed down my cheeks. I wished I could remember more. But if I had to die with her voice in my ear, I would.

The melody and numbness both climbed, two crescendos racing for two different peaks—one of light and one of darkness.

I closed my eyes, giving in to her hum, feeling guilty for the smile that twitched underneath the lingering agony.

She'd never know I gave up. But that didn't lighten the guilt as I rasped, "I'm sorry, Mom."

I let the music and light take me under.

My body limply moved from an uncomfortable tug. An unnatural sound and a hiss spliced through the music. Weight lifted off my chest, and I figured I was seconds away. Sound was the last to go, but I swore I heard my name.

"Did she do this?"

"Reduce a Hellhound to particles of dust. Looks like it."

"But the cuffs," someone said, shocked.

There was no answer to that. The humming jazz faded along with their voices.

Something tugged at my legs, bringing me back.

"She's still losing blood."

"Just leave her. We'll find another one."

"No, we'll take her to the closest healer," the voice said through my fuzzy hearing. I couldn't tell who it was, but I heard the irritation.

Pressure tickled my back and knees.

"Fine. I can carry her for you, prince."

"I'll carry her. She is my duty." He paused. "My duty to her."

My sides stretched and bent in his arms, and I screamed bloody murder. He stiffened, adjusted me, and I flew back to the unconscious world—or possibly death.

THE DARKNESS I WITNESSED in our mind connection and the sense of contentment from her emotions confirmed that my Soulhound was sound asleep.

Rune!

Nothing.

Rune! I yelled again, sending her a sense of urgency and anger.

She blinked open an eye and slowly opened the other, irritated with me for waking her up.

Bark bordered her peripherals, and a forest spread out before her. She was bedded down in a hollow tree, her favorite place to sleep.

Where is the female? I snapped. It was like dealing with a damned teenager. I'd make Rune come home and take her place if I could, but that wasn't possible.

She sent me a feeling of annoyance and walked over to the clearing she was supposed to be watching, finding it empty.

Fuck!

Find her!

"HEY, SWEETIE, WAKE UP. I need you to drink this," a gentle, high-pitched voice coaxed.

Too much pain and *worry* remained on the other side of this dreamless world. The worry felt off, but I didn't have the energy or clarity to pinpoint why.

"Come on." A hand tilted my head up. Barely aware, something pressed to my lips. "That's it. This will help your bleeding." A terrible taste entered my mouth. I took in some liquid, but most of it slid past my lips as my head lolled to the side.

There was a deep sigh as I settled back into something immovable but warm.

"Wasn't she supposed to drink all of that?" A voice accused behind me, hot and sharp.

"Yes," she said with concern. "Hopefully, it will be enough for now. After I stitch her, I'll have to make her bindings tight. Once conscious, she'll have to drink more of the coagulation serum. Until then, she will have to be checked frequently."

Something moved from underneath me, making me groan.

"Will she live?"

Silence.

"Will she live?" The voice demanded. I cringed. The volume of their words snapped into my ear.

I heard another heavy sigh and then felt a lot of agonizing pressure. My head rolled back and forth as I whimpered, wanting the pain to stop.

"I'll do my best. Now let her go so I can start."

The ground moved a lot more this time, and my pain sky-rocketed. Retreating from the pain, their voices softened.

"You will save her."

"Careful, it sounds like you're worried, Aspen."

There was a grunt and what sounded like a door opening. "Only because she needs to be whole for my queen."

"Your excuses seem to be weaker and weaker each time you visit." Silence. "Nice job on the tourniquets and bandages," she said be-grudgingly after a moment.

"Learned from the best."

An amused huff was the last sound I heard before fading to a numbing blackness.

CHAPTER SIXTEEN

Unearthly beauty reeled me in like a sucking black hole. Her hair was the color of a starless night, flowing in long waves down her tight, black bodice. She was regal. Her ebony eyes had scarlet rings and were washed with a purple film.

It was another dream-walk, similar to the one of my mom and—I gritted my teeth remembering bits and pieces of that man. I didn't invade any bodies. Here, without vertigo, my skinny body was my own. A big difference from my last dream-walk, where I was toned, my breasts weren't pancakes, a strange guy helped warm me, and my mom confessed to—

"The infamous Saraqael is summoning me?" I jerked back. *Saraqael?* That was my mom's name. "What would your precious angel say about this?" She smiled. But there was nothing friendly about it.

"How is it done?"

I peeked around a large pillar and found my mom on the other side of a circle of prominent red symbols. Her body shimmered with a pure white light. Glory.

They were opposites. One dark and sinful, the other light and pure.

"How is what done?" The dark one asked, intrigued. She prowled inside the symbols. Mulberry lips tilted in a predatory smile.

"Children."

The dark woman laughed, filling the air with a lilting melody. "Saraqael, you can't have children. You know that."

"I heard different." She paused. "And I heard you've helped others."

Swirling black silk grazed the white slippers of my mom's feet. Long-painted nails attempted to reach for her chin, but the dark woman couldn't breach the circle of symbols. "Did you now? And did these others happen to have names or locations?" Danger edged her questioning tone.

"No."

"Are you sure?"

"Shouldn't you know who you've helped?"

Her lips twisted. "I've helped many. But your kind? Very few. And none have proven to be successful. Or so I've been told." Her fake smile dropped.

My mom kept quiet.

"You want to know how to have a child. You will give me their name. And do not lie to me, for I know your other half would never allow you to associate with the likes of us, and I wouldn't want him finding out," she said sweetly, sounding like she wouldn't care one bit if he found out.

The light on my mom's skin guttered. "Miriam," she whispered.

A genuine smile spread on the dark woman's face. "Very unexpected of you, Saraqael. Twice today. First summoning me and second, giving up the name so easily." Black silk swirled, trailing the circle of glistening writing. "But a deal is a deal. Although, I'm not sure you'll ever have a child. And not because it is still difficult with my methods. But because you and whoever the father will be will need to tangle with a lot of dark energy," she tittered. "That purist you're with would send you to hell himself before doing that. You could see my husband."

My mom lifted her head, determination in her stiff shoulders. "Tell me."

PURPLE LIGHT FLASHED, AND my eyes opened.

I *was* born. My mom was an Archangel, and she found a way to have me with the help of the creepy, dark woman. *Did that make me the first-born angel in existence? Was that why I had Glory, and they took me?* All these questions made my head hurt.

I surveyed my surroundings, trying to block the blue moonlight streaming in, which was making my headache worse. The moonlight shed its light onto a small minimalist room. A table to my right held a flickering candle lamp and a bowl of pink water with a washcloth. The walls were plain with no adornment, no extra furniture but the cream bed and side table.

I pushed myself into a sitting position and gasped. My sides burned, and my legs throbbed with the slightest twitch. Pushing past the pain, I pulled the quilt down. A loose shirt pulled up to my breasts showed a bandage wrapped tightly around my ribs. Lower yet, two tight bandages circled my thighs, painfully so. Tempted to unwind them, I fingered the edge of the gauze. It was *sticky?*

A substance oozed from the corners. I rubbed it on the pad of my fingers. *Was that*—I sniffed it. *Honey?*

More curious than ever, I unwound the gauze at my ribs, then stopped and stared at my wrists. How I didn't notice before was beyond me, but my cuffs were gone. My wrist and finger splint were not. Or they had been rewrapped.

Continuing my unraveling, the gauze turned pink, darkening with each pull.

"Stop—" I jerked at Aspen's voice, covering myself. "Your wounds need to stay tightly bound!" he snapped, almost sounding panicked.

He stood in the open doorway, tense. I was so immersed in my head that I forgot about him and the others. But, of course, they were still close by.

"Where am I?" I rasped, throat dry.

He glared at my hidden ribs. His cloak appeared fresh compared to the splattered green gunk of his leathers. The candlelight flickered across the sculpted muscle of his tensing arms. Blushing, I clamped down on my cheeks and turned my face away.

"We brought you to a healer named Hana." He waited for that to sink in and continued. "You've been unconscious for two days. We didn't think you were going to make it at first. But Hana's one of the best healers around. She worked tirelessly on you, and you're undermining all the effort we put into saving your damned life!" he spat, drilling holes into my partially unwrapped sides.

I could hear the respect he had for her in his voice. Who knew he respected anyone, as big of an asshole as he was.

"What are you staring at? Rewrap your damned wounds!"

His demanding, arrogant tone grated on me. Perhaps I should unwrap the rest of my ribs and stuff the bloody cloth into his mouth.

Unfortunately, I listened to his forceful words, but not without taking my unnamed frustration out on him. "Have you ever thought about a gag?"

Nonplussed, his lips pressed into a thin line as he raised a skeptical brow.

Oh, he wasn't going to like this. I held back my anticipatory smile. "You know, to keep the condescending shit from spilling out of your mouth."

His eyes darkened. I threw him one of those smug smirks he'd given me the last few days. It dropped when he didn't react. I guess the smirk didn't affect him like it did me.

"Once Hana gives the go-ahead, we'll be back on our way to give you to our queen," he said point-blank.

"Your queen, as in your mother?"

Something strange flashed through his eyes—like confusion mixed with horror. But it tightened his face for less than a second before a soft red light flashed beneath his chin, and his cold mask eradicated the emotions.

What was that light?

Unable to sit in silence as he scrutinized me, I snarked, "You're finally giving me answers?"

"Figured I'd gift you a small slice for not dying on us."

I huffed. "Oh, right. Because dealing with my dead carcass would be a hindrance."

"You're more important to her alive than dead. For—" He stopped himself.

Did he really think I was that stupid?

"For now? Your queen, mother, whoever the hell she is," I was getting worked up. "Wants me alive, for now."

He didn't confirm or deny, but his silence answered for him.

My head dropped back against the headboard, defeated and tired.

The prince walked into the room, white knuckling the hilt of his sword. "Maybe you should've listened to me," he barked, branding me with his glare and his hot, apple-scented breath. Inching away wasn't an option, so I had to live in his angry proximity.

"This again?" The fabric in my hands scrunched in my fists. "Why the hell would I listen to you?" I scoffed. "You just admitted that my life was only as valuable as whatever I could provide to your *wretched queen.*" My head thrust forward in cadence to the last two words, ignoring the tug on my stitches, just in case he didn't hear the vehemence in my tone.

His grip tightened on his sword as the muscle in his jaw pulsed. He didn't like me insulting his sovereign, but too bad.

"I'm not going to your vile queen. I want nothing to do with you and your pack of whatever Cacus and Bael are." The throbbing in my side intensified, forcing me to sit back with a grimace. It was proof that my words were more bark than bite. If I couldn't even sit up without support, there was no way I was getting away from them.

Quietly, he stared, watching me with an intensity that made me squirm. The blues of his eyes forced me to hold my ground even though I wanted to look down.

"Demons." He voiced at last.

"What?"

Crossing his arms, he tilted his head to the side. "Cacus and Bael are Cambion demons. They explode on the brink of death, killing anyone near them." There was another stilted pause as he waited for my reaction.

"Cambion..." I trailed off, my mind going a mile a minute. It wasn't a stretch to think those two hulking beasts were demons, but I never thought—I shook my head—no wonder the Hellhounds wouldn't approach them. Fighting the demons was tantamount to suicide.

"You didn't know," he laughed with disbelief. "What do you know about Elora?"

Glaring, I bit into my cheeks. There was such arrogance in his tone, like he knew what my answer would be and couldn't wait to rub it in my face. If he continued like this, I'd either end up chewing through my flesh, gagging him myself, or worse, I'd dissolve this quilt.

But he was right, and that had me tasting copper.

I was brought to a world I knew barely anything about, with someone I just met, all because some voice in my head told me to.

And look where I was now.

I would not answer his question. Giving him that satisfaction would end me, even though my silence would condemn me.

Aspen grunted, looking at me with disbelief. "Your ignorance is going to get you killed." His words were salt in an open wound.

"Excuse me?" My nostrils flared.

His next grunt nearly tripped the strings of the melody that lurked beneath my rage.

"Who in their right mind would come to a world they know nothing about?" he seethed, the muscle in the back of his jaw throbbing.

"Why does what I do or don't know even matter to you?" I spat back, feeling itchy.

He stepped forward, knees hitting the bed's wooden frame, towering over me. My back straightened in response, trying to look strong and not wounded and slumped against the pillows. But I could only do so much as my stitches pulled with my movements.

"What the hell were you thinking? Why didn't you stay on Earth? Elora is dangerous! It isn't a place for a senseless, wimpy female." There was so much angry disbelief in his tone that I bristled.

Stretching further against my stitches, wishing I could stand, I attempted to look intimidating. "I am *not* senseless or wimpy!"

"Your actions speak otherwise." He glared.

My anger simmered. I lifted my chin, forcing us nose-to-nose. "If you bring me to your wretched queen, I will gladly burn her face off."

Blue flame flashed in his irises, and the light under his chin flickered. A half-smirk pulled at my lips, happy to have hit a nerve.

"Listen to you," he whispered with a deadly tone. "Spewing this arrogance around creatures you know nothing about. You don't even have the skills necessary to save yourself, which you proved by barely surviving a Hellhound attack. You'd be dead if it weren't for me and my queen. You know nothing of this world. You know nothing of your powers. You are an ignorant, untrained, senseless, helpless female." The force of his heartless words hit my face. They were brutal, needling at my insecurities.

I pulled my legs off the bed, making myself sit up and forcing him back a step. Water pooled in the corner of my eyes from the pain, but I wasn't about to let him get away with what he said. It hit too deep, and the itch wouldn't let me.

"At least I'm not a bitch's bitch."

Blue and red light erupted, and metal ripped free. A flaming sword came toward my neck, but before it reached me, stabbing pain erupted through my body, and the sword clattered to the ground. He came at me.

"What are you—"

He tackled and swaddled me in his heavy cloak. Unlike my disintegrated clothes, the cloak withstood the white and purple flames on my skin.

"Get off of me!" I yanked the cloak off my flameless face.

"Hana did a lot for you. The least you could do is not burn down her house," he yelled back. This considerate act wasn't for me but for Hana. And based on the indignation that replaced the flames in his eyes, he hated that he had to help me.

No longer wanting to meet his gaze, I glared at the hands that touched me. Too bad I couldn't burn things with my eyes. Maybe then he'd let me go. Not that the leather on his arms needed any more holes or tears. The Hellhounds had scored gouges into his uniform, and when I tilted my head just right, light gleamed on blood beneath the shredded folds. The wounds were shiny slivers, almost healed. He acted and fought against the Hellhounds, and I just hid like an untrained, senseless, helpless female.

The words were like a poison, repeating an endless cycle in my mind. Only the more I heard it, the less it sounded like the mocking tone of my princely jailor. There was someone else who used to call me a helpless little wimp, but I couldn't remember who.

Shame and anger colored my face, fueling my flame. The cloak had a threshold of how much power it could withstand as a shimmer of dark violet leaked through the seams. The white slowly dimmed along with my fear. But calming the rage wasn't working with Aspen's swaddling. It practically proved his point. His seething gaze only made it worse.

"Leave," I said, trying to pull away, but he wouldn't let go.

"Are you sure?" he asked, sounding almost concerned. He had to be mocking me.

"I said *leave*!" I screamed, purple flame spiking through the material.

Holding in a gasp of pain, I rolled onto my side, forcing his hands off me. The bed moved under his weight, and his sword scraped against the floor and slid back into its sheath. Once he shut the door, I let out the strangled gasp. The physical pain was just as bad as the emotional pain. Tears fell without the audience, rolling down the side of my cheek and over my nose, soothing the haunting melody and itch. My purple flames dimmed beneath the cloak, sinking back to where they came.

I shifted, thinking it'd help the painful heartbeat in my sides. With my clothing burned to nothing, the sticky honey slid against the heavy fabric of the prince's cloak. The throbbing worsened.

My fingers lifted the fabric, and I winced. It was stuck, possibly to the honey. Taking a deep breath, cringing, I jerked it off like a band-aid.

Blood seeped down my ribs and around my back.

The fabric had slowed the bleeding, but now my open wounds were exposed. My stomach turned.

"Shit," I said. Not only were my cuts freely bleeding down my side, but I had to find help, and I was naked.

I searched the room for something to wrap around my wounds, finding no extra supplies. *What kind of healer didn't have extra supplies?* Muffling my cry, I swung my legs off the bed. My hands pressed into my sides, trying to stop the bleeding. It barely helped, but it was better than nothing. My legs, though—there was nothing I could do for them. They throbbed with the same fiery pain my sides did and bled.

Working up the courage, I stood. The floor swirled before I gained my bearings and shuffled toward the door. Trickles of blood slid down the backs of my thighs. With slick fingers, it took two tries before the knob turned, and he was already there.

"Aspen?" I whispered, voice hitching. A sudden chill overwhelmed my body, and my knees buckled.

Without a word, he had me in his arms. My sides burned as he jostled me. I hadn't expected him to pick me up but was grateful even if it was agonizing, and the room swirled.

"Hana!" he called, laying me in bed.

"Why didn't you say something immediately?" he demanded, touching the opening of the cloak.

"I didn't know." I rested my head back against the soft pillow, my mind loopy.

What was he doing?

"Hey!" My vision blinked out, then back in, and my cloak opened. I was bare in front of him. "Stop!" Anxiety seized me as I felt pressure. I slapped his hands and whatever he was doing to me.

"Lucille, you're bleeding out. I'm trying to help. Please." The glacial hard tone he usually used melted into something soft and resigned.

He knew my name. *How? And why was he looking at me like that?*

Two beautiful mountain lakes glistened at me with concern—not hate, not the arrogant sneer or cold mask he wore, but genuine concern, like he had a heart.

I was hallucinating.

Stunned and dizzy, wanting Aspen to stop vanishing behind a black cloud, I stopped slapping him.

At one moment of clarity, I wondered if he sneaked a peek at my pebbled breasts.

"You're hurting my sides," I said weakly. "And my legs hurt, Aspen. They hurt so much," I cried. *Why did I keep saying his name?* "I hate his name."

"Whose name?"

"Your name. It's nice. But you're an ass. You shouldn't have your name."

Did I say that out loud?

"Hana!" Aspen's voice had to have carried through the whole house. The sword at his hip flashed along with his distorted eyes.

Down the hall, footsteps pattered. A lady barged into the room, frantic, holding a black bag. "What? I was stitching another patient. What's wrong?"

My muddled brain decided to hallucinate green skin onto the lady and shrink her down to the size of a dwarf. Odd.

Aspen stood as she entered. "She's bleeding out. Help her." Long gone was the male with melted seas of worry, replaced by the authority of a commanding prince. The arrogant asshole was back. I snorted to myself.

"How? She was finally stable!" Hana exclaimed, astonished, ignoring his tone. She lifted something from my sides, gazing at my open wounds. Quickly, she set down her black bag and grabbed supplies. "This is going to hurt. Deep breaths, okay?" Tender ruby eyes nodded down to my torso.

"Okay."

"And I need you to drink this. It's a coagulant serum. It will counteract the rest of the Hellhound's saliva." She held a vial to my lips, and I let her tip the bitter liquid into my mouth.

"How did this happen? And why didn't you get me the moment she woke up? Did you want her to bleed to death after nearly biting my head off to save her?" Hana did not sound happy—more like downright pissed off.

I giggled. Aspen was getting scolded.

My thoughts turned disjointed as everything blurred together. I squeezed my eyes shut, relieved by the lack of weirdness. Their words became softer.

"I don't know. We were talking. I got distracted." He paused. "I said some things and her powers did the rest."

He said a lot of things.

"You never thought about the stitches, bandages, or serum." It wasn't a question.

"No."

Was that regret in his tone?

Hana huffed. "Well, hopefully, her accelerated healing can replenish what she's lost. The serum should help soon, too," she sighed. "Does she know?"

My sides burned as Hana poured something into each slice along my ribs, then turned me with Aspen's help to do the same to my thighs. They moved me back, and I lay limp and barely conscious. I could feel my body twitch in pain, but my eyes never opened, only aware enough to hear the fading tones of their conversation.

"No," he said, frustrated. "She knows nothing about Elora either. Why would she come here?" He stomped back and forth. "Why doesn't she remember? Why didn't she fucking listen to me?"

"Did you ever think of asking her?" Hana supplied.

He scoffed, "Why would I do that? Her memories are gone."

"Maybe to help her?"

There was a long pause before he answered. "Hana, I think you need to stop drinking the earthly wine. It's obviously messed with your mind." He sighed, a sound I never heard from him before. "She's here now. Magda said..."

"She's a witch who plays with emotions for power. Her words can mean many things."

"True."

"Will you tell her? Help her?"

He laughed, a bitter, ruthless sound. "No. The queen will either use her or lose her, like all the others."

"Always so loyal."

Aspen gave another bitter laugh. "Either loyalty or death."

"Or taking my advice from before. Get out. Find a different life. Let her—"

"Stop! I won't listen to your pointless advice. It's too late. I will never betray my queen," Aspen declared.

"So she'll be another Nalini?" she whispered.

My ears started to ring with how quiet it became.

"Don't ever speak her name to me again." The door opened, then slammed.

"Oh, Aspen, what did she turn you into?" Hana whispered sadly to herself while her soft fingers applied pressure on my wounds. I let myself drift off, wondering about which *she* Hana was talking about.

CHAPTER SEVENTEEN

"If you don't do it, darling, then I will," a sickly sweet feminine voice said. Burgundy manicured nails, overlaid with a purple haze, pointed in front of me at a beautiful girl backed by a wall of ancient pillars. She was young, maybe seventeen, with dark freckled skin and copper hair. Eyes of piercing amber stared at me while silent lines of water slid down her cheeks, dripping off her chin to the rusty stone.

I didn't recognize her.

"Please," she said, voice cracking, shifting her attention behind me.

My head shook back and forth, shifting the purple haze. I couldn't stop the movement of my head or control it. Which meant I was invading the body of a past version of myself, reliving a memory. But I couldn't tell how old I was. My gaze never strayed down to my torso. It stayed on the tragic bronzed beauty I couldn't remember.

Tears pooled in my eyes as I nearly broke my jaw clenching it so hard, further confusing me. A great wall separated me from fully connecting to my emotions and this moment. *That was a new development.*

"I will not ask again. If you do not lift your hand, I will do it for you. And you do not want that," a voice said behind me, sounding like caramelized sugar over razor blades.

Out of everything in this dream, the ancient courtyard, the ominous black sky, the curvy sobbing girl, that voice was the only thing I recognized.

The alluring, dark sound was hard to forget. It was the woman with sinuous curves and dark features who was in my last dream-walk. I remembered everything from that dream-walk and the one before of the stranger and my erupting powers. But the rest were fragmented pieces of my amulet, someone after me and my mom, and a deadly conversation about my dream-walking powers.

If that man who spoke of my powers was right, then there were two aspects of my dream-walking abilities: one where I relived memories and the other where I gave memories the power to change. *But did that mean I changed just the memory, or was it bigger than that?* He also said something about time and jumping dreams.

The last dream-walk wasn't my memory. I wasn't born yet.

Whose dream did I jump into, and could I find my mom this way?

A sharp cry pulled me from my renewed hope. Regret wrinkled the forehead of the girl in front of me, and sorrow twisted her lips. If I could climb the wall separating the connection between my thoughts and emotions, I bet I would better understand the water threatening to overtake my eyes.

"It's okay," she said, crying harder. "It's okay."

From my tears, it wasn't okay.

Rusty brown stained the rock beneath the girl's leathered shoes, only in that spot. Against my will, my fists trembled as they attempted to rise, lifting a couple of inches before falling back to my side. I released more soundless tears, so unlike the sobs that burst from the curvy, freckled girl.

"It's okay." She nodded like she believed it. "Don't let her win."

A sense of apprehension hit me as she tried to keep the wobble from her legs. Something terrible was about to happen, and I officially wanted to leave this puppeteering dream.

"But I always win," the woman behind me stated.

The sobs that overtook the girl changed abruptly to ear-piercing screams. Her limbs stretched wide, pulled by invisible strings. Dark red smoke manifested around her spread-eagle body, lifting her into the sky until she was the size of my hand. At a certain height, the young girl stopped screaming. The wisps of red undulated and changed shape, holding her in place.

"Please," I begged, my voice a faint and broken whisper I didn't recognize.

It wasn't my voice, and this wasn't my body.

"You've made your choice, love," she sighed. Her breath brushed the back of my neck. "I told you time and time again. If this is what I need to do to acquire your obedience. So be it." The rolling red smoke that surrounded the girl vanished.

"No," I shouted, jerking forward as if I'd catch her but stopping short as the same power that held the girl wrapped around my wrists. My eyes narrowed on it. Flames jolted from my skin, burning away the red smoke chaining me in place. But each time I burned it away, a next tendril would take its place. I used more of my power, dragging my bloody knees against the stone, draining myself to reach the girl with copper hair plummeting to her death.

I fought to cover more ground, stretching out desperately until my fingertips grazed her copper hair just as she slammed into the unforgiving ground. Bones broke, flesh tore, and her blood sprayed into my face.

The force fighting against me released. I crawled toward the heap of green cloth. Her orange hair glistened, soaked through with blood. Brushing back the strands that covered her face, the air in my lungs stilled. Her amber eyes were dull, unseeing.

An anvil of power struck the wall that separated me from my emotions, turning it into dust. Agony flooded my mind, stabbing my chest and piercing my soul.

I brushed the wavy strands further from her face, smearing blood and tears, bowing my head against her forehead as a sob crawled up my throat.

"Nalini," I cried.

No. Not me. *Aspen.*

Before I could think about the implications, pressure, unlike anything I'd ever known, filled me—and so much blinding anger.

Fury intertwined with all-consuming agony. They pulled at something molten writhing inside me. The pressure swelled. With one last look at the stunning face, feeling a shattering in my soul, I whipped back my head and raged to the skies. Ungodly heat barreled to the surface of my skin. Bright light erupted, shaking the ground before a dark red cloud snuffed it out.

"You will obey me."

"HEY LUCILLE, TIME TO wake up." A gentle hand pressed into my shoulder. I jolted, looking around. Hope and agony tightened my throat.

Was that real? Did I just witness that girl's death through Aspen's eyes? And how did I dream-walk to his memory? I needed to figure out how to control this power.

"Lucille? Are you okay?" She touched my shoulder again.

I glanced over to a head of frizzy red graying hair, freezing.

She actually was short and green. I didn't hallucinate it. She was a foot taller than the bed. Her white shirt hung to her knees, covering loose pants rolled up to her scaly ankles.

My eyebrows scrunched. The scales weren't there last night, or maybe they were.

"The blood loss had you addled. You passed out, but the serum should be taking effect. Although it will take time to remove the toxins of their saliva completely." she said, assuming the expression on my face was about my state. I was thankful she couldn't read my thoughts.

"What are you?" I asked, staring at the red surrounding her yellow-slitted pupils.

She smiled, nodding down to my torso. "May I?"

I slid the covers off my body. Someone clothed me in loose blue pants and a white t-shirt. Hana, I hoped. My cheeks started to heat at the memory of my exposed breasts.

She lifted my shirt, peeled back the gauze pads, and surveyed the stitches. They were still bleeding slightly and very red, but by her nod of approval, that was okay. Moving to my legs, she pulled up the loose pants and had me turn. "I'm a half-breed. Part human and part serpent demon." She talked as she took something out of her pocket, lightly dabbing the sticky substance on my cuts. "Hence the scales and the eyes," she said with a soft laugh.

I didn't know what to say to that. First angels and angel half-breeds, now demons and demon-half breeds? Imagining a human and a demon together was horrifying. *If this was what Hana looked like, what did her parents look like? Did humans willingly want to breed with demons?* I bit my cheeks hard, attempting to school my features before she found the horror on my face.

Her gloved fingers slid over my stitches with the sweet-smelling substance. A safer question popped out of my mouth, "Why are you applying honey to my cuts?"

She dabbed a little more before wrapping my legs with gauze. "It's to prevent infection. Angel or demon, quick healing or not, you can still get an infection."

"Isn't there something better to use?"

Pale green lips revealed a flash of sharp teeth. My Glory prickled at the sight.

"You'll come to find Elora is nothing like your Earth. We healers don't have the same medicines and machinery. We don't even have electricity. Plants, herbs, skills, and magic are our resources. And if we are lucky, sometimes we can get human medicine. But can you really see someone like me going to a hospital and asking for antibiotic ointment?"

I couldn't see a lot of things, or unsee, as I watched her forked tongue flick out and again wondered about her parents. "No."

"You don't have to be scared." Her tongue flicked out once more. It was such a small thing, and yet I couldn't control my out-of-control heart and painful skin. *Please don't erupt.*

"I can sense it. It's a useful skill when you're a healer."

Her words were meant to console me, but her razor teeth and slitted eyes kept capturing my attention.

She carefully tugged my pant legs down and had me sit back. "We aren't all bad. Many, yes. But not all."

Smooth scales touched the top of my hand, patting me. Her black-tipped fingernails grazed my knuckles. I stared at them as my vortex of panic stole the last of my minuscule restraint.

My hands erupted when she pulled back, only catching the tip of the white flames. She hissed.

"Heavenly shit! I'm so sorry! Oh my gosh!" And like a complete and utter idiot, I waved them around to put them out like it'd actually work this time.

Hana gave me an amused smile, dabbing a little honey on her blisters. "It's okay. I have children in here who don't know how to control their powers either. Here"—she rummaged through her bag—"take a sip of this," then held a vial near my lips. "It'll suppress your flames for a few minutes."

I took a sip. The clear liquid tasted sweet against my tongue; a lot better than what she gave me last night. Immediately, warmth pooled in my chest, silencing my flames. The tension in my shoulders eased, and I sighed, at peace. It was easy, like my amulet was.

"Thanks."

She smiled. "Your injuries are stable. It'll take two to six days for them to fully heal. Check them each day to see how they're fairing. As for your broken bones, your pinky suffered a tiny fracture, but it's healed now. Your wrist may need one more day."

"That fast?"

The kindness never left her eyes, but a hint of worry made her smile vanish. "You're at least part angel, and I suspect a high-level one, or you wouldn't have made it through the first night. The Hellhound's saliva is designed to invade your bloodstream and stop coagulation so they can drink you dry. If you were human, you would've gone into multiple organ failure the moment Prince Aspen reached my door. It was only through your accelerated healing you survived. So yes, once the serum removes the rest of those toxins, it'll be that fast. As for your bones, they usually take longer, but Aspen told me you received them a few days ago. Still, last night put you back, but as long as you don't use your flames for a day or two, you should be fine."

I nodded in understanding. But that was a big ask.

"Can't I just take some of that serum?" I pointed at the small vial on the bedside table. The calming liquid filled half the bottle. I'd probably need more than that.

She gave me an odd look. "It suppresses your power. You'll take weeks to heal instead of days."

"That's okay." It could help me hide my powers if they got out of hand while I attempted to practice with them.

Her eyes narrowed. "Sorry, Lucille. This is the last vial I have until I go to buy more from Magda, and since she lives a couple of days away, I can't give you it."

I jolted. "Did you say, Magda?"

Hana nodded.

This was it. This was the help I needed. I latched onto Hana's arm. "I was told to find her. That she can answer my questions. Can she? Where is she?"

Hana looked at me warily.

"Please, tell me. I have to find her." I didn't know if it was the eagerness in my voice or the desperation in my eyes, but with a glance back at the closed door, Hana bowed her head and sighed, coming to some conclusion.

"Lucille, her answers come at a steep price and are not always clear. Plus, you won't be traveling that way. As the human walks, it's two days North of here, and you're traveling Southeast."

"Then help me escape. Tell them I ran away," I pleaded.

Hana bowed her head, dropping her gaze from my begging eyes. "I can't."

Sagging back, I stared at the ceiling as tears leaked from the corner of my eyes. Of course, she couldn't. Why would it ever be that simple for me?

"But in the Drune Forest, which you will go through on the way, there are creatures there called Drunes. No one knows what they are, but they've been here longer than most. They've seen a lot and know even more." Pity and kindness wove around her resigned words.

"Do they have a price?"

"Yes. It usually comes in the form of blood."

I fiddled with the hem of my shirt. "How much blood?"

Hana stepped closer, gripping my bicep. "Don't be so eager. Blood is a dangerous currency to give away. In the wrong hands, it can do a lot of damage. Make sure the answers you want are worth it before seeking them out."

She shifted her ear toward the door like she heard something and released me. "There are some extra clothes in the closet I found for you. Get dressed. Aspen is ready to leave as soon as you are." She handed me a ball of gauze and a small pouch filled with something. "Your rib stitches should be fine with the gauze pads, but if you'd like them covered more securely, you can wrap more around your body. That"—she pointed at the pouch—"is if, for some reason, you don't heed my warnings on using your power and end up bleeding again. It'll clot your blood long enough to allow your fast healing to kick in. I gave Aspen an extra sterile needle and thread, too." Hana shook her head. "I may have taught that male how to stitch, but trust me, it's better if you heal without his grumpy ass."

"Thank you." I held the gauze and pouch, studying her face. It was odd hearing anyone talk about Aspen so *fondly*. Especially when I could see the guilt in her frown lines. Hana may not approve of Aspen holding me against my will, but she'd do nothing to stop it. She cared for him, and by what he said about her, he cared for her, too. Or at least respected her.

After last night, I couldn't think my princely jailor was heartless anymore. But he wasn't far off.

Hana put the calming liquid in her bag, unfortunately, and walked to the door, hand on the knob. "Aspen is loyal to his queen and is the commander of her armies. He has ninety years' worth of swordplay and magic."

I jolted, forgetting angel blood made you immortal. Aspen looked young, like twenties young, not somewhere near or over ninety.

"Brock has the power to sense more than you know. And now Aspen can too," she muttered the last part to herself.

What did that mean?

"Why are you telling me all this? You don't want to help me escape, but you'll give me information?"

Concern lined her pinched brows. "I want you to escape. I just can't be the one to do it. Even if I wanted to betray Aspen, they'd know. It's nearly impossible to escape them. Females before you have tried. Either the forest creatures kill them, or Brock beats them to submission. But I despise his queen and everything she stands for. Aspen," her voice cracked. "Has been through hell and survived it, both because of her. It's changed him. Yet his loyalty remains sound, and I don't know why. He is good. He is. I swear." She urged as if trying to convince me, then gathered herself. "Aspen told me you have a lot of power, Lucille. His queen wants it. She's been searching for the key to her cage for centuries. She thinks you're it. Protect yourself and find a way out before you cross into the Tenebrous Kingdom." That was the last thing she said before walking out.

Holding back tears, I unwrapped myself from the blankets. My body throbbed, but the soreness would be my new constant companion until I healed. I walked gingerly to the closet and opened a mirrored door. Inside hung a white t-shirt similar to the one Hana wore, a black jacket made of the same heavy material as Aspen's cloak, and a pair of black pants with red accents.

Once dressed, I stared at myself and the hollow despair leaking into the purple bags under my eyes. They stood out against my fair skin. "What did you get yourself into?" I whispered to my reflection.

Gingerly, I sat down on the bed, scanning the uncomfortable shirt. My pancake chest shoved at the tight material more than I wanted. The jacket was at least semi-comfortable. But now I looked like Aspen. *Why couldn't I stop thinking about his name? Was I so starved for attention that the thought of the crinkles creasing his eyes as he saw me bleeding out moved me?*

But it was difficult not to sympathize with him for what he witnessed. Someone murdered the girl he cared for.

A knock sounded at my door.

Since when did anyone knock? "Yes?"

"I have your food," Aspen said.

I stared out the window. "I'm not hungry."

Aspen opened the door, standing with an unyielding expression, a hand behind his back, and an egg and cheese sandwich in his other. Dark, wet strands of hair clung to his forehead and curled near his chiseled cheekbones. His skin gleamed flawless against the crisp, black uniform that showed no trace of dirt or Hellhound gunk. *Why did he have to look like that? Why couldn't my captor be ugly?*

"You will eat, Lucille."

At least the ominous red glow under his chin, coupled with his glare, served as a reminder that appearances meant nothing.

"How do you know my name?" He shouldn't be allowed to use it.

For a moment, he stayed quiet, and then he walked to where I sat. The red glow lessened the closer he came. He set the plate and sandwich on my lap. "You told me."

"No, I didn't."

"Eat. You need nutrients to heal."

I glared up at him.

"Why do you care when your queen will either use me or lose me?" Yeah, I remembered that little phrase. However, the word lose confused me. I understood *use* all too well. If he cared for my well-being, it wasn't because, in the last week, I somehow got under his cold exterior; it was because I needed to be whole and ready to be used by his queen.

His jaw muscle pulsed, and a faint blue glow hovered in his eyes. I raised a brow in challenge. When he said nothing, I scoffed and gazed at the rising sun behind the dark forest.

I hated him. I hated this. I hated that I had no one.

Small vibrations tickled my chin as Aspen jerked me to face him. His mouth opened, ready to spew his next demand, then stopped. At first, I thought the unnatural tingles from his touch surprised him. But that wasn't it. Not as his gaze roved over me, taking in my sponge-bathed face, my peculiar eyes, and the tight white shirt under a black jacket. His pupils dilated. My cheeks heated.

"Like what you see?" I snapped.

His lips pursed into a hard line. A deafening silence charged the air between us until he let go of my chin and picked up my sandwich, pressing it against my lips.

"Bite."

"No."

"Lucille."

"Aspen."

He flinched. I grimaced, hating myself for the slip-up. He wasn't anything but a cold asshole, taking me against my will. I bit the sandwich then, hoping to take off his fingers. To my disappointment, my teeth only grazed them, sending a jolt I wasn't expecting into my lips.

I jerked back at the same time he did. The large mouth of food was hard to chew. Eventually, it sank like a tasteless lump in my stomach as we glared at each other.

Satisfied, Aspen brought forward his hidden jangling hand. I broke our glaring match as I took in the sight of a pair of black metal cuffs.

"You're not putting those on me."

"And since when did you think you had a choice?"

I hated him.

"Do you ever tire of the constant arrogant mask you wear? Or have you been wearing it so long you forgot what it's like not to be a princely asshole?"

With the cuffs in hand, he dropped to my ankles. "These won't electrocute you, but in exchange, they suppress everything but your healing," he said, unphased by my insult. "You won't be able to feel your powers or melt them off like the last ones. These cuffs only come off by key."

"Don't put them on me. Please."

I needed to practice my powers and learn how to control my dream-walks. I also needed to find my mom and then escape.

My Glory woke up from my panicked thoughts, poking me.

Aspen's eyes flashed, like my begging pissed him off. "You should never have come to Elora."

"Aspen," I pleaded.

Before my Glory could surge and I could use it against him, he tore open the cuffs and hastily snapped them onto my ankles, brushing the sliver of my skin exposed between my pants and socks. My Glory vanished, and tingles skittered up my legs from his touch.

"Put your boots on, and let's go," he demanded. But his demand seemed guilty and painful. Yet, I didn't gather that from his tone and couldn't see his expression. *So why did I think that?* Before I could analyze his face, he luscelered out the door.

I clanked my way down the hall, taking small steps to prevent pulling on my stitches, feeling more like a prisoner than ever.

Hana was in the kitchen washing a pan. She glanced up at the noises of my chains, yellow pupils narrowing. "He wasn't always like this," she said.

But it didn't matter what my princely jailor used to be or that he had moments where he may be one percent less of a terrible person. He was still an asshole, bastard, and every other curse word. I glared at the black metal around my ankles—and I was still his prisoner.

"Thanks for saving me," I said, bitter.

"Don't give up, Lucille," she whispered.

Ignoring her comment, I touched my frizzy waves. "Do you have anything to keep my hair out of my face?"

After putting my hair up with a rubber band and bobby pins, my ankle cuffs dragged along the threshold, quieting when I walked out onto the grass. The soft clinking turned to a harsh clanking when I hit gravel. I stumbled as my chains caught on rocks, righting myself before I face-planted. When I looked up, I saw my absolute *favorite* angel.

Brock stood at the front of an upgraded carriage, and by upgrade, I mean less boxy with a fancy paint job and two small windows instead of one, but it still appeared old and rickety. He met my glare with a cocky lift of his mustache and a smug glimmer in his pink eyes. "Nice cuffs."

My fingers twitched, wanting to flip him off. But I wasn't feeling another injury just yet. I trudged to the back of the carriage. Cacus and Bael, the demon grenades, were already huddled inside. Dreading the pain I'd soon feel, I placed my hands on the wooden ledge. Before I pushed myself up, a hand grabbed my shoulder.

"You won't be back there."

I turned to glare, quite done with Aspen's touches. Not understanding my clear as day *back the hell up eyes*, Aspen continued to grip me firmly. The tingling sensation hid behind my barrier of clothing.

"Did you hear me?" he *asked*. "I want you in front with Brock. It won't jostle your stitches as much. You'll be in less pain despite the company."

"Are you going to let go of me so I can move up front?"

He let go, only to grab my wrists. His stupid hands tingled against my skin, and it felt good. The tingles always felt good, and I hated that just like I hated his gentle hold.

I pulled, trying to get away. He dropped my unwrapped wrist to rub at the stubble on his jaw but didn't let go of the other. "Is it feeling better?" he asked.

Out of all my wounds, my wrist gave me the least bit of pain.

"Stop acting like you care."

His expressionless stare narrowed, and he let go of my broken wrist. I met his irritation with a smug smile. Holding his gaze, I found his purple ring, which told me he was part angel and one other.

It was the color of the sky right before the sun disappeared behind the horizon—a dark cobalt sitting next to a deep purple.

If I cared enough, I may have asked him what it meant. Instead, I left to climb into the carriage. My jangling links caught on each step, making me grind my teeth. At least I had a cushioned seat.

Brock clicked, urging the horses on with the reins.

Golden light shone through the trees as we moved, signaling early dawn. Rays swallowed up the leaves. The dew-covered forest shimmered like faceted jewels. Hundreds of specs of light reflected on my skin, and not only my skin, but Brocks, and the horses. All around us golden rays reflected and refracted. It was breathtaking and other-worldly.

It was the first glimpse of the Elora I had hoped to see when I first arrived.

But now, it was difficult to care about the beauty.

"It's called Aurum Forest. It's a word for gold. The name's pretty explanatory at this time of day," Brock stated.

I ignored him.

"Take it in now. It'll be the last pleasant thing you'll see."

"Ah yes, your bitch queen." I mirrored his goading tone, hoping to rile him up.

To my surprise, Brock laughed. His throaty laughter shook his long gray beard. "I hope you didn't say that to the prince."

I glared. That wasn't the reaction I was hoping for. "I did indeed."

His laughter stopped, bushy eyebrows shooting into his hairline. "The prince doesn't take kindly to insults to his queen."

No kidding. The almost sword to the throat and flaming blue eyes weren't a dead giveaway or anything. But that didn't mean I was going to stop. They both deserved every insult I had.

"Where is this horrid queen of yours?" I asked.

Brock took his time answering. Clip clops and jangling chains stole my attention until he spoke. "The capital Deava. Most likely tearing apart the last couple of prisoners we gave her."

"Tearing apart, how?"

A gruesome smile lifted his mustache as his eyes transitioned to a blood red. "I've never seen what's done. You'd have to ask the prince. I only clean up the aftermath." He rubbed the red beads decorating his beard, looking thoughtful. "She's pretty gruesome to her victims. Her pit is a mess of limbs and torn bodies. It's almost full. After she discards you, we'll have to make arrangements to clear it out."

I stared at him, taking in his apathetic words. *My fate was to be discarded and left to rot on top of a pile of shredded bodies?*

"So how much longer do I have with my pitiful life?" I asked, glancing down at my cuffs.

"Three days. Two until we hit the boundary line."

"Boundary line?"

He focused back on the road. The carriage creaked and groaned as it moved across the rough ground. "Separates her kingdom from The Divide."

Two days until I was in her impenetrable land. Two days to figure out how to unlock my cuffs, practice my powers, dream-walk, and escape.

CHAPTER EIGHTEEN

Time passed, and minutes felt like hours. Bugs that resembled green mosquitoes buzzed around our lunch–a simple meal of bread, cheese, and apples. I nibbled on the apple. Drops of juice fled down my wrist. I licked up the drops, noticing my Blocking Rune. I glanced at Brock's wrist, finding only veins and liver spots.

"Why do you look so old?" I hoped my question insulted him.

A whip of the reins and a grunt were his only reactions. Pity. "Is there a different way I'm supposed to look?'

"Young, immortal?" I shrugged.

"I am immortal."

The wrinkles in his face and his worn, leathery hands told a different story. Even the roots of his gray hair were speckled white—grays and whites, the colors of a burning piece of wood on its last leg of life. The only sparks of energy were in the red beads of his white beard and ever-changing eyes.

"I'm Fallen. This"—he waved a hand around his head—"was part of my punishment." That was bitterness in his tone.

I opened my mouth to ask why his wings had been torn from his back, craving to poke at the old wounds. Before I could get a word out, a deep divot in the road slammed me against the metal railing. Searing pain shot up my side, and a whimper caught between my clenched teeth.

"Any more questions you'd like to ask?" He smiled, all teeth and spite.

"Would you knock me out so I didn't have to see your ugly face anymore if I did?"

He jerked the horses to the side, slamming me back into the side rail. I gasped.

"No, that'd be too nice." His mustache twitched an inch. "But these horses are difficult to steer. Never know which way they'll jerk." He lifted the reins, ready to twist them to the side. "Best keep your mouth shut."

Two taps sounded inside the carriage. Brock brought the horses to a stop.

"Why are we—"

"I'm taking over," Aspen said, walking up to stand on the other side of Brock. His cold gaze shot to my arm, gripping my side, then to Brock's face. If possible, his expression grew colder.

"But we still have an hour before change."

"I said I was taking over. It wasn't a negotiation."

Brock squeezed the reins once, then threw them to the ground. "Whatever you say, Prince Aspen," he shouldered past him to the back as Aspen took his seat.

"Are you okay?" he asked.

"Would it matter if I said no? Would you release me?"

"I can't," he whispered as a red light pulsed beneath his chin. Then, he more forcefully said, "I won't."

"Didn't think so." I gave his chin a questioning look and turned to face the dirt road, ignoring his presence.

"Why did you come here?"

Did his demanding tone never cease?

"Lucille!" he snapped after my continued silence.

At first, I resolved to stay silent, not caring about his impatience. But then the perfect response slid into my head. "Your questions aren't worth my answers, asshole."

That shut him up. *Thank goodness.* Like I wanted to explain anything to him, he deserved nothing from me.

I glanced down at the keyhole of my cuffs. My fingers twitched, knowing what to do but unable to in my princely jailor's presence.

A jerk snapped me from my plan. My head turned to side-eye Aspen. He pushed his broad shoulders back, posture stiff. The reins wrapped around his fist turned his skin pale and slightly blue. He gazed over the heads of the black mares, never moving his head. I would've guessed he was a statue if not for the flutter in his jaw. He didn't even blink. At first, I thought he was angry about what I said, but now I didn't know.

"What?" he snapped, feeling my stare.

I raised a brow. "Are you scared of horses?"

He snorted. "I've been around horses longer than you've been alive."

That wasn't an answer, and now I wanted to know his age. Hana mentioned he had 90 years of training, which was indeed a lot longer than I've been alive. But Aspen didn't look it. There were no liver spots or wrinkles for him. His skin was tight from his chiseled jaw to his perfect forehead. There wasn't even a gray hair in his silky dark waves. If I had to estimate, I'd say he chose to stop aging in his early twenties.

Immortality had its benefits.

"How old are you?"

He released a long breath from his nose, "Old."

That also wasn't an answer. "How old?"

"Couple of years from one hundred."

Damn.

"How old is Brock?"

"Around four hundred."

I gaped. "Four hundred? I mean, he looks old, but not..." I trailed off.

"Brock's appearance is punishment." Aspen never took his eyes off the road, veins popping in his clenched hands.

He was definitely afraid of horses or driving.

"For what?"

He shrugged, but it was short and quick, like moving his hands too much would veer us into a tree. This arrogant, commanding prince could slice and punch Hellhounds, but steering horses was a scary feat.

"Not sure. I never cared enough to ask. But it was bad enough that they tore his wings off and stole the agelessness of immortality from him. As a result, he turned himself over to my queen."

His queen. He spoke of her with such reverence, like she was some saint or a high and just queen who didn't devalue life in pursuit of her wants and needs.

I shifted my head away from him, scratching my hand. "Your queen can rot in hell," I muttered.

Aspen jerked his attention from the dirt road. That same odd red light flashed under his chin. "What did you just say?"

The horses veered toward the center, walking at an angle. He was so engaged in glaring at the side of my face that he didn't notice. I almost let the horses continue until we tipped into the ditch by the trees, but my stitches already hurt from Brock's abuse.

I lifted my hand to point at the horses. "I said your queen can rot in hell. Also, we're about to go off the road."

Aspen jerked the carriage hard, overdoing it. I flung into his side as the horses whinnied.

"Get off of me!"

"Learn how to drive!" I yelled back, wincing from my stitches, pushing off.

"Learn how to keep your mouth shut!" The red glow continued to flicker.

"You wanted me to talk before. I figured after letting you stew, I'd impart my wisdom. So, on top of learning how to drive, why don't you learn how to be loyal to someone who doesn't steal girls and shred them apart? That'd be a good first step in becoming less of an evil, demanding asshole."

Aspen snorted, slowly nodding his head. "Your ignorance is showing, Lucille."

"Maybe, but at least I can sleep at night," I said, remembering the tight planes of his face as he dozed. "Bet your dreams don't particularly agree with all the lives you've destroyed."

The red light vanished, and for a moment, pain pulled at the lines of his mouth. But not just pain; I also glimpsed his guilt and shame, too. I rubbed at the ache pressing on my chest as if I could feel his pain. Bile crawled up the back of my throat. Confused, I swallowed hard, clenching my fist to resist the impulse to soothe the deep creases on his forehead. He deserved the glassy look in his eyes.

After a few more hours, Aspen veered off the road. This time on purpose, driving us to the center of a sizable, circular plain of grass.

"Why are we stopping?" The orange-veined trees on white flesh captured my gaze. Their vibrant colors stood out against the dull brown. They wrapped themselves in a half-circle around us.

Aspen stood and stepped off the carriage, ignoring my question.

Brock walked toward the horses, unlatching them.

"Are we staying here?" I asked.

Brock gave a curt nod. He guided the horses to the edges of the orange-veined trees, likely going to the river trickling nearby. The wooden carriage rocked as Cacus and Bael got out.

Standing, blood returned to my bottom and legs after sitting for so long. I stepped off the carriage and almost face-planted. It was one thing to get used to the tingling sensation and a whole other to maneuver cuffed ankles. By the time they jangled, I was already falling, arms whipping out to grip anything I could. One hand found purchase on the rail, swinging me into the carriage side with an oomph. The itching of my power traveled up my arms as I contemplated punching the wood till my knuckles were bloody.

But I thought I wasn't supposed to feel my powers.

I stepped down to the grass, glaring at Aspen, who sat on a stump far enough away not to hear my mishap. And, of course, he pulled out his sword, lying it across his lap, preparing to sharpen it.

Taking a few steps, my chains made little noise against the plush grass. Aspen didn't acknowledge me. His whetstone clashed against the metal of his blades, covering the rest of my cuff noise. Brock was still gone, and the demons vanished into the trees, probably to hunt for food.

I glanced behind me at the forest, down to my chains, and back to my jailor.

Hana said Brock could sense things, which was part of the problem with escaping. But this time, it was only Aspen. This was my moment. It didn't matter if the forest was dangerous and filled with Hellhounds. Aspen's threat of chasing me down if I ran was only valid if he knew of my escape. But if he did catch me, he couldn't do anything. His precious queen needed my powers. Armed with my bobby pins and the cover of the forest, I could remove my cuffs. After that, I'd lusceler away, find a safe place to practice my powers, and find my mom. The details would fall into place later.

But if I didn't take this opportunity, my life would be forfeit the moment I stepped on Tenebrous's soil. Any hope of finding my mom, even if she were in the Tenebrous Kingdom, would be crushed under the sureness of the queen's abuse. But who knew if my mom was there? She could be in the Ethereal Kingdom. With the flickering image of both kingdoms surrounding her, I had no idea who had her. The only way to find those answers was through my dream-walking abilities or, if that failed, Magda.

So, if my only options were to brave the deadly forest and possibly die to find her, brave the deadly forest and get abused by my captors once caught, or sit back and wait to die at the queen's hands, then why not attempt escape while Brock isn't here?

If the forest killed me, if I was captured and broken again, so be it.

With one last glance at the asshole prince, I walked. My craving to escape begged me to run, but it'd make too much noise. So, I kept my steps slow and quiet, avoiding leaves and potential tripping hazards.

When I reached the halfway point, I glanced back at Aspen, covered partially by the carriage, still sharpening his stupid weapons. Good. At the three-fourths mark, something dark flashed in the forest. I might've stopped if it wasn't for my need to escape and the lingering itches of my power riding my angry determination.

But I didn't.

My boots reached the forest line, pausing in surprise. Sure, it's only been a couple of minutes, but I figured my princely jailor would've investigated by now. Maybe after the Hellhound attack, he thought I was too frightened to attempt to go into the forest. Little did he know how badly I wanted to find my mom. The only thing keeping me going was the thought that my mom was alive and in need of help.

Ominous shadows flickered in the forest's colorful depths. The oranges, whites, and greens were a curling finger beckoning me in while the shadows spoke of trouble. Without a second thought, I entered. Walking a ways in, I pulled a bobby pin from my hair. I crouched to pick up my cuffs and froze.

A Hellhound stepped out of the shadows.

Was it a Hellhound?

Its shadow fur resembled fur more than the ones that attacked us. Gold specs mingled with the black, moving between the wisps, matching the color of its eyes. At least this beast looked less skeletal, closer to a black wolf than a skeleton of death.

Maybe it was half-Hellhound.

I stood, knowing right about now I'd be feeling the stabs of my Glory. But unlike the itches I felt seconds ago, my cuffs suppressed them.

We stared at each other. It tilted its head to the side and sat back. The glow in its golden eyes was less murderous and more curious. Not that that meant it wasn't going to eat me, or more accurately, drain all the blood from my body. Just because it seemed less threatening didn't change the fact its gigantic fangs peeked from its black lip, glistening with poorly contained saliva.

I peeked to my left, seeing a road through the unique trees, knowing I couldn't escape that way or to my right, where the river trickled somewhere in the distance where Brock and the horses were.

That left straight ahead past the half-hellhound—or whatever it was.

Swallowing, I gave one last glance at my cuffs and put my bobby pin back in my hair. I'd have to un-cuff them after I got past the beast. I raised my hands and took a step forward and to the side. It shifted to its legs, raising back up to all fours.

Heavenly hell, why did they have to be the size of small horses?

I stopped, hands shaking. "I just want to pass. Let me pass."

I'm not scared. I'm not a wimp. I'm not scared.

The mantra was shit against the giant beast shifting forward, sniffing.

The beast tilted its head, sniffing again. I bet it smelled the delicious angel blood running through my veins. I took another couple of slow steps. This time, it didn't move.

Its gaze pinned me, never once leaving my face as I continued my incremental shuffle. I was just waiting for it to stop playing with me and lunge.

I didn't have to wait long.

It quickly obliterated the yards between us. I gasped and squeezed my eyes shut. The claw-tearing pain I was expecting turned out to be a long, smelly, wet lick up half of my face.

I didn't dare move, suspecting this was a twisted game. But when it licked me twice more and whimpered, I relaxed the slightest bit and opened my eyes.

"Does that mean you like me, beastie? Or are you tasting the goods before sucking out my blood?"

The beastie sat back and tilted its head a few more times.

Okay. That had to be a good sign. I hoped.

It rose and butted its wet nose into my hand, whining. It wanted me to pet it. *What the actual hell?*

I raised my hand against my better judgment to brush the shifting shadows near its ear when it let loose a vicious growl. I scrambled back.

It was going to eat me. I knew it. *Why was I always so trusting?*

The beastie turned. The vicious growl wasn't for me but for the blurring figure that shoved me back, making me fall and the beast attack.

I expected obscuring steam and red flames, but the half-hellhound fought like any normal wolf. But it was as fast as Aspen.

They blurred around each other, barely discernible to the naked eye. At moments, I caught flashes of blue fire, heard animal whines, and a couple of masculine hisses. The hisses made me flinch. I hated the sound as much as I hated the whine from the beastie. No part of me understood why. Or why I wanted to intervene to stop the fight in hopes it'd fix the dreadful bottoming out of my stomach.

Reasoning finally slammed back into me when I looked down at my cuffs. *Dammit. I needed to get out of here and get them off.*

Jerking to my feet, avoiding the blurring bodies of black, I slipped behind a tree and shuffled my way forward.

I screamed at myself to hurry, switching my shuffle to a noisy jog. The fact that I didn't know where I was going didn't concern me. Only that I got away from them and the weird pain pushing me to reconsider. There was nothing to reconsider when my mom was out there.

After tripping and bruising my knees over and over, I lost Aspen. Their noises of pain faded to the ominous rustling of leaves and my heavy breathing. Switching directions, I attempted to find the noise of the river after avoiding it. A water source would be necessary until I found someone who wouldn't kill me or use me when I asked for help.

As the tension left my shoulders, I slammed into a hard, unyielding chest, my bubble of space obliterated.

"Going somewhere?"

Shit.

CHAPTER NINETEEN

BLOODHOUND AND RUNE

Rune sent me a feeling of panic. I tuned into her sight.

I don't know how she managed it, but the female had escaped.

Stop her, Rune.

Rune stepped out from the shadows, and the female froze, scared. I didn't blame her since Rune resembled a Hellhound. The female recently got attacked by them, which we didn't know until *after* the fact. It was the price we paid for sending Rune out on missions like this as young as she was. She got distracted easily, slept too much, and had a difficult time listening to commands if it didn't suit her whims. But we had no choice.

Understanding the female's fear, Rune sat. The female paused, then raised her hands and took a step.

Don't let her get past you, Rune. Distract her until the pet notices her absence.

"I just want to pass. Let me pass," the female pleaded.

Rune walked over to her. The female squeezed her eyes shut and acted like Rune was about to eat her. Bothered by her fear, Rune licked her and whimpered.

"Does that mean you like me beastie? Or are you tasting the goods before sucking out my blood?" the female asked.

From the unusually strong emotions I received from Rune, she more than liked the female. Rune whimpered for more pets. The moment her hand brushed against Rune's shadow fur, I felt the hum of her contentment until Rune sensed another presence in the woods.

She let out a vicious growl, scaring the female, and turned. She pulled at my power through our connection and attacked the lusceler-ing figure. Blue flames flashed, and she yelped as it singed her shadow fur.

That's the pet! Stand down, Rune.

But she didn't listen, and the female got away.

Rune! Let him get the female before it's too late, or he kills you!

She dodged a flaming punch, got hit by another, and then finally listened to me and ran away.

You're lucky you can't come home, pup. Observe only and stay hidden unless I say otherwise, I seethed.

ASPEN'S HANDS DUG INTO my shoulders. The width of a hand scarcely fit between us.

I stared at his leather-covered chest, heaving up and down, trying not to feel like my life was ending.

I thought it'd be okay if they caught me again. I would despise it but be okay with it because escaping was nearly impossible. I went into the forest, convinced of that. But knowing something and ex-periencing it was entirely different.

Stupid, utterly traitorous tears pooled in my narrowed eyes. I didn't lift my head. I didn't give him anything but my stiffness and silence.

His hands dropped towards my face, hesitating a breath from my cheeks. His warmth breached the tiny gap separating his skin from mine. I swallowed, unsure of what he planned to do, when his calloused fingers brushed away my escaping tear. Tingles followed the trail of his soft, gentle touch.

"How'd you do it?" he whispered, fingers lingering on my face

What?

I snapped my head up, hating the way his touches confused the pain and bitterness poisoning my mind. "How'd I do what?"

Sweat instantly slicked my palms. Blue eyes and plush pink lips were mere inches away. Too close. Way too close. I tried to take a step back, but he grabbed my waist. The heat of his hands seared through my leather jacket. But it was nothing compared to the heat that flushed my body as he glanced at my lips for longer than I liked.

"How'd you get so far without either of us knowing?"

I scrunched up my face, unsure of what he was talking about. "I walked. Quietly."

He shook his head, staring at me like he was trying to figure me out. "It wouldn't have mattered how quiet you walked or if you were invisible. Brock can sense intention. Sense emotion. He can hear the difference between a nervous heartbeat and a calm one. But we didn't sense a thing from you."

So that was what Hana had meant by sense. Pissed at the invasion by the worst man in Elora, I opened my mouth to rage when an unbidden thought entered my mind.

This really was my only chance. Because now they knew I could somehow sneak past Brock's power, they would start chaining me to trees, that or never leave my side.

Holy hell, this was it.

My chest cracked in half as my tears fell in streams.

I met Aspen's tight eyes and begged. "Let me go. Please, just let me go."

He stared at me, fingers digging into my waist and chin erupting in that weird red glow. "I won't."

I went further and clutched his face. I needed him to see me as a person, not a thing. I needed him to have a conscience. "Please, Aspen."

The red glow stuttered.

Pain flashed through his eyes, and for one unbelievable moment, his forehead dropped to mine as his hands came up, sending distracting vibrations into my cheeks. He squeezed his eyes shut as the red glow vanished. "I never wanted you to come here," he said, sounding broken. "Why did you have to come here, Lucille?"

The rough ache in his voice and his confusing words paused my tears. *What did that mean?*

The way he spoke sounded like he knew me. But he didn't. "What mind games are you playing?" I said, jerking out of his tender hold.

In the next second, he lifted his bowed head, and the scar beneath his chin glowed with a blood-red hue. His agonized expression changed right as his arms wrapped around my waist and picked me up. He luscelered us through the forest, back to camp, and against the side of the carriage.

My heart stopped. My breathing stopped. My thoughts fled.

Every inch of his body pressed against mine—leather to leather, knee to knee, chest to chest, and it would've been hip to hip, but his belt of daggers separated that connection. I couldn't even breathe out a relieved sigh with his muscles entrapping my small form and shocking me with the heat of his body.

"Remember what I said if you ran, Lucille?" he whispered. His hand slid around my neck, making it tingle at the contact. "Did you want me to catch you? Punish you? Is that what you wanted when you created your mindless escape plan?" He went from cold to broken to filled with vindictive arrogance so fast my brain was trying to catch back up.

With my heart beating out of control, his body heat consuming mine, I had to take a second to gather myself.

"How is it mindless when the risks are the same? I either die with you or escape and die on my own in the forest," I said, pushing back my useless tears and drowning in a deadly sea of blue.

That same flash of pain blinked in and out of his eyes. Once it left his expression, it was like I could still feel it. I didn't understand. *Why was he in pain?* We didn't know each other. I was a prisoner going to my death because of him. He shouldn't feel any pain from my words. *But more importantly, why could I feel it?*

Sensing emotions wasn't part of my powers, not that I knew of. Plus, why now, and why only him?

Focusing on the softly lit navy and purple ring and not the confusing emotions lurking in my battered chest, I interrupted whatever he was about to say.

"What does the blue ring mean?"

One side of his plush lips tugged. A predatorial gleam sparked as he tightened his hand around my neck, uncomfortable but not suffocating.

He lowered his face to the side of my head. "Would you believe it if I said demon?"

The movement of his lips sent little flares of electricity into my ear and crawled down my spine. I shivered.

"No," I said, not expecting that answer to come out of my mouth. It was instinctual, with absolutely no evidence to back it. He controlled my life. He held it in his dangerous hands and was about to give it over to be snuffed out. I hated him, his tingles, his eyes, how worthless he found me. He handed over multiple girls to be killed. So my answer shouldn't have been no. Yet it was. When I opened my mouth to take it back, something tickled in my brain, holding me back.

He stared at me with an utter look of shock. I was pretty sure my expression mirrored his.

He recovered fast, lowering his head to the side of my face. "Stay the fuck out of the forest, *sweetheart*." I flinched as air pushed into my lobe. "I have one job to do, and I won't fail."

Tilting my face up to his ear, I reached the pulse underneath his jaw—a vulnerable, throbbing spot that worked in my favor. I still didn't know if the tingles only tormented me, but if they didn't—I smirked, brushing my lips to his neck, feeling his muscles tense. "Go to *hell*," I whispered. The pounding of his heartbeat bounced against my lips and pebbled nipples before I leaned back.

For a minute, there was absolute silence as he stayed frozen, no comeback nor arrogant retorts, only a feathering in his jaw.

I had to admit I was pretty impressed with myself.

His hand came up from my neck and gripped my chin, stealing my attention with his touch. "So help me, Lucille. If you try to escape again, I will chain you to the carriage."

"I could just melt..." I trailed off as Aspen stiffened, and my head throbbed. I forgot what I was about to say, and the throbbing quieted.

Weird.

Aspen took a step back, gazing at me with an odd expression. "Stay here. Stay safe," he whispered so softly I wasn't sure I heard him right. I was almost positive I didn't.

The moment he dropped his hand, ceasing the tingles, a red light pulsed beneath his chin, and whatever pain I sensed from him vanished.

"Why does your chin glow red?" I asked.

"What are you talking about?"

Overcome by an urge to touch him, I brushed my thumb against his scratchy stubble and the raised mark. It sent a shock into the pad of my finger, making me jump. He latched onto my wrist, pulling my hand away.

"It's a scar. I've always had it."

"Scars don't glow."

Disbelief indented the lines of his forehead. He opened his mouth to reply, then shut it as he noticed Brock returning. Releasing my wrist, he considered me for a second more before limping away to the despicable fallen angel.

He was hurt, and a part of me fiercely didn't like it.

I walked over to the stump Aspen vacated, staring at his cloaked back, and sat on the edge.

It looked and felt like a scar, but last I checked, light did not gleam from scars. Maybe he was a demon. But that thought seemed wrong. The cobalt ring didn't signify demon. I swear it didn't.

"Prince Aspen went hunting. If you want to eat, you need to set up camp," Brock snapped. It surprised me—not the snapping itself, but that it was all he did. I attempted to escape. I figured he would have broken my next wrist. *Unless Aspen didn't tell him. But he made it sound like he did when he explained Brock's sensing abilities.*

I kept my eyes on his boots, refusing to look at his disgusting face. "Good thing I don't want to eat."

"Too bad," he pushed me off the stump. "I'll shove squirrel down your throat if I have to."

Only if I can shove a knife down yours.

My knees knocked into the hard ground. "Is squirrel the only damned animal you have to eat around here?"

"Unless you want to puke your guts up or hallucinate from eating something else, I'd keep your trap shut."

I wished he'd take his own advice.

"Hurry up," Brock threatened, striding away.

Torn between staying on the ground to see what he would do and following orders, I listened. I stood, refusing to brush off the grime digging into my palms and knees, and I set up camp for *Brock*.

Aspen returned later with four giant gray squirrels, skinned and ready to be cooked on a wooden spit. We ate. Or they did. I nibbled every time Brock glanced up from his meal, not wanting his grimy fingers anywhere near me, and shredded the rest. It was hard to have an appetite when I lost my only chance at escape.

The sun sank. Our clearing turned multiple shades of orange.

After the show I put on, I laid my head on my stiff pad, gazing at Elora's blue moon. Goosebumps pebbled my skin underneath my leathers despite the glowing fire I lay next to, but no matter how close I scooted to it, warmth never reached me.

Brock slept soundly to my left. The demons had yet to return, and Aspen—I shot him a glance. He sat on his stump, sharpening his knives and keeping watch.

Feeling my stare, he looked over. For a moment, as he held my gaze, not smiling, but not glaring either, something wiggled beneath my bitter hate. I shoved the feeling away by flipping over and closing my eyes.

CHAPTER TWENTY

I invaded the mind of yet another past version of myself. The cuffs didn't block my dream-walking abilities. Ready and hopeful to find more information about my mom, I let the memory unfold.

IT WAS A MONTH after the big reveal of who I was, the prophecy of my life, and my explosive episode. A month, and still, we hadn't worked on my emotions or powers. Instead, she had been monitoring my state like a helicopter parent and finally caved to give me an iPod to appease my restlessness. Last week, after getting sick and tired of wearing turtlenecks and baggy sweatshirts, she found out I no longer had my amulet and had a conniption, like full-on took a couple of her favorite chicken plates and slammed them to the floor. Afterward, she screamed at me for being so reckless and *losing* it in the forest at our previous house. Things went downhill from there, which was why, after another screaming match, I was in another forest next to our fourth house, listening to music to calm down.

She allowed my space because her powers couldn't break through the itches—not one bit. I both loved and hated it. So, the next best thing was storming out of the house with my headphones and calming down away from her. Plus, it sucked to see the absolute terror on her face when the flickering purple fire took hold.

I wasn't sure who she was more scared of—me, my father, the council, the queen, or the one with the ability to sense when I used my power.

A snap in the forest stole me from my musings. I pulled out a headphone, searching between the tall pines. When something moved, I jerked to my feet.

"Who's there?" I squinted, making out a figure hiding behind a trunk. My hands prickled, signaling my Glory. "Come out. Or I'll..." *What? Erupt in flame because I'm scared and hope they see me as a threat while my legs wobble uncontrollably? Yep, I could already see it going in my favor.*

When the figure stepped out, my thoughts took a sharp turn and dropped me off at Fantasyland, where handsome princes came and stole away girls from their terrible lives. But in my life, shit like that didn't happen. *But just damn it.*

Rough leather hugged the contours of his muscular body, and wavy brown hair fell across his forehead brushing his sculpted cheekbones. He was handsome and alluring in his unusual uniform, with a sword at his hip. And those eyes? Those azure pools sparkled like sunlight dancing on the surface of our tranquil pond behind our house, reflecting a depth of emotion that stirred my soul.

"Who are you?" I asked, suspicious and intrigued.

He didn't respond, watching me.

The prickling of my Glory traveled up my arms. I was about to lusceler away and tell my mom we were compromised by a handsome stranger when I noticed a flash of silver reflect in a ray of sunlight. Surprised, my fear and Glory vanished.

"It's you."

He was wearing my amulet. The sparkling, ruby wing clasp rested against his exposed neck. It was an angel wing my mom gave me as a birthday gift. She explained the color signified my birth month, according to humans and their made-up system. She loved the quirky things humans made up and created. I, on the other hand, was indifferent and a little bitter. Probably because while she got to go out and experience said human quirks and creations, she kept me locked away at home, threatening me if I ever followed her.

I stepped closer until only a few feet separated us as he watched me with a wary expression. With each step, he seemed to stiffen more. Part of me feared he'd run away. But I wanted to know who he was. I always imagined this moment, meeting the stranger who warmed me after my outburst.

"I'm not sure how you found me. But sorry, we moved. It wasn't safe to stay. Do you have a name?"

A muscle throbbed in his jaw.

I gave him a tentative smile. "It's only a name, right? For all I know, you could give me a fake one."

His lips pursed, considering, then said, "Aspen."

Shit. He shouldn't have talked. I forgot what he sounded like, and the smooth, low tones did nothing for the fantasies I created about this mysterious male.

"Lucille."

He gave a sharp nod, still stiff. "I know."

"Right." I told him the first time we met when I was naked. My cheeks flushed. "Why—why were you there that night?" *Why was he here now?*

The chirping of birds settled the fluttering of my nerves from his silence. I took a slow step forward, and he took one back.

"I swear I don't bite." I smiled, unable to hide the laughter in my eyes. He stared at me like I stunned him. The flush increased under his intense, curious gaze. "You do know how a conversation works, right?"

He gave another sharp nod, making me laugh. It sure didn't seem like it. When I stopped laughing, his gaze traveled down to the pocket of my sweats, to my dangling headphones still playing my music.

I pulled out my iPod and watched his eyes narrow in confusion. "It's an iPod." When that didn't clear the puzzlement, I said, "It plays music."

How didn't he know that?

I lived hours away from civilization, without a TV or phone, and I knew what an iPod was.

Bold, I stepped into his stiff bubble and placed an earbud in his ears. He jerked up as if to fight me off, grabbing my hand, then stilled. But I wasn't sure if he stilled from the music playing in his ear or from the strange, tantalizing tingles erupting at his touch.

"Who are you? What is this?" I whispered as the tingles enticed the butterflies in my stomach.

He pulled back his hand and shook his head. "Stay here. Stay put. Stay safe." Then he luscelered away.

"What the hell?"

He was an angel, or part—an angel who made no sense. *Stay put? Stay safe? He couldn't possibly know our situation, could he?* I hoped not, but he wanted me safe, so that had to be good. Although, if my mom found out what happened, she'd find an island and lock me away in a basement with bubble wrap and every Binding Rune she could think of. It was a good thing she couldn't use an angelic feather anymore, or she would have another horrible Binding Rune on me.

Yeah, that was a big hell-no to telling my mother. Plus, I wanted to see if he'd come back.

And he did, two weeks later. I might've taken up the habit of running in the forest every day to check.

I sat on pine needles, soaking in the rays of sunshine sneaking through the canopy as I listened to music and ate my favorite chocolate bar. When I saw movement, my lips twitched, hoping it was him and not the wolf who somehow followed us to this house.

He stepped out with a half-eaten apple, and I stood, taking him in. He wore the same outfit, the same closed expression, and the same drop-dead gorgeous looks.

"I was wondering if I'd see you again." I walked over to him, and he didn't back up. That was progress. Now, I just had to figure out how to make him talk. "Are you always this quiet?"

He shook his head.

So just with me. Damn.

When we first met, he talked, asking questions about me, but now, if I asked questions about him, he barely answered. Maybe I needed to talk about myself, and then he'd reciprocate. *But where did I start?*

"The first time we met, you asked about who I was. Well, if you want to sit, I'll tell you a little bit."

He gracefully sat against a tree as I crossed my legs and faced him.

"Obviously, I'm part angel," I said, pointing at my eyes. "Like you."

He tensed when I acknowledged what he was, so he really hated any conversation related to him. That didn't bode well for getting to know him.

I sighed. "I'm—" Nope, I couldn't tell him my age without too many questions popping up. "I have—" I couldn't tell him about my powers, who we were running from, or why we stayed isolated.

"I love chocolate," I laughed at myself at the pointless fact I provided.

His lips twitched, making me smile again at almost getting him to drop the closed-off expression with my dweebish behavior.

I looked down, playing with the hem of my t-shirt, thinking of something better to mention. Something a bit more real that wouldn't give away anything too important but still let him in. Why I even wanted to let this handsome stranger in, I didn't know. But something told me I should.

Or I was just lonely.

"I told you last time I hated my father, and my mother lied to me. Nothing's changed since then. I've..." I glanced up at him, then back down. "I've had a pretty difficult life." What a freaking understatement, but that was the most he'd receive. "Because of things that happened, my mom's gone overboard on the protection. To the point, running away sounds pretty good."

"Don't you dare. Stay here and stay safe," Aspen demanded.

Was it weird I found it endearing that he wanted me safe even though he snapped at me? Probably. I shouldn't let him affect me. We didn't know each other. I didn't know his intentions or how he kept finding me, but I couldn't help it. I'd blame it on the fact that my only friend was my mom. This was the most I'd ever talked to someone, besides my mom, since middle school—let alone a guy. *Nineteen-years-old and I haven't even had my first kiss.*

"You want me to stay safe, which is curious in itself, but what exactly do you want me to stay safe from?"

Surprise, surprise, he didn't answer.

I glanced at the ruby angel wing at his neck, smiling. He kept it. I should ask him why he did, but he probably wouldn't answer. "The necklace I gave you. Did you know it was an amulet to *protect* me?" If that was what you called it.

"No." He looked like he was about to take it off.

"Don't. It doesn't work anymore. Nor do I want it back. Once upon a time, it had the ability to..." Calm me was my go-to description, but I no longer liked that definition. "Take away extreme emotions that could trigger my powers. My mom doesn't want me to use them because I'm a danger to myself and all the hiding and running we've been doing. But I'm so sick of it." My voice cracked. "It's been fight after fight with my mom about my powers, our life, my isolation." I stared hard into the layer of golden pine needles, refusing to bring my blurry gaze up. "I'm tired. I want to live, to be normal," I whispered, throwing my burdens at this stranger and most likely freaking him out.

Pine needles crunched and shifted. Tingling fingers tilted my chin until I met the soul-wrenching blue depths of his eyes, finding his angel ring next to a cobalt one. He was double-ringed, like me, meaning he was extremely powerful. Double-ringed angels were rare, or so I read. Each color represented something. But for the life of me, I couldn't remember what the cobalt signified. I'd have to sneak my mom's texts again when I got home and check.

"I'm here."

"Except you don't talk. Two to three words seems like your limit."

"I said eight before. Plus, I'm a good listener," he said, smiling with a lightness I could bask in forever. I was in trouble when he lit my skin on delicious fire brushing my cheek.

I was pretty sure my stomach fluttered out of my body. Aspen had dimples. For one moment, I contemplated that all my isolation made me insane and he was a hallucination. I lifted a hand and poked his cheek. His abrupt laughter did untold things to the hollow ache I'd been living with for most of my life.

Shit. So much trouble.

"Tell me something about yourself." He stopped laughing. "I've lived a life filled with lies and secrets. For once, I want to be in the know. One thing. Tell me one thing," I begged.

His flat expression and silence killed me. I was so sick of not understanding my life. Things always happened to me, and I was always left in the dark. My mom just started giving me answers, but I lived in a constant state of half-truths and mysteries. I wanted it to stop. I needed it to.

After seconds of watching his jaw clench and unclench, I decided I couldn't do this and pulled back from his touch.

He latched onto my hand, following me as I stood, making me stay. "The night I found you, I was there that night because"—he heaved a sigh—"I'm your guardian."

"That's a bond, right? But what else does it mean?" I remembered seeing the word listed in my mom's old text. It was in the section of vinculums, right under the word cordistella. But I was too busy reading everything on the romantic cordistella bonds that I never read the two sentences under it for the guardian bond. Before I could, my mom found me and ripped the book out of my hands, locking it away again.

Aspen shook his head. "All I know is we're bonded, and it's the reason behind the tingles. I've been looking into it with little results."

I bit my lip. "I think the bond is rare."

He raised a brow. "How do you know that?"

"I saw the word once in my mom's old texts, but I only remember seeing how small the entry was, and I've come to find that small entries mean the scribes don't know enough or have enough information on the topic."

"Can I see the book?"

I snorted. "Not until I find my mom's new hiding place and unlock whatever new locks she put on her books. Then I'd have to sneak it out of the house without her knowing." The locks I could handle. With how much time I had on my hands, lock-picking, reading, and training were my main hobbies. But finding the hiding place and sneaking it out, on the other hand, with how close an eye she had on me these days, would be the issue.

He frowned.

"I can try and sneak it out if you give me a week." That way, we'd get our answers, and he'd have to return.

"Okay," he said.

I smiled. "When did you know we had a bond? Is that how you found me? Where are you from?"

His frown came back in full force. "You said one thing, Lucille."

I raised a brow. "You expect to drop a bomb like that on me, and I'll just shut up? You could've given me anything else. I wasn't looking for the whole moon, only a sliver."

Those too-blue eyes of his narrowed to slits. He dropped my hand and stepped back, about to bolt.

"You know I could follow you, right?" I already told him I was part angel.

His eyes flashed with fire. "So help me, Lucille. If you follow me, I will chain you to these trees," he seethed.

I swallowed, taking a step back. "I could just melt them off."

That was the wrong thing to say.

"I will never come back if you follow me. Never. Stay here and stay safe, and I'll give you some slivers next week." Then he left, blurring into the trees, and leaving me with itchy skin at his demanding words.

I POPPED OUT OF my dream self. The scenes vanished as I sat in a dark area. That was the best way I could explain the odd sensation of not waking up and leaving whatever the hell that was. Maybe, my brain needed a safe spot alone to make sense of all the bullshit I witnessed. Aspen couldn't be my guardian, whatever a guardian was, not after everything.

But my dream-walks were memories, not dreams.

So much wasn't adding up.

My mom and I were running from everyone because of what I was. But even after remembering my last dream-walks, I wasn't sure who *everyone* was. Was it my father, the council, the queen, or whoever could sense my powers? Past me remembered my mom's fear of these people, but were they all after us? Did one of them take my mom?

I needed to control this power and jump to her memory. Maybe all I needed to do was focus on her.

Before I could try, the temperature in my head dropped, and it didn't feel like I was alone anymore.

My muscles spasmed from the subzero temperature. I didn't think that was possible without a body.

"Hello?" I called out.

"There you are," a deep voice said, echoing in the cavern of my mind.

"Who's there?"

He didn't answer at first, giving me a moment to question my mental stability. Actually, I didn't think I ever stopped after the first instance of voices in my head.

"My sweet Lucille, it's been a long time since we last talked," he stated calmly, temperature plummeting. Frostbite was a real possibility.

"How do you know my name? Who are you?"

"No one you know yet. We've talked once before, like this. Don't you recall?"

"No," I said.

He hummed as something cold prodded my mind. "No, I suppose not," he said as the temperature plummeted further. I couldn't feel my hands or feet. "You have Nerium poison lingering in your system."

That's what Marcus put in the IVs?

"You said Marcus did this to you?" The slow, vicious words had me wishing I could wake up. Especially since he just read my mind, and I wasn't a fan.

"Yes. To weaken me for his queen." Or so I assumed.

"He no longer works for the Tenebrous Queen."

"How do you know that?"

"I have eyes and ears everywhere. There's very little I don't know." Little picks tormented my arms at the ominous way he spoke.

"Do you know who he does work for? Or how long he hasn't been working for the Tenebrous Queen?"

"Months. But they only found out he was a traitor recently when he fled."

Months? So the queen didn't have Marcus lock me in that room. But if it wasn't her, then who was it?

"That's what we're trying to figure out."

"You're trying to figure out who took me? Why?" How did I know this wasn't all a lie or a game?

"I have no reason to lie or play games."

The fact that I couldn't think without an invasion of my thoughts made me itchy. Ice cracked in my ears like an iced-over lake warming. My teeth stopped chattering. *Thank heaven.*

"I'd rather not."

"And I'd rather you explain why you're here, who you are, and why you're looking for who took me," I snapped.

The slightest bit of warmth I garnered fled.

"I don't take *kindly* to your tone," he said, inches away from my face. His breath slithered into my nose and froze all the moisture. Every time I breathed, it felt like I inhaled gaseous ice, freezing me from the inside out.

"I just want answers," I whispered, afraid that if I pissed him off further, I'd die of hypothermia in this dark dream landscape and never wake up.

"You will not die. Although the fact you do not use more of your gifts is off-putting and quite concerning."

I opened my mouth to snap back at his patronizing tone, forgetting my fear, when he cut me off.

"I don't care to hear excuses. Let's get on with your answers. Who am I? Irrelevant, for now. Why are we looking for who took you? Because my sweet Lucille, we have similar interests. One being on who took Saraqael and why. The next being why I'm here now, which is to help you escape, and there are others, but you're not ready for them."

My heart raced at his words. He was looking for my mom.

"I've been looking for both of you. But after Marcus's slipup and my gain, it seems that the worthless underling has learned his lesson because we have yet to find him or his new employer, who we believe may have Saraqael."

"Why do you care about my mom?" Or me, for that matter.

"I have my reasons."

Goosebumps slithered down my neck at the smile in his words, while the words themselves had me curling my lip. I despised the fact that I had yet another puzzle to figure out. The constant mysteries and lack of control I had over my life enraged me.

"I despise your weakness and ineptitude. I guess we're both found wanting."

The tickling itches intensified, strumming the cord of crashing ice, eradicating the cold and my fear of this man. My purple flame sprung from my fingers, licking up my metaphorical hands.

"Well, well, well, she has a backbone after all. Good. If you're going to escape, you'll need it."

"And how the hell am I going to do that?" Brock can sense me. He had caught me twice now, and Aspen—*How* did *Aspen catch me?*

"Is this what I have to work with? A weak-willed little wimp who tried to escape a few times and is now giving up?"

I was getting really sick of this whole invasion of my thoughts. Did he not realize from invading my thoughts that the last escape was my last chance? They would never let me out of their sights now.

"Go to *hell*"

He laughed. Abruptly, icy fingers gripped my chin, making this seem more real. "What did I say about speaking to me with that tone?"

I almost cursed him and his punishing grip. To hell with him and his manhandling claws of ice. I didn't like being degraded by some condescending voice in my head, real or not.

The music of ice and its glorious destruction pounded in my ears, spreading the itch to my shoulders and up my neck to my chin. Instead of icy claws gripping my face, they turned to warm fingers. Odd.

"There she is," he said, smug, letting go. "She is who I'm looking for. She is who will get you out. With my guidance, of course."

"What about Brock and Aspen?"

"I'll take care of the Searcher. The prince I'm still working on."

"The Searcher?"

"Brockalian. His powers were used to find dissenters and spies in angel ranks. When he fell, the disgusting angel switched sides and used his skills to cart unsuspecting angels to the Tenebrous Queen."

"Okay, say I believe everything you're saying, and you can help me escape. What about after? Where do I go? We don't know where my mom is yet. And what if I don't remember this when I wake up?"

Although, lately, I'd been remembering more of my dream-walks, if not all.

"The Nerium poison only disrupted your past memories. But seeing as it's still in your system, I'll have my general make sure you don't forget this. As for the rest, we'll talk more tomorrow and plan your escape for tomorrow night. Let's see what you're capable of."

That sounded ominous.

"Then we'll find my mom?" But as the frigid air warmed and the silence grew, I knew he was gone.

The dark cavern of my mind released me, and my eyes opened.

Groaning, I shifted on my back. Small pebbles and sticks dug into my spine and bony butt, and now my side. I glared at the single pad and blanket underneath me, noticing a layer of white coating my area. My brows scrunched.

What—

A flash of purple caught my eyes right before it sank into my skin.

Ice crystals spread out from where I lay, dispersed in a circle. Inch by inch, it melted, retreating to me.

I looked over at Aspen and the frost surrounding his sleeping form. I remembered all the thoughts and feelings from my dreamwalk—the handsome stranger, my mom, our fights, our potential enemies, the fact that I had a father my mom was scared of, and worst of all, an unending desire to leave her for the stranger who now held me captive.

The only thought left in the mess of my mind as I stared at the little spec of silver glinting from the coals around Aspen's neck was, *what the fuck.*

CHAPTER TWENTY-ONE

I didn't wake up. Only because I never went back to bed. It wasn't for a lack of trying. I focused on my mom, closed my eyes, and tried to dream-walk to a memory of her, but my mind wouldn't shut up.

The last dream-walk left me with a lot to think about.

Aspen flung off his blankets, standing. He yanked his sword belt to his hips, buckled it, and barreled off into the brightening forest.

Guardian, my ass.

I stood too, removing my blanket in a less forceful manner. I ran a hand through my hair, removing the bobby pins and rubber band. At my nape, my fingers yanked on a ginormous knot. Wavy strands tangled around my hands, ripping out, making me cringe. Looking at the loose strands, I grimaced at the dirt and grime under my fingernails and in the creases of my fingers.

Gross.

I bent down to wipe off the dirt on my bed when something slammed into my butt, making me face-plant. A rough hand wrenched my head back, pulling me from the ground.

The lovely itches that enjoyed tormenting my skin came to life, but this time, I didn't hear the musical sounds of ice. No, what I heard was the dark and seductive music that came alive when I wanted to strangle Oliver.

Brock whispered into my ear. "Sometimes, when the prince goes hunting, I enjoy sharpening my knives on our prisoners."

A tiny coil of black flame circled my pinky. That shouldn't happen with the cuffs. But that was twice my powers had breached them.

Brock jerked my head back, exposing my neck and pressing a dagger to my skin. "Did you hear me? You wouldn't mind that, right?"

This was one time I didn't want to feel the seductive rage of my power. Not when it had the habit of making me indifferent and impulsive with my words. Brock didn't let insults slide. He wanted to punish and abuse with every chance he got. In the back of my mind, I knew that. Yet the compulsion of my power leaking through the cuffs said I didn't care.

"Actually, I don't think there's a time I've ever enjoyed your disgusting Fallen hands and their wrinkly creases."

See, rational Lucy would've steered clear of poking that wound. The Lucy who suffocated on her breaths would've kept her mouth shut. But not this Lucy. Nope. I couldn't even feel the fear of what Brock would do because of how easily I succumbed to the addictive song.

He started to saw into my neck as he ripped at my hair. I bared my teeth against the pain, hissing out spittle.

"If I could, I'd kill you right now. I'd carve off each appendage as slowly as I could, and seeing as your new cuffs block all your powers but healing, I'd let you heal. Then cut again." He pressed harder on his knife as he moved it, smiling as blood trickled into my shirt. "Then let you heal." He took away the knife and waited for my skin to knit back together the slightest bit before pressing it back into the wound.

Dots speckled my vision as I fumed with both pain and rage. Right before I either erupted in the dark flame attempting to consume my finger or pass out, a blur of black slammed into Brock and ripped him away.

"What did I tell you about touching her?" Aspen seethed. His fist gripped the collar of Brock's shirt, bringing them nose to nose.

"The queen said *mostly*."

Aspen scoffed, shoved Brock away, and slammed a string of squirrels into his chest. "Cook these," he demanded.

Brock sent him a heated glare, but Aspen didn't see it as he turned to me. His eyes latched onto my neck, making the blue of his eyes spark. "There's a river," he said, gesturing behind him. "To clean that and wash yourself."

Aspen held my gaze for a long moment before crouching down and pulling out a key. "Give me your ankles."

I glared at him, having difficulty coming down from my rage.

"Come on, Lucille. Turn over."

His voice seemed different now that I remembered the sound from before, when he'd say, *"Stay here, stay put, stay safe."*

I glanced at his neck, finding the chain and the peeking ruby wing. The deadly music and rage quieted, replaced by a fragile confusion.

I turned to my bottom and placed my ankles in front of him, watching as he unlocked one and re-cuffed it to my other leg. Maybe away from Brock, I could work up the courage to ask him about the memory, if he'd even tell me the truth. He went from spewing words of safety to taking me against my will.

He pocketed the key with his eyes drilling into the cut on my neck like it personally insulted him.

"I'm not undressing in front of you."

He stood, pulling me off the ground. "I know how to turn around and close my eyes."

I eyed him skeptically, then gestured forward. "Lead the way."

We walked into the forest. Aspen kept close by, panning left and right in search of Hellhounds or other creatures I didn't want to know about. His hovering behavior lasted as long as the walk did, which wasn't long.

Red grass stretched from the ground, brushing against our leathered thighs and weaving between orange and white trees. Large rocks with moss the color of Aspen's eyes jutted into the slow-moving water. I may hate everything about my situation, but Elora made it hard to hate its beauty.

We stopped by one of the large rocks. I turned to him and pointed to a tree far enough away. "Go stand there and turn around."

He clenched his jaw. I could see the protest stewing in his eyes.

"I am not undressing with you this close even if I am your prisoner. So, we can stand here and glare at each other all day, or you can go over there and wait until I undress and splash into the water to turn back around."

Surprising me for the second time today, he conceded, giving me a sharp nod.

"If you run—"

"Yeah, Yeah, big bad Aspen will come and chase me down. I got it. I won't run," I said, huffing.

His lip twitched, almost like he was about to smile, but he turned around too fast for me to know. I waited until he neared the tree before I undressed, watching him the entire time.

My jacket and shirt came off easily, as did my boots and socks. My pants were another story. Gently sliding the stiff leather over my stitches, I pulled them down. The first leg slid off with no trouble, but when I did the same to the second, it wouldn't budge. I tugged and kicked, cursing the cuffs.

"Do you need help?" Aspen asked, voice muffled.

"No," I snapped. "You could've tightened the damned cuffs."

"You could be grateful I took them *off* at all," he called back.

I rolled my eyes. This wasn't exactly *off* in my book.

Toes needing a break from the cold rock, I plopped on the ground, letting out a squeal as my warm butt hit the stone.

Did not think that one through.

"Sure you don't need help?" Aspen asked. And I swore I heard a smile in his voice. But my arrogant princely jailor didn't smile or offer help. Maybe the Aspen from before would, though. *So, which Aspen was this?*

"I'm fine."

I fussed with my pants and cuffs. When that didn't work, I stood, placed my freed foot on the loose material, and wrenched my leg back.

My pants shucked off. I smiled for a split second before my wobbling balance had my arms pinwheeling in the open air.

Squealing, I splashed into the river.

It was cold. So cold.

Breaking the surface, I sputtered.

Aspen stood on the rock I fell from, took one look at my face, and laughed. Dimples indented his cheeks, and joy sang in the creases of his face.

My eyes grew twice as big as my stomach fluttered at the throaty noise. I knew that laughter. I knew those dimples. I knew the playful tilt of his head and the wonder soothing his normally tight-lipped expression as he held me with his vibrant blues. I was drowning in a sea of pure manifested joy—all light, all goodness, all him—the Aspen Hana spoke of—the Aspen I once knew.

So, what the hell changed? What happened to him?

I wanted to ask, but I feared what he'd say or wouldn't say.

"Did you want to wash your pants too? Or did that little shriek and flailing limbs mean what I think it meant?" He pointed at my pants floating next to me.

I balled them up and chucked them at his face, keeping an arm around my breasts. "I said not to look!"

He dodged them and shrugged. "You yelped. I had to make sure you were okay."

Had to make sure I was okay? I haven't been okay since the moment he took me.

He pointed again. "I think you forgot something."

The tail of the gauze wrapped around my ribs and floated beside me. I unwound it, curious about how well the wounds were healing.

"No blood. That's good," he said, nodding at the soppy fabric.

Yes, it was.

"Can you turn around again so I can check them out without your prying eyes?"

He did but didn't look happy about it.

I inspected my rib stitches. They still had a little blood on them, but they seemed to be healing nicely. In another day, I bet they could come out. Now, I didn't know about my thigh stitches. They were tender to touch, more so than my ribs, but I wasn't about to ask Aspen to look at them, so I assumed they were fine.

While he continued to look the other way, I wiped down my skin and combed through my hair, wishing for a bar of soap and warmer water as I stared at the ruby gem glinting on his neck. I wanted to ask about it. I just needed to say a few words to figure out what was happening. But they stayed trapped in my throat, forced down there by all he'd done and hadn't done in the past week.

"You have about two more minutes, then I'm turning around."

After one, I yelped as something long and slimy slithered between my thighs, and he turned around anyway.

"What?" he asked.

Spinning, I looked for the creature that had my heart stuttering. After a few anxious moments of not seeing anything, my heart and breathing calmed, like nothing happened.

"There was something in the water."

He relaxed his grip on the hilt of his sword. "Yeah. Fish."

"I don't like fish."

His eyebrows rose.

"They're slimy and have sharp dorsal spines," I exclaimed.

I could see the difficulty he had holding in his laughter. But it burst out in a light chuckle, sobering me. The words caught in my throat, tickling the tip of my tongue as I stared at his dimples and all they hid.

His smile flattened. "Get out."

"No. Go back to your tree, turn around, and then I'll get out."

"Lucille, get out of the damned water!" he bellowed, pulling at his sword.

I swam as fast as I could toward the bank, nakedness forgotten. Movement splashed a few feet away, sending another rush of fear through me but doing *nothing. Why did my purple powers work but not my Glory?*

I tried to shove my fear away and latch onto my anger to bring my purple power to the surface, but my fear doubled. Whatever it was, was coming fast, and I wouldn't reach Aspen in time. Inches from the bank, a slimy tentacle suctioned to my leg. I latched onto a root protruding from the water.

It pulled. I whimpered as my Hellhound wounds screamed at me to let go.

"Aspen!"

My hands slid against the decaying bark, nails gouging lines in the root. Squirming and kicking, I tried to dislodge it, only succeeding in making it squeeze harder. Then, the squeeze turned into a razor-sharp bite.

I cried out. It yanked. My hands slid.

"Lucille!"

Rage and determination pierced through my fear, feelings that weren't mine, as water hammered into my mouth and up my nose. I was drowning as the tentacle pulled and pulled, not just dragging me, but pulling something inside me, too.

The cloudy river fizzled behind black specs. The lack of air staked its claim as the noise of the beast and a masculine bellow resonated through the thrashing water.

"LUCY, SWEETHEART, IT'S TIME to wake up," she said.

"Nooo. Why?" What was it, four in the morning? The birds weren't even awake yet.

"Sweetie, come on. You have to train and study."

I groaned, shoving my face further into my pillow. "Why? Because of the deal you made with father?" That reason was getting old. "Let me sleep."

She pulled my hair to the side, pressing her calloused hand into my back, rubbing circles. I knew what was coming next. A gentle warmth seeped into my spine, sending an arrow of calm straight to the heart of my grouch monster.

"That's cheating," I mumbled.

She laughed. "But it makes getting up easier, doesn't it?" Then something changed. Her hand on my back tingled, or maybe it wasn't my back. And the bubble of happiness in my chest turned to burning pressure.

"COME ON. BREATHE, LUCILLE."

Electricity tickled my lips.

"Breathe, dammit!"

Pressure built, and within seconds, I heaved and hacked up gritty liquid.

"That's it. Get it out," he said as a wet hand rubbed my back, sending that absurdly pleasant tingle across my entire torso.

Wait...

I shifted around, wide-eyeing Aspen who looked soaked through. His surprisingly dry cloak covered my bottom half, which I yanked up to cover my chest.

The river rippled, bringing me back to the cause of the watery puke lingering on my lips. I scurried back, crushing grass, until I hit a tree, curling my knees up to my raging chest. Huddled in his cloak, I watched tentacles undulate in the murky blue. Aspen assessed it, sword out, until the river settled, and the razor-sharp wormy limbs disappeared.

"What—" I heaved.

"Tusoteuthis, a giant ancient squid," Aspen supplied, sheathing his sword and walking over to me.

"You—sent me into that river—knowing there was a giant—killer squid in it!" My breathing, already uneven, came in and out in angry pants.

Aspen squatted in front of me, composed in the face of my outburst. "Breathe." He demanded.

"I am," I yelled, clenching my fists.

The water rippled, and I half expected the creature to fling out its slimy limbs and grab Aspen from behind.

"That squid is an ancient protector of this river. I didn't expect it to be this far down. It usually stays far North. Now breathe."

"I'm trying!" I waved around my hands, hyperventilating.

Aspen squeezed the hilt of his sheathed sword. Chaotic thoughts pounded to the beat of my erratic heart. A giant ancient squid of Elora bit me in the leg with tentacle teeth. *Wait, my legs.*

I lifted Aspen's cloak, peered down, and touched the back of my thighs while covering myself from view. My fingers came back smeared with blood.

"Shit."

"Hey, breathe. It's okay." Aspen watched me with a solemn expression.

"It's okay?" I paused to inhale quick breaths. "I drowned." I inhaled again. "I almost died!" And my wounds were bleeding, which meant I needed to ask for his help once again, proving for the umpteenth time how pitiful and defenseless I was.

"Breathe," he said, emphasizing his word with a slow breath, like I didn't know what he meant.

Heavenly hell. "I can't help it." Air, I needed air. "This panic stuff—happens!"

Aspen's face lightened. "Panic attacks?" he asked.

Was he holding back a... laugh? "Are you—mocking me?"

"No, reassessing. I knew you were naive, but I didn't expect you not to know what a panic attack was."

"I know—what it is."

He tilted his head to the side. "And?"

What did Oliver say? "Has to do—with—thoughts."

Aspen grunted. "More accurately, your fear. So, what are you so scared of, Lucille?"

Him, the man in my head, my mom, this world, the lack of information I had, the queen, my father for reasons I couldn't remember. *Everything.* But like hell I'd tell him that. None of this was supposed to happen. I was supposed to go to Elora, find my mom, get my answers, and return to the normal life we were living, not become a prisoner and learn about all the enemies I had. Or learn about how weak I was because my mother refused to train me and my powers.

My vision speckled.

"Breathe, dammit. Stop panicking."

"That—doesn't—help!" I heaved.

"What are you so scared of?"

"Why—would—I—tell *you*?"

He grabbed my face between his palms, forcing me to lock eyes with him. Pleasant electrical shocks tingled my cheeks.

"I said breathe, not stop breathing."

"You—should've thought of that—before grabbing my face," I snapped, hating that his touch reminded me of before.

He stared at me, blue eyes illuminated, pressing more firmly. Unusual warmth joined the tingles, soothing my chilled skin. A sense of calm washed over me from him. The pressure in my chest eased, and Aspen's handsome face stopped blurring.

"There, that wasn't too difficult, was it?"

His soul-piercing gaze rattled me as much as his gentle hands and my uncanny ability to sense his emotions at random. I closed my eyes, wanting to hate every single thing about him. I didn't want to be attracted to my jailor, nor did I want the tingles against my cheek to affect me so. But as his hands sent tantalizing fire into my skin, I was, and it did.

"How'd you do that?" I whispered, happy that my breaths were back to normal.

"Do what?"

Give me a sense of peace I haven't found in a long time. I couldn't say that to him, though. This was the Aspen who took girls to his queen to be tortured, who left me with Brock to be abused. This wasn't the stranger I met in the woods who wanted me to be safe. No, for some reason, that Aspen disappeared.

"What do you mean, sweetheart?" He brushed his thumb along my cheekbones and tucked strands of my wet hair behind my ear. My slowing heart rate fluttered, ignoring my rational mind.

The nickname didn't have its usual mocking tone. This time, it was gentle and kind, melting my insides. That wasn't okay. But in between the melting and my whirling thoughts, the throbbing screamed louder.

"Aspen?"

"Sweetheart?" he whispered back.

Stop. I just wanted him to stop with all his mind games. But I didn't say that either.

"I need you to get my jacket. There's a small bag in one of the pockets that I need for my wounds. It's by the bank."

"What's wrong with your wounds?" he demanded, looking down, but his cloak covered me.

"I think my thighs are bleeding more than they should be," I admitted. My ribs were fine, luckily.

He immediately dropped his hand, the tingles ceasing, and went to grab my jacket. When he came back, he nodded at my legs. "Let me see."

"But I'm naked," I said.

He sighed, frustrated. "Fine," he put the small bag into my hands. "Put that on your wounds. I'll be back with the needle and thread."

"What? But the cuffs won't hinder my quick healing." *Didn't Hana say this would clot my wounds long enough for my power to kick in?*

He shook his head, clearly annoyed. "The Tusoteuthis drains power. It latched onto you briefly, so you'll be practically human for a bit."

"How long is a bit?" I exclaimed.

I needed to dream-walk. Plus, when I got these cuffs off and escaped, I would need my flames. I couldn't be helpless anymore. I almost died from a giant squid because I couldn't control my powers. This was what Oliver was talking about. I either learned to control them or continue to hurt myself and others.

I loved my mom, but her fears stunted me, and I allowed it. Sure, I understood she was protecting me. *But look where we were now.* Although I still craved her forced calm and the easy way it silenced my doubts, fears, and hatred, I no longer could be the weak girl who took the abuse. I wouldn't be, especially when a deadly man I didn't fully trust invaded my head. He may be looking for my mom; he may even help me escape, but if not, I'd be as ready as I could be to catch the knife before it stabbed me in the back.

Aspen nodded down to my body. "Put that on your wounds. I'll be back." Then he left without telling me how long it'd take to get my powers back. It had better not be long. I needed to start practicing my powers *now*.

"Put that on your wounds." I quietly mocked while pouring the powder into the cuts on my thighs.

I jumped as Aspen luscelered in front of me. "Don't do that."

He threw my shirt into my face. When I pulled it off, the slightest twitch in his lips slowed my movements. The potential view of his dimples filled me with an addicting anticipation and a sadness I couldn't articulate. But with his smile, he radiated light, drawing me in to understand him again.

"Put them on. I'll turn around. Tell me when you're clothed."

Them?

I looked into my arms and found my shirt, pants, and undergarments. My cheeks flushed at the thought of him touching them, especially unwashed. Mortification tempered the fluttering in my chest. I watched his back while I took off his cloak and dressed.

"Okay," I said, already hating what was coming next.

Aspen faced me, keeping his eyes level with mine, as he crouched, needle in hand. "This will hurt, but I'll try my best to make it as painless as possible."

I searched his face, noticing the soft planes, the openness of his eyes, and the gentle sincerity in his voice—a night and day difference from the guy who withdrew behind a cold mask.

"Okay."

He nodded to my thighs. "May I?"

For reasons unknown, I gave him a small smile despite my nerves and said, "Oh, are you actually asking, princeling?"

"I do, in fact, know how to do that, sweetheart."

"Hm... could've fooled me with your grabby hands."

Oh, hell no, I was flirting.

Long lashes hooded his eyes as he peered up at me with twinkling amusement. "Ready?"

"Yeah." *No.*

My wounds were inches away from my bottom, inches away from an intimate area, and about to be touched by fingers that vibrated against my skin. I almost hoped for pain, scared of what else I might feel.

"Turn around."

I bit into my cheeks and turned.

His fingers grazed around my wound, sending tingles into my skin and masking the painful throbbing. The sensation was—was—I couldn't focus on it without feeling a different throb in a different area. I was lucky Aspen couldn't see the flush in my cheeks or the way I bit my lip.

"Here I go," he said, voice sounding shaky.

I tensed. The same odd warmth mingled with the tingles as he held my thigh and then stabbed.

The warmth and buzz pulsated into my body, distracting me from half the pain. Each insertion made me cringe, but I couldn't imagine what it'd feel like without his help. When he moved onto my next thigh, his hands shifted higher—an inch from my butt. I could not go through another tingly, slightly painful thigh stitching in silence.

"Whose Nalini?" I blurted out. Not the question I originally planned, but my habit of refusing to face the things I feared wasn't about to go away because of my pretty mental speech from before.

He jerked back, and I winced as he poked me.

"I heard Hana mention her name when you two talked over me." I didn't want to mention the gruesome dream-walk I witnessed.

Silence.

I turned. "Aspen?"

Agony tore into his face, bleeding in his eyes and my mind before disappearing right as a red glow flashed and haloed his chin.

"No one," he said, resolved as if she meant nothing.

I would've believed him if I had not seen and felt his pain or remembered how he brushed her hair back and bellowed to the sky.

He returned his hand to my skin, resuming the stitching, and the red light faded into his mark.

I should've let it go. But I had a sinking feeling I knew one reason why he might've changed.

Back aching, I turned to face the tree again. "I want to understand. One thing. Tell me one thing."

His hands froze, and utter silence greeted me. *Did that mean he remembered my words? Remembered that day?*

"Just a sliver," I whispered.

"Not the whole moon," he whispered back in a broken voice.

An ache built in my chest from our combined pain, bringing tears to my eyes. He remembered. I almost wished he didn't. I wished I didn't, because it changed nothing. A heavy weight filled the quiet as he sewed the last few stitches, resting his hands on my leg.

"Nalini was the first person I ever loved." His voice grew hushed. "Then she was murdered."

A crushing weight enveloped my chest. I could taste his sorrow as it bled off my eyelashes and hit the corner of my lips. My hands twitched, wanting to push off the ground and comfort him. But he was my captor.

"All done," he said.

Nervous, I flipped over and met his face. "Who did it?"

He stood. "Who did what?"

I furrowed my brows. I couldn't feel his pain, and his chin glowed. "Who murdered Nalini?"

The red mark darkened from crimson red to red the color of dried blood.

"Nalini died because of crimes against my queen," he growled.

I narrowed my eyes at his chin. "But she was murdered."

He ignored me and turned to leave. I shot out my arm, stopping him. "Aspen."

He stared at my fingers on his as I watched the red light fade back into his skin. The mask covering the destruction in his face fell, and the block on his pain, like my touch brought him back to himself and reinforced our connection.

When he looked up from my touch and I saw the glassy blue, it was difficult to think of him as my captor. He looked more like a guy ruined by his past.

"Don't look at me like that." He pulled away from my hand, picking up his cloak to crouch down and cover my bottom half. "I'm your enemy, Lucille."

He was right, and yet I already needed another reminder as he double-checked that he'd covered every inch of my exposed skin.

"Is this you giving me the moon?"

Aspen lifted his head and gripped my chin, staring at me with a severeness that stopped my breath. "If I could ever give you the moon, I'd start by taking you away from here. Then I'd ensure no one ever found us and destroy anyone who did. But as you can see, Elora's moon is blue, dyed by the sorrows of failure, broken promises, and power. So I can't give you the moon, Lucille. I can't give you anything." He punctuated his words with the drop of his hand. Brock rounded a bush just as Aspen stood and said, "Stay away from the water."

"Everything alright?" Brock asked, glancing between us. I watched him note my state and pants off to the side.

"Yes," Aspen said, then left, worsening the ache in my chest.

"Get dressed, we're leaving," Brock ordered.

"Drag your wrinkly ass back to camp, and I will."

Shit. Why'd I say that?

"Watch yourself. Just because Prince Aspen's had a change of heart about playing with our prisoners doesn't mean accidents can't happen."

That tidbit didn't bode well for the butterflies confusing my mind about my princely jailor—not after his speech, when his words made poetic sense, but the emotion in his eyes told a different story. He was the enemy. I knew that, and yet something prompted me to reconsider.

Brock chuckled. "Don't think that means anything, angel. The prince received correspondence after the Hellhound attack stating the queen wants you mostly intact and healthy."

Is that why he continued to save me? For his worthless queen?

"Now you understand," Brock smiled, sensing my emotional downturn. "Hurry up, or I'll drag you back half-naked. She said *mostly*."

At the tip of my tongue lingered curses and insults I wanted to spew into his loose-skinned face. Knowing his threat wasn't empty, I kept the hateful words in my eyes, and my lips pressed together.

Like the despicable old man he was, he watched as I shimmied on my pants underneath Aspen's cloak. My power tickled my fingers at the leer twisting his lips.

Why did Aspen leave me with him?

To my horror, I had to have Brock hold my arm to keep me steady on our way back. He didn't trip me for fun like I thought he would, but he got in some shoves, laughing when I winced.

At camp, he dragged me past the doused fire and the demons, then shoved me into Aspen's back. "Here, your prisoner," he said, forcing me to latch onto Aspen's arms so I didn't fall.

Aspen turned, taking my arm to steady me, and eyed Brock. "You're driving first, and she's sitting up there with you," he stated, dropping my arm to leave.

Brock grabbed him. "You need to re-cuff her, Prince Aspen. She can't think she can escape."

The chill morning air heated to suffocating levels. A pulse vibrated through the building tension. Flames licked Aspen's neck, trailing down to his leathered arm. He turned to face Brock, smiling with malicious intent. "If you want to keep that hand, I'd remove it, Brockalian."

He snatched his hand back.

The heat died down, bringing relief to my sweaty forehead. Aspen pulled back his flames, only keeping them in his irises. "Do not touch me. Do not give me orders. I know how to treat our prisoners." He stepped chest to chest with Brock. "You work for us. Go to your position."

Brock licked his yellow teeth, fisting his hands. "Yes, Prince Aspen," he finally gritted out, whirling around to the front of the carriage.

The flames calmed when he addressed me.

"Don't you dare," I said, not caring he almost incinerated Brock's hand. If double-cuffing one leg still blocked my power, I didn't need them attached to both. It mortified me to trip and shuffle around. But really, I needed to be able to run when the time came.

Aspen dropped to the ground, lifting my pants leg. He made quick work of unlocking and cuffing my other ankle.

I seared my gaze into his coffee locks, wishing to burn it all off.

He stood. "There's leftover squirrel in the back."

"To hell with your squirrel." I turned and jangled like the prisoner I was to the front of the carriage.

"You need to eat."

I snorted. "And you need to stop acting like you care, enemy. Your worthless queen will be just fine with a half-starved prisoner."

If I turned around, I'd bet all my currently inaccessible powers on the fact that the prince's eyes were back to flaming. That thought alone brought a satisfied smile to my lips as I sat on the driver's seat next to the most loathsome fallen angel.

Brock may want to slice and dice me, and some part of me understood that. But Aspen, with his random laughter, the way he touched me, the way his voice broke—I honestly felt like it was all a twisted game.

I stared at my ankle cuffs and let the image and meaning pound reality back into me, wiping away the useless feelings attempting to surface for a guy who only wanted me for his queen.

Bastards. All of them.

"Always so angry or sad," Brock commented.

"I can tell that pleases you, Searcher."

He jerked. "How do you know that title?"

I smiled to myself, thinking about the man in my head, and shrugged. "How indeed."

My smug smile dropped at the fist he slammed into our seat, missing my leg by inches. Two raps on the wood diffused the tension, signaling Brock to drive. He gave me one last menacing stare and picked up the reins.

"Accidents happen. Remember that."

I'd have to be a lot more careful with my words around Brock, or I wouldn't be able to escape if I was beaten to a pulp. But confirming that the man in my head wasn't lying or a figment of my subconscious dreams was reassuring. Which meant I'd be gone by the end of the day.

Let's hope my powers returned by then.

CHAPTER TWENTY-TWO

The first half of the day was long and uneventful. The orange trees were pleasant to look at. But my eyes grew heavy after the first couple hours of the same scenery, lack of threats or unpleasant conversation. With thoughts of my mom firmly in my mind, in case my powers returned, I let the soft clip-clop of hooves put me to sleep.

THEY WERE ALWAYS PURPLE, which kind of annoyed me. But I suppose it helped to distinguish between a dream and a dream-walk. This time, I dream-walked into the body of my five-year-old self.

"It hurts, Mommy."

She crouched in front of me, holding my tiny hands, frowning. "What does, love?"

"The flames," I whispered, like talking too loudly would make them come back.

She tilted her head to the side. "What flames?"

I rubbed my arm up and down. "The white ones on my skin."

Her eyes widened. "But you're only five."

"Almost six!"

"Yes, almost six in two months." She gave me a small smile, but a tiny line formed between her eyes. I didn't know why. She hadn't found my stolen brownies yet. I checked under my pillow.

"Are you upset, Mommy?"

"Just—" She pushed a strand of my wavy hair behind my ear. "Confused."

"Why?"

"No reason." She stood, patting my bed. "Do you want to hear a poem, love? And when you're older, I'll tell you the story."

I really wanted to eat my brownies, but a poem wouldn't take too long. Nodding, I scurried underneath the covers, making sure not to lay on my pillow.

Mommy grabbed my hands, smiling, looking sad.

"There once was a daughter of seven circles, hidden, protected, avoiding the hurdles. There once was a palace of crystalized ice, awaiting the daughter to sacrifice. Unbalanced and sorrowful. Hopeless without tomorrow. There once was a world concealed from her, vibrant in color, awaiting a shudder. When the ice whispers. Be prepared for the fissures."

"I don't think I want to know the story when I'm older," I said.

"It'll stay a story, baby. But only if you promise Mommy something?"

I nodded.

"When you feel the little pricks, before they really hurt, I need you to come to me. I'll take away the pain, so the poem never comes true. Can you do that?" She rubbed my arm.

And I smiled, nodding, until her warm hand tingled.

"Mommy—"

MY EYES JERKED OPEN. Aspen gripped my arm.

"You were sliding out of your seat," he said, only half his attention on me, letting go.

I reached up to my neck, rubbing the healed cut, surprised Brock didn't add more while I let myself dream-walk. Except it wasn't the memory I was looking for. I ended up with my mom, but not at the right time. *How did I jump to the right memory?*

Disoriented, I sat straighter, taking in my surroundings. I bobbed out of the way of a patch of dangling moss. The branch it hung on twisted into a dark canopy of entwining limbs, blocking the sun. Without its warmth, the damp air easily breached my jacket, prickling my skin. The aroma of decay filled the air, not like the earthy smell of leaves decaying, but more like the decay of spoiled meat.

"Where are we?"

"Drune Forest," he answered, scanning the woods.

The forest Hana mentioned.

Spiders crawled up my spine as Aspen, who was most definitely scared of driving, willingly took his eyes off the road. The smell didn't help. Neither did the shadows of the trees that moved when they should definitely not be moving.

"Are the Drunes out there?"

"Yes," he whispered, gazing over my head.

Shadows interspersed between the trees flickered as if they heard him. My grogginess completely wore off.

"Will they attack?"

He narrowed his eyes. "They won't." But the arrogance that usually graced his words wasn't there. And for once, I didn't like that.

"But they could?"

"They won't. I've sent Brock, Cacus, and Bael to talk to their leader for safe passage. They should be back soon." That didn't mean we had safe passage now. "Plus, they're scared of me. Drune's go for easy kills unless otherwise commanded, or they're with a group."

Ahh, there it was.

"And what if you're an easy kill?" It wasn't an admittance, but I wasn't exactly a warrior.

"Weak beings have a difficult time surviving in Elora, Lucille. No matter what side you're on." His gentle tone shocked me.

I expected a, *then you will die,* with a nice glare to hit me where it hurts. Not that.

"Well, I think I'd have a better time surviving in the Ethereal Kingdom than the Tenebrous."

His gaze drilled into my cheek. "You know the names?"

"I know a few things."

"Not enough. The Ethereal Kingdom isn't much better than the Tenebrous. But I suppose we do have the Mother of Demons as our queen."

His queen was the mother of all *demons? That's who he was taking me to?* Now I knew why he scrutinized my cheek. He wanted to know my reaction.

But he wasn't finished.

"Which is why your cuffs aren't just cuffs that bind your magic. They're made from the metal mined in Dark Embers hot pits, where demons are first created, and they're infused with demon energies. And seeing as crossing into The Tenebrous Kingdom requires demon blood, and we're not sure what you are besides part angel, you need to wear them, or you'll die before we reach her."

I laughed, unsettling the ancient forest, and probably making the Drunes and Aspen wonder if I'd lost my mind. But I couldn't help realizing how unlucky I was, how every step of the way had been one terrible thing after another.

Did I need any more proof of why I shouldn't be attracted or moved by his stupid laugh or pain? Like he said, he was the enemy, not a handsome stranger in the forest, not my guardian angel. My enemy.

I closed my mouth, reining in my disbelieving laughter, letting it sink in.

If I crossed that boundary line, I'd never escape. I'd never be able to remove the cuffs without killing myself.

"I told you not to come here."

My head whipped around, eyes narrowing.

"I told you to stay."

Stay here. Stay put. Stay safe.

He never meant to *stay put* at my house. We moved, and he didn't care. No, he meant stay put *on Earth*. He never wanted me to come to Elora.

I scoffed. "You told me to stay put. To stay safe. And now look at you, handing me over to your queen to be slaughtered."

He flinched, and I laughed, feeling a creeping itch. I focused on the sensation and analyzed it. But it wasn't just an itch. It was a ruthless energy coiling beneath my skin, begging to come out. Soon, I'd let it.

"You're a liar. Your words mean nothing."

Aspen jerked on the reins. I flew forward at the sudden stop, catching myself on the wooden ledge.

"I am no liar, Lucille."

Right.

"I remember those sweet words you'd say right before you ran away. You probably went straight to your queen to give her all the intel she needed. Is that it? Or are you Marcus's new employer, and that's why he gave me over to you? Do you have my mom, Aspen?"

"I don't know what the hell you're creating in that naive mind of yours, but we didn't take anyone but you. I intercepted Marcus before he took you to wherever he was running away to and reported the traitor to our queen."

So, the chilling voice was right. Marcus worked for someone else, and if he took my mom, the queen wouldn't have her.

"That doesn't change the fact you're a liar and play twisted games. I'm just calling it how I see it."

He stood, towering over me while I sat on the edge of the carriage front. "No, you call it how you want to see it. There are reasons I did and said the things that I did."

I held his searing stare and grasped the coiling energy that itched my skin. I didn't want to show my power. I only wanted to practice for when I was ready to show my hand. "Says the male, taking me to his queen. I will be another Nalini, won't I? Murdered and forgotten."

He shook his head, gripping his sword hilt as the scar on his chin darkened. "Maybe if you'd stop being the ignorant, helpless wimp you are for one second, you'd survive!"

They were his words. I saw his lips move. But the voice that said *helpless wimp* wasn't his, even if they were spat in the same way and just as demeaning and arrogant. It wasn't Aspen. It was— The memory was at my fingertips. But it stayed at the edges of my mind, taunting me. So I was left with the bitter taste of fear and an unending loathing I didn't quite understand.

But that word. That damned word. My hold on my power slipped as my rage took over.

"Do not"—the itch surged—"ever call me that again." Pressure pushed behind my eyes. The sense of deja vu overwhelmed me.

He smiled, the red glow making him look vile and wrong. "I call it how I see it." Throwing my words back in my face, eyes flashing blue.

The call in my blood sprung to my hands as I swung at his face. He dodged deftly, smirking. "Careful Lucille, wouldn't want to find you naked again..."

Low blow.

I jerked my knee up, going for the source of his arrogance, and was stopped by my chains.

"What would that be... the second—no, the fourth time I've seen you naked because of your lack of skill?" he continued, smug.

Every inch of my skin raged with the itchy energy.

Mindless, I pushed off the floor planks with all my strength and tackled his royal ass off the side of the carriage, catching him off guard.

He took the brunt of the fall, letting out a grunt as we landed in a heap on top of a soft patch of moss. Straddling him, hands covered in a deep purple, I placed one around his neck, threatening to squeeze as I bared my teeth, ignoring the tingles.

How dare he?

I wrenched my arm back, ready to wipe the pretty smirk off his stupid, handsome face. Ready to make him feel the overwhelming, itchy, fiery pressure of whatever this was. Because what coiled in my core felt different from all the other times my purple flames erupted. It was hot and lacked the crackling noise of ice.

My chest heaved in and out, purple flames spreading from my hands up to my neck and pushing behind my eyes.

His smirk fell. Now he saw them.

"How—"

I clawed into his hair, ripping his head back with my other hand, hoping to dissolve some of his stupid soft locks.

He flinched, and I thought I saw a purple wisp slowly eat a piece of his hair, but then the coiling in my core changed to burning.

Everything my undulating darkness touched, I felt ten-fold.

No longer was his hair just soft. Instead, it slid between my fingers like a satin caress. His skin went from smooth to a vibrating velvet. It took all my strength not to move my hand against his neck to caress him. And his smell. Heavenly Hell. Sweet apples mixed with my favorite piney scent. I swallowed back a moan but couldn't stop my body from arching against him.

The heat in my cheeks reached the tops of my temples as Aspen's frown changed to a look of hunger I didn't understand. But I didn't need to. Not when my pelvis rubbed against his. Not when the hard length of him grew beneath me and pressed into a place I only gave thought to earlier today. A place that now throbbed with an urge I never knew I had.

Aspen's eyes glowed, flames hovering on the edge of his irises. He lifted his hands off the moss and grabbed my hips. The contact was pure ecstasy.

"Lucille, what are you doing to me?" he whispered. His voice strained, fingers digging into my sides.

The heat growing between my legs made me crave for him to press harder.

"Nothing. I'm doing nothing," I spat, attempting to hold onto anger that wasn't even there. My unwanted desire for him fueled my purple flames, somehow covering the intact leather of my jacket.

Aspen moved one of his hands up my spine, returning the favor of gripping my hair. But instead of jerking me back, he jerked me toward him—nose to nose. The scent of him wrapped around me, addictive and sweet. I squeezed my eyes shut in pleasure.

"Lucille, wait," he groaned as his nose trailed along my neck. I felt his unending desire for me swallow his confusion. "Dammit, you always smell like winterberries and sunshine. It kills me. Every. Fucking. Day."

My eyes snapped open to pure starvation.

He jerked his hips, hitting the ache between my thighs, and I couldn't help the moan that escaped.

"Dammit, Lucille, do you know what you do to me?" he whispered.

"Enlighten me," I replied, equally as quiet.

His lips were centimeters away, moist and pink, ready.

Would he taste as sweet as he smelled?

Tempted, I wanted to bring his face up to meet mine. Instead, I gripped his hair tighter, loving the feel of the satin silk, torn between overwhelming temptation and confusion.

He tightened his hand in return, bringing my face lower like he wanted to bridge the gap, but moved out of the way at the last moment. "Lucille, if you do not rein in whatever this is, I am going to strip you naked..." he paused. "And fuck you, like I've always wanted, against this soft moss where anyone could see," he finished, voice low and grating. His hips ground into mine to emphasize his words.

I bit my cheeks hard to keep back my moan, failing terribly. I wanted—but I couldn't, but I wanted more.

Losing myself, I slid against the hard bulge of him, hating myself for it and for the breathy noises that escaped my mouth. It was—was, I couldn't think or breathe. I just wanted more. The need hit me hard.

He pressed into me like he heard my thoughts, giving me the friction I desired. My purple flames flared, bringing even more sensation. It was strange and all-consuming—addicting.

"Fuck," he rasped, flipping me over like I weighed nothing. Somehow, I still managed to grip his neck and arm, his velvet skin too addictive to let go of.

I licked my lips. Aspen gazed at my tongue, little blue flashes flickering in his eyes. The hand that held my side crept up until it touched the side of my breast, rubbing delicious circles.

Heavenly Hell.

"Are you sure you want this to be how our first time goes?" he asked, breathless.

"You want to stop?"

"Fuck no," Aspen moaned, giving in at last, lips crashing down on mine.

My first kiss and it wasn't gentle.

Aspen devoured me, tasting sweet and tangy. But there was also another flavor, almost as if fire had a flavor. The electrical tingles from his skin only intensified my desire. When he opened my mouth, I was lost, so utterly lost in the exquisite pleasure of the tip of his tongue.

I never wanted it to stop.

He groaned, sending a pulse of need to my core, making me wet and throb. I needed more. Our leathers were too restrictive. I wanted to feel all of him, all of his tingling skin against mine. I trailed my hand down his chest and palmed his length, needing, craving, wanting that. His rough leather scratched my palm as his hardness throbbed against me, shoving itself against his restraints. Aspen jerked back, eyes flashing.

"Lucille, are you sure? I won't stop if we start." I could tell he battled himself. He pressed harder into my hand but kept his lips away from mine even as he gazed at them with such heat.

A smile twisted my swollen lips. Now, it was my turn to be smug. "Why?" I said as I rubbed him over the fabric. Finding the buttons to the tops of his leathers, I released one while staring into his devouring gaze, pleased that I affected him so.

"Because..." He lowered his head. I released another button. "Whatever..." Another button. His gaze hooked onto my lips like they were his saving grace. "You are doing..." He lowered further, and I was two buttons away from unleashing him. "Is disarming me." His tongue licked the seam of my mouth, tingles making my eyes flutter.

What would that feel like down there?

I opened my mouth, letting him slip in, to taste, to tease, to consume, and when he crushed his mouth into mine, I broke our kiss and slipped past him to his ear. "Prince Aspen rendered powerless by a naïve helpless female," I said, licking his lobe. He shuddered and grabbed my glowing arms, pinning them above me, smothering any space between us. With his pants half undone, the heat of his tip hit the apex of my thighs.

It undid me and urged me to do the one thing I shouldn't have. "Please," I begged, grinding against him. I didn't want to beg, but at the same time, I'd do anything to feel what comes after the ache.

"If," he panted. "If you do that, there is no going back." His forehead met mine as he restrained himself. One hand slipped away from my pinned arms, cupping my breast over my jacket.

I wrenched one of my pinned arms free, wiggling it between our pressed bodies. The rest of his buttons were more challenging to open, but I managed, desire spurring me on. Only a thin layer of his undergarments held in his large length, the fabric moist. I grazed my thumb over it and heard his strangled groan. Smiling, I replaced my thumb with my core, going off basic instinct, rubbing him in slow circles, feeling his body shake, his heartbeat, and the blood pumping under his skin.

Was that normal?

"Lucille," he moaned, doing things to my insides. I savored the way he moaned my name and reveled in the way I controlled him so thoroughly with my touches.

His hands released me, sliding into my hair, jerking me to his lips, where he devoured me once more.

My hand moved to the clasps of my jacket while the other trailed down his spine. One by one, I plucked them open, my white t-shirt exposing my arousal. He pulled back, zeroing in on my nipples peeking through the fabric. I held back my smile at his ravenous look. Aspen's restraint was fracturing.

I wanted to fracture it completely.

Slowly, I lifted my shirt, then circled the protruding dark pink tips, giving him a show. The blues of his eyes flared, and he broke.

Diving down, he replaced my fingers with his mouth, sucking and circling.

"Aspen," I breathed. "More," I moaned, feeling the pulse of his tip, needing the rest of our clothes removed.

Understanding, he sat back, removing himself from me so he could remove his weapons belt that still held his pants in place, watching me as I trailed my fingers down my stomach. His eyes were eager, all heat, looking like he wanted to replace my fingers with his lips. But at the lack of contact, the smoldering heat changed. I watched as the hunger dimmed, blue flames returning to a soft glow. Aspen fell back, then luscelered away.

The distance shocked my system. All the heightened sensations I gained returned to normal as my flames sank back into my skin. The intense desire pounding in my chest extinguished like a weak candle. Yet, I sensed Aspen's lingering desire and didn't know what to make of it. To make matters worse, a set of boots crunched against gravel coming around the carriage.

"If you're going to enjoy yourself, at least wait until we reach our destination," Brock said.

I yanked down my shirt, grabbed my jacket, and stood.

Aspen stared at me, chest moving up and down, still irregular.

"I felt her emotions a ways out, almost interrupted, even thought about joining." Brock came around and shot Aspen a wink.

I held back my gag, watching Aspen's eyes flash to flames for a split second. Whatever desire I felt from him turned to anger.

He removed his eyes from me and gave Brock a grimace. "Don't bother. She's not worth it," Aspen replied.

Ashamed, I stormed off, needing to get away from these feelings. I couldn't believe what happened. I couldn't believe how much further I wanted it to go.

But it couldn't have been me. It couldn't have. Seduction wasn't a part of my powers. Fire and ice, that was it. It had to be something else. But he asked what I was doing to him. He sped away from me the moment he stopped touching my purple flames.

Don't bother. She's not worth it.

He didn't want me.

With everything he'd said, everything I'd learned, I shouldn't want him either. Yet, I had been attracted to him since the beginning. I wanted him to be the handsome prince who stole me from my life. Too bad I never expected this to be the outcome.

"Go get her," Aspen said, sounding unsteady.

Brock was in front of me before I could get any further. I was starting to hate the fact that all angel-blooded beings could lusceler. He had a malicious smile on his face that I hardly noticed as two shadows moved behind him.

CHAPTER TWENTY-THREE

One shadow zipped past on all fours. I squinted, unable to tell what it was. The second shadow materialized. Goosebumps spread along my flesh as I tilted my head from a wispy dark robe to a bloody skull covering its face.

The shadow made me question why Hana decided to share information about the Drunes in the first place. Because that was what the seven-foot creature had to be.

Brock turned when the Drune lifted its sharp, bony fingers and pointed at me.

I backed up, hitting the back of the carriage with my legs. My chest heaved up and down. Brock snatched my arm, dragging me around to the front, as I begged myself not to have a panic attack.

The Drune's frayed sleeve dangled as it continued to point at me until Brock pulled me out of sight and into the driver's seat.

"Prince Aspen, we need to leave. The leader of the Drunes gave us a limited time to leave their forest, and there's one behind us as our reminder."

I laid my wide eyes on Aspen. He stood off to the side, staring at me. That was all he did, stared, like Brock's words didn't reach him.

Shocked, I realized his eyes were glazed over. He wasn't registering what was around him. Aspen, a formidable warrior and commander of a military, wasn't mentally present.

"Prince," Brock snapped. "The Drunes." He gestured behind us and took the reins like he thought it was best he drove.

Aspen finally nodded, quiet and distracted, like he didn't particularly care whether there was a giant skeleton-wearing creature behind us or that he had to go near it to get into the carriage.

When he walked back and the doors slammed shut with no incident, I heaved a sigh. It did nothing to relieve the tension in my shoulders or change the past few minutes.

Brock smacked the whip at his side into the horse's rear. They took off at a canter. The carriage squeaked and rattled as we barreled through the forest. I gripped my seat, cringing as each bump shot into my newly stitched legs, and hoped not to be overrun by skeleton-headed creatures. Eventually, Brock slowed the horses when we covered a good amount of ground.

"They didn't chase us," I said, surprised.

"No, they said they'd give us time to leave before they did, and Prince Aspen's a good deterrent," Brock said, face twisting into a leer. "Speaking of... was it everything you hoped and dreamed?"

I stilled. He felt my desire. Just like he felt every ounce of embarrassment, anger, and mortification I felt afterward. So, he only asked that question to be cruel. This was his payback.

I had never wanted to escape them both more than I did now.

After what felt like hours of occasionally dodging moss, plugging my nose from the stench of the forest, and worrying about everything, my bladder was about to burst.

"I need to relieve myself," I stated.

Brock grunted. "You couldn't have done that before?"

"When was there time?"

He smirked. "You're right. It's hard to find the time when the prince's needs need to be met. Although he seemed pretty put out, you must've only met a quarter of his needs. Don't worry, he'll find someone else later, per usual."

Itches surged along my fingers, but for the first time, I shoved my energy down before the purple flame could burst out or take over. It wasn't easy, and my head throbbed from concentrating, but what happened with Aspen would never happen again. But that didn't mean I leashed my anger.

"At least a quarter is better than none. Which is the quota I assume you meet, with your wrinkly old-man skin, salt and pepper hair, and saggy balls." I spat back.

Brock luscelered and slammed me to the ground. I gasped as pain split my ear. He straddled me, leaning down next to the side of my face.

"Talk to me like that again, and I'll remove the rest," he whispered, licking a dribble of blood off my neck and spitting it into my face.

The point of his dagger threatened to take my eye. So close, the blood slicking the silver blade gathered in my eyelash with each blink I couldn't hold.

"Oh, and say anything about this to the prince, and I'll give you a matching set." He lifted off me, delighted. "Go pee, I'll let his highness know. And if you get out of range, I'll send him after you. I know how much you'll love that."

Once he retreated to tell Aspen, I stood on shaky legs. Long trails of warmth slid down my arm as I clutched the throbbing cut. Shock held back my tears.

He cut off the tip of my ear.

I walked away from the carriage and all its psychotic occupants, rearranging my bobby pins to keep my hair out of the blood. I glanced down at the keyhole of my cuffs. If only I could escape now.

Out of view, I squatted behind a large tree. After I relieved myself, I ripped some plush moss off the trunk, using it to wipe off my bloody hands, and pressed it against my open slice, seeing no other options.

White mist rolled in, snaking along gnarled roots and rising to the first shelf of branches.

That wasn't creepy at all.

I rushed to wipe off more blood and leaves, but before I moved, a bony finger slid through a new line of blood dripping along my neck, freezing me.

The air in my lungs died as the skeletal finger slid underneath a brown-speckled deer skull. It was a Drune. A Drune that lapped at its finger with slow, languid sweeps.

Mmmm. Such an exquisite flavor.

No, not another one. I didn't need any more voices in my head. Especially ones moaning about the taste of my blood.

Mmmm. So many secrets. And so much hidden power. No wonder she kept you suppressed and hidden, the Drune said, stepping closer. Its voice sounded like old trees creaking in the wind. Drawn out and deep.

I jerked my attention to the skeletal holes where its eyes should've been. The dark depths curled with mist. "My mom?" I asked.

The frayed cloak hanging on its bony shoulders snapped in an unseen wind, skimming my boots, much too close for comfort.

"Are you talking about my mom?" I demanded.

The skeletal mask jerked down, sniffing. *Mmmm. It smells as delectable as it tastes. Give me a few more drops, and I will answer a single question. But the forest whispers of the stolen prince's approach, so hurry.*

"What about two?" But even two wasn't enough.

Let me taste the sunshine and the circles, and I'll answer one.

I had no clue what it was talking about.

"You already had a taste. If you want another, I want two questions answered."

It raised its robed arm, gesturing to the ear I pressed moss to.

Let me suck it, and we have a deal.

Suck my bloody ear? First, gross. Second, that didn't seem like a good idea.

Hurry. Or you'll have no answers.

"Fine!"

It bridged the gap to press against my side, robe traveling through my legs. My already wide eyes widened further.

It chuckled, plucked my hand away, and descended on my wound. Bumpy wetness slid over my cut, stinging. It groaned. I shuddered, wincing as its tongue lapped with more force.

What are your questions?

"How do I escape?" Nothing else mattered unless I escaped. Crossing that boundary line was *not* an option.

Hmmm, it hummed, tongue vibrating against my ear, gaining volume, gaining words. Hundreds of voices echoed in my mind: soft, loud, feminine, and masculine, a cacophony of noise and life. But the loudest of all said, *The king in your mind. Follow his instructions.*

"The man in my dreams? He's a king?"

Male, not man. This isn't Earth. Is that your next question?

"No! Where's my mom?"

"You'll find her when you find Magda."

"So she's at Magda's?"

Was that Marcus's new employer?

I didn't say that. I said you'll find her when you find Magda.

"I'm letting you suck the blood out of my ear, and that's all you're giving me? That's not a location!" I yelled.

It gave one last long lap and pulled back.

Yes.

"No. That's not good enough. You owe me a location!"

"I owe you nothing, child of the sun and circles. But I will give you something else in return. Advice. Beware of the greedy witch. And do not give her the emotions she seeks."

With that, the Drune's incorporeal robe gave one last snap before he walked into the large trunk at my back, fading into the surface as a flash of blue thunked into the wood. I stumbled back, tripping over a root.

Aspen yanked his sword out of the bark and glared at me. "Tell me you did not give it any of your blood!" The flames on his sword vanished as he leveled me with his blade. "What did it say?"

"Nothing," I said, lying, wanting to grab the blade that hovered in front of my face.

"You never give your blood in Elora. Never."

"I didn't."

"Then what the fuck is that?" He took a step forward. The tip of his sword pointed at my cut ear.

I shrugged, not ready to have a matching pair if Brock found out Aspen knew who did it.

"Did you fucking let the Drune bite you?"

"I had questions!"

He stared at me in horror. "Do you have any idea what Drunes do with your blood?"

I opened my mouth and shut it, having no answer.

"Dammit, Lucille!" He swung his blade into the trunk as if he could kill the Drune that vanished inside it. "The moment you give them your blood, they know everything about you, which they can sell to the highest bidder. They steal a piece of your power you'll never get back, and the more blood you give them, the more power they take. That's how they survive as long as they do!"

Shit. "I didn't know—"

"Of course you didn't! You don't know anything. Why the hell did you come here?"

He had a point, and it was a bitter pill to swallow. But even though I came here as naive and innocent as I was, I'd do it all over again. One way or another, I would find my mom and all this hell would be worth it.

"For the only person who ever gave a damn about me," I spat. "For the one person who doesn't play games with my mind and act like they care, when in reality my life expectancy is what? Two days? More? Less? What do you think, Prince of the Tenebrous Kingdom?"

Itches surfaced to the tips of my fingers, and instead of letting the sensation control me like I always did, I latched onto it. I pulled at my power, allowing the itches to take over my hands and arms, but not yet summoning my purple flame. I reveled in the energy coiling under my skin, smiling at my control. Curious, I dove deeper into my power and discovered a delectable song. It whispered in my ear, eager to respond to my call. All I had to do was touch the black cords in my core. So, I did.

Dark and foreboding flame licked up my hands—pure black. With my white and purple flames, I never felt what they could do. Of course, before release, they stabbed me or sent me into an itching frenzy, but with the black flames, their sweltering heat pulsed off my skin. They slowly ate my socks, my shirt, and the frayed wrap around my wrist but didn't touch my jacket or pants—yet.

"Is this what your queen wants? Does she want to use this?" I stepped toward him and smiled as he stepped back. "Scared?"

Overcome with the melody and resentment, I enjoyed how his face washed of color, how he didn't even think to lift his sword. Even more, I savored the words tingling in my ear, urging me to raise my arm and wrap it around his neck despite the fact sand pooled in my body.

"Let it go, Lucille," he whispered, as if speaking too loudly would set me off.

Too late.

The music was too difficult to ignore. It didn't care who stood in front of me or why. The tune only wanted revenge and blood.

Listening to the seductive words, I raised my hand. But before I came close to his neck, the heaviness took over. I stumbled as my vision blurred, seeing two Aspens. Swaying, I closed my eyes as my legs gave out, waiting for the pain of the ground when he caught me.

Aspen cradled me to his chest. "You're not just an angel, sweetheart," he whispered as I blacked out.

CHAPTER TWENTY-FOUR

I woke to fuzzy voices and a stinging in my ear.

"A few more minutes. If she doesn't wake up, we'll leave."

"Whatever you say, prince. I'm just the backup."

"Go corral Cacus and Bael from their joy hunt."

Footsteps faded, and the pressure on my ear resumed. I winced, daring to peek through my lids.

Aspen knelt over me, focused on the side of my face and ear. I stared at him, refusing to shift against the lumpy ground, while he was oblivious to my awareness.

He pressed a cloth against my tender skin and used his other hand to wipe away dried blood.

"If I ask you a serious question, will you answer me with the truth or lie to me?" he asked, continuing to tend to my ear.

So much for being oblivious.

I stayed silent.

He shook his head. "The Drune didn't do this to your ear."

"That's not a question."

He slowly met my gaze, intense and drilling. "This is a clean cut. Done by a knife."

"Those aren't questions either."

"Brock did this to you."

Well, he may be deadly, arrogant, and ruthlessly loyal to a terrible queen, but he wasn't dumb.

"Lucille did Brock do this to you?" he demanded.

"Does it matter?" I sat up, making him push back.

Soon, I'd be rotting in a body pit. That was if I didn't escape.

I stared into his face and let him hear the bluntness of my thoughts. "I don't know who you were before or what other confusing, contradictory memories I've forgotten. But I'm glad they're gone. I've had enough of your flavor of *caring.*"

He lapsed into silence, gazing at me with a pissy expression. His chin strobed with a red light until it held firm to a soft, menacing glow.

Standing, I swayed, my exhaustion momentarily forgotten. Aspen's tense stance hinted at an internal struggle as he battled conflicting emotions. Eventually, the red glow subsided, and he stepped forward to steady me. I recoiled, pushing him away.

"I don't need or want your help."

His chiseled jaw tightened like a vise, each muscle visibly straining under the weight of his mounting irritation. "We're leaving. Brock!" he called out. "I'm driving, and our prisoner is sitting next to me."

Wonderful.

I sighed, plopping myself down up front, emotionally and physically drained. Aspen took his place. The carriage wobbled, the back doors shut, and the horses moved.

He ignored me. I ignored him to concentrate on my power.

When I was angry, the energy coiled at the surface, making itself known through the itches. But now, I had to concentrate and dive deep to find the coiling power. It hummed faintly. I tried to pull at it, but my eyes drooped with the effort. I released it. Whatever I did earlier had taken a lot out of me. Those black flames were something else entirely, and the music—the addictive, vengeful melody—consumed every thought and action. If not for the drain, Aspen and I would've fought to the death. I wouldn't have stopped. I wanted to kill him. Guilt, anger, joy—none of it sparked at that thought. Only numbness remained until the lingering effects of this drain faded.

We drove through the Drune Forest into a field of long golden grass. Its metallic strands reflected in the beating sunshine, brushing away the moist, cool air of the lightless forest. I just reached my hand out, slightly curious if they'd feel metallic. But nope, the softness tickled my palm.

I leaned my head back against the wooden planks of the carriage, peering up into the clear blue sky. Two black specs flew high above.

"Why don't we eat birds for a change?" I pointed, curiosity loosening my lips.

Aspen yanked on the horse's reins, jerking them to a stop, about knocking me out of my seat. "Those aren't birds."

"Then what—"

"Brock! We got company," Aspen called out.

The doors to the back of the carriage slammed open. With the lack of side-to-side swaying, it seemed the demons were staying inside.

"Do not speak, understood?" Aspen said, taking off his cloak and handing it to me. "Cover yourself."

I stared at his outreaching hand and dangling cloak, wondering what would happen if I didn't, gazing back at the sky. The black specs were larger and coming fast.

"Lucille!"

I snapped my attention back to him and rolled my eyes, putting it on.

Two loud resounding booms echoed in the field, causing a cloud of dust. Once it cleared, one man and woman—or male and female—sauntered over to us. Aspen stepped down the stairs of the carriage, blocking me from view, while Brock stood off to the side.

"Look what we have here, Milda. I told you it'd be entertaining to see who was with this carriage."

I peered around Aspen, wanting to see who spoke. He looked to be in his thirties, not that that meant anything, with short golden hair and smooth, tanned skin—average. What wasn't average was the armor they wore and the female standing next to him.

She stood tall, covered in the palest blue, almost white, colored armor. Silver rivets held together each tiny piece of metal that made up the body-hugging uniform. Red corkscrews tumbled behind her head, held back by intricate braids. The vibrancy of the color melded well with the deep caramel of her face, her ruby lips, and the three red-hilted daggers at her side.

"Yes, Brocky boy seems to have aged since we last saw him. And we get the attractive, worthless demon prince to add to the disappointing Fallen scum," she tittered.

"So nice to see you, General Tavean and Colonel Milda," Aspen said, sounding the least bit amused by her condescending tone.

Colonel Milda approached him, poking him in the chest. "Does that scowl ever come off your face, Prince Aspen? Or do you need help with that?" The salacious tilt to her ruby lips screamed desperate.

A bolt of bitter jealousy spear-headed through my drained state—a feeling I did *not* like.

"Remove your hand before I do it for you, colonel," Aspen said as he gripped the pommel of his sword.

But she didn't remove her hand. No. She dared to place her entire palm on his chest.

"Oh, no, no, prince. We wouldn't want to start a war, would we? Not with your queen a prisoner to her own land. We'd slaughter you." Her words may have been a warning, but the eager gleam in her purple-ringed eyes told me she wanted war.

Aspen's spine stiffened. "Back up, Milda."

"Oh, dropping my fancy new title so soon?" she pouted.

I hope she didn't think that was cute.

"Don't test me, Milda. Back up," Aspen warned.

But the foolish female didn't.

"Milda, let the poor defenseless prince go. We are here for a job, you know," Tavean said, moving closer.

"Oh, but I think the prince needs some fun," she said, rubbing the stiff leather covering his chest.

My eyes zeroed in on that hand. "Remove your gaudy nails," I snapped, glaring over Aspen's shoulder.

Milda jerked her gaze to mine, still touching him.

"Who do you have behind you, prince?" Tavean asked. He leaned to the side to get a better view.

Aspen shifted, finally side-stepping her unwanted touch, blocking me from Tavean's view but opening more space for Milda to scrutinize me, especially my eyes. Before I could duck my head, she smiled. "Oh Tavean," Milda sang. "I think I found who we've been looking for."

"Fuck!" Aspen snapped, pulling out his sword before either one could grab me. The metal erupted in vicious blue flames, pushing Milda and Tavean back. "Guard Lucille, if something happens to her, the queen will kill you, and if she doesn't, I will." Then he swung his flaming sword at Tavean and sent a fireball at Milda's face, forcing them back further.

Heavenly shit.

Brock took Aspen's place as he faced off against the two angels. I glanced up into the darkening sky. Thunder boomed with the first clash of sword on sword, snapping my attention back to Aspen. This fight was different from the one with the Hellhounds. All three luscelered, dodging each other's swords and daggers. Lightning shot down, hitting the spot where Aspen last stood.

Aspen smirked at Milda.

She shrieked. More lightning streaked to the ground, each flash hitting the previous spot Aspen stood in.

Why is the Tenebrous Prince fighting a Power and Dominion from the Ethereal Military for you?

I jolted at his chilly voice, surprised to hear his voice in my head while awake.

Can you see what I see?

Yes, while we're connected. Why do they want you? he demanded.

I don't know. But I wondered if I'd be better off with them since they were angels.

He scoffed in my head. *You wouldn't. You'd be a prisoner in a different kingdom I couldn't help you escape from. Now turn your head to the left,* he said.

I did.

Do you see that path past the field and in the trees?

Yes.

A little further in is the Tenebrous tripwire.

Why does that matter?

I'm getting you out of your mess. The angels won't take you if you cross it.

Why?

It's a declaration of war.

I stared at the path. It wasn't too far away, but it wasn't near either.

The only problem you face is you need the prince with you to cross it, he said.

I glanced at Aspen right when two daggers slipped from his belt, and two more daggers flew from Tavean's hands toward his face.

"Behind you!" I called out at the same time Brock yelled, "Telekinetic bastard!"

Aspen blocked the first two daggers with his sword and dogged one of the ones hovering in the air, only to be stabbed in the side by the fourth.

How do I accomplish that when he's busy fighting?

They're fighting over you. So take yourself out of the equation and sneak to the tripwire first. Then play your hand. Afterward, stay with the prince, and I'll help you escape tonight. Hopefully, I'll have answers about Saraqael by then. If not, I'll at least have other answers you seek, he finished. His icy presence faded, giving me back my warmth and a difficult task.

The first part of my difficult task was getting away from Brock.

"Why don't you help Aspen? And where are Cacus and Bael?"

Brock twisted his head slowly, raising a brow in disbelief. "You heard him. I'm here to guard you. And the demons are most likely hiding in the back."

"Hiding? They are giant bombs, and they're hiding?"

"Exactly. They'd level this entire field and kill every one of us if accidentally struck."

Right.

"Well, I don't need guarding. Help your prince."

"He's fine. It's all for show. They can't kill each other, or they'd start a war."

Another dagger sliced into Aspen from behind, sinking into his leg.

I glared at Brock. "They look hellbent on starting a war. What will your queen do if you return with a dead prince?"

Brock met my glare with his own, but something in his expression told me my words struck.

"That's what I thought."

He eyed Aspen, now covered head-toe in blue flames with his uniform still intact.

"If you move from this spot, I'll take your whole ear," he said, unsheathing his sword.

"I hope you die," I said, meaning every word.

He smirked. "They always do."

Brock leaving me was easier than I thought it'd be. Although, playing on his fear of the queen helped. It was a game of who was the lesser evil—Aspen or the queen who'd most likely kill Brock if anything happened to Aspen. To Brock, I was another female in the long line of females they'd kidnapped. I was disposable to him. Aspen was not.

The next tricky part was sneaking to the tripwire, luring two dangerous pissed-off males to me, and not dying.

A ball of blue flame flashed through the air toward Tavean's chest. It distracted the Dominion long enough for the dagger swinging in front of Aspen's face to drop. Tavean's second dagger melted on contact with Aspen's flame-coated leather. Relief released the tightness I didn't know squeezed my chest.

Brock faced off with Milda and her lightning, dodging it as he swiped with his blade. Truly, I hoped the wench won. Because if she didn't, I was about to be earless.

Sliding to the other edge of the carriage, I jumped down and hurried to the horses. They blocked most of my body as I gazed at the gap in the trees.

I glanced at my cuffs and made the smartest decision I could. Dropping to my hands and knees, covered by the metallic grass, I crawled as fast as I could through the field.

Lightning struck, hitting randomly, giving me mini heart attacks every time. I already tempted death with one lightning strike. Let's hope death didn't want me today, either. When one came a foot within reach of my hand, blinding me, I froze.

Ether drove into my nose. The hair on my arms and legs stood erect. Every inch of my mind screamed at me to turn around.

I stayed there staring into the little flames on the ground, seriously reconsidering everything.

"Lucille!" Aspen bellowed.

Shit. I needed to hurry. I couldn't stop.

"Your mom's out there. Be brave, Lucy," I whispered, closing my eyes, and drove to my coiling power in my core. It hummed with a little more energy than before. I pulled at it, and nothing happened.

Another lightning bolt struck nearby.

"Come on. I can do this." I grasped the humming energy and willed it to listen to me. It was challenging without the prompting from my anger, but I forced it to the surface. A restless energy tingled beneath my skin, accompanied by the faint melody of ice cracking in my ears. When I opened my eyes, purple flames swallowed my hands. A triumphant smile curved my lips as I beheld my accomplishment.

Thunder boomed above my head, reminding me I needed to move.

I scrambled. Fast.

The tiny flames created by the lightning hissed as I crawled over them, leaving icy handprints behind. Despite the danger I was in, I couldn't keep the grin from my face at the site. I had finally used my power without help from my anger, and I wasn't overwhelmed by the music or consumed by the desire to kill. If this were any other time, I'd probably jump up and down. *I did it.*

At the tree line, I found the path and stood, letting go of my power. My smile dropped when I assessed the vicious fight.

Aspen dodged another knife and dragged his sword against Tavean's leg. Tavean stumbled back. I waved at Aspen, capturing his attention for a second before Tavean attacked. A flash of surprise, worry, and anger overpowered my emotions. I didn't know why I could feel his emotions at random times. It had to be the guardian bond, but I knew nothing of it. *Did I ever end up getting the book for*

Aspen? If so, I wasn't sure a couple of sentences would give us much to go on.

I motioned for him to hurry, hoping he saw it and understood what I was trying to say. Then, going off a hunch, hoping he was true to his word, I ran away. More like jogged. Maybe shuffled.

Cuffs sucked.

Up ahead, the dirt road forked into two paths. One shimmered with iridescent light, and the other swirled with darkness. It was a good thing I didn't have to guess which one was the trip wire. Turning my back on both paths, I waited to see if his highness would come.

Two panic-inducing minutes later, he did, pulling me over his shoulder. He luscelered us through the screen of iridescent colors and into a sweltering landscape of blue-tipped bushes.

"Are you out of your fucking mind, Lucille?" He plopped me on the ground, blue eyes swallowed by flames, seething.

I stood, refusing to let him lord over me. "Obviously not, seeing as we have no raging angels on our tail. I just saved your sorry asses and myself in the process."

"I had it handled, and you almost got fried by lightning!"

Wouldn't be the first time.

"Yeah, it sure looked like you had it handled with the knives stabbing into your legs," I deadpanned, nodding down to his bleeding wounds. If they bothered him, he didn't let on. Or the rage fueling his fire disguised it.

He took a step toward me. "You are the most infuriating—"

"Naive, ignorant, stupid, helpless, wimp," I gestured with my hand, acting unphased, bored. A lie hiding the anxiety I came down from. "Any other insults you want to add to your list?"

He squeezed his eyes shut and let out a long breath. "Why are high-ranking angels after you?"

Apprehension twisted the nausea in my stomach. "I don't know."

My mom and I had a lot of enemies.

He opened his eyes, staring at me with an unreadable expression until the planes of his face softened. My heart picked up speed as he opened his mouth, nervous about what words would come from such a gentle expression. But before a sound left his lips, something silver flashed through the air.

I flinched to the side, expecting pain. Only to see Aspen jerk, catching the object. The cool metal tip of a knife poked my ear.

For a second, I thought the angels found us. But when I looked over Aspen's shoulder, all I saw was Brock standing just inside the shimmering barrier, bruised, bloodied, and vengeful.

When I glanced back at Aspen, I didn't dare breathe.

The veins in his neck popped from how tightly he clenched his jaw, similar to the knuckles erupting from his tightly squeezed fist. He stared with glowing eyes at the knife he caught millimeters from my tipless ear. A hue of red illuminated his chin. But the more he stared, the brighter his power became, and the glowing scar throbbed. Once fire breached Aspen's eyes, the scar's light weakened.

"Aspen?" I whispered, afraid to startle him.

He shot his flaming gaze to mine, and pure loathing ravaged his eyes. I stepped back, and that little movement catalyzed his rage. Hot and powerful fire burst from his hands, turning the knife in his palm to molten metal and extinguishing the rest of the glowing red light.

I took a few more steps back, my exposed skin burning from his heat.

In the next breath, he unleashed his sword and channeled the flames into the steel blade. He plunged his sword into the ground, leaving it to turn to Brock.

The sword flickered before me, a viscous inferno separating me from them. I dared a small step toward it, and the blue flames pulsed, marking the ground in a dark line. To cross would be to suffer the consequences of Aspen's wrath.

He strode to Brock, hands loose at his sides, no longer covered in his power.

Brock retreated a step. "Prince Aspen, I told her to stay in the carriage. She disobeyed my orders. I told her what would happen if she did."

Aspen swung. A loud crack resounded through the air as Aspen's fist made contact with Brock's face, sending the old male to the ground. He jumped on top of Brock, straddling him. "I told you what would fucking happen if you touched her again!" Punch. "I should kill you." Punch. "The only reason you're here is because she ordered it." Punch. Punch.

Brock tried to retaliate, but Aspen's fists were too fast, stunning him with the force of his blows.

"Always following your own orders." Punch. "Insubordinate." Punch. "Fallen scum."

Brock sputtered, trying to get out words, but Aspen wrapped his hand around Brock's neck, leaning close. "I swear, the next time you so much as lift a finger at her, I will obliterate you. And don't think our queen will mind one bit because I'm protecting her asset."

Aspen leaned back and stood. Brock heaved himself off the ground, eyeing the flaming sword and me. "I don't remember you being this protective over the other *assets* we brought in," he spat. A glob of red landed next to Aspen's boots.

The flames on the sword leaped. I jumped back.

"I don't answer to you."

Brock took a step toward him, a fiendish smile on his face. "No, but I bet the queen would be interested in hearing about the odd feelings I've felt from her," he nodded to me. "And your change of heart."

I stiffened.

Aspen, an inch taller, met Brock boot to boot, sneering down at the old male. "Will that be before or after I show the queen the tip of her ear?"

Brock sent me a murderous look. "The queen said, mostly intact. She'll end up torn apart, regardless."

Aspen corralled him in with a hand, jerking his face. "And I told you completely intact. Touch her, and next time, I won't hit you with just my skin. Now go get the demons and the rest of our stuff." He shoved Brock away, waited till he left, and limped over to his dimming sword.

"Come on, we're not far now," he said, pulling up the intricate metal. His hand brushed against my palm as he passed me, sending tingles shooting up my arm. "Not getting any younger," he called when I still didn't move.

"You're technically not young at all," I yelled back.

He laughed. My heart revolted in the best way.

"By angel standards, I am. Now come on, sweetheart."

I turned to face his back, keeping my feet planted. "Why do you call me that?"

He stopped. "Because I want to."

"Do you call all your *assets,* sweetheart?"

A heatwave rustled the hair around my cheek as I waited for him to answer. He refused to turn around and meet my gaze, so I drilled holes into his cloaked back. The same cloak he swaddled me in at Hana's and used to cover me after the Tusoteuthis attack, calming me with his touches and sewing up my legs. *Why was he so contradictory? Was it all for his queen?*

"No, just you." His three words carried on an air of breath, floating to my ears and stabbing a resurfacing ache.

"Well, stop," I said, finally following him.

We walked in tense silence. I distracted myself by analyzing the unique bushes. Their blue-tipped spikes jutted into our path, looking ready to stab anyone who dared to touch their velvety blue leaves.

"They're Blue Morsus bushes, lined with microscopic bumps that will cut you and burrow into your skin. They slow an angel's healing process."

I veered to the center of the road and thought I heard a chuckle.

Eventually, the feeling of being cooked in an oven lessoned.

"We're close."

Goosebumps rose along my arms. "To the boundary line?"

"Yes, we'll make camp tonight and be there by late morning."

The tension withdrew from my shoulders. I still had one more night.

"I'm sorry, Lucille."

I stopped, utterly stunned. Never in my wildest imaginings did I believe sorry was in his vocabulary. He turned around, and I swore if I were still moving, I would've tripped over my feet at the openness that lay in his eyes and the sorrow bleeding through our bond.

"I'm sorry for—"

"Stop."

He took a step toward me. "Luc—"

"Stop apologizing for something you could change!" I snapped, putting distance between us. He followed me until the strides of his legs gained on mine, and he grasped my elbows. The moment he touched me, I lost it.

"I do not want your moon. I do not want your slivers. I want *nothing* from you. In one moment, you trick me with your sweet little words and actions, then the next, you call me names and let Brock abuse me. My guardian?" I scoffed. "We may have a bond, but you are no guardian."

His face paled, and I saw and felt a split second of guilt and horror wedge between the indifferent mask he was trying so hard to put back on.

I tried to wrench out of his grip and away from the feelings that had infiltrated my mind at his touch. He soothed something in me, something I thought only my mom could do. But his touch was a lie. Everything was.

"You'd think a guardian would be someone who risked everything to keep the other person safe. Everything." I spat. "If anyone was ever my guardian, it was my mom." An ache traveled up my throat, and dammit, I didn't want to cry in front of him. "But someone took that from me. And now you're taking the rest." This time, when I yanked on my arms, he let me go. "Your apologies are worthless when you are in control of my freedom or my death."

His chin erupted in a deep red light, and his lips flattened.

"My queen wants you. I am loyal to her."

I took in the twitch in his eye, the red glow beneath his chin, avoiding his plush pink lips. "Why? Why are you loyal? What could she possibly give you? Is it just because she's your mom?"

The exuding red light flashed off for a moment as agony tore into his eyes and through me.

Did the red light somehow affect our bond? Was that why I only got blips of his emotions at random times?

"She's not my mom," he said, jaw fluttering as he gripped his sword so tightly I thought his knuckles might pop out. But the unending pain and guilt making his eyes glassy vanished as his scar illuminated. "I am loyal to my queen."

"So, you're blindly loyal?"

"No!"

"Then what? Does she have your mom?" Because the pain and guilt I could taste coming off him was a lot like how Oliver was talking about his sister.

"No, she doesn't." He took a step forward, eyes lit up with softly repressed rage, and I, for once, held my ground.

"Does someone else have your mom?"

"No."

Why was I even trying to figure this out? The damage was already done. But I stared at the flickering light beneath his chin.

"Why does your scar keep glowing?" I asked.

"What?"

Against my better judgment, I placed my thumb over his scar. It zapped me on contact, and he flinched. But the glow receded.

Going off a hunch, I met the hovering flames in his gaze and asked, "What happened to your mom?"

His face dropped as a sickly color washed away the rosy pink of his cheeks. Agony and guilt reared their heartbreaking heads, urging me to rub my sternum. "Murdered."

I swallowed back my tears, hating that he confused me so thoroughly. *Why should I care that his mother and first love were murdered? Isn't it what he deserved for what he did to others? To me?* And yet, for some reason, a deep-seated part of me hurt.

"How?"

Aspen's eyes glinted. He knew how she was murdered.

"She—"

The scar zapped me as he fought to get the words out.

"Lili—" He tensed.

"How Aspen?"

"Lilith!" he seethed as the scar sent a bolt of searing pain into my thumb and up my arm. I gasped, letting go.

"Who's Lilith?"

He straightened, composed his face, and stepped back. "I am loyal to my queen."

I panned between his face and the thing beneath his chin. Goosebumps danced along my spine at whatever the hell that was. It controlled him and what I could feel from him. He didn't know it. He thought it was a scar.

"Who's Lilith? She murdered your mother?" I asked again.

Aspen didn't respond.

But how much did it control him? And why did it fade sometimes but not others? Before I could ask questions or test my theories, clip-clopping and rolling wheels invaded our moment.

We climbed in the back next to Cacus and Bael, who were crunching on—I didn't want to know.

I sat away from them, glancing at Aspen's chin as he rested his head against the carriage wall. Then, I took in the rest of him, finding glistening red on his leg.

"You're bleeding," I said, keeping any traitorous concern out of my voice.

He grunted.

"So, you're not going to do anything about your leg?"

Aspen side-eyed me. Any lingering tension from our heated exchange was safely shut away, forgotten, or ignored. *How was it so easy for him? Did our conversation blip out of his mind, or did the scar force away his emotions?*

"It'll heal," he said, taking me out of my puzzling thoughts. "Just like your ribs, wrist, neck, finger, and ear have."

He was paying close attention.

I raised my finger to my ear, finding smooth skin.

"We heal fast, Lucille."

"Can you at least put a cloth to it?"

The corner of his lip twitched. "Sure." He did, up until the carriage stopped.

I climbed out, eyeing Aspen as he winced jumping to the ground. I winced with him. So he could bind and tend to my wounds, but not his own. I shook my head and grabbed my blankets from the back to set up my bed. It was best to keep up pretenses.

Brock, swollen and bruised, set up a fire as he shot me glares where I rested on my blankets. Aspen skinned the meat Cacus and Bael caught. It still surprised me they could catch anything without shoving it down their giant gullets.

When the meat was ready, Aspen limped over with a plate. I peered up at him from under my lashes, the heat of the fire blocked by his body.

"Heals fast?"

"It was deep. It won't heal in a couple hours, Lucille," he said, exasperated.

"So, sew it up."

He handed me the plate of squirrel and ignored my comment. I grabbed it, but he wouldn't let go when I tugged. Masked by the shadows, I couldn't see his expression. I dropped my chin to the plate, hoping he'd get the message, and instantly regretted it.

Buttons.

Buttons I ravenously wanted open hours ago stared at me. They were barely visible, but I could still see their silver outlines. My cheeks flushed as an unwelcome shot of desire hit me, along with the mortification of the direction of my dirty thoughts. I looked back up at Aspen, palms slick against the warm metal in my hands.

"Scared, Lucille?" he mocked.

"Only of the truth," I whispered. *What would I do with the unwanted attraction I had for him if somehow he wasn't the reason behind all his terrible actions? Would it change anything for me?*

I didn't know, and that scared me more than if I did.

He stumbled back, letting go of my plate as if he could read those thoughts in my eyes.

We all ate silently, one of us glaring, one of us staring, and me questioning.

When night fell, there was no king.

CHAPTER TWENTY-FIVE

My head whipped to the side, forcing me to look at the vanity mirror and the angry hand mark on my cheek. I stared at my young reflection and the wobble in my lip, knowing I didn't want to witness this memory, but my dream-walks were the best way to fix my memory loss.

"YOU ARE A DAUGHTER of an Archangel. I will not see you behave this way; do you understand me?" His eyes glowed white.

It always seemed like Dad was mad at me. *But why?*

I nodded, trying to choke back tears. Dad hated tears. They'd only make him angrier.

He inhaled a long breath and blew it out, eyes returning to their normal gray.

Dad's eyes, right after they lost their white glow, were the worst. The first time, a couple of birthdays ago, I thought it meant he was happy again. I thought it meant the storm was over. He'd smack me and then hug me. I learned how to hold in my tears, and it was okay. But then, something changed, and the smacking wasn't enough.

"I'm sorry. Sometimes my temper gets the better of me; come here," he motioned with his hands.

I paused, looking up at him. *I won't cry. I won't cry. I won't cry.*

"Come here. Don't be a wimp. It's fine," he insisted.

He was my dad—or father. That was what he liked to be called now, no longer daddy or dad. Those words got me hit. Now it was father.

But in my head, I called him Dad.

I walked into his arms. My head rested against his stomach, wrapping around his waist. I let a couple of tears leak out onto his shirt, fisting my shaking hands into the fabric. But the hug didn't stop the sliding noise. My tears turned to quiet streams.

"Why, Dad? I was only playing. I didn't mean to let my light shine through. It only hurt him a little." I pulled out of his arms, picked up Thumper, the stuffed animal rabbit, and shoved him into his face. Plastic black pieces speckled Thumper's head where his ear used to be.

Smack!

My stinging face pressed into the fur of Thumper, hiding the leaky tears and snot from my dad. Needles prickled my skin, pushing out at my tiny body. Tears came faster from the achy feeling.

Don't let it show. Don't be a wimp. Maybe he won't use it.

"Remember what we said about the word dad? You're older now—none of that. Now, don't be a wimp; turn around and lift your shirt. You know what I said about your powers last time this happened."

I didn't want to turn. But I didn't want to be a wimp either. Hugging Thumper, I stared down at my dad's white shoes. Maybe he'd let it go. Maybe he could just hug me again.

"Turn Lucille, or there will be more than one this time."

The feeling under my skin increased along with my tears. *Don't show it. Don't be a wimp.*

I turned. *I wasn't a wimp.*

"Put your bunny in your mouth. Remember, no noise unless you desire your mother's anger. Then you'll never see me again."

Bunny to my mouth, sniffling, I nodded. I didn't want my dad never to come back. I wanted him to love me like Mom did. But he was always mad at me, and I think that was why he left us for so long. Mom was never mad at me. She always told me how proud she was of me. But I didn't want her to leave, too. So I bit Thumper and made sure to clench hard enough no noise would come out for her to hear.

I bit into Thumper with all my strength. When he pressed the buzzing knife in harder, sliding it down my skin, I couldn't hold back my scream. I couldn't help being a wimp. It hurt. So much.

I stared with blurry eyes at my purple bed and the other stuffed animals next to my pillows. Their fuzziness looked like home. I wanted to curl up and cry in them.

Once the knife stopped making its line, Dad cleaned up the sliding warmth and bandaged it like last time.

"Now, we won't tell your mother about this. She wouldn't be happy with you. Tomorrow, it will be healed, and you can take your bandage off."

My pink floral shirt dropped back into place, and I turned, nodding into Thumper.

"Wipe those tears. We don't want helpless wimps in this household."

I sniffled once more and drug my fisted hand across my face, still staring at my dad's shoes.

The door opened. "There you are, my darlings," a pleasant voice said from the hall.

I turned to the voice of my mom.

"Oh, sweetheart, what happened?" She came and knelt next to me, holding my chin. Her hand pushed away my wavy hair, looking at me with concern. I looked up at my dad. He raised his eyebrow in expectation.

Swallowing, "I—I was playing and fell off my bed," I mumbled.

"Hmm. Next time we need to be more careful, okay, baby? But look, it's already healing up nicely. The redness is almost gone." My mom tenderly touched my cheek, replacing the sting with a sense of calm.

"Do you want to give Dad a hug before he leaves for a while?" she asked.

I didn't want to. But Mom was right. I wouldn't see him until next year on my birthday. He was my dad, after all, and I still loved him even if he hurt me. I wasn't a wimp. Turning, I swallowed and then hugged him. His fingers pressed into my bandage.

A chill infiltrated my mind, blurring the dream-walk and taking me out of the memory of past me and my *father,* if that was what you'd call the abusive bastard. At least now I knew where my scars came from. The coldness steadily increased to the point of pain.

I jolted awake, clutching my throbbing head as my teeth chattered. The king *finally* arrived.

You fell asleep, and I couldn't find you in your dreams.

I held my head tighter. By the sound of his voice and the intensity of the chill in my brain, he wasn't thrilled.

Could you possibly bring down the sub-zero temperatures? I asked as I shivered.

Tiny embers glowed in the fire pit, giving only a little light in the pitch black. A couple of feet away, Brock was little more than a faint outline.

I needed to wake you up.

I'm awake. Now what?

Now, things become a tad chillier. Laughter and delight lightened the irritation in his voice.

What the heavenly hell does that mean? If things got any colder, I might pass out from hypothermia.

My sweet Lucille, it is time you realize you possess more than your Glory in that scrawny body of yours.

Scrawny? I glared inside my head.

He laughed.

I know I have more than my Glory, I snapped.

But what were my dark flames? Between the itch, different melodies, wanting to kill, ice, seduction, and black flames—I had no idea what they were.

Black flames? he asked with a smile.

Get out of my thoughts! I yelled.

The temperature dropped. *Careful.*

Goosebumps crawled along my spine from his deadly tone.

Have you frozen things?

No. I was being a brat.

I don't appreciate lies. You are wasting time.

You can read my mind; can't you just figure it out?

I am only aware of the thoughts that occupy the forefront of your mind, provided they linger long enough for me to discern them.

Maybe you need to discern faster then.

You want to escape and find your mom? he threatened.

That got my attention. *Fine, yeah, I have.*

Good, he emphasized by dropping the temperature further.

I don't like this. My thoughts chattered like they would if I said it out loud. Since he knew what was at the *forefront* of my mind, I knew he knew exactly what I was talking about.

Don't test me, Lucille. Later, you can learn how to build barriers, but now, you need to stand, he commanded.

I slowly stood and peered around for Aspen, ensuring Brock didn't wake.

Walk to the carriage.

I held my hands out and shuffled to the wooden box on wheels. At the driver's seat railing, I waited for the next direction.

Hello? I asked, standing as still as possible while my nerves were jumping out of control.

How did you freeze things?

Most of the time, my anger prompted it to come out. But I've gained some control.

He chuckled, low and deep. *Interesting. Bring it forth.*

How is this going to help me escape?

Do it.

I sighed. *Okay, but it may take me a second.*

Closing my eyes, I dove to the center of my core, finding the writhing mass of dark energy. At my presence, it perked up, humming with anticipation. I grabbed the mass and tried to force it to the surface. It moved, but slowly. *Come on.*

It'll be easier if you don't force it. Your Infernus is like your thoughts. They come to you naturally. You don't need to force yourself to think because your mind is ready to help and work for you. Your Infernus is the same. It wants to work for you. Give it your intentions, and let it flow like your thoughts do. Stop forcing it.

At the word *Infernus*, I lost my grasp on my power. *That's what it's called?*

Yes. Now, bring it forth.

One of the horses tethered to a tree snorted, making me jerk. My ankles gave a slight jingle. Shit. I needed to get these cuffs off me.

Cuffs? he said, oh so very slowly. *What. Cuffs?*

I swallowed. *The ones around my ankles. They stop my Glory—*

A sudden ice storm raged in my head. I yelped.

Ember Manacles. That's a problem. Fortunately, they don't block your Infernus, only angelic power. But you needed to be able to run.

I have a bobby pin; I can unlock them quickly.

Ember Manacles can only be unlocked by one key. They are spelled to resist tampering.

Shit.

We'll have to make do. Bring forth your Infernus.

"What are you doing?"

I whipped around to find Aspen standing behind me. *How didn't you know Aspen was there?*

I only know and see what you do. Clearly.

"Lucille, what are you doing by the carriage?" Aspen demanded, stepping closer. The moonless night masked everything but his soft, glowing eyes.

What should I do?

A long breath of cold air somehow tickled the hairs on the nape of my neck. *Let your power flow, then touch him.*

What? I think my brain short-circuited.

Do it.

I dove into my core, and instead of forcing the whirling mass of energy to the surface, I relaxed into it and shared my wants. Eager itches rushed to the surface of my skin, then settled when the purple flame covered my hands.

"Lucille?"

I'm going to help you with the rest. Touch him.

A gale-forced wind of ice made every hair on my skin stand erect. The ice pushed and pulled, coalescing in the back of my mind. But rather than experiencing the frigid temps, it was only slightly cool, feeling more like pressure than anything. The tidal wave of pressure gathered strength.

"What are you—"

Touch him now!

Startled, I reached out to Aspen, gripping his biceps. The tidal wave crashed. I screamed. White stars disrupted my vision. As the stars cleared, the pressure eased. I opened my heavy eyes.

Ice attached me to Aspen's fully encased body.

I stumbled back, skin ripping from my hands. Numb, the stinging I should've felt got lost in the horror of what I'd done.

He couldn't breathe in there. He'd die like Marcus's soldiers.

I panicked. Nausea pushed at my gag reflex. *No, no, no, I didn't want to kill him.* I covered my mouth, about to be sick.

Run!

I—but Aspen—

His ice-covered body turned blue, intensifying, and reflecting prisms of light through the crystal casing.

Relief gave me breath before reality decided to take it.

Run! The male said, his words weak with strain.

I moved, tripping over my chains, and managed a pitiful shuffle-jog as I stumbled over every root and rock.

To the right. Now your left, he yelled, directing me in the dark.

I followed his every word, missing the silhouettes of trees by mere inches. There was no time to doubt. Trusting the Drune and this male, I emptied my mind and solely focused on his directions.

"Jump."

CHAPTER TWENTY-SIX

My feet tangled together, chains wrapping and clanging against the stone slab. I fell stomach first, skidding across the ground, stopping with my head just over the ledge, tender palms burning from the scraping grit.

I heaved a strangled breath.

"JUMP? JUMP?"

Dirt continued to rain down on the shadows below. The tinkling joined the sound of moving water hidden by the lightless night.

The prince won't stay solid for long. Stand up and jump!

Relief penetrated my achy heart once again. I didn't kill him. He was alive.

Yes. He's unfortunately alive. I can't kill unless I am present or am able to infiltrate their mind.

I couldn't control the worry that manifested from his words. He had infiltrated my mind.

I have. Now jump! He expected to be obeyed.

Go to hell! I snapped back and shivered as the temperature dropped.

Do not speak to me in such a way. Jump.

Grimacing, hands raw but healing, I stood. Dirt spilled into the black pit as I toed the ledge of the open space. Butterflies committed suicide against my stomach. I didn't want to die.

You'd choose death over what the Mother of Demons will do to you if the prince catches up?

The wind whipped my black waves. I stepped closer to the unseeable waters, digging my toes into my boots as if to puncture through and claw into the ground to keep me here.

What about Brock?

He's not an issue right now. Stop stalling. The prince will be coming, and I'm losing my patience.

This was for her. I couldn't stop now. My unmoving legs didn't agree. But I'd be free to find her. That was worth it, right? Unless I went splat on a boulder, or another monster squid attacked me. Yeah, this wasn't working. I'd never jump if I continued down that thought path.

Jump!

Please, say it one more time. It worked so well the first few tries.

Watch it.

Don't intrude on thoughts you don't like, and I would.

When you jump, do not under any circumstance take in any water.

What's wrong with the water?

Something rustled in the background. I whipped around. Spindly black shadows rested against a blacker background. No one was there.

Do you want to be a prisoner again?

Of course not.

Then jump! His voice shot an ice spear into my mind, sending the chilling command all the way to my legs.

I leaped into the abyss, plummeting with my stomach pushing into my throat.

"Lucille!" Aspen boomed.

His raging voice followed me as I dropped, increasing my nerves. Boots first, I struck the river, jolting my spine and submerging into ungodly frigid water. My yelp bounced off my clenched lips, getting lost in the rush of water flooding my ears.

Underwater, screaming into my closed mouth, my limbs struggled to move. It took the entirety of my focus to lift my arms. Stroke after heavy stroke, I breached the surface, gasping.

This is what you wanted me to jump into?

Stop whining and swim.

He wanted me to swim when every brain cell worked overtime to keep my head above water. Shaking, I lifted my ten-pound arm to wipe away lingering droplets. This was insane. And I wasn't even including the ankle cuffs restricting my movements.

Swim!

How?

Aspen splashed in behind me.

Shit.

Lucille, swim!

I whimpered with my first arm swing. Who cared if I sounded like a baby? Liquid ice lapped at my body, leaching off my warmth. Each stroke moved me a couple of inches, if that. My only saving grace was the current helping to push along my feeble attempts.

The moisture in my nose burned. Not an, it's freezing out burn, but more like a gaseous acid eroded my nose hairs burn. Plus, it smelled like bleach and rotting vegetables.

What is that smell?

Vibrations tickled my mind with his creepy laughter. *You don't want to know. Just keep the water from your mouth and nose.*

I'm pretty sure it's already in my nose.

Then let's hope you don't die.

My stroking arm paused. *That's not funny.*

I wasn't laughing.

No, he wasn't. Not anymore.

What's wrong with this river?

It has a dark history. Very dark.

And what? It's poisonous?

There was a gesture in my head equivalent to a shrug. I didn't know how to process the nonchalance.

No history lessons today, my sweet Lucille. I'll give you your answers if you survive this.

My teeth chattered together. *You better. And why do you call me that?*

I can call you whatever I like. Now swim. The prince is catching up.

I had no energy to snap back, plus he was right. In an aura of blue light, Aspen swam behind me like this was his morning routine.

Why? I groaned.

I can help slow him down, but you must swim as fast as you can.

My palms pounded through the water, splashing with frustration. I already was! A drop of water landed on my lip, and I quickly let go of my irritation, changing my stroke. When I thought it couldn't get any worse, the water became colder, and so did my head. Too painful to fully extend my arm, my swimming turned into smaller doggy paddles.

Don't stop!

"I'm trying not to," I breathed. Sparing a moment, I peeked behind me. Light surrounded Aspen, bright in the pitch dark, reflecting off a white surface.

I snorted in disbelief. "You have got to be kidding me."

Layers of ice spread, holding Aspen in place for only long enough for him to flash with blue flames. Each time, the layer of ice grew thicker, taking him longer to melt through. It slowed him but didn't stop him.

"Lucille! Swim to me!" Aspen yelled.

Like hell, if I didn't move any faster, I'd become a Lucille-sized ice cube sinking to the bottom of this poisonous river. My hands and feet already cried out for help, and if my limbs reached that point, well, I'd neither be a prisoner anymore nor a daughter.

Maybe I would die.

Do you always give up so easily? Is that who you are at your core? he asked, voice strained.

Who said I'm giving up? I snapped. It wasn't my fault the icy river stole my breath and energy.

You haven't touched your Infernus. You haven't even tried to fight against the cold. You're just whining and taking it like you've been doing since the moment they captured you!

How can my Infernus help with his? I yelled at his sneering, judgmental tone.

If you can manage to surround your entire body in flame, you'll be immune to the cold, just like you were immune to my power when I froze the prince.

I slammed my fist into the water. *You could've said that in the beginning!*

Yes, I could've. But there is a reason for everything I say or don't say. Like the fact I never told you, you were jumping into a river that kills 99 percent of the creatures who touch it. You're definitely naive. But that's easily remedied. I can give you all the information you need. What's not easily remedied is your will. Remember who I said I was looking for? It wasn't the whiny, weak female. It was the one with a backbone who was willing to do whatever it took to survive. Show me you're a fighter.

I'm sorry. What the actual *hell? 99 percent of creatures? I'm going to die?*

I don't know, my sweet Lucille. You tell me? Who are you at your core? His frigid claws raked down the muscles of my mind. I tensed at the sharp sting and dove into my Infernus. Listening to my desires, it spread into my head and hands. Flames erupted on my skin, returning sensation to my fingers and shoving at the icy claw gripping my mind.

Who the hell are you? He knew stuff about me and my mom, or at least thought he did. He definitely knew things about Elora and the creatures who lived here. So, who was this king the Drune told me to listen to?

"Lucille!" Aspen sounded closer.

I'll tell you everything I know, but only if you survive this. He was dead serious. There wasn't an ounce of guilt in his tone for the fact he sent me into a river that killed almost everyone.

Have you found my mom yet? I let my Infernus spread from my hands to my neck and down to my toes, warming every inch of me.

Who are you at your core, Lucille? Where does your Infernus come from? he asked, ignoring my very important question.

Why don't you tell me, king? I glared into my mind. *Then answer my question.*

Prove to me that you aren't some weak-willed, naive wimp, and I will.

Am I not already? My Infernus covered my entire body, and my strokes eased through the deadly water.

Maybe. He smiled. I couldn't see it, but I could feel the smug, conniving little thing.

"Lucille!" Aspen bellowed once more.

But I didn't care or take the time to think about the waver in his voice as it got lost in the resonating crash of ice filling my ears.

Swim faster, he said, voice even weaker than before.

I did, but not because he said to. The flashing continued behind me, picking up speed. Aspen melted the ice faster than the male in my head froze it. With only meters away, he gained a lot of ground in my silent argument with the intruder king. I pumped my arms faster.

"Lucille! Please. Please stop," Aspen begged. It was almost like he was scared.

He is. Keep moving, the king said, no longer using his claws or insults to get under my skin.

Does he know about the river?

Yes.

Then why'd he jump in after me? He could *die.*

I have a suspicion he may be a part of the one percent.

I stilled, staring over my shoulder at the blue-hued prince struggleing against the ice. A red light glowed within the blue flames. Did he risk his life for me or for his queen?

Why would a scar pulse with a red light? I asked.

Did you say red? His slow rage attempted to steal the warmth of my Infernus.

Yes.

It's a hell rune.

What does it do?

Precisely what you've guessed, it controls the wearer in any way the carver decides. The rune is rare. Not only does it take immense power to carve with it, but unlike angelic runes that can only be carved from Archangel feathers, a hell rune can only be carved with one specific feather.

Whose? Who did that to him?

They're not one and the same.

Explain, I demanded, looking at Aspen pounding his glowing fists into the thickening ice, trying his damnedest to rescue me.

Or to claim me.

Drop the tone and swim out. Then I'll give you answers.

And my mom?

Silence.

You don't know where she is yet.

Stubborn, treading water as I stared at Aspen, my heart pounded with a crackling anger. I hadn't reached the right memory of my mom to find her. But I knew Magda had what I needed. The king may have helped me escape, but I came here for one thing, and if he couldn't give me those answers, give me my mom, then this may be the end of the road for us.

Don't you dare. I have what you want without risking your life for that witch's words. But only if you swim to that bank, Lucille.

I despised how he thought he could control me with his threats almost as much as I despised my warring feelings holding me in place as I watched Aspen.

Do you genuinely care so little about yourself that you'd risk your life for his?

No. But it was a lie, especially when his blue flames flickered, and the swing of his arms slowed.

I said leave him!

I've decided to stop listening to voices in my head and letting them dictate my life. Melt the ice.

No. The vicious snap of his denial sent another layer of ice toward Aspen. His dangerous flames vanished.

That pissed me off.

I said melt the ice!

You do not order me around. I am trying to save your life.

And I'm trying to save his.

You will not.

Well, it seemed the king and I had something in common. We both hated being ordered around.

My Infernus could create ice, but that wasn't all it could do. It also had vicious, hot black flames. I dove deep into my power, finding the dark black cords, and strummed the tune of my desires. A haunting melody whispered in my ear, changing my purple flame to black.

The circle of water surrounding Aspen crept toward him as his body dropped lower in the water. He was going to drown.

I swam toward the ice with everything I had, even as the ebony flames sapped my energy.

You're not strong enough to hold them. Let it go.

I ignored him, having no patience to listen to reason.

Aspen's head dropped beneath the water. I touched the ice, and my black flames ate little chunks here and there.

"Come on!" I screamed, letting the music wash over me.

It ate faster, but the creeping weight of sand filled my feet.

You won't reach him in time.

Then melt the ice!

My Infernus devoured the cold, reflective surface. Only a few more feet and it'd reach Aspen.

As my hands grew heavy, I knew I didn't have long before the rest of my body would give out. But then all the ice vanished.

Hurry, he seethed.

The music's addictive melody begged to stay, but with Aspen sinking in the poisonous water, I let my power go and dove.

Keeping my mouth closed, I wrapped my arm around Aspen and struggled to the surface. When we broke through, I gasped a lungful of air and swam with his dead weight.

There's a bank up ahead. Swim to it before you both freeze.

He didn't sound happy. But I didn't care.

I doggy-paddled through the poisonous water, refusing to stop or think about Aspen's lack of rising chest. When I rounded the bend in the river, barely holding our heads above water, my numb feet hit the sand. I dragged us the rest of the way to the bank and heaved Aspen across pebbles until my body gave out, and I flopped next to him.

Let him die.

Don't say pointless shit. It downgrades your intelligence, king.

He dragged an ice claw across my mind, and I cringed. Refraining from cussing him out, I felt for Aspen's pulse.

He didn't have one.

Do you think he has the water in his lungs?

I hope so.

My vision dotted as I stared at Aspen's lips.

Your powers are about to claim the price of their services.

He was right. Without another thought, I placed my lips to Aspen's, ignoring the rancid taste of the water, ignoring the horrifying lack of tingles, and breathed for him.

I gave him the last of my strength as I pumped his chest, gave him the fate of my life as I tasted the poisonous water, wondering if I was too late. I gave him every last ounce of myself, not even knowing why. And when he finally coughed up water, rolling over to puke it up, the weight in my body took its claim.

I fell forward, slamming my cheek into damp rocks. Aspen's soft rasp and the king's disapproval slithered into my head before darkness claimed me.

"Why, Lucille?"

Stupid female. How will you escape now?

CHAPTER TWENTY-SEVEN

A shiver woke me up to a muddy puddle. Dazed and drenched, I felt something shift when I sat up to scan my surroundings.

A black cloak blanketed me, but that wasn't as surprising as the comforting, warm weight of Aspen's arm latched around my hip.

He seemed dead beside me despite the warmth of his body. I pressed two fingers into his neck, relieved to feel the tingles and his pulse.

Well, I'm glad to see he hasn't taken you to his kingdom yet.

I started at the chilling voice.

Were you waiting around until I woke up?

Yes.

Why?

To do this.

Before I even assumed what that meant, a wave of agonizing icy power slammed through me and into Aspen. I screamed and forced my Infernus to the surface. The pain ceased, but the damage was already done by the time I recovered and jerked my fingers back. Ice layered Aspen's body again.

Why the hell did you do that?

It needed to be done, he said weakly. *He survived the waters like you. After he heals, he will wake up and take you to his queen. I can't have that.*

Why? Why am I so important to you?

Go North, and I'll help you find your mom and give you answers, he said, voice and chill fading.

Great. I couldn't even ask him which way was North. Not that it mattered. I wasn't going North. I was going to find Magda.

With one last glance and doubtful thought, I wiggled out from under Aspen's iced-over arm and placed his cloak back over him. Knowing he'd live, I dragged myself away and into the forest.

The loud swooshing of my feet jammed into the stillness. I needed to lift them. But between my difficulty seeing and lingering exhaustion, I couldn't seem to care enough. What minuscule energy I gained from my drain nap revolted against my movement. That was the second time I drained myself into passing out. *How long would it take me to drain myself to the point of death?*

I sighed. It didn't matter right now.

Eventually, dried bark turned to wet moss. It squished into my hands each time I steadied myself. When a uniquely unpleasant smell overpowered the scent of my wet clothes, I knew I entered Drune Forest.

A delirious part of me hoped to stumble upon a Drune so it could point me in the right direction, and another part wanted to sleep more. Yet, the only part I listened to was the one that moved my fifty-pound feet, eyes glazed over, half paying attention to my surroundings for what seemed like forever.

Sometime later, my knees gave out. I fell flat into a moist pile of moss, missing a protruding root. Splaying my hands, I planned to push myself off the ground. That plan backfired when the sweet bliss of sleep took over.

I WASN'T IN MY body. Either that or I grew a bulge where I knew, for a fact, I did *not* have a bulge before this. But as my fingers adjusted my relatively small situation in my nether regions, and I glanced at the flat expanse of my chest out of the corner of my purple-hued vision, I knew I was in a dream-walk. Although, as my scrawny arm scratched my tiny balls, I think I preferred invading my own body.

A door slammed, jerking my hand away from my crotch. *Males.* I took in my surroundings as much as possible without controlling this young boy's head while he rose off the gaudy red settee.

We stood in a jewel-toned sitting area filled with golden ornamentation and fancy wallpaper. The only piece of furniture without patterns was the coffee table in front of us, holding a stack of books and a pile of marbles. I couldn't decide if the flamboyant room was a poor style choice or if my dream transported me to the Victorian era.

"Mom! Someone's here," he called out. I winced, not liking the vibrations of the little boy's voice in my head. *In his head? In our head?* This trapped in not your own body experience seemed more straightforward with Aspen. But I rather invade my own body. Then, I didn't have to contend with two sets of emotions.

Two purposeful sets of shoes click-clacked against the hardwood floors on the other side of the walls. An older blonde female entered the room, rubbing her hands on a towel and giving us a curious look.

"I wasn't expecting anyone," his mom said as another set of shoes rushed down the hall and into the room.

A dark-haired female stood in the doorway, panicked. An unusual white suit with buckles and sheaths hugged her body. She clutched the hand of a young boy in plain black pants and a grey shirt. They both had short dark hair, vibrant blue eyes, and a similar bone structure.

The blonde dropped her towel, face pale. "No, you need to go!" she said, pointing at the dark-haired lady.

Confusion that wasn't my own wedged in between my curiosity and apprehension.

Trapped, I watched the dark-haired female storm toward the blonde, leaving the dark-haired boy in the doorway. We stared at each other, neither moving from our spots. Or, more accurately, the dark-haired boy stared at the boy whose body I invaded.

"Emily, you don't understand."

"I understand just fine!" Emily pointed at me, then gestured to another gaudy red chair in the corner where a little girl with ebony hair slept cuddling a porcelain doll.

The dark-haired female shook her head. "I know since you're human, you never wanted this to be the safe house for our children. But—"

"No buts, Miriam! How am I supposed to protect them like this?" Emily gestured to her petite frame, clothed in a blush dress—the opposite of Miriam's lethal attire.

Our concern spiked. We walked to her, side-stepping the other female, and grasped her hand.

"The safe house doesn't matter anymore," Miriam said. "Originally, my son and I came here for that, but I had a vision at your front door. They know. Someone sold us out."

We stared at Miriam's panicked face. A navy ring circled her pupil, butting against the vibrant blue. She wasn't human. But without the tell-tale purple ring, I didn't know what she was.

Her panicked eyes peered down at us.

Hello, Oliver.

We jerked. Her eyes drilled into his soul, and her brows lowered with her lips.

Hello, Lucille.

Her lips never moved, but her voice was clear as day. The boy's shock and confusion amplified my own. I was not expecting to hear words in this head, or that name, or my name. We shifted our attention to Emily, eyes wide. She looked ready to faint.

"Mom?" We squeezed Emily's hand.

Frozen stiff with horror, she stared at the sleeping form of the tiny ebony-haired girl.

Miriam touched Emily's shoulder. "I'll stay with our children while you pack a bag. But make it quick. I don't know how much time we have."

Emily nodded, unable to speak. She released our hand, and someone banged on a door.

We all jumped. The chandelier above the coffee table shook. The dark-haired boy scurried into Miriam's arms, and the little girl woke up.

"Mama?" she said, sitting up with her doll.

"We're too late," Miriam whispered, tightening her grip on her son.

Emily ran to her daughter, pulling her off the couch. "We can go out the back!"

But before anyone could move, an explosion shook the house, sending us to the red-carpeted floor. Miriam covered Oliver and her son from the raining debris, while Emily covered her daughter. We coughed into our arm as Miriam pulled us up, dragging us into an antique kitchen.

"Get to the hall. We'll run out the back." Emily nodded to a doorway on the other side of the kitchen.

We ran behind Miriam, following her down a long hallway, and smashed into her back as she stopped. Peering around her, we found my worst nightmare stepping through the back door.

Marcus was here. And if the body I invaded belonged to back-stabbing, jokester *Oliver*, and we were with his sister and mother...

This was about to be another tragic dream I wanted no part of.

"Well, I just love it when things are made easy for us," he laughed.

Miriam pulled her son behind her and backed us up.

"We're surrounded," Emily said.

Oliver gazed behind us to the exploded foyer and back at Marcus.

Figures covered in blood-red leather crowded into both sides of the hallway. Emblems of different colors decorated their chests.

Marcus prowled closer. A pulse resonated the air, and two balls of blinding white light formed in Miriam's hands. She threw one toward his face and the other to the figures behind us. Marcus dodged it, but it didn't stop the balls of light from obliterating two of his armed soldiers—no blood, no flesh bits, no ash. They were just gone.

Our eyes widened.

Miriam formed two more balls of light. The color reminded me of my Glory, only brighter and hotter, and the core appeared blue. She flung it at Marcus's chest, but again, he dodged it, and two more soldiers died.

"I can do this all day, darling," he smirked beneath his hat.

Miriam didn't rise to his baiting words, throwing ball after ball down each side of the hall until four soldiers remained. Sandwiched between her and Emily, we grabbed our little sister's and Miriam's son's hands.

"Mathew, give some incentive," Marcus said, shrugging his shoulders with nonchalance, unphased by the ball of light that almost singed his cowboy hat.

I didn't know what that meant, but I found out real quick when Emily screamed and collapsed to the floor.

"Emily!" Miriam yelled, turning to throw both balls of light at the two remaining soldiers behind us.

"Mom!" Oliver scrambled to her side, horrified by the two knives protruding from her stomach.

That was all Marcus needed—a split second of distraction.

Miriam shrieked, and something sizzled.

We whipped our head around. Marcus latched onto her wrist as deep red shadows seeped from his glowing marks and devoured the flesh on Miriam's arm—inch by inch. The sight of her bloody bones and the smell of her burning muscles turned Oliver's stomach.

The air pulsed, and a blue ball of fire formed in Miriam's hand. Sweat slicked our arms from the uncomfortable heat. But before she could smash it into Marcus's face, it fizzled.

"Having issues?" Marcus taunted.

"No!" she screamed, pulling a knife from one of her many sheaths. It plunged toward his side. He clawed into her burning flesh, pulling her forward. She cried out but managed to stab the horrid male in the leg.

"Bitch!" Marcus seethed, stumbling back.

Miriam unsheathed another dagger, holding it out as her half-eaten arm dangled by her side.

"You'll pay for that," he said, forming another cloud of red smoke between his hands.

Miriam retreated, Marcus limped forward, and Miriam's son decided to play the hero, positioning himself in front of his mom with clenched fists raised. Beside him, Oliver's sister stood frozen, mere inches from Marcus's swirling red smoke.

We jerked back, nicking our finger on the blade protruding from Oliver's unconscious mom as we applied pressure.

"Melanie!" Oliver whispered.

By the eager gleam in Marcus's eyes, Oliver should've never brought attention to his sister.

The cloud of red split. One went high, the other low.

Time slowed down, and Miriam spoke to me.

Lucille, if you can hear me, if you're in there, save my son. Save them all. You're the key.

I stilled.

Tell your mom I forgive her. And remember, Lucille. Remember, she was only trying to do her best by you.

Then, as if time paused to give Miriam that moment, it sped back up. She grabbed her son and turned them around. The cloud of red hit her back. She arched from the impact of Marcus's power and screamed. Her son stared up at her with watery eyes, watching her agony until she reined it in enough to press a hand to his face and mumble soft words only for him.

I didn't want to be here anymore. I didn't want to watch as a little boy witnessed his mother's death while she held him, and he shed silent streams of tears. *Please, I want to wake up now. Release me.* But my temperamental powers didn't listen to me.

The other cloud came for us. But before it hit, Emily managed to push to her knees and shove Oliver out of the way. Surprised, we fell into the wall, banging our head. Our vision blurred, and our ears rang. Warmth dripped down our forehead as we tilted our head up. Black dots interrupted the picture of Marcus's retreating steps. Blinking, it took us a second to see two little bodies being dragged out of the house.

Miriam's son was knocked unconscious, and Oliver's sister cried in Marcus's arms.

"No! Mom!" Oliver yelled, looking back for help, and froze. "Mom?" His voice broke along with my tender heart. He blinked, unable to comprehend the sight. More than anything, I wished I could control his arms and cover his eyes to shield Oliver from the horrendous sight. Tears helped to blur the two half-eaten bodies. But nothing could stop the sound of the sizzling flesh or the smell of burnt meat and hair.

"MOM!" he wailed, then puked.

I WOKE, GASPING FOR air, and puked into the leaves.

"Oliver was telling the truth."

That didn't make what he did to me okay, and I didn't forgive him for it, but after witnessing and feeling what he went through, I hated him a little less.

What I didn't understand from my dream-walk was how Miriam talked into my mind.

Lucille, if you can hear me, if you're in there, save my son. Save them all. You're the key. Tell your mom I forgive her. And remember, Lucille. Remember, she was only trying to do her best by you.

Invading the body meant I invaded the memory. I didn't give power to the memory for anyone to change it, or that was what the male said. But then how was it possible that Miriam spoke to me? And how could I save her son?

I assumed her son was the boy with her, but I didn't recognize him, and depending on when that memory took place, he could be dead or older.

Save them all? You're the key?

That didn't make sense either. *I could barely save myself, and she was telling me I had to save them all?* Who is *all*?

At least the last part I was doing. I know my mom was only trying to protect me in the only way she knew how. I already forgave her for isolating me and refusing to teach me control.

Sighing, I pushed myself off the wet ground and rubbed at the mud on my face. Everything looked lighter, but I couldn't see the sun as it hid behind the thick foliage.

I stilled.

The sun.

Cursing, I peered around. Trees, dangling moss, and large patches of carpet moss filled my vision. I moved, jangling at a brisk pace. There were no amount of curses I had left at the noise my cuffs made. The king said I couldn't unlock them, but once I found a safe spot to rest, I would try anyway.

I hid behind trees, searching for movement. My ears were useless when it came to Aspen, or the Drunes, for that matter. Both were silent as death. But I figured I'd at least try to sneak, ignoring the fact that I jangled like a dinner bell to anyone in the near vicinity.

After a couple of hours of walking, I sat behind a tree and took out both my bobby pins. I bent one in an "L" shape for the tension wrench and curved the tip of the other to create a small hook. Inserting the tension wrench with one hand and applying rotational pressure, I added the hooked bobby pin and pushed at the pins. When a couple of pins released, I smiled.

"Temper resistant, my ass."

At the final pin, the keyhole flashed, sending a searing heat into the bobby pins. I yelped and coated my fingers in purple flames. But even as my Infernus soothed the searing heat, it did nothing for the melting metal.

I slumped. *Damn.*

Resuming my walk, I stressed over where I was going. A Drune wouldn't be half bad right now, at least to point me in the right direction to Magda's and food for a drop of blood.

At the mere thought of finding food or water, I nearly sent myself into a panic attack. Alone, hungry, and tired, and I had no idea how to hunt or provide for myself. If I found a berry bush, I could pluck some off to eat. That was if Elora even had berry bushes. As for the water, Elora had rivers, but based on the poisonous one I was just in, who knew if they'd be safe to drink? It looked like I was back on the starvation train until I found help.

Foot by foot, tree by tree, I traveled through the Drune Forest with no sightings of Aspen, Brock, or Drunes.

Eventually, the trees widened until they were the width of a small compact car. Unsurprisingly, there was still moss. But this moss was fluorescent orange, swallowing the thick roots that erupted from the ground like tufts of fur. In between the tufts were bright blue mushrooms. But I most enjoyed the little clusters of white flowers blooming in the spaces between each car-sized trunk. Yet, my gaze kept training back on the mushrooms.

Were they edible? Probably not.

With my stomach a twisted mess, energy leaking out of a hole created by the lack of food and water, my thoughts took a dive. I was either about to starve out here, collapse and get eaten by some hellish creature, or collapse and get caught.

With heavy eyes, I paused against a tree to take a break, then jerked back.

It hummed.

I placed my hand back on the rough bark, feeling the vibrations tickle my hand. Each tree I touched resulted in the same sensation. Strange.

It took twice as many steps, but I weaved around the giants, marveling at their vibrant foliage and curious vibrations. When my stomach cramped with pain, I grabbed a mushroom, desperate. Blue residue brushed off on my fingertips as I turned it, contemplating. Brock mentioned something about things I couldn't eat unless I wanted to puke my guts up. But as the spongy mushroom pressed into my fingers, and my stomach craved sustenance, I brought it toward my lips.

With no warning at all, someone tackled me from behind. Air fled from my lungs as my face planted into a cluster of white flowers. Panicked, I squirmed and thrashed at my captor. Their hands dug into my arms, and their body pressed against my back, holding me to the ground. Once I realized I couldn't get out of this, my ears registered a noise. They were talking to me.

I froze, recognizing the voice. He must've noticed the change in my body because he released me. Turning around on the ground, I looked up into emeralds.

A devilish grin lit his face. "Hey, Luce."

CHAPTER TWENTY-EIGHT

No words. I had no words as I gazed up at Oliver. He stood in nothing but a green pretty boy sweater vest and dark jeans. He shoved one hand into his pockets, and the other ran through his wind-blown hair, the streak of black mixing with his blonde strands. He continued to rub his head nervously, smearing the cut along his forehead. A cut I secretly hoped I gave him in our struggle.

"So, did you miss me?" he asked.

One phrase. That was all it took to entice the coiling power in my blood. I scrambled off the ground, letting my Infernus cover my hands, and moved toward him.

Oliver's face paled. "Lucy, come on. You don't want to do this," he said, backing up, hands raised.

"I don't?" My voice was quiet. Lethal. Similar to the male's voice who liked to invade my head.

I backed him into a tree. "Last time I saw you, you placed me into the hands of the same male we were running from in the first place," I spat.

He laughed and looked everywhere but my eyes. "About that... I had no choice."

"You had no choice?" I shouted. "That's your excuse?"

Oliver's gaze hardened the tiniest fraction. He didn't look angry, only determined, as if he had something to prove.

"My excuse?" he said and laughed. The fear shot right out of him. "That's what you think it was? An excuse?" He took a step forward, and I yielded a step. The shift in his emotions startled me. "I regret that I played you. I regret that I had to lie to you. But when I say I didn't have a choice. *I didn't*. You have no idea."

"*I* have no idea? I've been through hell because of you!"

"Welcome to my world." He walked around me, no longer concerned, like I wasn't a threat.

I grabbed his arm and whipped him around to face me. "No! You don't get to walk away this time!"

He wrenched his arm back, brows furrowed. A small patch of icy crystals attacked his skin, turning it angry and pink. He was lucky that was all I did to him after he shoved a knife in my back.

"I almost died because of you! A pack of Hellhounds almost killed me!" I jerked my shirt up to show him my scars and had the pleasure of seeing shame in his eyes. "I almost died because you set me up. I trusted you, and you handed me over to the Mother of Demons! You turned me over to be used and tortured!" I shrieked. "The only reason I got away from Aspen and Brock was because of some male in my head."

I let my Infernus crawl further up his arm, surrounding his skin in ice. His face pinched. Seeing his pain helped a little. I thought about letting it consume him or at least leave angry patches all over his body, but without food, water, or proper rest, I felt the toll it was taking to hold the ice on his arm. I let my Infernus flow back into my body and sat against a tree.

Oliver's eyes widened. "Looks like you've been practicing."

"Well, when you're shoved into enemy hands and have no other defenses, it's kind of hard not to."

"I'm sorry, Lu—wait, did you say Aspen?"

"Yeah, Aspen. The Tenebrous Prince. You know him?"

His expression hardened. "The prince has a knife with his name on it."

"What'd he do, steal your favorite toy?"

"No, but him and his wretched court have my sister, and he works with a monster who killed my mother."

"Marcus."

He rose a brow. "How do you know that?"

I laughed, refusing to explain myself. "That's rich." I dug my nails into my palm, near to breaking my skin. "You tried to hand me over to a male who murdered your mother and sister." I might've kept the flames at bay, but not the vitriol in my tone.

"She's not dead!" he screamed, eyes flashing.

"Why would you let that piece of shit live!" I raged back. My Infernus opened an eye, eager to come out, but I pushed it away, not needing it.

Oliver's eyes turned to emerald fire. "I tried! I tried to kill that murderous fuck and get my sister back, and this is what it got me!" he yanked his vest down and showed the mangled flesh on his chest. "He held a ball of his hell flame against my skin. He forced me to hear and smell the sizzle of my flesh and live in the agony of his slow torture so that he could hear my screams. Marcus could've killed me. But instead, he laughed and told me I was too pathetic to kill. He marked me. Here and here." Oliver pointed to his chest and then to the strip of black hair. "Told me it was so I always remembered my place and that I'd never see her again." He sank back against a tree opposite of me. "I tried," he whispered.

I almost felt for him—almost. "How do you know she's not dead? And why hand me over to him? I was going to help you, and you betrayed me to a male who is a lying scum bag." Marcus wanted Oliver to suffer. He didn't just leave him alive so he knew his place, but so he always suffered with the knowledge that his sister was either dead or in a kingdom that was unreachable without...

I glanced down at the cuffs at my ankles.

Without something infused with demon energies.

I had the one thing that could get him over the border to his sister, yet I said nothing. They wouldn't come off without Aspen's key.

"Why take her if they were only going to kill her?"

I could name a few reasons, but I kept them to myself.

He sighed, head falling back to gaze up at the body of the giant tree, squishing some blue mushrooms in the process. "I found a way to rescue my sister. But the help I gained came at one steep-ass price." He flicked his gaze to his wrist, staring at his tattoo. "You're not the only one with an angelic rune. Except mine is still active and forcing me to keep the deal I made." He laughed. "I sold my soul."

Did he mean he literally sold his soul or something else? Either way, it didn't sound good.

He continued. "I've lived long enough where I'm not as naïve as I used to be. I called Marcus, told him about you, and acted like I believed he'd return my sister in exchange for you."

I squinted at him, not yet understanding.

"It was a game—all of it. The male who had one of his cronies put this on me," he shook his wrist forcefully. "Told me my next move was to hand you over."

"Your next move?" I didn't like the sound of that.

He sighed, again running his hand through his hair. "My first move was to find you. There was a reason I was in those woods."

"You were looking for me?" It was a suspicion I always suspected.

"No. *He's* looking for you. I just happened to be in the area, and he sent me because of some intel he found."

Oh...no... I didn't like the direction of this conversation.

"He who? So, you knew about me?"

"No, yes!" Oliver slammed his fist into the ground. "I haven't met the male. I made the deal months ago through his cronies. The messages I receive aren't in person. He doesn't give me much to go on except a when and a where. And I listen because the way he speaks, even if I didn't have the rune, I feel like he could kill me with his voice." Oliver shuddered. "He sent me to those woods without telling me what I was searching for, only if I found anything suspicious to intervene and help. And there you were, a tangled mess, seeing me despite my shadowing. It was suspicious. You shouldn't have seen me, so I figured you were the target he wanted."

"But that doesn't make sense. I was in the woods because I escaped from Marcus. If he wanted to hand me over again, why not take me back to where I escaped from? Why take me to Elora?"

"He told me you needed to be tested, and he needed incriminating intel about Marcus." His hands scrubbed at his head.

I had a feeling I knew where this was going.

"The male contacted me when I went into the cafe without you. Originally, I told the male no to his instructions, and instantly, it felt like icicles were stabbing into my body. It was the rune, he said. It'd force me to whether I wanted to or not. But for some reason, he took pity and told me that doing this could help them bring down Marcus. I called Marcus to tell him I had his escapee and said I'd hand you over, but only in Elora. The male said you had to cross the portal into The Divide to alert the Mother of Demons." His emerald irises flashed with hate and disgust.

I closed my eyes, wanting to laugh at all this absurdity. "He set it all up."

That derailed Oliver. "What?"

"You said you've never seen this male, so how is he speaking to you?"

No answer. I opened my eyes. Oliver stared at me, but I couldn't tell what his expression said.

"My head."

I nodded. "He wanted you to take me through the portal so it'd alert the Mother of Demons, so she'd send Aspen to intercept us. He wanted Aspen to take me over Marcus. Marcus must've not known about the portal."

"You know who the freezing asshole is?"

"Yeah, he's a king, I guess."

Oliver raised his brows at that. "Huh. But why did he want Aspen to intercept you?"

"To prove that Marcus was betraying his queen. Right before I was knocked out, Marcus was surprised that Aspen had shown up. You were already out for that part."

Oliver grunted. "Okay, but why the prince?"

I thought about that for a second. Why would he want Aspen to take me and not Marcus when he may be the one who had my mom?

I'll tell you everything I know, but only if you survive this. Prove to me that you aren't some weak-willed, naive wimp.

"The river was my test."

"The Corruptible River? He told me you were headed that way, but not why."

Of course it was called that.

"He told me that ninety-nine percent of people die in it."

"Yeah," Oliver scoffed. "I'm pretty sure everyone is taught not to go near it while in their mother's womb or incubating up in heaven in their little creation pods."

I laughed, shaking my head. "Well, he told me to jump into it."

Silence.

At his disbelieving eyes, I nodded.

"You didn't die," Oliver said, stunned.

"Nope. And he didn't seem to care either way," I shrugged.

"Or he knew you'd survive it."

Oliver had a point. The king didn't want me going to the Mother of Demons to be torn apart. He didn't want Marcus to have me. So what did he want, and how did it tie in with the test I believe I passed because I survived against all odds?

"Has he told you anything else?"

I glanced back at Oliver's suspicious face, wondering what to say. I didn't forgive him. Rage still faintly poked at me. But I understood why he did it, and that helped the need to wrap my hands around his neck. "He's been searching for my mom, but I don't know why."

Oliver rubbed at the rune on his wrist. "Well, that's kind of helpful. He seems creepy enough to have all the right resources, especially if he's a king."

"Yeah," I sighed.

Oliver stood, walking over to me, and reaching out a hand. "So, assuming your memories haven't returned yet, have you somehow figured out a place to start looking?"

Blankly, I panned between it and his face. "Who says I want your help?"

He flinched and twisted over his wrist to show me the black rune. "Sorry, sweets, but you don't have a choice. He directed me to you. I found you. Now you get to keep my ass."

"Fine. But only because I know I can't survive in Elora without help, so I'll call a truce and not burn you in your sleep." Despite my threat, Oliver still held his hand in front of my face.

"Don't worry, Luce. I'll get back into your good graces soon enough."

I wasn't so sure about that. Ignoring his hand, I stood, wiping off the dirt on my pants. "Where are we anyway?"

"You wandered into a graveyard," Oliver said, crossing his arms and smiling around at the area.

"What does that mean?"

He winked, keeping his cheerful attitude. I didn't like it.

"Why are you smiling?"

"Because we actually are in a graveyard, and I'm enjoying your reactions."

Great. No wonder it was so silent, and the trees hummed like they were alive. Everyone was probably too scared to venture into this part of the forest and I wandered in, welcoming it with open arms.

Oliver laughed. "Relax, Lucy. It's not like they will pop out of the ground and grab your leg."

I gave him a nasty look.

He snorted. "Even though dead bodies are underneath our feet, and ghosts are possible in a place like Elora, this forest is pretty cool. The remaining essence of dead angels, Nephilim, and Fallen are buried here."

Not sure how that made it cool. A burial ground creeped me out, no matter who was buried there. And ghosts—yeah, I would rather not.

Oliver flung out his arms toward the trees. "They're what makes these so ginormous. Whatever powers we have left over seep into the forest floor and affect the nature. Enchanted and haunted, or so they say." He waggled his eyebrows, and I refrained from smiling. He wouldn't get under my skin that fast.

"Why is it so silent?"

Oliver's eyes lit up, and before he could say anything outrageous, I stopped him. "A serious answer, please."

"You can't feel it?"

"Feel what?"

"The energy around us."

We slowly walked, not going far but wandering around the giant beasts. My fingers grazed the rough bark. "No, but I can feel it in the trees."

"It's in the air too."

I stopped. "I can't feel it."

He shrugged. "Well, I can, and I'll tell you no insect or animal with enough survival instincts would come near here. I wasn't joking when I said this place was said to be enchanted. Weird stuff happens here."

"Does this weird forest graveyard have a name?"

"The Forest of Damatha." He gestured wide and spoke dramatically. "It's an old word for weeping. The Forest of Weeping, fitting for a graveyard."

It was almost too perfect of a name. "So, we aren't in Drune Forest anymore?"

Oliver side-eyed me. "They connect, but no, which is a good thing. You don't want to mess with those Drunes." He shuddered. "Blood-sucking beasts."

Reaching my hand up to my ear, I touched the spot where the Drune sucked. Even if I lost some of my power, it was worth it. Partially. I escaped but still didn't have any information on my mom. My mood soured.

With each step, I bounced between thoughts of my mom, the king, and the dead angels beneath the moist ground, especially when flowers moved without cause. After the third time, I showed Oliver, but he just shrugged.

"So...can you get those cuffs off, or will I have to suffer through the sounds of a jail yard for the foreseeable future?"

I shot him a glare. "The king said they can't come off without the key."

"Super."

A seed of guilt grew within my annoyance at his attitude. But I shouldn't feel any guilt. I didn't have the key.

"You do know if we are going to try to evade Aspen, we need to muffle those. I might dislike him a whole lot, but he isn't some stupid brute. He's trained to track, among other things. She made him into the perfect weapon."

True. Plus, with how fast he melted the ice last time, we needed to move faster.

"I don't have anything to muffle them."

"Have you tried to burn them off?" he asked.

"I can't. They block my angelic powers, so save transforming into a monster for someone else." I couldn't try my black Infernus flames yet with how little energy I had left. Not that I thought it would work. The king was right about the tampering and everything else, so I doubted anything would unlock them but Aspen's key.

He raised a brow. "I don't transform into a monster."

"But when we camped—"

"That's not my power. It's much worse than that," he said.

"Then what is it?"

Oliver paused, staring into the darkening forest as the sun we couldn't see lowered. "It's fear." He met my questioning gaze. "I can sense it and invade anyone's mind and pry out their worst fears. Or any fears. It depends on how far I go in. The farther I dive, the more power I use to dredge them up. Surface-level fears are easier to manipulate, and I don't have to touch someone to use them."

"The monster was one of my surface-level fears?"

He nodded.

"Why are you so reluctant to talk about it?"

He let out a breath, running a hand through his hair. "Because I hate it. The surface-level ones are easier. But my power isn't some pretty walk in the park. No, I have to suffer through nightmares to pull it to the surface and scare the living shit out of them. Sometimes, even break them. I have to see the horrors in their minds." From the little light left, I watched the blood seep from his cheeks. "I've seen unimaginable things that still haunt my thoughts."

If my surface-level fear could demolish a tree, I couldn't imagine the damage a deeper fear could create.

"It's... terrible. This power was never meant for someone like me. So, I try not to use it. Unless, you know, we get chased by crazy ass Powers." He gave me a weak wink, finally revealing how he managed to get us away. "But shadowing. That's the only part of my power I like."

I gestured for him to explain.

He smiled, one of those sneaky ones he had. "I can hide from demons, humans, and most angels. Everyone's a little scared of the dark, so when I wrap that fear around me, they subconsciously don't want to look. It's very handy."

"But it doesn't work on me," I said smugly.

His smile dropped. "Yeah. But the moment I met you, I could tell you were strange."

I rolled my eyes. A piece of bitter tension chipped away from the wall I put up between us. I forgot how much I enjoyed Oliver's sarcastic commentary.

With the sun's departure, the forest turned black. Oliver became a barely visible silhouette beside me. But it didn't last long. The tiny flowers on the forest floor glowed with a white light. And they weren't the only nightlights. The blue mushrooms erupted, glowing neon, along with the orange moss. Their glowing colors lifted my lips, but the trees dropped my jaw. Each trunk erupted in light-blue shimmering veins of light, stretching to their leaves.

"Did you know this happened?" I asked, feeling like a little girl lost in a fairyland.

A genuine smile lit Oliver's face. He marveled at the spectacle as much as I did. "I heard stories. I've even made up some of my own and spread them. So, I never knew which ones were true or superstitious shit."

I was curious about the other stories, smirking at the thought of what rumors Oliver spread when that same feeling of urgency reared its ugly head.

"Where are you leading me?" I asked. We needed to find a place to hide, food, and water.

"I was following you."

"You just told me how skilled Aspen is at tracking, and you're choosing to follow me nonchalantly through a forest in a world I know nothing about?"

The glow of the trees illuminated a funny look on Oliver's face. "I asked you if you had any ideas! You never answered, so I assumed you'd take us somewh..." He trailed off at my disbelief. "Okay, okay." He threw up his hands. "So, where do you want to go?"

"To find water, food, and Magda. In that order. Do you know where she lives?"

He whipped his head to stare at me. "The wicked witch of Elora?"

"That's what she's called?"

"No." He snorted. "I just liked the ring of it. But yeah, I know where she lives, and that's where my knowledge ends, not counting all the rumors about her."

"Bad rumors?"

He mulled over my question. "Yeah, I'm trying to figure out how a fence full of decapitated skulls could be a good rumor, but I'm coming up blank."

I side-eyed him. What an Oliver thing to say. "She answers all your questions, though, right?"

"So I've heard. If you can pay her price."

"I've already paid plenty of prices. What's a few more?"

Oliver groaned. "Come *on,* Lucy, you can't possibly be thinking of going to that witch. She has a fence of skulls! That doesn't exactly scream, *please come and join me for a cup of tea and answers,*" he said in a high-pitched voice, holding an imaginary teacup.

I threw my hands in the air. "How else am I supposed to find my mom?"

"Oh, I don't know. Maybe from the nice male who likes to invade our minds?"

Nice? Yeah, that wasn't the word I'd use to describe the male who used ice claws to stab my brain.

"We have no idea when he's going to contact us next. What if we go to Magda, ask her questions, and if I can't pay the price, we leave?"

He opened his mouth, clearly about to protest, and I said the only thing I knew that'd convince him and take my guilt away.

"I know a way into the Tenebrous Kingdom. But I'll only tell you after you take me to Magda's," I said.

His jaw dropped. "You're serious?"

"Dead."

"You have a way?"

I nodded. "Yes, I have a way, and it doesn't include any angelic runes." *Just a pair of cuffs and a key we'd have to steal from Aspen.*

Oliver held out his hand, and I shook it. "Deal, but if we're going to Magda's, I'm having a full belly, so if she decapitates me, she has more to clean up than just blood."

"Seriously?" I scrunched my face, disgusted. "You couldn't keep that to yourself?"

He shrugged, strolling forward with a hop in his step like the little hope I gave him made his entire day. "Nope. Where's the fun in having a filter? Life's more enjoyable this way."

Maybe for him, but not for my ears.

"So, fill our bellies first, then go possibly die at the hands of Ms. Decapitator, then finally get my sister back?"

"And my mom," I added.

Oliver nodded. "And your mom."

"Sounds wonderful. Now lead the way," I motioned.

CHAPTER TWENTY-NINE

The night faded. Eventually, the trees lost their glow and became thinner. A bronze blanket of needles covered the ground instead of vibrant mushrooms and moss. The white flowers became the size of my fist, clinging to vines that wrapped around the trees and dragged along the ground. They were perfumed with vanilla, masking the horrid stench of my hair and clothes. Their velvet petals with little blue centers continued to glow as the night waned. The only light we had left. But it didn't matter since their size made up for the loss of light. Even in the distance, I could make out the glowing flowers.

"Tone down the crazy eyes." Oliver moved to nudge me and thought better of it. "Celestrus are beautiful though, aren't they? They only glow at night if someone with angel blood is in their presence. Then once they start glowing, it's a chain reaction, and they light each other up."

The flowers were now ten times cooler than before.

Oliver couldn't hold back his laughter at my dreamy saucer eyes. "Come on. We need to find a place to sleep for a couple of hours before we pass out from lack of squirrel."

"Is it safe to sleep?"

"Probably not. But Aspen hasn't found you yet, and we need to rest, or we'll be as good as dead if we run into anything. And if I need to use my fear on Aspen, surface-level fears aren't going to cut it, and that's all I'd be able to do right now."

"How do you know?"

"Searching for my sister, I ran into people who talked about him. Plus, I've seen him from a distance sneaking up and down the Tenebrous border."

"You never approached him?" I asked.

Oliver shot me a disbelieving glance, scanned himself up and down, then glanced at me again. "I'm sorry, but in what world do you think my 150-pound ass can go up against a commander who can snuff me out with a fireball?"

I shrugged. "You did it to two high-level angels and Marcus."

"That was a last resort, do-or-die situation, and I wanted to murder Marcus. Plus, the demon prince is never alone. The ugly old male is always with him or a horde of soldiers."

"Suppose you're right." He'd never stand a chance against Aspen.

We walked away from the forest. The flowers dimmed the further we went, shutting off as we stopped next to a foggy pond illuminated by Elora's moon. We plopped onto the bumpy grass and tried to settle in without gear. From the way my bones ground against the ground and my breath clouded the air, comfort was unlikely. I curled up into a tight ball, conserving my heat. The moment I laid my head down, I focused on thoughts of my mom and the present day and let exhaustion drag me into another dream-walk, hoping it would show me where she was.

AFTER I DECIDED I shouldn't follow Aspen, he was true to his word and returned every week, giving me slivers. He never returned on the same day, but he was at least consistent with the time.

That morning, huddled in an oversized baggy sweatshirt, making my rounds through the forest to see if he'd show, he luscelered in front of my face.

I flinched, falling on my ass, making him laugh. "Don't do that!" I exclaimed, irritated but unable to hold back my smile.

"How many times have I scared you? And yet, you still end up on the ground," Aspen snorted, holding out his hand to help me up per usual. It had become our irritating routine.

"Maybe one of these days, you'll be kind enough to catch me before I fall." I grabbed his hand, enjoying the way the tingles tightened my stomach.

He lifted me, then smoothed a piece of my long hair back. "But how else will I come by my weekly chuckle?"

I pushed him and his delicious hands away, trying to act indignant, but it wasn't easy when his dimples came out to play. They didn't grace his face often, usually because of my prying words, but when they did, I melted.

"So, what sliver will you give me today?" Yep, and there they went. Unlocking anything from Aspen was like attempting to find where my mom hid her old text about bonds. I had searched everywhere for the damned book and still couldn't find it. Aspen was disappointed when I told him, but I said I would keep looking and tell him *if and when* I found it. Until then, he visited, we talked, and I tried to learn things about him.

So far, I had learned that Aspen loved apples and possessed a bonded sword, which was a weapon *he* could only touch and channel his power into. After he explained, I demanded an example and watched as his eyes and intricate sword lit with blue flame. I also learned he enjoyed fighting because he was excellent at it, his words, not mine, and that he wasn't from here. But when I asked where he was from, he said those same six words and left me. So, I now resorted to letting him choose what to tell me. For the most part, my curiosity got the best of me at times and bit me in the ass half the time.

He stepped closer, brushing more of my wild hair from my face, which he did almost every time we met. I gazed up at him, smiling because I had officially become addicted to his tingly touch, stupid dimples, and even the thin-pressed scowl and frown he wore every five minutes.

"Tell you what, sweetheart." He started to call me that after I accidentally leaped on him after he surprised me with one of my favorite chocolate bars. I didn't mind one bit. "I'll make you a deal. If you answer a question of mine, I'll answer any question of yours."

At first, I wanted to jump with joy at his offer, but then my smile dropped. Aspen liked his secrets, or at least thought he had to keep them, and I wasn't much better with my own.

"Who is after you?"

I stepped back. Out of all the questions he could've asked, it wasn't the worst, but it'd only spawn more. However, he was my guardian, so maybe he needed to know. I decided to compromise and give him a half-answer.

"Everyone."

Or more of a non-answer.

He snuffed out the distance I had created and grabbed my hand. I wondered if he knew how easily he could sway me with his touch and the tingles that pitter-pattered their way into my lonely heart.

Maybe that was why I said it. For once, I wanted someone else to know the secrets of my past. I'd keep it vague enough he'd be safe if, for some crazy reason, he was questioned by the wrong people, but I'd give him a sliver.

"I was never supposed to exist, and my—" I gathered my thoughts before I spewed something I shouldn't. "We've been hiding from my fathers."

"Fathers?"

"Yes, plural."

A soft glow illuminated his eyes, like he despised the fact someone so close to me was after me. Or someone was after me to begin with.

"Where are they now?" he demanded, clenching the hilt of his sword.

My lips pressed into a thin line, holding back my smile. *What was he going to do? Kill them for us?*

"My mom hasn't shared that information with me."

Determination rested in his brows. He opened his mouth, likely about to ask more questions.

"Oh, no. My turn, Aspen. Where are you from?"

He shook his head vehemently.

"We made a deal," I said, releasing his hand to brush his cheek, giving him a taste of the delicious torment.

He squeezed his eyes shut as if battling himself or possibly the influence of the bond between us. "If I tell you, you must promise never to follow me there."

I nodded, all too eager to know.

But when he opened his eyes, they were all flame.

"I mean it, Lucille. You are not to ever go there. Ever. Promise me."

"I promise," I whispered, noticing fear and agony behind the demand in his flaming eyes. The emotions were so powerful it was almost like I could feel them.

His jaw pulsed for a second before he answered. "Elora."

Stay here, stay put, stay safe. He never meant the house we lived in. He meant on Earth. Stay here and safe on Earth.

Oh, he should *not* have said that. Currently, hiding under my bed were four bobby pin-unlocked books about Elora—the angelic world I was forbidden from. Just knowing the name nearly gave my mom a heart attack.

FATHERS. I HAD TWO fathers. *How was that possible? What else was I missing from my memories?*

I feared that answer—and the lingering ache I had for Aspen.

In my dream-walk, he was everything to me. I adored the way he brushed my hair back, his tingly touch, and the cliche nickname he gave me because of my obsession with chocolate. He made me feel seen, bringing life to my isolation. Every time he left, my chest ached to follow him or make him stay. *Why couldn't I have met that male when I came to Elora?*

Uncurling from my ball, I glanced around. The Celestrus from the forest glowed with warm light. *Weren't we too far away for them to glow?*

I grabbed Oliver's long leg and shook.

Nothing.

"Oliver," I said.

"What?" he groaned, rolling over.

"Weren't the flowers normal when we went to sleep?" I continued to stare, muscles tense. But underneath the fear, my worry felt foreign and overwhelming.

"Yeah, why?" he mumbled, stretching out before glancing toward the forest. "Shit." He sat up, grabbed my hand, and pulled me up with him.

"But what if it's not him?" I asked, knowing I sounded foolish.

"You really want to risk it? Say it wasn't the evil prince. If the queen knows about you, then there's a good chance others do, too."

He was right. "Earlier, we ran into a blonde Dominion and a redheaded Power. They were after me. Do you think those were the ones you scared off when we were still on earth?"

Oliver nodded. "Sounds like it. And before I touched them with my power, they mumbled about a reward for finding you. That some *he* would be pleased. They were so focused on you that they didn't stand a chance against me."

"Who do you think *he* is?"

Oliver stared at the glowing Celestrus. "The king?"

I shook my head. "Unless he's playing a bigger game than I've realized. He's not working with them."

"I wouldn't put it past him. But we don't have time to mull over why everyone wants you. We gotta run."

"I can't. My cuffs!"

He glared at my ankles. "I really hate those jangling bastards." He swooped down and picked me up. "I'm not risking my neck because of your stupid cuffs. Hold on."

Squeezing my eyes shut from the wind, he luscelered us away from the pond. We ran over flat grassy lands and continued into another forest. A typical, average-looking, non-glowing forest. Squirrels and all.

He stopped when we reached a golden field and put me down, breathing unevenly.

"Why'd we stop?" We couldn't possibly be far enough away. But if they never saw us leave, they would never know what direction we went.

He gestured in front of him. "Because we need to walk through that, and I figured I'd tell you what to expect first."

I stared at what he pointed at. Near us, metallic golden strands swayed, but halfway out, a shimmery haze split the field, changing the gold to silver.

"Why does the grass look like that?" It reminded me of the field near Drune Forest.

Oliver chuckled. "It's the barrier that makes it that color."

I craned my head up to him. "What?"

"The Ethereal Kingdom is on the other side of the golden grass. There is a barrier in place that separates The Divide from the kingdom. It keeps out unwanted species."

I stilled, staring at the swaying silver grass, as a chill brushed my spine. "I can't cross that."

He looked at me funny. "Your legs look fine to me."

My eyebrows shot into my forehead. "We just said angels were after me, and now you want to go into their territory? Do you plan on handing me over to them, too?"

His mouth opened and closed. "But that's where we can eat food," he whined.

What a child.

"Aren't there other places we can eat? Or hunt more squirrels?"

Oliver frowned. "This is the closest place to find real food. Aren't you sick of squirrels? Wouldn't you like some homemade bread or stew or anything else?"

I threw up my hands. "Of course, Oliver. I'd love to have my fill and not be on the brink of starvation! That doesn't change the fact I, *for some reason,* have everyone after me!"

"Okay, okay, don't have a panic attack." He mulled over the rest of what I said. "I promise if we see any angels with armor, we leave. But they normally don't come to this village. Plus, it's just over the border. Then, after we eat, maybe we rest a second. Magda won't fly away on her broomstick before we arrive," he said, bottom lip sticking out as his blonde lashes fluttered.

Such a baby. But my stomach rivaled with the need to reach Magda.

"I swear, Oliver. If we run into trouble..."

He hugged me. "You'll love this place, trust me. Plus, I'd never risk our deal for a second time."

We walked to the edge of the golden grass. A hum of energy vibrated into my feet and up my spine. "So, we just walk through? Easy peasy?"

Oliver nodded. "As long as you have angel blood, you should be good. But once we cross, we need to move fast again. I only stopped to be considerate and let you know what the barrier was."

I was sure that wasn't the *only* reason.

"Okay, what about my cuffs?"

"What about them? I'll be carrying you."

I bit my lip. "But what if they have demon energies in it? Do you think the barrier would pick up on them?"

Oliver glanced at my cuffs, analyzing them. "I don't think it'll register with border control. They may like to make sure what walks onto their side is angel, but I've seen mix-breeds in the villages, some even part demon. They're not as strict about their rules in this area, but once you pass the villages and near their capital, they'll hunt you down if you're not pure angel."

"You're sure?"

He grabbed my hand, the devil sneaking a peek through his bold smile. "Any danger, and we're out, I promise. Plus, you already agreed. Too late to back out now."

"Okay," I sighed, trusting him.

He pulled me through the shimmery barrier before I could finish my sentence. It tingled against my skin like pins and needles.

"Did you feel that?" I whispered, awed by the golden field butting up to a stream that bordered a forest of pink trees.

"No dilly dally, remember? We need to run."

Oliver swooped me up and luscelered us over the stream and through the pink trees. His puffs of hot morning breath hit my cheek until it changed to sprays of spit. After nearly missing a couple of tree trunks, his long strides shortened, slowing our pace to a jog. A pink root caught his shoe. He tripped, and I landed in a bush.

"Oliver! What is with you and dropping me?" I yelled, swatting away the branches trying to rip out my hair.

"Sorry, jailbird," he panted, laying stomach first on a bed of pink leaves. "Olivmobile is out of commission. It's time to use those scrawny legs of yours. It's just by those trees." He pointed without looking.

"Get up. Someone promised me bread and stew," I said, walking over to his sprawled body, holding out my hand to him.

He smiled like an idiot as he looked at it. "Does this mean you forgive me?"

"No. But I want food. For that, I need you."

His goofy smile widened as he latched on. "I'll take that."

I rolled my eyes. "Come on."

We shuffled—okay, I shuffled while Oliver strode—until we arrived at an edge of thinning pink trees and a view of the village—a very unmodern village, with thatched roofing and wood siding. Some, very few, were made from plain stone.

Oliver noticed the look on my face and chuckled. "It's not Earth, Lucy."

"Well aware. What are they doing?" I asked. Figures moved about, but from this distance, I couldn't tell why.

Oliver grinned as he rubbed his hands together. "It's their daily market, with lots of food."

Thank heavenly.

He stepped into the clearing. I hesitated. I'd be completely exposed the moment I stepped away from the forest. They'd see us coming. They'd see me.

"I promise, I got your back. Any trouble and we're..." Oliver turned back to me, words trailing off as he gazed at something over my head. "Fuck-a-duck."

I turned, gaze landing on a piece of paper at my back, and almost sank to the ground. We should've never stepped over that border. Crushing pressure gripped my chest at finding my face on a piece of paper with the words WANTED ALIVE at the top and an outrageous sum of money on the bottom. But before I had another panic attack at the fact that someone named Michael put a bounty on my head, something flashed through the clearing.

There wasn't enough time to warn Oliver as the red blur luscelered toward him at top speed. I shoved him out of the way as the figure, meant for Oliver, slammed me into a tree.

I cried out, feeling a snap in my ribs. A scrawny redhead with dark skin grabbed my neck and held me against the tree with one arm. I latched onto his wrist, summoning my Infernus.

"Michael wondered if you'd be stupid enough to enter Elora and come to Etherea. I guess it's a good thing he had me stationed here," he said, unfazed by the ice spreading across his skin as he reached to his belt and took out a feather. "Don't worry, I'll take care of your parlor tricks with a Binding Rune." Then he slammed my head back into the trunk.

CHAPTER THIRTY

I stood at the edge of an endless, shadowed space, and at its center, a purple-white ball of light twisted and turned, flickering with images. Intrigued, I stepped closer. Dread, pain, and betrayal enveloped me in a vile caress. Swallowing, I took a giant step back.

"Touch it."

I jerked to my right. A cloaked figure stood there.

"Touch the ball," she said again, her voice familiar.

"I know you," I said. "You're the voice who told me about Oliver and Magda."

She circled behind me, no longer just a voice. Her red and black cloak flowed around her combat boots, illuminated by the flashing ball. "And did you find them?"

"Oliver, but not Magda, yet. Did you know what would happen to me when I came to Elora?" I demanded.

She snorted. "You don't want to know what I know. But it's time you learned the truth."

"Truth of what?"

"Your mom."

I perked up. "What about my mom?"

"You'll know soon." She prowled around me and gestured to the ball. "Touch the core of your dream-walking abilities, think of the memory of your mom when she was surrounded, and face the truth," she said, then vanished.

Eager, I faced the colorful ball of light, understanding the emotions and flashes of images were memories. I gripped the image of my mom surrounded in my mind's eye and stepped into my power.

I LUSCELERED TO OUR safe spot in the forest, forced out by my mom's powers, trying to fight through the calm to no avail. I sat against the weird, gnarled tree we discovered and designated as our meet-up spot if anything were to happen and waited. Worry nudged at the calm, but the flickering emotion did little to overcome the relentless intrusion of her damned powers. I wished Aspen were here. He would know what to do. But after our huge fight, when he found me following him, he didn't come the last few weeks.

A snap made my head jerk to the side, where my mom stood in her black and red rooster pajamas. I stood, scrambling to her, happy to find her safe and unscathed, but stopped as I noticed her arm raised and palm open, cupping something black.

Nerium powder.

It was only one dose, strong enough to put an angel to sleep for about a week. We kept it in case my father found us, so I didn't understand why it was in her hand. Or why, when I glanced at it, she started to sob.

"Mom?"

That only made her cry harder.

"What's happening?" Uncertainty pounded in time with my heart, disrupting the forced calm.

She stepped forward as I took a step back. Something wasn't right. My mom loved me. She'd never do anything to harm me. That particular skill was left to my father. So what was going on?

Her shoulders shook with each step, and her hand wobbled, spilling dark powder onto the forest floor.

"Why are you doing this?"

"You know why."

I took another step back, feeling an ache work its way up my chest at the reality of this situation. The one person I loved and trusted was about to knock me out with poison.

"This is about our fight? About Elora?" *How did that deserve this?*

"Partly. I can't have you following me. I need you safe."

"How is poisoning me keeping me safe?" I screamed at her. *Hasn't she taken enough from me?*

"I'm sorry, Lucy. I'm so sorry," she said over and over. Her words were like a hammer, shattering everything I trusted and believed in. When she blew into her hand before I could move, and a male with a cowboy hat appeared beside her as I breathed in the poison, I decided the poison could take me and keep me forever. I never wanted to wake up.

OPENING MY EYES, HEAD-throbbing from the slam, I lay there staring up into a blue sky, wishing the physical pain would drone out the crushing pain beneath my sternum.

My mom poisoned me. And by the slow smile peeking beneath the cowboy-hatted male behind her, she was working with Marcus, which explained why I woke up to him guarding one of the doors.

It made sense now. My mom's betrayal made me give up my miserable life. It was the last straw. As the poison infiltrated my system, my powers fought for me and battled against the Void until I didn't want to fight. *What was the point when I no longer had anyone? When I was alone?* I gave memories of myself to The Void to forget. But with each dream-walk I remembered more and now wish I didn't.

"Lucy! Help!" Oliver yelled. "Fuck-a-duck, how are you so strong you look like a damned twig!" I heard more cussing and smacking flesh.

Disoriented, I shifted my throbbing head right as the redhead slammed a fist into Oliver's face, knocking him out. Footsteps approached, and I tried to move but gasped from the pain in my ribs.

The redhead blocked out the dreadful blue sky with a satisfied smile. "Gabriel's spawn was a lot easier to take care of than I thought, which only leaves you," he chuckled and crouched down, fingering my chains as he smiled. "Cuffs, broken ribs, no access to your powers—today's an easy day for me." His gaze roved over my body, starting at my calves, lingering on the zipper of my pants and breasts until he reached my face. "You're a lot prettier than I thought you'd be. The poster doesn't do you justice. My cock's been lonely of late, and it needs a nice ride."

"If you come near me with your cock, I'll—"

"You'll what?" He nodded down to my wrist. "Even if you had your powers, you're no match for me."

I glanced down. Blood smeared my entire forearm, partially covering the black Blocking Rune.

No, no, no.

"I'll scream," I said, glancing at the village. "They'll hear me from here."

The redhead smirked. "No, they won't." He leaned in and unzipped my jacket, desire overcoming him as he stared at my exposed nipples peeking through my holey shirt. I reared back and slammed my forehead into his nose.

"Damnit!" he seethed, spraying the blood that dripped into his bared teeth. "You know what's worse than being fucked when you don't want it?" He yanked on the laces of his pants and pulled them down. His cock sprung out, surrounded by red curling hair. "Being fucked when your ribs are broken."

My breathing turned uneven. This couldn't happen. I gazed over at Oliver, desperately seeking help. Though his chest still rose, he wasn't conscious.

"Help me!" I screamed, whimpering as I scooted away from his naked thighs, hoping the villagers would hear me.

"Michael won't mind if you're a little used." He grabbed onto my chains and yanked me back. Pain tore into my ribs as I tried to kick out of his hold.

"Help! Someone please help me!"

He slid his sweat-slick thighs along my leathers until he straddled my lower legs, pinning me. I swung at his bloody nose, connecting. His head whipped to the side, and he spit a big glob of blood out of his mouth.

"I guess you don't have to be conscious," he said, slamming his fist into my jaw. My head snapped to the side. The force of it stole my gaze for a moment. I came to when he finished unfastening my pants. He pulled them down, exposing me. I sobbed, screamed, and squirmed fighting against the agonizing pain in my sides. But it was useless.

He chuckled. "I'm going to enjoy this."

A bright light flashed right before his cock pressed against me, and warmth splashed across my skin.

The bounty hunter's head flopped to the ground, detached. Blood spurted onto my chest from his tipping, lifeless body, and a black boot kicked it before it fell on top of me.

And I saw him. My savior and damnation, standing there, seething with unrestrained fury.

CHAPTER THIRTY-ONE

Aspen.

Relief washed over me like a tidal wave, and tears streamed down my cheeks as he draped his cloak over my body.

I cried for the close call, for my helplessness. I cried for Aspen's safety, though I should have been fleeing from him. I cried for myself, for what my mom did, and for all the pain I endured in Elora. Every bit of it.

Aspen sank to his knees, wordlessly brushing my hair from my face and tears from my cheeks. Flames engulfed his eyes, and his jaw muscle pounded with lingering fury. Minutes passed, yet he remained by my side, soothing me with his tingly touch while I grieved. Even after I cried myself out, he continued to comfort me, like he needed it. Like he needed the reassurance that I was safe and here. When the flames finally dimmed in his eyes, I worked up the courage to speak.

"Aspen?" I rasped.

"Yes, sweetheart?" he whispered, brushing his knuckles down my face.

That nickname. Damn, I loved that nickname and shouldn't.

"Can I ask for a sliver?" I almost started crying again, but I held the ache back.

"If I could, I'd give you the moon," he responded, reverently taking in every inch of my face.

"Back on Earth. Was any of it real?" My voice was small and broken, scared of the truth.

"Yes, Lucille. Every second."

I swallowed and nodded. "And Elora?"

He bowed his head, and I sensed his pain flickering along with the red rune under his chin. "Some."

"What changed?"

"Everything."

"Was it because I tried to follow you?" It was ironic how I desired to go to Elora when I was on Earth, and now all I wanted to do was leave.

"No."

"Can you tell me why? Why on Earth you were... you. And here, you're..."

"An evil bastard," he filled in for me. At my silence, he nodded. "I'll try. I can't always say what I want."

I brushed my finger underneath his chin, feeling a zap. "Because of this hell rune?"

Confusion and clarity waged a war in his gaze. The rune beneath his chin attacked my finger, but I kept it there, taking the pain to see if it'd allow him to talk. No matter how painful it became, I pressed my thumb into his chin until he unclenched his jaw, and the clarity won.

"I know she carved something there. Sometimes, I can remember the pain and the ebony feather moving against my skin, but then it fades away like a bad dream." He took my free hand and interlaced our fingers. "But around you, its influence dulls. I found that out the first time I met you."

"Why were you there? You said it was because you were my guardian, but you never explained further."

"That's because I've only been slowly figuring out what it means after you showed me the sentences from your mom's book."

I scrunched my brows. "I found it? What did they say?"

"Born of imbalance, destined to right the wrongs of the past, a force written in ink shall emerge. Sacrifice will pave the way as voices whisper the secrets of the Fallen. I've figured out—" He started to stand, and I panicked, releasing his hand, and cringing as I reached to clutch his face. "What happened?"

He didn't know my ribs were broken, and right now, I didn't want to derail the conversation and lose whatever clarity he had.

"It's nothing. But I think touching you helps more than just being present."

"It does," he said, still gazing at me with questions in his eyes.

"Then why are you moving?"

"I wasn't going to let go of your hand, Lucille. But I need to show you what I've figured out."

I put more pressure on his face, refusing to let go. "Can you do it down here?"

He looked ready to refuse, but either from how tightly I gripped his face or from the worry he saw in my expression, he nodded. "Okay. But I need to move."

One of my hands dropped as I slowly settled back on the ground, holding back my cringe so Aspen didn't notice. But by his expression, I had a feeling he did. With my hand on his face, he sat back, unbuckling his stiff uniform. Shucking them off, he noticed my furrowed brows. "Just wait. It'll make sense in a second."

When he untucked his undershirt, pulling his arms through the holes, heat flushed my face at the view of his sculpted body. It brought me back to the moment I writhed against him, wanting to feel his skin, and the terrible words he threw in my face after my power released us. Shame pulled my gaze away. Ever since I met him, I was attracted to him, and each time he returned to the forest on Earth, those feelings only grew. When I tackled him off the carriage, and the music amplified, my feelings amplified for him. I may have felt his desire, seen it in his eyes, and heard it from his lips, but I wasn't sure I believed it. And if I forced those feelings onto him, if I made him want me, made him kiss me, then I was no better than the redhead.

"Lucille," he said, gently tilting my chin back toward him. I attempted to resist, but he didn't allow it. "I don't want to see that shame in your eyes. If anyone is going to feel shame, it'll be me."

"I almost raped you like—"

"Don't you dare compare yourself to the piece of shit. You hear me? Your powers elevated emotions that were already there. I've always wanted to share that moment with you. I just wasn't sure you wanted your first time to be in a forest crawling with eyes or under the influence of your power. I wasn't worried for myself, only you."

"But you said I wasn't worth it." Out of all the things he said to me, that one hurt the most.

He grimaced. "Because I couldn't stand the thought of Brock even thinking about you that way. You are worth it, Lucille." He dropped a kiss on my forehead. "You are worth it. I'm sorry for ever making you think you weren't. For everything."

His warm, tingly lips mended my shame, at least a little.

"Now let me give you a few more slivers and explain the rest. But know that not everything I did was influenced."

"Okay," I whispered.

Aspen took my hand from his face and shifted around. Two giant indigo wings inked his back.

"Can you see them?"

"They're hard to miss," I said.

His shoulders seemed to relax at my words. "No one else can see them, Lucille," he sighed. "They appeared nearly twenty years ago during my training. The searing pain was so abrupt and intense that I thought someone had attacked me from behind, but there was no one there.

"The infirmary found nothing wrong and assured me I was fine. It wasn't until I returned to my chambers that I saw what no one else could.

"I searched through old texts and discreetly questioned others but found no answers. Frustrated, I gave up searching, even as the sensation prickled sporadically over the years. Then, on Earth, during a mission for"—he tensed, hesitating before spitting out—"Lilith, the tingling erupted, bringing me to my knees. I could no longer ignore it. Desperate, I confronted the Drunes, threatened their forest, and demanded they tell me the origin of the tattoo. They did.

"When I returned to Earth, intense tingles scorched down my back as I entered a rainy forest. The sensation stopped when I found you surrounded by melting frost and mud."

As he placed his arms back into his sleeves, before he let his shirt fall, I noticed raised scars hidden within the wings tattooed on his back.

No, not scars, hell runes. Hundreds of them.

With my free hand, I winced as I reached to touch one, relieved to find them devoid of ominous power. They were all inactive.

"I saw that," he said, turning around and glaring.

He positioned himself beside me and returned my hand to his face, where the rune flickered with light. I covered the vile glow as Aspen placed a hand on my ribs. I gasped at his touch, and he immediately removed it.

"I should've made him suffer," Aspen muttered, casting a sidelong glare at the redhead. I sensed the tumult of his rage, worry, and guilt through our bond.

Pulling him away from the gory scene, I smiled weakly. "Decapitation is close enough. Explain the tattoo."

He frowned, his lips tightening, but eventually gave a reluctant nod. "When I was with you in the forest on Earth, there was a moment I didn't understand. One where I had a quick flashback of a face I didn't remember."

From the despair in his tone, I could guess who.

"Nalini?"

"Yes. And when you gave me your necklace, I don't think you realized, but it glowed black. The moment I touched it, the amulet unlocked more of the memory I had been forced to forget. Somehow, it countered the rune's power."

But I used all my mom's power up unless it absorbed mine when I erupted.

"When I left you, I had more questions than answers. I couldn't return to the Drunes, so I went to a witch, and she gave me some answers and a word."

"Guardian," I guessed.

He nodded, playing with a piece of my hair, lost in the past. "Your amulet gave me the memory of Nalini's murder. But every time I thought of who did it—" He hissed, and the rune burned my thumb. I gritted my teeth, refusing to let go. "It'd burn through the power, making me forget until the amulet no longer worked. After that, I decided I needed to see you again."

"How'd you find me?"

"Through the tattoo. *A force written in ink shall emerge.* Our bond began when I received this tattoo. That's the only part of the sentences I've figured out. We're tethered together through my ink. I can track it to you at any time. Except for when you almost escaped, and I found you next to that Soulhound." Seeing my puzzled expression, he elaborated. "They're ancient creatures related to Hellhounds, though less dangerous since they're usually bound to an angel that keeps them in line. I thought they were extinct, but after almost losing you to Hellhounds, I didn't care what creature it was. I lost it. So, I fought it until I scared it off."

I sighed, relieved he didn't kill the Soulhound. It seemed sweet until Aspen showed up.

He bowed his head to mine, his voice thick with emotion. "God, Lucille. A month after our fight, I felt the tether between us shrink, like you were moving further away. I thought nothing of it until I decided to search for you and couldn't find you. I couldn't fucking find you."

My eyes stung with the intensity of his voice and the pain I could sense.

"Something blocked the ability, and then our tether faded as if you were slipping away from me. The panic I felt didn't go unnoticed. And then she sensed you come through the portal just as the tether reestablished." He shook his head, rubbing it against my forehead as if trying to erase the memory. "She knew she found her next power source to drain and knew my behavior was connected somehow.

"That night, she carved the rune on me as she had done for years, but this time with more commands. When Brock and I portaled to The Divide and saw you..." He pulled back, locking his glowing gaze with mine, gripping my face. "When I saw you, stick-thin and all bruised, I nearly leveled everyone in the clearing.

"But I'm under orders not to kill those loyal to her, and I didn't want to hurt you or the Nephilim. Except, when I discovered Marcus was a turncoat, I happily killed her soldiers and almost Marcus, but he jumped back through the Earth portal. In my rage, I *accidentally* obliterated the portal to the Tenebrous Kingdom's boundary line."

"To buy more time until you had to hand me over," I stated, putting the puzzle together.

Sadness doused the blue glow in his eyes, and he nodded. "I was so enraged—with you, myself, our situation, the fact that you couldn't remember anything, and her fucking commands. I couldn't fully protect you, yet I had to ensure you stayed alive. I couldn't intervene with Brock, but I had to prevent him from accidentally killing you. I couldn't remove your cuffs or allow you to escape. The only place I could take you was the Tenebrous Kingdom, so I destroyed the fastest way there. I couldn't show any sign that you meant anything to me, not with Brock monitoring my every move. Yet, every time I played that role, it hurt you, and I just wanted someone to stab me in the heart and get it over with.

"I wanted to resent you for stepping through the portal, so I took it out on you, but deep down, I resented myself for failing to protect you. Then your presence stirred up memories that the rune repressed."

I wiped away the tears trailing down his cheeks, not sure what to say to all that. His confession didn't exactly excuse his behavior. He didn't have to say the horrible things he did. It didn't sound like that was one of his commands. Even if Brock was watching his every move, Aspen took out his rage and fear on me for coming to a world he couldn't save me from. I understood it but didn't forgive him for it.

"How long until you're back to the evil bastard," I joked, kind of.

"Maybe if we continue to always touch, he'll never come back."

Oliver groaned a few feet away, and a shot of guilt hit me. I forgot about him. "Not sure how that'll work, seeing as Oliver's waking up, and soon his knife will be at your throat."

Aspen sat back, sweeping a deadly gaze over Oliver's moaning and groaning form. At his severe expression, I looked at his rune under my thumb, relieved it wasn't glowing. This was a facet of Aspen. The utter confidence, as he sized up Oliver, that I once thought was arrogance was really self-awareness. Aspen grew up in Elora. He knew this world. He had years of experience. And yeah, maybe he was a little arrogant, but most of it was backed up by the fact he could kill someone without a thought.

"You can't hurt him," I said, not exactly sure where we stood but hoping he listened.

Aspen glanced back to me and nodded before taking my hand from his face, placing it on my chest and almost releasing me, but I squeezed it in a death grip.

"What are you doing?" I panicked.

"You're right, we can't touch forever. I need to put my gear back on if your friend is gearing up for a fight, and you need to put your pants back on."

Dirt and sticks dug into my exposed skin. I swallowed. If Aspen hadn't shown up or he was even a second later... I squeezed my eyes shut.

Warm, calloused hands smoothed away the frown between my brows.

"Hey, sweetheart, look at me." I did, staring into his vibrant blues. "I will always come for you. I will always find you."

"Can you sense my emotions?"

He cocked his head to the side. "No, but I'm intelligent enough to put two and two together."

I was wrong. He was arrogant.

"I can sense yours," I admitted, knowing he needed to know the other facet of our bond. *But why couldn't he sense mine?*

"What?"

I nodded. "It's true, but I think your rune affects when I can and can't sense them."

"For how long?"

Thinking back to my dream-walks, I remembered a couple of instances I sensed emotions that didn't feel like my own. "From the beginning."

"I wonder—"

"Ahh, fuck-a-duck, how did that twig knock me out?" Oliver groaned, interrupting our conversation.

Aspen grabbed my chin, turning my attention back to him, and ignored Oliver. "The male I decapitated was an Archangel bounty hunter. Grab the feather from his belt and the cuffs from his pocket. I want you to cuff my ankles. They'll stop my power and make it harder for me to take you." He fished something out of his pocket and handed me a black key—the one that matched the color of my cuffs. "Then I want you to run as fast as you can back to the Earth portal and get the hell out of Elora."

"And leave you?" I asked, pocketing the key so I didn't lose it.

He nodded, earnest.

I smacked him across the face.

CHAPTER THIRTY-TWO

"Are you out of your mind?" I yelled, winding up to smack him again.

Aspen snatched my wrist before my second hit landed. The smack wasn't hard, but it stunned him. Oliver scrambled to push between us like he would save me from the big bad prince who told me to leave him in Etherea, cuffed and without his powers.

Just as I noticed Oliver's eyes glowing green, I threw out my hand to block him from Aspen. But Oliver ended up touching both of us. Aspen's murderous blue flames evaporated, and we both fell into our fears.

I STARED AT MYSELF in the full-length mirror, body clad in a white dress that hugged my innocent body and flared out into glittering tulle. Sparkly white shoes from last year pinched my toes, and crystal artfully tamed my dark curls. My mom wanted me presentable. My father was coming to visit. He only visited once a year, on my birthday, like today. And the sparkly white display was all for him—his favorite color.

I glowered. It's not that I didn't like white—although the sparkles I could do without—but I hated that this was all for him.

"Honey, are you almost ready? Your father will arrive soon." My mom's voice was tender, but I could hear her nerves in the lilting sounds.

Biting my cheeks, I gave into my distress, and immediately soothing calm pushed it away as she placed her hand on my shoulders. "Come on, honey."

I smiled at her, grateful for her influence. She smiled back, a sadness lingering there, and popped out of my room to tend to dinner. The horror of what was to come sank in.

Once a year, he came, inflicting confusing emotions on both of us. Of course, I wanted the father I hardly knew to love me and care for our family. But he was never here, and when he was, well, I wished he wasn't.

I couldn't remember much from when I was younger, whether the trauma was stuffed in the back of my mind or he was a nicer father, but as my birthdays passed, his abuse became worse.

For me, it started as hitting. Anything that displeased him was a hit. But then he needed to take more—like throbbing hot slices out of my back. And if I struggled or cried, he'd call me a wimp and make another permanent line, taking his sweet time as he drew out the agony. Only that still wasn't enough. He had to have another outlet.

My mom.

At first, when he abused her, it was just hateful words spewed behind a closed door. They didn't think I could hear it. But when the walls were paper thin, it was hard not to. Things changed when I winced from my mom's hug. She forced me to show her the lines carved into my back. He hit her the following year after confronting him about it, black and blue bruises smattering her jaw. Yet my warrior mom never did anything back, which I didn't understand. She was strong and fierce. Part of me hated that she never fought back. So what held her back from retaliating or leaving?

I often imagined running away on this day. This oh-so-special day. That was what my friends at school told me. What a lie.

I reached my hand back to trace the scarred lines, forever tormented by his brutal abuse. My stomach rolled at the thought of my mom talking to him for a second time. She said this birthday would be different. But if she didn't stop her own abuse, how would she stop mine?

"Lucille, your father has arrived, and the food is done. Come set the table for me," she called.

I walked down the picture-lined hallway, secretly happy that every frame was only of us two. She took down the ones of the three of us a few months ago. He may taint all my birthdays, but it was only one day.

Our quaint kitchen held drying herbs and chicken decorations. I teetered between laughter and eye-rolling every time the hallway opened to the chicken-themed objects. Even the wallpaper sported black and white roosters. My mom had an obsession. Since we were too close to town to own them, she made up for it with statues, antique signs, bowls, butter dishes, and whatever else she found on her trips into town. I will give it to her, though; she had an eye for design. Any other person would be accused of being a hoarder or an old lady antiquer, but not my mom. It was tasteful, and yet still a hilarious obsession.

I grabbed our nice, white plates—ones without chickens on them—and set the table. My father disliked my mom's obsession, claiming it defied her principles. Enjoying silly human pleasures and emotions was beneath her, he often remarked. According to him, it was the very reason we found ourselves in this situation. I didn't fully grasp his meaning until last year when his gaze fixed upon me.

This year, who knew what damage would be done?

"Lucille, come take my coat for me." His tone suggested I should've already been there to relieve him of the heinous duty. Placing the last fork down, I walked over to my father's imposing form, refraining from tensing at being near him. The white tweed coat scratched my fingers as I placed it on the hook beside our door.

His gray gaze fondly flicked to my mom, who placed food on the table, then to me with distaste. He never smiled. I doubted he ever laughed. I knew he oversaw some angel military and had to be strong, but my mom was once a part of the same military, and she smiled every chance she got. It made me wonder how the two came together in the first place. I had asked, but like the topic of my birth, it was never talked about.

"Anything new?" he asked, sitting in the wooden chair at the table, waiting to be served. It was the same old song and dance—the same questions, the same actions, and, for dessert, abuse. I could probably recite this conversation by heart now.

"No. Shields are still holding well, and there's been no unwanted attention," my mom replied in a monotone, as if she, too, risked dying of boredom from the same conversation. I'd come to an age where I continually questioned why she put up with it—with any of it. She may have only found out about the cuts last year, but how many years was she abused? And yet, here we were.

"Good," he said, waiting for my mom to finish piling food onto his plate. Once he had his food, we were allowed to sit and serve ourselves as he ate.

"Lucille, how is your training?" He asked the same question, and he expected the same answer.

"My training is going well, Sir. My powers are in check, and Mother has been educating me as required."

"Lucille, why do I sense a lie in your words?" he demanded.

"I'm not lying—"

He slammed his fist on the table, rattling the plates. "You are. I can sense it!"

Out of my peripherals, my mom's back stiffened. The gray in my father's eyes flashed white like lightning, signaling a brewing storm. He turned to my mom.

"What is she lying about?" he said, quiet words laced with a hint of a threat.

"I put her in school," my mom said, holding his gaze.

"You did *what*?"

"She still trains every other day, and we keep her powers suppressed. She needs socialization and to be with kids her age." she pleaded. A plea that my father ignored. There was no way she'd have a conversation about his abuse now.

He stood, napkin slapping the table, fork clattering against his white plate. "You knew the deal we agreed upon." Each sound out of his mouth was a step in her direction. The blush in her cheeks faded to an ugly white fear.

"You will take her out of school. You will move. She is not allowed to associate with the creatures of Earth, or else I will take you both to The Council of Righteousness."

The whites of my mom's eyes were wide with horror. I didn't know what The Council of Righteousness was, but it wouldn't be good for us.

Red flushed my father's face in his rage. "She should've never been born," he spat, latching onto her upper arm. "Look what your selfishness did to us!" The echoes of his bellows were a shock to our systems.

Faster than I'd ever seen my mom move, she stood and slapped my father, sending him stumbling back. My eyebrows raised in surprise, not because my mom couldn't hit. My mom did the training my father always spoke of. She was well-versed in the art of war from her previous life, yet she never used it against my father.

Until today.

Shining flame overtook the deep gray of his eyes. The air deadened as it pulled toward his fury. Ears popping, the pressure changed and turned to a brilliant white flame on his hands—Glory, like mine and my mom's.

In the book I stole from my mom, I read Angelic Glory only had one purpose and one purpose only.

To burn away evil without mercy. To snuff out life. It consumed the object, burning brighter and hotter than any flame created on Earth. Another translation in the angelic texts was Heavenly Virtue. It's what singed my stuffed animals not once but twice.

This "Heavenly Virtue" was pointed in the direction of my mom.

My heart dropped to my feet, and a new feeling crawled under my skin. He wanted to eradicate the only good thing in my world.

His flame shot out with a flick of his wrist, and I screamed as the ball of fire changed directions. It would've never hit her, even if she hadn't moved. And she did move, faster than my eyes could follow, barreling into me and knocking us to the floor. The large ball of flame disintegrated into particles of light.

My father didn't want to kill my mom. Only me.

"She will be taken to the Council of Righteousness, and we will finally take care of your mistake. We will see if you told me the truth all those years ago." The words echoed in their absoluteness.

His words should've broken me. Instead, they fueled my bitter hatred toward him. No matter what I did, he never gave me any love or warmth. If I turned back time to when I was seven, when I still hoped I'd receive my father's affection, then I'd be a crying heap on the floor. But ever since he hit me, an untethered seed of hate grew with each encounter. The fact that he wanted to punish my mom for creating and loving me made me realize I was capable of deep loathing.

The air around me deadened. My ears popped, and my mom's hands erupted in the same white light.

"Over my dead body." She stood, acting as a barrier between me and him.

"There will only be one dead body at the end of this. And darling, it won't be yours unless you're found guilty again." My father threw a white ball of flame at her face. She dodged it, realizing too late it was a distraction. Blurring behind her, he grasped her hair and yanked her to the ground right before slamming her head against the floorboards, knocking her out cold.

Rage burned through me. *How dare he.* Tasting copper, I let my cheeks go and clenched my teeth instead, glaring up at his face as I sat on the ground. I hated him. From the tops of his buzzed blond hair all the way to his pristine white shoes. My soul cried out for revenge to make him hurt as much as he made us hurt. The seed of hate blossomed into something tangible. An itch I never felt before scattered across my hands, and a coldness invaded my mind.

"What do you have to say for yourself?" My father pointed to my mom like I caused her unconsciousness.

And what do we have here?

I jerked. "What?" Not sure where that voice came from.

My father's eyes narrowed. "Don't make me repeat myself!"

Not out there. I'm in here. It felt like a frozen finger dragged down the inner workings of my head as the male spoke.

In my mind? I asked, shuddering.

Yes. What's your name? he asked.

Lucille. Who are you?

My head ripped to the side as my father smacked me, causing me to miss the male's words.

"I told you I would not repeat myself!"

Tears stung my eyes, and the seed grew further. My anger made my skin itch more severely, and a crackling noise started.

He will regret that. The angry voice matched the pulsing rage in my blood.

Slowly returning my gaze to the gray eyes of my nightmares, I glared. "You can't blame me for your sins."

I shouldn't have said that. My father was pure, an angel of renown who did no evil and brought justice to the worlds. Sin was reserved for the weaker, the lesser, for demons. Never him. Or so I was told. I knew saying the word would tip him over the edge, but I was so angry I wanted him to suffer. To prove him wrong.

The hand came faster and harder than last, sending my head into the floorboards. Dots pixelated my vision, only to disperse to a hand filled with white flame. My mind dropped to even colder temperatures, making my body shiver.

Touch him. Now. A cold fury seeped out of each syllable. The stranger's rage was a welcome companion, watching and wanting what I did.

Revenge.

So, when he told me to touch my father, I grabbed ahold of his glaring white leather shoes and *screamed.*

I screamed for all the words he spoke to me about how worthless I was, how I was a mistake he never wanted. I screamed for each bruise I received from his hands, for each puckered scar on my back. I screamed for all the mistreatment my loving mom received. And I screamed from the pain.

The freezing temperatures in my mind were a different kind of agony. One I wasn't in control of. The penetrating cold had to come from the stranger, but as much as I wanted it to stop, I suffered through it for the satisfaction of what came next.

Snapping my hands back, I glanced up to see an expression I'd never witnessed. My father's gray eyes widened in shock, completely encased in ice.

It's temporary. It won't hold him for long. You need to leave. The chill in my mind no longer hurt. Instead, it was a soft snowstorm that raised goosebumps on my flesh.

I can't go—my mom. I thought, scrambling on my hands and knees around my father's frozen figure.

Then hurry, he said with no bite to his words, only urgency.

I placed my hands on my mom's shoulder and shook her gently. "Mom. Mom. Wake up!" My head swiveled back to the frozen statue, noticing a white light shining through. *No, no, no.*

Hurry! he yelled.

"Mom!" We were running out of time. The ice dripped down into a puddle. We couldn't be here when he freed himself. If he smacked me only because of words, I couldn't imagine what would happen after my attack.

My hands shook harder, rolling her limp body across the hardwood like a rolling pin. "Mom!" I begged.

Leave her. She'll survive, he said. But I could hear the grains of regret putting doubt in my mind.

I felt stabbing icicles and gasped. "What are you doing?" I said.

Leave her! The sliver of regret I heard earlier vanished. It reminded me of my father and how he spoke, expecting everyone to hang from his every word and do anything he asked.

I ground my teeth together. *I won't leave her.*

The stranger didn't understand. My mom was all I had. She held me when my first dog ran away, calmed my nerves on my first day of school with humans, listened to every story I came home with, wearing a smile on her face, and guided and soothed me when bullies tried to mock my strange eyes. She read to me every night, and on special nights, we had hot chocolate. She was my teacher, my rock, and the kindest person I'd ever met, except when she taught me hand-to-hand fighting, which I sucked at. But my mom was always there, calming my emotions and Glory with her soft touches. I would never leave her because she never left me.

The gnashing of teeth echoed through my thoughts. *How old are you?*

Eleven. Today, I turned Eleven and hated every second of it.

He said a harsh word I couldn't understand. *Fine. We do this the hard way.* He paused, thinking. *Grab the heaviest pot on your table and smash it into the back of that despicable angel's head the moment the ice melts.*

I started at his words. *What?*

There is no room for questioning. You have already made your bed. It's time to grow up and lie in it. Now, make that angel bleed.

He was right. But that didn't make it any easier.

I tried to hold onto my anger as I grabbed the cast iron skillet filled with cold potatoes. The pan required two hands. Feet slapping into the wet puddle, I stood behind my ice-encased father. Parts of him remained iced over, while others were thoroughly soaked. The white of his clothing hung close to his muscular frame. Potatoes slopped onto my sparkly flats and into the water as I raised the skillet. Winding back, I waited. Drip by drip, my father thawed. Each drip made me flinch.

I couldn't do this.

He hurt you first, he said.

But... The doubt continued to seep in. My wrists shook with the weight of the iron. Hovering over his neck, sweat forming with my increasing heart rate, the last of the ice melted. And it might've worked. Maybe we could've left with no one the wiser, but the moment the glistening sheen fell away to soppy clothing, I hesitated. In that moment, I truly realized the value of my mom's lesson on hesitation.

His movements blurred. My body slammed into the pans and plates of food on the table. A broken plate cut through my dress and into my back, staining my no longer pure white dress with blood. Black and white spots dotted my vision from the force of my head hitting the pot. My father used one hand to pin both of my wrists down. He moved so fast I didn't even notice the large white feather gripped in his hand coming for my arm. Its needlepoint was dipped in black, like a quill, and as if my arm was the missing parchment, he stabbed it into my skin, dragging it up and down.

"You will never have access to your powers again, and once the Council of Righteousness is through with you, I'll not only be rewarded, but I'll never have to see your sinful face again."

Shrieking from the hot agony, I tried to squirm out of his hold. But I didn't stand a chance.

He sawed at my skin with his feather, warming my mind and taking my energy.

Fury that didn't belong to me erupted without its piercing cold. *I will take pleasure in seeing him burn in hell for his sins. Mark my words, child, his days are numbered.* The stranger's voice weakened the more my father carved.

I will find you again, my sweet Lucille. And maybe by then, we'll both have an explanation. The last of his words faded.

A deafening bang echoed through the air. My father fell to the floor, taking his angelic feather with him.

"Lucy? Lucy?"

I gazed into her glossy eyes, now green, tears mirroring mine. "Mom?"

"Oh, heavenly. My sweet girl." She hugged me and pulled back. "We need to leave." My mom hauled me off the table and dashed into the bedroom. Tired and dizzy, my legs gave out. I scrambled back from my father's unconscious body, winced at the pain in my wrist, and looked at the damage.

A bloody Binding Rune cut into my soft flesh, taking away all my powers. I was practically human.

My mom rushed out of her room with two backpacks and a pair of keys.

She hauled me from the floor, shoved calm emotions into my body, and dragged me as quickly as she could through our front door and to our only vehicle. Not a word was said, not an explanation of where we were going or what had just happened. She pushed me into the passenger side, buckled me, ran to the driver's seat, and we left.

Him. The house. Everything we owned.

We left it all. I had no words as my mom broke all the speed limits to escape, hoping he wouldn't catch up.

I GASPED, JOLTING UPRIGHT from the horrible memory Oliver put me through. Beside me, Aspen writhed on the ground, not yet out of his own hellscape. He didn't moan or cry out. But the reflective lines leaking out of his tightly squeezed lids were evidence of his pain. A pain that I shared with him as I remembered a mom who loved me and betrayed me and a father who wanted to kill me.

"Wake up, Aspen." He jerked on the forest floor. I could feel his pain and couldn't stand it. "Oliver, wake him up, stop this." But Oliver was on his hands and knees over a pile of puke.

"Oliver?" holding my side, I cringed as I stood and approached him. Whimpers interrupted his heaves. "Oliver?" I touched his shoulder.

"I forgot," he said in a broken whisper.

I sank behind him and gasped as I pulled him away from his puke. He let me, slumping against my chest. His weight made my ribs throb, but with the heart-aching noises coming from his mouth, I couldn't help but let him rest against me.

"He was just a boy. He came to our house," he whispered.

"Who? Who did you see?"

"My mother," his voice cracked. "Being burned alive by Marcus's flame."

Goosebumps pebbled my arms, and I stilled, knowing exactly what memory he was talking about.

"I never saw it happen. I was—she pushed—" Oliver heaved in between his cries.

"She pushed you away, and you hit your head on the wall," I whispered. I glanced at Aspen. The small blue-eyed boy was Aspen. *That's who she wanted me to save.*

Oliver jerked up, eyes puffy with tear streaks on his cheeks. "How—"

"I have the power to dream-walk into memories," I admitted. "I saw that one before you tackled me in Damatha Forest."

Stricken, he stared at me. "How is that possible?"

Aspen moaned. I jerked my head around, pushing Oliver to get off me so I could return to Aspen. I moved to crawl back to him, and Oliver grabbed my arm.

"What are you doing, Lucy? He's the enemy. We need to bind him or run or kill him or something! I could hit him again, but it'll take the last of my juice after hitting both of you when you shoved in front of him like a lunatic!"

"No! We're not killing him or binding him and leaving him here." I shoved Oliver's hand away. "But we might need to cuff him. The bounty hunter had some. Go search his clothes." There was no way I was going near that male. I shuddered, crawling over to Aspen as Oliver rifled through the dead angel's stuff.

I reached out to Aspen, about to touch his face, when he snatched my hand, jerking me toward him. My ribs screamed, and I whimpered. He immediately let go of me, only to grab me again.

"Fuck," he spat as he fought against the glow. "Lucille, you need to leave. Cuff me and run."

Oliver stepped next to me, jangling the cuffs in his hands. "I agree with the princeling, except I'm not sure why?"

I ignored them both, scooting closer to Aspen. "Let me touch you. It'll help," I said, pressing my hand against his face.

Aspen clenched his fists. "It won't work. Not after what the Nephilim did." He flung his head back, crying out as every muscle in his body tensed. I wasn't even touching the rune, yet I felt the searing electricity attempting to take over. "I'm not supposed to remember my mom's murder. It's her failsafe. Anytime I tried, the rune would attack and weaken me until I forgot and obeyed again. But you made me remember the whole *fucking* thing, and it's battling me," he said through gritted teeth.

"So, what do we do?" I asked, putting my thumb on his rune. It shot into my hand, sending a path of unbearable heat through my entire arm. I screamed and let go.

"Stop touching me, Lucille!" he said softly before snapping at Oliver. "Put the damned cuffs on me, Nephilim."

With wide, puffy eyes, Oliver glanced at me and then back to Aspen, trying to understand the situation but failing miserably.

"Do it! Before it's too late," Aspen bellowed, flames flashing in his irises.

Startled, Oliver dropped to the ground and locked his ankles together, then pocketed the key. "Now what?"

"Now you take Lucille and leave," Aspen moaned like the cuffs that took away his power made the struggle worse.

I grabbed for his fist, but he pulled out of reach. "I'm not leaving you here."

"I can't promise you what I will be like when it takes over. You need to go."

"No."

"Luci—" His eyes rolled as he fell back, writhing on the ground.

I snapped my gaze to Oliver as he retched into the grass. "Why did you do that?"

"How many people has he watched get murdered?" he moaned as he grabbed my arm, lifted us off the ground, and pulled me away. I almost jerked out of his hold, thinking he was about to run with me, when he said, "I'm just getting you away from the stench of my stomach acid. Relax. I'm buying us time to make a plan."

Defeated, I gingerly sank to the ground. "What kind of plan, Oliver? I have no idea what to do or where to go anymore."

He looked at me funny. "What do you mean? We're going to Magda's."

I scoffed, wincing as I unlocked my cuffs and handed them to Oliver. "Here. That's how you reach your sister. They'll allow you to cross their border, but it'll suppress your powers. I don't need to go to Magda's anymore. The memory of why I was taken returned. My mom poisoned me. She's working with Marcus. She doesn't need to be found."

Oliver stared at the cuffs, quiet. Then he took a step back, refusing to accept them.

"Oliver?" I asked, surprised. "Take them. This is what you've been dying to find. Go get your sister back."

"You're right. For ninety-five years, I've been trying to find a way to Melanie." He lifted his gaze from the cuffs. "But we made a deal. We're going to Magda's, then you can give me the cuffs. Your mom isn't working for Marcus, Lucy. You need the rest of your answers."

"How would you know that? Do you have another super-dandy power I don't know about?" I asked, throwing out my hands and regretting it instantly.

"No, but I saw your fear too, Lucy. I saw your scum-bag father. I heard creepy iceman, which we will have to revisit later. And I saw your mom. I saw the love she had for you."

I rolled my eyes and stared at Aspen. Oliver stepped forward, gripped my chin, and forced my attention back on him.

"No! Listen to me. I may not have a mother anymore, but I know what love from one looks like. Jumping in front of a fireball for you and standing in front of you, ready to duel it out with another Archangel, is love. So whatever memory you restored in your head isn't the whole picture. You're missing something, and we are going to that damn decapitating witch and getting you answers," Oliver stated, practically stomping his foot.

"But what if it's all true? What if my mom's—"

"What if my sister's dead? What if, even with the cuffs, I can never get to her? What if, what if, what if? I get it more than you know. But the difference between you and me is that I'm willing to face any outcome just to know I tried for her. But you, Lucy, based on what I saw by touching you, you have a habit of ignoring your fears or having your mom suppress them, which was why you were shit at controlling them in the beginning. She did you no favors even if you were hiding from a scum-bag father."

I didn't want to listen to his rational words, not after what I saw. I didn't want to go to Magda's and face the truth, whatever it was. My mom sobbed in front of my face and poisoned me with Marcus.

"Lucy, you went straight to the worst what-ifs and forgot to ask, what if your mom's in trouble? What if there was no other option? Are you really going to forget about her and go on your merry way? Was surviving this shit place all for nothing?"

I didn't want to face my past—my abusive father or my mother's betrayal. But also, I didn't want to remember how badly Aspen made me yearn to escape. Every time he met me in those woods, I longed to leave my mom behind and experience life in a different world. But the guilt wrecked me after thinking of everything my mom had done for us, which she always soothed away when I walked back from the forest.

Her touch was a comfort and a cage.

But it wasn't just her betrayal that hurt. It was hating myself for wanting a different life and partially resenting my mom. If she truly was an evil mastermind, then all the guilt and self-loathing I had for myself was a lie. But if Oliver was right, and my mother was in trouble, I needed to help her like she always did for me, no matter how misguided her help might've been. If he was wrong and we found her... I didn't know what I'd do.

CHAPTER THIRTY-THREE

"Okay, but how are we carting Aspen around?"

Oliver glanced at the cuffs in my hands, then Aspen's wrists. "We're not. He's walking, and we'll cuff his hands so he doesn't get any ideas."

"You want Aspen to have the cuffs that'll take you to your sister?" I asked, raising a brow.

He shrugged. "Not really. But I also rather not have an enemy prince with the ability to use his hands and chop off my head with his sword."

"Good point."

I stood slowly and handed the key and cuffs over to Oliver.

Oliver turned to Aspen's twitching form, weighing the cuffs in his hand and contemplating.

Assuming what he was thinking, I said, "Lock them in front. If we run into anything, we may need the little help he can give."

"I was thinking the opposite. But with your Binding Rune and my sapped powers, I guess we could give the evil princeling the ability to choke us in our sleep," Oliver mumbled while securing Aspen's wrists in front of his body. Then he proceeded to search for and remove every dagger stored on Aspen's person. As he was about to touch his sword, Aspen came to, lurching up and smashing his forehead into Oliver's nose.

"Fuck-a-duck!" Oliver fell back, blood seeping through his fingers. "You're lucky she wants you alive!"

I scrambled forward before Aspen could use the cuffs he was glaring at as a weapon. "Stop!"

The rage on his face had me stepping back. "I don't let anyone touch me, prisoner."

Prisoner?

"Aspen?" I whispered, staring in horror at the rune underneath his chin. The red looked almost black.

"Do not address me in such a way. It is Prince Aspen, prisoner."

I just stared at him, listening to the haughty disgust in his words. *What the hell did the rune do to him?*

"The way I see it, *princeling,* is you're our prisoner until we figure out what to do with your sorry ass. If I had it my way, I'd leave you here to be pulled apart by the Ethereal Kingdom." Oliver glanced at me, making a face. "Speaking of, we should probably leave so that doesn't happen."

He was right, but how the hell did we get Aspen to follow us? At my concerned face, Oliver took the lead, putting a knife in one hand and thrusting the other forward. "Get up, unless you want me to hit you again, princeling."

"With your fucked up illusions?" Aspen snarled, wrists wrenching against the cuffs.

Oliver shrugged, wiping away the last of the blood dripping from his nose. "Whatever helps you sleep at night, princeling."

Did he think the memory was fake? From the certainty I felt from him and the disgust curling his lip, I think he did.

"Aspen?" I tried again.

"I am not Aspen! I am the Prince of the Tenebrous Kingdom and the right hand to the queen. And when I remove these cuffs, you will be coming with me."

"To the queen who murdered your mother?" I asked, needing to see if he was in there.

"You have no idea what you're talking about."

I took a step closer. "Marcus murdered your mother. The queen murdered your first love!"

"I will *obey*! They mean nothing to me!" he raged.

"They brainwashed you!" I yelled back, begging him to remember. I had the real Aspen back for a split second, and she was taking away the male I met in the woods, who gave me the courage to want more, who made me see there was more to life than hiding away in fear.

"How would you know, Lucille? You're barely surviving in a world you know nothing about that will only use you up and spit out the useless pieces."

My mouth dropped open. He had said other terrible things to me, and I knew this was the rune talking. It had to be. "Says the male being used. Let's go, Oliver."

Aspen's glare darkened. The muscle in his jaw ticked as he gripped the hilt of his sword.

Oliver eyed the intricate metal. "I feel like I should confiscate that."

"Even if you thought you could take it from me, it's infused with blood magic."

"Let's go, Oliver," I said, walking away as I clutched my sides.

Oliver pointed his dagger at Aspen. "Oh no, he's walking in front. Lucy, you'll stay by my side. We shouldn't be far from the border, but let's not dilly-dally."

I agreed, clutching at my ribs.

"You okay?" Oliver asked.

I should be asking him that after he had to rewatch the memory of his mother's murder.

Aspen walked in front of us and turned back to stare at me.

I ignored him. "The bounty hunter broke my ribs."

Oliver frowned. But Aspen... He turned around and glared at the lifeless body like he'd like to set it on fire. For a moment, I thought he cared, until he spoke.

"No one damages the queen's property."

How could my mom do it? Watching Aspen right now, listening to him, and seeing how thoroughly a magical symbol controlled him, I didn't understand. Sure, my mom pushed the positive on me, but how was that any better? We were both puppets. But I hoped I finally had learned my lesson. As for Aspen, I needed to figure out how to remove a rune. That'd be another question I asked the witch.

Oliver hip-bumped me, making me gasp. "Shit, sorry. I was just trying to get the glazed look out of your eyes. Do you want me to stab him?"

I snorted, blinking away the blur of pain. "Let's not give him any opportunities to steal your weapon and use it against you. At least he can't remove his sword cuffed."

"True. Did you want to find a healer before Magda's?" Oliver asked, following Aspen as he walked further ahead, never straying too far from us. Aspen would never leave the *queen's property*.

"I don't think there's much to be done about broken ribs. They'll heal eventually." I lowered my voice. "Has *he* said anything?"

"No. You?"

"I don't think he'd be able to reach me with the Binding Rune."

"You're probably right," he said, his eyes drilling into Aspen's back as if the option to stab him was still under consideration.

"You want to ask him about your sister, don't you?"

"It crossed my mind a few dozen times. But the princeling seems quite put off. I doubt I'd get anything from the bastard."

He wasn't wrong. A brooding cloud of anger swallowed Aspen. Between his tight shoulders and the dark red light casting a vile halo beneath his chin, it didn't matter his steps were soundless; someone could feel him coming a mile away. I was glad we walked behind him, and I pitied the person who stumbled into his path.

We sloshed across the shallow river, Oliver holding my elbow to steady me and Aspen on the edge of the bank, watching our steps with guarded eyes. Once we reached him, he turned his back and stepped through the barrier. We followed, stepping into the field of metallic gold grass, back into The Divide.

"So which way to Magda's?"

Aspen stopped. "We are *not* going to Magda's."

"When we need the input from our princely prisoner, we'll ask. Otherwise, best to keep your thoughts to yourself," Oliver chirped back.

The muscle in Aspen's jaw pulsed as he strode back to us and pushed into my space. "I said no. She's dangerous."

"More dangerous than Lilith?"

He grimaced as the rune flickered to red but didn't go out. Confusion furrowed his brows before the rune reverted to black and shifted his frown to an expression of displeasure. "My queen will be the only one to claim you." His arms jerked up, attempting to encircle me with his cuffs, only to freeze when Oliver pressed the tip of his knife against Aspen's neck.

"*Lucy* will be *had* by nobody. I think she's had enough cages to last her the rest of her life."

I agreed, gesturing forward, glaring into a face I barely recognized. "How about you return to your useful spot up there and lead us to where we want to go."

Flickers of his rage and panic intruded on my mind. "I can't—" He clenched his teeth, forcing out words, and the rune pulsed between black, red, and skin. "Protect—you," he gasped out.

Immediately, I placed my thumb on his rune, hoping to help him. The same agonizing pain shot up my arm, making me whimper. My Aspen, the one that peaked through for a moment, wrenched his face out of my grasp to save me from the pain.

"Don't touch me."

I couldn't tell which Aspen spoke. The one who stared at me with scorn, thinking I was an object to be used or the one who wanted to murder the queen's army after finding me malnourished and bruised. But from the emptiness I felt from him, I assumed it wasn't my Aspen.

It hurt to look at him while he was like this. I didn't know what to say or do.

"Start heading to the Damatha Forest, princeling, and leave protection duty to me, seeing as you're looking at her like she's a thing again," Oliver said, keeping the knife between us and him.

Surprisingly, Aspen complied after looking Oliver up and down and sneering. He jangled his way through the golden field, heading towards the trees, as I stared at his back, feeling hopeless.

Oliver lightly placed a finger under my chin and turned me to face him. Blonde and black wisps of hair tickled his light eyelashes, bordering his intense gaze. I swallowed.

"I know we agreed to go there. But in all seriousness, if the prince is right and it's too dangerous, we leave and wait for the king to contact us." I didn't know what to think about this Oliver—fierce and somber, holding me under his penetrating gaze. "Because he'd probably freeze my balls off if I let anything happen to you. So, let's try and keep out of danger if we can." He wrapped his arm around my neck and gave me a noogie, like an annoying older brother.

I laughed and batted him away, then gasped. "Shit."

"Might as well get used to it, Luce. If you broke your ribs, you got a while with that pain without your fast healing. Unless we can find someone to remove your rune."

I sighed. "I hope we can find someone then."

"And I'll hope for a bowl of stew and the chance to stab the princeling. One's more likely than the other."

Looking up, Aspen stood waiting for us in the distance, watching our exchange with narrowed eyes.

"You know he might've been good once. Before she brainwashed him."

I bit my lip. "He still is."

Oliver gave me a sympathetic look. "Lucy, he's been with the queen for his entire life. He's carted female after female to her. He may not harm them, but he's still guilty. Even with some magical rune compelling him, does that truly excuse his actions?"

I followed Oliver, having no answer for him. But he was right, and I didn't want him to be.

Still a few yards away from Aspen, Oliver stepped in front of me, gripping my shoulders, and captured me with the sincerity on his face. "I see how you look at him." My cheeks flushed. I tried to look away, but Oliver held me there, forcing me to hear his words. "I'm not judging you." He reconsidered. "Okay, maybe just a little bit. But Aspen will never be what you want him to be. You need—"

"Someone who doesn't cart females against their will? Someone to sweep me off my feet and catch me when I fall?" Although, once upon a time, he had swept me off my feet back on Earth when it was just us in the forest with all our secrets.

Oliver shook his head, his gaze intense. My stomach flip-flopped. I so wasn't used to this Oliver.

"No. We all fall, Lucy. It's a part of this strange life we live. We need to fall. You don't need a knight in shining armor or a broken prince to catch you on the way down. You need someone to hold you in the mess. Someone to find strength in you as you mend your broken pieces. From the ground up, not the sky down."

"But what about his broken pieces?" I whispered.

Oliver wiped away my tears, pursing his lips and shaking his head. "What if he's broken beyond repair?"

"What if your sister is? What if my mom is? Are we going to just give up on them?" I demanded.

He sighed. "Not give up, but distance ourselves. I said, find *strength in* as you mend *your* broken pieces. But you can give a person only so much strength before you're giving too much. You aren't obligated to sacrifice yourself for someone else."

I opened my mouth to protest.

"Lucy, you said you had the Binding Rune on you for years. Don't you think your mom could've taken it off or found someone who could've?"

"She was scared of people finding us," I explained.

He nodded. "So instead of helping you to be excellent in all that power you have and give you the strength to stand on your own two feet, she kept you suppressed and then poisoned you."

I frowned.

"She let her broken pieces win. She let her fears win."

I threw up my arms. "So what? I need to give up on my mom now, too?"

Oliver gave me a dry look. "No, my point is that you should value yourself as much as you value others and vice versa. If the other person is too broken or taking too much from you, it's important to let them go so they can heal themselves. It's called taking care of yourself, and it's not selfish; it's necessary. Okay?"

"Okay," I sighed, even if I didn't entirely mean it. He lifted one side of his lips, leaned in, and kissed my forehead.

Who was this male, and where was the carefree insufferable Oliver?

He kissed my forehead once more before wiping away the rest of my tear streaks. "So, when you kick Aspen's ass to the curb, I'll be your wing-woman."

I gave a wet laugh at his wiggling eyebrows. *There he was.*

"You?" I asked. He was pretty bold with his methods. I wasn't sure I wanted his help, even if I was giving up on Aspen. Which I wasn't.

"Yeah, me! I've got years of practice. Where do you think all that sound advice came from, huh?" He shot me a look. One that had my cheeks heating once more. It was easy to forget how old they were when they looked so young. I didn't even want to think about all the females Aspen's been through. And how inexperienced I was compared to... Well, most.

Oliver pulled me closer. "You need a wing-woman. Lucky for you, I have all the time in the world to fill that position—when we aren't running for our lives or finding answers. And as of right now, I'm saying Aspen's off the potential getting Lucy laid list."

I sputtered, the flush reaching my forehead at how loud he said that.

He full-bellied laughed as we walked toward the glowering prince. I hoped that whatever god was out there, Aspen did not hear that because underneath the evil prince was the Aspen I hoped to set free.

But was he a prince? He wasn't related to the queen. He was no demon. His mom had blue rings in her eyes, not purple, so what did that make her? Aspen was part angel, but what was the other part?

Aspen turned and led us to the witch. I hoped she held our answers.

CHAPTER THIRTY-FOUR

The further we walked into The Divide, the thicker the trees became.

"Think if I threw a stick at the princeling, he'd explode?" Oliver leaned over to whisper to me.

I held back my laughter. "Please don't. We've come this far with no incidents."

Before we were deep in the Damatha Forest, Oliver found some interesting green fruit that he swore was edible. He didn't want to hunt and leave me with Aspen, so it would have to do. I finished the large, sour morsel before the thick canopy swallowed the sunlight and the trees became car sized.

"Think I could eat those blue mushrooms?" I asked, still hungry.

Oliver laughed. "Yeah, that's a great idea if you want to turn into a glow-bug or die."

Aspen scoffed like we needed our brains reevaluated when actually we needed more food and for our lives to be simpler and not the object of everyone's malicious desires.

A slight twitch hit the corner of my lips as we passed a batch of Celestrus. They lit up one after another like a runway guiding us to the darkness ahead. Distracted by the strange beauties, I ran right into Aspen. I jerked back, not wanting to touch him, and backed into Oliver.

"Why'd we—" I started to say until Oliver covered my mouth. Shooting him a glare, I noticed his face had paled. Confused, I side-stepped Aspen and stopped.

It was so much worse than I could've imagined.

The dilapidated cottage crawled with browned vines and fog. Pikes were placed in a ring around the cottage with skulls of animals and humans in different states of decomposition.

"What'd I tell ya? Ms. Decapitator," Oliver mumbled, eyeing the skeletons with wariness.

Aspen's jaw bounced in time with the flicker under his chin. "Uncuff me."

"No," Oliver and I said in unison.

"If we go in there, and it goes to hell, who will help us escape?" By his tone, it sounded like he already had an answer. *So arrogant.*

"Oliver's got enough juice to take down a witch. Right, Oliver?"

I peered back at him. He nodded, but his scrunched, pained look did nothing for my nerves. Turning back to Aspen, I hoped he didn't see. The last thing I needed was some posturing fight over powers and strength. But as I watched a piece of left-over flesh plop to the ground from a freshly spiked skull and smelled the rancid scent that a swarm of flies flew to, I prayed I wasn't making some mistake.

Staring at his chains, I contemplated. Would it be so bad? Maybe... I shook my head, snorting at my asinine thoughts.

"We can't un-cuff you. The moment we do, I'll just be fodder for your queen. Oliver and good old-fashioned wit will have to be enough."

"You'll be fodder if you go in there, as weak and useless as you are."

I whipped around, eyes wild. So many hurtful words sat on the tip of my tongue, ready to explode in his black-runed face. I had to remember this wasn't him. But it was hard when our relationship, or whatever you'd call it, was fragile to begin with.

I stormed toward the skin-crawling cottage like I had a death wish, hearing Oliver at my back.

"I'd be careful what you say to her, princeling. Because if that rune ever comes off, you'll be one sorry bastard when you wake up." His tone held an unmistakable threat.

Before I got to the first wooden step, Aspen jerked me back with jangling chains, stepping in front. If we weren't about to be on the porch of a flesh-eating witch, I would've shoved him off. I didn't need his protection. It was only a guise for the need to keep me whole for his queen. Even if part of him wanted to keep me safe, he remained loyal to her.

We stepped onto the decaying threshold, the boards creaking with the shift of our weight. Aspen lifted his hand to knock, and the door swung open before his knuckles could touch, but the doorway appeared empty.

"This is starting off like every horror movie ever, and we're the stupid people walking into the haunted witch house when we all know we're going to die."

I shot Oliver a pointed look that said, *shut the hell up.*

He shrugged, mouthing, "It's the truth."

The smallest, most infinitesimal part of me had the urge to step closer to Aspen, but I dug that traitorous bit a grave. Although, I wasn't enjoying the tension in his shoulders or the sound of scavenging flesh flies.

"Darlings, don't worry, I only kill when there isn't a fair exchange," a pleasant voice called out. "Please, enter, and tell Magda what you wish to know."

Aspen scoffed. "Don't die." Then, as a shot of overwhelming worry hit me, he added a strangled, "Please."

I couldn't help but stare at his back as the Aspen I cared for peeked through. I needed to find a way for him to stay.

He moved through the door, Oliver and I at his heels. Once through the threshold, my face went slack.

I glanced at Oliver, who surveyed the small cottage with a similar surprised expression.

"Wow, it's pretty nice in here," he said, admiring the living room.

There were no dilapidated moldy boards to be found. The oldest thing in the cottage were the trinkets and gems lining shelves near a well-crafted fireplace. Even then, they were well-kept. Although, they stood apart from the rest of the interior. The rest appeared to be straight out of an interior design magazine.

Light feminine laughter pealed to our side. "The skulls and decaying wood help to keep the riffraff away."

The voice belonged to a sensual female. She stood in her pristine kitchen under a ceiling decorated with herbs. She looked young, which meant nothing in Elora. But by the surprise on Oliver's face, we were both expecting an old hag. Not a female with long golden hair in a tight ice-blue dress with no warts, moles, wrinkles, or scars to be seen on her skinny frame.

From the sneer lifting Aspen's lips, I think he was the only one unaffected by the unexpected appearance.

Magda smiled at his sour expression. "I'm surprised to have you back, prince, after the last time." Her eyes flicked to me and back to his glare.

I shot him a side glance. "This is the witch that told you—"

"That the female I'd have a guardian bond with would destroy my world."

"What?" He never mentioned that part in all his slivers.

Magda smiled, delighted by his answer and my shock.

"Figured you wouldn't want to know that part. But I no longer care. Soon, it won't matter."

It's not Aspen talking. It's the rune.

Magda laughed, enjoying our tension. "Well then, take a seat. Rest. Let me hear your questions." Keeping her smile, she gestured to the cushioned chairs by her fireplace. "Would anyone like tea? Or apples?" she asked, like a doting host.

Oliver shot me a questioning glance, and we both sat across from each other. I shrugged, wincing at the movement. We were both hungry. *But was her food safe?* I eyed Aspen, who stood behind me, his narrowed gaze all for Magda.

"They're not poisoned, just your average apples. And, sweetness, I have a tea to help soothe whatever ails you," she added, bustling around in her spotless white kitchen.

I guess not much got by her.

Oliver shrugged and nodded. "We'll have apples, and she'll take the tea. The princeling..." he glanced at Aspen, who continued to glare. "He doesn't matter."

Her silky dress swayed back and forth as her dainty hand released two apples into Oliver's lap. He handed me one. Not correcting Oliver, Aspen took nothing, hands more occupied with digging into my chair.

"So," Magda handed me a painted teacup and gracefully sat beside Oliver. "This is how I work. You ask a question, I'll give you a price for the information, and you accept, or you leave."

I let the steam of lavender and herbs hit my nose and took a sip. Its warmth spread into my skin and bones, soothing and mending. The relief eased my tension, making me wonder why everyone considered her dangerous. The witch was helpful, gorgeous, seemingly kind, and had a home most people would die for, at least in the interior.

"Okay, I guess I'll start," I said between sips.

Magda waved to my cup. "Please, finish. It's best to drink the tincture all in one sitting to receive the full benefits. We will wait." She smiled, gentle and encouraging. Any apprehension I had left slipped away.

They all waited patiently for me. Oliver's obscene crunching and my twitching feet hitting the leg of the chair filled the awkward silence. Drawing out the last sip as long as possible, I thought of my questions. My stomach twisted into a knotted mess.

At the last drop of tea, I set my cup on the coffee table, ignoring how it clattered against the wood.

It was now or never.

"Is Oliver's sister alive?" I asked.

I was such a chicken shit.

Oliver choked on his apple, caught off guard by my question. But I wasn't ready to ask about my mom. I needed a moment to work up to it, plus we needed to understand her price.

Magda fingered a small, glowing pendant on her chest. A crystal surrounded by five other crystals in varying shades of white pulsed with light before settling back to its dim color.

"The price for that answer is your name," she replied, still fingering her pendant between her cleavage.

Easy. I opened my mouth to respond when Aspen's chains clamored against the back of my chair, and his hands clamped down on my shoulder. His fingers alternated between squeezing and releasing, as if uncertain whether to offer reassurance, protection, or exert control. Regardless of his intent, I shrugged him off.

"Lucille," I stated.

Magda's gentle smile widened, and another pulse of light throbbed from her pendant. "She is."

Oliver slumped back in his chair, running a hand through his duel-colored bangs. He gave me a relieved smile and twisted to face the witch. "Did Marcus bring her to the Mother of Demons?" he asked, butting in. Not that I blamed him.

"Your price for that question," Magda said, pausing. She pursed her lips, rubbing her necklace. "Tell Lucy your deepest, most coveted desire. That you would do anything for."

He squinted at her. "Why'd you make that sound dirty?" Oliver snorted. "I'm pretty sure, Lucy, and now everyone, knows what I want most. It's my sister."

Magda softened her expression. "Yes. The Mother of Demons has her."

Oliver flew at Aspen. I jerked to a stand and held out my hands to stop his approach. Aspen may be vile and cruel, but I couldn't help but feel the urge to protect him.

"He doesn't know of her, Nephilim. He never has," Magda said after a tense moment.

My stuttering heart slowed. We both settled back into our seats, eyeing each other.

"How?" Oliver whipped back to the witch. "How could he not?"

Magda slid her hand from her necklace up to her mouth, rubbing her dainty lips and exposing her white pendant, which turned pink. "Is that your next question?" she asked.

Oliver shot Aspen a scathing glare, fingering the tiny knife sheathed at his side. "Yes," he said, green eyes flashing once before returning his focus to Magda.

Magda rubbed her pink, slowly turning purple, pendant. "What lengths would you go to rescue your sister?"

"All of them," he answered immediately.

"Would you kill for her?

Oliver looked at Magda like she suddenly turned into an old hag.

She smiled. "You've never killed anyone in your life, have you? So would you kill for her?"

"It depends on who I'd need to kill. Marcus, yes. The princeling, maybe. Lucy, no."

Magda pouted. "I suppose that's a fine enough answer. Yes. The prince doesn't know about her because she's kept in a secure location only the queen knows about."

"Where?" he demanded.

"That's a question."

"I'll pay the—"

She waved her hand. "Don't bother. My amulet won't show me. Next question."

Oliver ran two hands through his hair and nodded to me.

It was my turn.

"How do you get rid of a hell rune?" I asked, avoiding the big question and the reason I was in Elora. But faced with the prospect of learning what my mother had done and where she was, stole the air from my lungs. I wasn't ready. And I needed to fix Aspen.

Magda's eyes glittered. "Your price is to tell the prince how you feel about him."

Every muscle from my toes to my jaw tensed. I shoved at the flush threatening to overtake my face. "What do you mean?"

Magda smiled big and bright, almost like she enjoyed my discomfort. "You know exactly what I mean." Her smile dropped. "Tell him."

Needing a moment to think, I dropped my gaze to her chest, ignoring the creaking of wood and rattling chains. Her lavender pendant changed colors again, darkening to blue. At first, I thought the pendant changed colors with each question and answer, but that didn't seem to be the case. Something else triggered the color change, though that detail seemed irrelevant as I avoided the question.

"What if... I'm not sure?"

Magda lifted a brow, lips flat. "That'd be a lie. Lies are not part of the deal, darling." Her pendant flickered between purple and blue as her nostrils flared. "Do you want your answers?" she threatened.

I did, but I could hardly deal with my emotions myself. And telling him... It didn't feel right. Not now. Not like this. But I haven't asked about my mom yet, and we couldn't get kicked out now.

Oliver grimaced like he knew exactly what I was going through. Magda sat and stared, waiting with a severe expression. And Aspen, I didn't dare look behind me at the sneer or disgust waiting on his face.

"I—"

Dammit.

The tips of my ears burned, along with my neck, cheeks, forehead, and pretty much everything else.

Shutting my eyes, trying my best to ignore everyone, I spoke. "I always thought he'd be the handsome prince to steal me away from my life." I scoffed. "In a way, he was. His dimples, touches, and actions all got under my skin."

The day he called me sweetheart, his mantra of protection, *stay here, stay put, stay safe*, even when he warmed my leg to help the pain as he sewed me up, it all got under my skin. I opened my eyes, gazing at Oliver with a sad, resigned expression, remembering his words.

"I have feelings for him, for the male I met in the forest. But not for the male ruled by the rune who takes helpless females to his queen," I finished with a terrible ache in my gut and a cement house on my chest. Part of me wanted to be swallowed whole by a Hell-hound right about now, especially feeling the heat from Aspen's hands inches behind me.

Magda's face transformed with a brilliant smile. Her pendant shone a steady dark blue, no longer flashing.

"Mmhmm," she moaned, shutting her eyes. "I quite enjoyed that answer."

I glanced at Oliver, who mirrored my *what the hell* expression.

When Magda opened her eyes, they were the same shade of color as her pendant.

"Unfortunately, there's only one person who can remove a hell rune, and he is locked away."

I frowned. *That's all?* "Who? That shouldn't cost extra. I gave you a good answer."

Magda regarded me with a perfectly plucked lifted brow. "I don't give out freebies. I give what I want. But I'll meet you halfway and answer with, the general to the Mother of Demon's husband."

"Say what?" Oliver jerked back. "There's a Father of Demons?" He held up a hand as Magda opened her mouth. "No, that wasn't a question. My mind is currently blown and trying to reconfigure. Please give me a moment."

He wasn't alone.

Slowly, not wanting to but forcing myself, I turned to Aspen. He met my gaze, jaw ticking away.

"Your queen is married?" I asked.

"My queen is bound to the male, but they despise each other. I understand the feeling."

I sat back, taking in his disdain, wondering how many more of these looks and hurtful words it would take to erase the Aspen who wiggled his way into an innocent female's heart, wondering if it was all lies or if some of his words held truth.

"Not hard to despise someone like her," Oliver muttered, bringing me out of my head.

Aspen clenched and unclenched his jaw. The queen's disgusting hell rune swirled with black light, coercing his loyalty and infiltrating his mind.

Even if there was a slight chance Aspen wasn't lying about what he thought of me, he deserved to be free of his queen. His mom asked me to save him. I don't know how it worked or how she knew I'd end up in the dream-walk, but she knew enough to tell me. She anticipated the consequences before Marcus took her son, and she acted in his best interests.

I turned from Aspen and faced Magda, not ready but as ready as I would ever be.

"What else do you have for me, darling?" Magda twirled a lock of her golden hair.

Was it shinier than normal?

A jangling hand latched onto my shoulder. "One last question."

I jerked around. "I have more than one."

Aspen shrugged. "Should've asked the important ones first. That's not my problem."

"Go to hell," I whispered forcefully, holding back tears at his indifference, wishing for his dimples and soft touches. "I've come this far, and I'm not leaving without knowing everything about my mother and the king in my head."

His hand dug into my shoulder. "What king in your head?"

"Ask me, Lucille," Magda said with a smile in her voice.

Aspen shot a glance at Magda before landing back on me. "One," he repeated. By his tone and the way his fingers threatened to tear apart my chair, he meant it. Kicking or screaming, he would make me leave. *Good thing we cuffed him.*

"Did my mother poison me to protect me?" I asked, hating the wobble in my voice and the way my lungs seized.

Magda's blue pendant changed to blood red, and the glee I witnessed on her face—like she somehow won the biggest prize—unsettled me.

"I'll tell you that interesting tidbit if you tell me what you are."

Why did she want to know that?

"I believe I'm a born angel, the first of my kind," I said. Oliver's eyes grew.

Aspen scoffed. "No, you're not."

"I am," I insisted.

Magda tilted her head, rubbing her pendant. "Yes, I sense you believe that, but that's not all you are."

"What else am I?"

She licked her lips. "Isn't that the question of the hour? But to answer your previous question, yes. She thought it was the only way." Magda crossed her ankles, smiling with shimmering hair.

Relief settled the queasiness in my stomach. There was a reason my mom did it. It wasn't malicious, so she probably wasn't working for Marcus, but why was he there, and where were they now?

"Do not ask anything else unless you want to be strangled," Aspen snapped, digging his tingly fingers underneath my arm, trying to force me to stand.

I wrenched at my arm, but his fingers only gripped harder. So, I grabbed onto the heavy wooden chair. It didn't stop him, but it made dragging me a little more difficult for him.

"Sweetheart, let go!"

I froze, twisting around to look at his chin, giving him the time to slide his arms over my head and haul me out of the chair and back against his chest. The rune remained black.

He tricked me.

Aspen gripped my chin, smirking as he pulled us to the door. "The only person who gets to maim you is my queen. So, keep your mouth shut."

"Now you sound like Brock," I spat before he covered my mouth. He flinched as the rune flickered, but it wasn't enough. My presence, my words, my touch, nothing was enough to get him back. I needed the general to the queen's husband.

Oliver stood, bouncing his attention from the scene we were making and Magda, who sat daintily smiling in her chair, golden hair gleaming.

I ducked, forcing Aspen's cuffed hands to choose between muffling my words or keeping me close. He attempted both by pressing a hand into my chest and mouth, failing to silence me.

"Where is she? Where's my mom?" I asked, voice muffled but strong.

"Sweetheart," Aspen gasped, awkwardly twisting my face toward his. The rune flickered between skin and red light, mirroring his emotions as they wavered between worry and emptiness. "Listen to me, please. I know you can't shield your emotions, but no more questions, or we won't leave, and I need you safe. Once I open the door, run."

His eyes. I reached up, tempted to touch them. They glowed. He wore two pairs of magical suppressing cuffs, and his eyes glowed with power.

"Did you hear me, Lucille? Run and leave us."

I pressed a hand to his cheek, realizing even with my Binding Rune and his power-suppressing cuffs, nothing stopped the tingles of our bond. "But I have to save you," I said, staring into the eyes of the male who wanted me to stay safe, staring into my Aspen's eyes.

He dropped his forehead to mine. "There's nothing left of me to save."

Magda threw her head back and laughed. "Sorry, darling, but I no longer need her questions with how much sorrow and hope she's throwing about. It's so raw and potent. Delicious," she tittered.

"Although I will say, Lucille. You won't have to wait long before you find your mom again."

What did that mean?

As Aspen approached the door, she dropped her head slowly, her gaze locking onto us with eyes that mirrored the color of her pendant—a hue that filled me with growing dread.

"Run, Lucille," Aspen snapped, pressing me against the door.

Even if I wanted to, the doorknob wouldn't twist.

Magda stood, hair floating around her in a glowing halo. "You've given me quite a meal. I'm not ready to let you go yet. Not with one last thing to do."

A strand of golden hair lengthened, floating over to Oliver, who scrambled toward us. It caressed his cheek. He flinched back as the glowing hair seared a line into his skin.

"You should've listened to the princeling, darling." She prowled forward. "But I'm quite glad you didn't. The last time the prince came, he gave me nothing. But you two. You don't shield your emotions. It's delectable."

"Uncuff me, Luc—prisoner." Aspen vibrated with tension and warmed my hands with his unnaturally hot back. The heat penetrated his thick leather uniform. Almost as if the rune sent its searing heat through his body or his power sought release. I couldn't tell which, or maybe it was both.

"She doesn't have the key. I do, and I think it may be best to leave your cuffs on," Oliver said next to me, trying his hand at opening the door.

"But Nephilim, don't you know what's on the prince's wrists?" Magda said, smiling like she was about to win something.

Oliver raised a brow. "I do know. They're called cuffs."

"But they can—"

"Get me to my sister? Yeah, Lucy told me."

"But my vision showed me she hid that information..." she trailed off and frowned.

"Sorry to ruin whatever chaos you had brewing, but your next emotional meal isn't on the menu."

Magda sighed as her skin shimmered like the glow in her hair. "Fine, darling. We'll do this the hard way, then."

"Uncuff me!" Aspen bellowed.

But before we could react, Magda sent a flare of golden light at Oliver, and it sank into his skin.

"I hate doing the dirty jobs." Magda pouted. "So please knock out the female and kill the prince for me. He'd make a lovely addition to my fence."

Oliver slid a dagger from the sheath on his hip and stepped toward us. He smiled in a twisted sort of way. In a way I'd never seen. "With pleasure."

"Touch Lucille, and I'll have you begging for mercy, Nephilim," Aspen snarled, shifting his body to protect me from Oliver and Magda. I wasn't sure if it was the queen's Aspen protecting me or my Aspen.

"How? You're cuffed?" Oliver sneered at him, stepping closer.

"Oliver, whatever she's done to you, fight it! You don't want to kill Aspen or hurt me!"

"The prince works for the queen who has my sister. That's reason alone for him to die." He stepped closer to Aspen, pressing his dagger into Aspen's neck, their chest nearly touching. An unnatural heat radiated from Aspen's shoulders.

My stomach dropped to my toes. I tried to squirm around Aspen to protect him, but he only shoved me back.

"Back up, Nephilim."

Oliver glanced down at Aspen's chin. "I think you look better with the queen's rune. At least then we know where your loyalty lies."

"My loyalty will always lie with Lucille."

Oliver snorted, lifting his gaze to me. "You only wish that were true. But your queen has you leashed like a good little pawn. How long do you think you'll have this time with her? How many sweet lies will you whisper into her ear before you turn on her because of that rune?"

Aspen nodded down to Oliver's wrist. "If that rune is what I think it is, are you not a pawn?"

"Sure. But the difference, princeling, is that I was her protection detail."

"And now you're going to betray her and knock her out to let the witch do whatever she wants with her?"

Oliver shrugged, eyes apathetic. "Not my problem."

I flinched back from Aspen and the sweltering heat coming off him. He raised his flameless sword to Oliver's neck, and my eyes widened. He couldn't have taken that out of its sheath with his hands cuffed. I looked down at his side and found melted leather and ash.

But how?

Then I saw a flicker of blue flame snake around Aspen's cuffed hands holding the sword. It wasn't enough power to transfer to the blade, but it captured Oliver's attention. Not that he seemed concerned about the sword at his neck or the flames that were trying to breach two sets of cuffs.

"I said back the fuck up, Nephilim. Or I will take your head. I don't care if the witch is controlling you or if Lucille hates me. I have taken enough lives to no longer care about my soul or what I have to do to protect what's mine."

I glanced at Magda and found every part of her glowing, gazing at Oliver like he was dessert, controlling my first friend and making him turn on us. I was so sick and tired of haughty power-hungry bitches thinking they could control anyone they wanted. And when her eyes flashed and both of Oliver's hands shot out, Aspen only managed to block the knife diving toward his chest. But Oliver had a fail-safe as he latched his other hand onto Aspen's wrist, making my guardian crumble. Pricks and itches tickled my skin, and music whispered in my ears.

I glanced down at my Binding Rune. It turned lighter. *How?* Then a piece of a dream-walk memory came to me, of me on my bed, bathed in flames, looking at a Binding Rune that my powers destroyed. At that time, I had no control; now I had some.

I smiled down at my rune and dove to the deepest depths of my power, finding a mass of brilliant light and coiling darkness ready to aid my vengeance. Pressure pushed at my eyes, and itches swallowed my torso until my rune turned white, and purple flames enveloped my skin.

Oliver crouched over Aspen, pressing a knife against his neck. A fierce protectiveness surged through me, and I threw out my hand. A ball of ice smashed into Oliver's forehead, knocking him out. I felt terrible for hurting him, but I had no choice.

I turned to Magda. She shot a flare of golden light at me, but it did nothing against my purple flame. I tsked. "You unleashed hell. I hope you're ready to freeze in it."

CHAPTER THIRTY-FIVE

Revenge pounded in my blood, wanting an outlet. My power shoved the gut-twisting horror of killing someone in a corner, barricading it behind a wall of black fire. I savored the wariness in the witch's face and how the seductive melody brushed away my doubts and fears. I should be concerned. I didn't know how to fight. Maybe at one point, but not now. But as I listened to the song of my soul, I didn't care.

I channeled my desires into the melody, shaping a sharp icicle in my palm. As I hurled it towards her chest, she lunged aside. Her golden hair whipped past me, leaving a stinging trail of blood on my hip. The icicle didn't sink into her chest as intended; instead, it struck her shoulder.

"That must be painful," I remarked.

She screamed, sending strands of golden hair flying towards me, Aspen, and Oliver. I dove out of the way of mine and threw myself on top of Aspen and Oliver to shield them from theirs. The strands grazed my legs, leaving burning slices up my calves.

Furious at the witch's cowardice in attacking Aspen and Oliver while they lay defenseless on her pristine floors, I immersed myself in the seductive melody and summoned my black flames. Sitting up, I conjured a flickering ball into one hand and hurled it at her, simultaneously launching an icicle with the other. She deflected the icicle with her hair but couldn't evade my fireball, which seared into her leg. The flames ate away her skin, leaving a patchwork of muscle and bone.

Steeling myself against the pain in my calves, I approached her and her terrible shrieking. "Oh, I'm sorry. That must've really hurt. But I think I need to give you a matching pair like you did me." I threw another fireball at her other leg, but her hair intercepted it, thwarting my attack and reducing her strands to cinders.

She choked on a chuckle. I hated the sound. By the gleam in her eyes and the twisted smile on her face, she still thought she had the upper hand.

That enraged me more. I formed two black balls of flame, and my feet became heavy. *Shit.*

Her glowing whips of hair hovered around her as her shoulders shook. I didn't understand why she didn't attack or why she continued to cackle after what I did to her leg.

I threw my two balls of flame, needing to let go of them before I passed out. They flew toward her chest as she let out an ear-piercing scream, but right before they hit her, a ball of red smoke intercepted my power, and a knife sliced into my ribs.

I gasped, clutching my side, and turning to find a pink pair of lips peeking from a cowboy hat.

Marcus smirked and took a pouch out of his pocket, scooping up a handful of black dust. "Your father's waiting for you, Lucille. He's been waiting for a long, long time." Then he blew a small amount of Nerium powder into my face, sending me into a dark oblivion.

I STOOD IN THE same shadowed space with the glowing purple-white ball hovering in the middle. It taunted me, wanting me to reach out and take hold of my power.

"Are you ready?"

She was back—the cloaked figure.

"Ready for what?"

She thrust out her hand to the ball of flashing light. "To see the bigger picture."

I swallowed. "But the last time I touched it, it showed me..."

"A memory of your mom poisoning you."

"Yes," I whispered.

"The truth is better known than not known."

I stared at the ball of images and emotions, nervous about what I'd find.

"We didn't rescue you from The Void, so you could chicken out now. You gave your memories away, you stopped fighting, and you didn't even know the whole truth. Now you need to dream-walk to find everything you're missing."

I knelt next to the purple-white light. "How do you know all this? And why'd you send me to Magda's? Did you want Marcus to find me?"

The cloaked figure crouched next to me, tilting her face to the ground to hide from the light. "It was supposed to happen this way for the best outcome. Touch your Infernus." She stood back up. "Touch it, and when you wake up, if you ever want to save Aspen, steal the bastard's knife. Put it in your waistband and survive." Her footsteps retreated, leaving me in this shadowed cavern with my power.

Eighty percent of me wanted to turn away and bury it all. I always wondered why some memories about myself were clear while others remained elusive. I never understood why it wasn't a clean swipe, why only my dream-walk memories had returned and nothing else. But the part of me that yearned to escape and live freely to master my flames, the part of me that listened to Oliver's advice and sought out Magda's dangerous answers all stemmed from the core of my Infernus. The untamed power within my soul insisted I take charge and remember.

I touched the core of my dream-walking power. Vertigo and purple light enveloped me.

"I WANT FRIENDS, MOM. All I have is you. Don't get me wrong," I held up my hand before she could be insulted. "I love you. I'm grateful for all you've done for us. But you can't keep me hidden away forever. I'm suffocating," I pleaded.

She walked over to me with a tender expression in her jade eyes and her soft smile.

I stepped back. "Stop. Don't."

My lungs spasmed, trying to find air as I backed into our living room wall, knocking down a painting of a colorful chicken.

"It's okay, sweetheart. Let me calm you down."

I put out a hand to stop her. "No," I heaved. "Wait." My hand flew to my throat. "Why can't I breathe?"

"Lucille, sweetheart. I'm serious. Let me help you before you pass out."

I gave in.

She took my shoulder, easing the strain on my lungs and heart, pushing away the dizziness. "Why didn't you tell me you depleted your amulet?" she scolded me.

"Because of this." I gestured, skirting around her before she took hold of my amulet. "That happens every time the amulet depletes, and I don't know how to stop it alone. You never let me struggle with it long enough to figure it out. How am I supposed to manage myself if you're constantly there? How will I ever learn?" I said, flopping down into my favorite armchair. "Mom, I can't even feel scared out of my mind at the thought of leaving you now. Isn't that wrong?" I glanced at her, seeing fear in her watery eyes. I didn't mean to make her feel bad, yet I couldn't even feel bad about it.

"Love, for a year straight, you woke up in cold sweats. You want to go back to that?" she whispered.

My head fell back against the cushion. "No, but we can't keep living like this. It's been eight years, Mom. He hasn't found us. I want to live."

She opened her mouth to protest.

"Mom, I'm nineteen and haven't even kissed a guy. I have no friends. I'm stuck here day after day, reading books and sparring with you. Can't you see what this is doing to me?"

I hated the wobble in her lip as she sank into the couch, head bowing into her hands. She would always sit in the same spot when her thoughts ate at her. She'd never tell me what upset her, but I had my assumptions. Like all the previous times, I approached her, sat on the carpet, and took her hands.

"Mom, I'm sorry. I know you're scared. But two, three, five more years of this, and I might literally go insane. We'll practice my powers. I'll learn the scope of my emotions with your help. If things go badly, we'll have the amulet or you, and we can always move. After that, I want to live near people."

"It's not safe," she mumbled into her hands.

"Mom, come on. Please," I begged.

She snapped her head up, face puffy. "You don't understand. It's not just Michael that's after us."

My brows furrowed. "Who else?" This was news to me.

"The Tenebrous Kingdom, The Elorian Military, The Council of Righteousness," she admitted.

I dropped her hands. Stunned. "So, all of Elora. Your entire world?" I'd read all about Elora in the four books I unlocked and stole from my mom's hiding spot. Although, she didn't know that until now. But she didn't even whip her head up at how I learned things about Elora. That scared me. "Why?"

"Because I was never supposed to have you."

I rocked back. "Why would you say that? You're sounding just like Michael." Father was too nice of a term to call him.

She reached toward me, dark hair sticking to her sweaty forehead. I scooted back. "What aren't you telling me?"

The pain and regret I saw in her frown set the calm she had given me teetering on a cliff.

"Angels don't have children, Lucille," she whispered.

I nodded. "I know. You said I was your miracle baby." And that was it. She'd never tell me anything else.

Tears filled her eyes. The calm she gave me was hanging on by a frayed thread.

"Angels are only created. We don't conceive because it goes against creation and the balance of our world. But I wanted a child so bad. I didn't want the life I was created for. And when I heard my friend Miriam found a way. I asked her about it. She told me Lilith helped her."

"That's the Queen of..." My mouth dropped open.

"You shouldn't even know who that is," she sighed, shaking her head. "I didn't care. I'd pay any price. Lilith said I needed to use the other side to conceive. And I did."

"The other side?" I asked. It couldn't be true. "Are you saying I'm part demon?"

She shook her head, black hair sliding back and forth over her shoulders.

"Then what?"

"Miriam used the blood of a high-level demon to conceive her child, but since she was a Serephim, the demon essence burned away. As an Archangel, I couldn't take that risk with you, so I found another way. A loophole."

Based on the pain and regret wrinkling her forehead and creasing her eyes, the loophole cost as much as using demon blood would've.

"Tell me."

My mom looked up to the ceiling as if asking for guidance and then looked back at me, tears spilling down her cheeks. "Michael isn't your father. And I think he's figured that out."

"Then who is?" I said, standing. The calm vanished, replaced by a building pressure. And my mom, so overcome by her own emotions and thoughts, didn't know.

"Do you remember the poem and story I used to tell you?"

"The Daughter of the Seven Circles? The one who destroyed Elora and lives in an ice palace with her father the..." I trailed off at her nod. Her face contorted in pain, tears flowing freely.

"It wasn't a story." She wrung her hands together. "The Daughter of the Seven Circles was a prophecy given to me at the time of Miriam's death. A warning to me about my future daughter as she died protecting her son."

No. No way. "You're saying I destroy Elora? That I'm Lu—" I couldn't say his name. "*His* daughter?"

I stumbled back, tripping over my slippers and falling into my chair.

"Does he know?" I asked. My heart sped up.

"Maybe," she answered, resigned. "He can most likely sense your power when you use it since you're his daughter."

Oh, my heavenly hell. "That's why you always suppress me, why we move the moment I so much as flame up. Not just so the entirety of Elora doesn't find me. But so he doesn't either."

"Lucy," her voice cracked, and so did my heart.

"How could you keep me so in the dark?" I cried. "I'm her. I'm, I'm—" The pressure intensified, needles stabbed at my skin. I sprinted for our front door, wrenching it open. She called out to me.

"Give me a *Minute*!" I yelled back before sprinting into the pouring rain.

THAT WASN'T THE ONLY dream memory I walked to. I walked further into the past, witnessing:

My father's torture.

My mom's pain.

Public school, then home school.

Lying on my father's cuts and crying myself to sleep.

Begging my mom to soothe the fear and pain.

So many verbal fights with my mom.

Meeting Aspen.

Then Marcus came—him and his small army.

They were the ones to surround my mom that day. But she forced me out of the house before I could listen and understand why she had chosen to poison me.

When my dream-walks released me, I found myself lying flat, staring into shadows, absorbing the radiance of my power.

All my energy drained away. Probably from all the tears that spilled on the ground. Or from reliving the worst and best parts of my past.

CHAPTER THIRTY-SIX

I groaned as I woke up, ears ringing, head pounding, ribs aching. I attempted to lift my arms to clutch my head, but they halted abruptly, clinking against metal. The sound and my immobility snapped my bleary eyes open.

"Mom?" I gasped, wrenching against the black chains wrapped around my body, holding me to a metal table. "Mom!"

She lay beside me, strapped to a table with a lone bag of black fluid feeding into her veins. My purple flames erupted, coating my body and spreading ice over my chains.

"No!" I slammed against them, ignoring the agony in my side. The ice shattered. I dove deeper into my Infernus, strumming the cords of the black flames. They replaced the purple, but no matter how high they flared or how hot they burned, they didn't help me. "Mom!" I screamed again, a heaviness seeping into my body from the extreme amount of power I used. I dove too deep.

A door squeaked open. I scanned the room desperately, hoping for help, but found only rusted hooks, chains, and knives. Blinking away the light-headedness, I released my power.

Where the hell were we?

"Funny, isn't it, that your Glory is the only thing that could melt Ember Chains, but it's the one power you don't have access to."

No.

"I figured you'd be out for longer. Shame about your mother. I had to sedate her with Nerium. She was inconsolable when we brought you in."

No.

"Speak when you are spoken to!"

I squeezed my eyes shut. Every word he spoke was a shard of glass slamming into my ears, filling me with an intense, visceral hatred.

He stepped into view. Not a spec of fuzz or color sullied his uniform. It remained white all the way down to his pristine battle boots. "Lucille, I didn't want to start your punishments just yet. But if you do not speak, I will have no choice."

I lifted my hate-filled eyes to his face, contemplating spitting on the stupid white metal of his armor. "What do you need me to say, Father?" I ground out.

His sneer flattened to a line. "Never call me that."

"Then what should I call you, Father?" I didn't know why I egged him on, but it had something to do with the fact of him knocking my mom out, cutting me up, and abusing us with his words, playing on replay in my mind.

I saw a flash of metal and flinched back. Except I had nowhere to go as the metal sliced my cheek. Blood slid down my face. My wrists yanked on my chains.

He held up a dagger with an ebony blade. "You will call me by my name." He smiled, twisting his dagger back and forth, gazing at the drop of blood dotting the tip like he won some prize.

I abhorred him—more than abhorred. There wasn't an ounce of daughterly affection toward him.

Oh, wait. I wasn't his daughter.

He strolled to the end of the table. "Do you not remember?" He paused. "Do you know what I am?"

"A bastard?" I goaded. The last thing Michael deserved was compliance, especially when that was all he ever wanted.

He chuckled. The hilt of his dagger flashed before the ebony blade sliced the arch of my foot. Tender flesh that never saw the light of day split.

I pushed against my chains. The cut stung but barely bled.

They were taunts. Little slices to satiate his craving for abuse until it wasn't enough. By the long scars in single file lines on my back, it was never enough.

"An Archangel. Pure and renowned," he said with his chest puffed out. "Just like your mother. Until you."

Gag. I attempted to hide my disgust, but it was as futile as stripping the sarcasm from my tone.

His gray eyes churned with malice and a sickening joy. "Lucille, do you know my name?"

"Nope," I said in a platonic, chipper voice that was as fake as the smile lifting his lips.

This time, his chuckle gained volume, sounding pleased. "Did your mother ever clarify my abilities to you?" His finger tapped against the table, waiting. I glared at it.

"You know, can't say we ever cared enough to talk about you," I said, looking over at her unconscious form. My purple flames itched to come out, but I was still light-headed, and every one of my limbs was pinned down. Even if I could manage an icicle, I wasn't sure how to slam it into Michael's face. But maybe if he touched me at the right moment... My thoughts trailed off, mulling over a plan.

He walked around to my arm, fingering my blood at the tip of his dagger with his gloved hand. The white remained stain-free as he smeared it down the middle, his ebony blade absorbing the red line.

What was that thing? Was that the knife I needed to steal? If so, that female had a lot of faith in my abilities to escape Ember Chains without a key or my Glory.

"As an Archangel, we all have a singular power. Mine is one of truth. So, my dear Lucille, we will play a game."

I was surprised he didn't keel over by saying the word dear.

"Oh goody, I love games." All the resentment I had stored over the years leaked out.

"Me too," Michael said in a low voice, pressing the edge of his dagger to my inner arm. "Let's start off with a truth of my own to set a good example for our game."

I bit my cheek to avoid letting out a loud scoff. He didn't know a good example, even if it came and sat at his feet like a sacrificial lamb.

"This dagger," he dragged it across my forearm, indenting my skin but not slicing through. "There is only one of its kind. Its name is Tsal-mawet. Shadow-death." He stared at it proudly.

So that's what that looked like.

"Since you most likely forgot. I'll recap what you've missed, and we can go from there." The dagger left my arm and tinked against the table. He walked around, letting the tip screech against the metal, outlining my body as he talked.

"After your mother hid you from me successfully over the years," he said begrudgingly, glancing at her with a sick sort of pride. "I bided my time, waiting. Because your mother may know me and my tactics, but I know hers as well." His lips curled up into a smile.

My father *actually* smiled as he gazed at her. A weird tenderness softened his murderous eyes.

"I knew because of *you*, she'd slip up." The soft expression he reserved for her twisted into revulsion when he turned to me. "And she did. So, I sent a message to a demon called Marcus. He needed to find you and secure you.

"But see, your mother thought the demon still worked for Lilith, the Tenebrous Queen. She thought Lilith was after you because we all heard of the queen stealing female angels to escape her prison. So, your mother made a rune-binding deal with the demon, a trade.

"She'd give up herself for you, but only if the demon would keep you sedated and safe so you wouldn't run off." He laughed. "They put you up in an abandoned safe house with one bag of Nerium poison until she could return to you. Little did she know the demon was under my command. I told him to up the dosage to three bags, enough poison to torture your disgusting sin-filled mind until I could come to finish the job."

She traded herself for me to keep me safe. Instead of being tortured by a queen, my mom poisoned me to keep me unconscious until what? She survived her own torture and retrieved me from Marcus, a demon who worked for Michael, who wanted me dead or to go to some council?

"If they made a binding deal about keeping me safe, how is destroying my mind defined as safe?" I glared.

He smiled with pride. For himself. "Because the only way to remove a rune of any kind is from an Archangel's feather, which only an Archangel or Seraphim can use.

"Your mother assumed no angel would dare remove a rune from a demon. They are our enemies, so if a rune has been placed on them, we know our brethren had reason to do it. But sometimes, in rare cases, we must get our hands dirty for the greater good," he shrugged, unphased. "So, I paid off an Archangel bounty hunter to remove Marcus's rune. Therefore, no more deal. Then all I had to do was wait for my appointed time to finish the deed.

"See, long ago, I petitioned to the Seraphims that I wanted to come to Earth once a day on your birthday. Archangels are too powerful to grace Earth with their presence more than once a year." The pride in his voice made my stomach roll. His shoulders were back, chin up like he was a god.

"My mom's an Archangel, though."

The corner of his eyes tightened. "No, she fell not long after you came to be. A Fallen angel who kept her signature powers because of *me*. I gave her everything, even after her sin stole her wings and forced her to live in Elora or on Earth." By his expression, I felt I was somehow the cause of her fall. "But she chose Earth. At first, I didn't understand, then I put the pieces together.

"The Council of Righteousness is comprised of Seraphims, and they aren't allowed there. However, they keep a close eye on the supernatural on Earth. So, your mother figured with *me*, we could keep you completely off their radar, and we did. Until the day I bound your powers, and you escaped. I told the council what happened, and we made a deal. But first, I needed to find you, which proved difficult because I reduced you to a human, so I employed anyone willing and available to complete the task for me.

"When the demon stole you two months ago, I had to wait until your birthday to come. Only a few weeks remained until I could do what I've always wanted. But somehow..."

The dagger stopped near my thigh, an inch away from touching my skin. Heat radiated off the metal, and a magnetic pull begged me to touch it. If the chains weren't holding my thighs in place, I would've pressed my skin to the knife.

"Somehow, you escaped Marcus. You even managed to evade all the other angels I sent to help fix his mistake. But luckily, he retrieved you on this celebratory day. So, here's the game, Daughter," he spat. Literally spat his saliva onto me. It globbed onto my shorts and sprayed onto my thighs. "You answer my questions the way I want, and you extend your life for a few more minutes or hours."

I laughed. I think it was shock. Michael talked about extending my life, so he meant to kill me, regardless, on my birthday, which I didn't even know until now, next to my unconscious mom.

Bolted to the table with my Glory bound, I had no way of escaping or helping my mom. Any hope of a rescue attempt from Oliver or Aspen didn't exist. Neither knew where I was. Who knew if they were still alive? So, here I was at the mercy of a fake father who hated me and waited all this time to eradicate me from his life with a flourish of his special dagger.

The laugh was not the response he wanted. He moved.

I screamed as the tip of his magnetic dagger stabbed into my thigh. He pulled it down in a straight line, splitting my flesh. Jerking against the heavy chains, my screams turned to shrieks, and my Infernus surged.

Michael spat on the purple flames. His spit turned to specks of ice on my skin. "Disgusting things. Put them away."

I didn't.

"I already owe you a slice for screaming. Do you want another for disobeying me?" He made another deep line next to the one he had just carved.

I ground into my cheeks, squelching my next scream and battling my flames, biting into my flesh so hard it was a wonder I didn't break through to the other side. Agony. Pure agony. Tears streamed out of my eyes as fast as the blood out of my leg, and I didn't know if my accidental surge, the blood loss, or both caused my shaking.

If he continued this, it really would only be minutes.

He eyed all the blood dripping down my leg, looking indignant. It tickled the backs of my legs, spreading onto the table. "You'd think with half of your disgusting power, you'd heal faster than this. I have other fun things I want to do to you."

Fun?

I let the silent tears roll, staring into the dim lighting, thankful my mom wasn't awake for this. My heartbeat wildly out of control, pounding in my leg. Each heartbeat forced my blood to ooze out, adding to the blanket of red in which I lay. But he didn't hit any major arteries. That'd put an end to his game too soon.

"First question. What do you remember of your past?" He circled me like a shark. White armor glinted with each step.

"Everything."

At that, he appeared relieved and very eager. He couldn't very well receive the answers he desired without my memories. *Overzealous psychopath.*

"What are you?"

"I don't know." After my dream-walk, I finally figured out who my biological father was. *But what did that make me? A born angel or something else?*

The dagger dove in my peripherals, slashing open the flesh of my arm. I shrieked, holding back my power but letting it build. Searing pain traveled up my shoulder from how deeply he cut. Then I received another just as deep. I ground my teeth together, muffling my scream by forcing myself against all my chains.

"I told the truth!" I whimpered, automatically tensing, readying for another slice.

"Tell me what you are! What hell dimension did you come from?" he spat.

"I didn't come from any dimension, you sick bastard!"

"That's not good *enough!*"

"Let my mom go, and maybe I'll give you more."

Wrong answer.

The dagger sawed through. Black specs threatened to swallow me from the agony of each tug that carved through the meaty part of my thigh. The wet sound of my flesh made me cough on my vomit. I fought to keep it from my lungs, gurgling it up and onto the metal table. It pooled with my blood, then dripped off the edge inches from Michael's white boots.

SMACK!

My head whipped to the side.

Dammit! That was my opportunity to attack him. But between the agony and creeping numbness, it was hard to stay focused and hold onto my power.

But I couldn't give up. I had to fight for my mom.

"You almost dirtied my shoes with your impurities. Who knew your mother raised such a deplorable, disgusting wimp?" He circled to the other side.

That word. That damned word. I had every memory of when he said it—his favorite endearment. I let my Infernus feed off my anger and held the flames just below the surface of my skin, ready to piss him off again. If it didn't work, I'd get sliced, but if it did, maybe I could freeze him solid.

"What are you hiding, disgusting little wimp?"

I smiled through the pain, blinked spots out of my eyes, and then lied. "Nothing."

"Stop lying!"

His hand came flying toward my cheek. I didn't flinch or move, and the moment his skin slammed against mine, sending my face into my puke, I released my Infernus in a rage.

Ice devoured his hand and raced up his arm with fierce intensity, consuming everything in its path until it reached his neck. I smiled, triumphant, but my expression faltered as the ice began to slow, its advance stalling while dark spots swam into my vision. *No, no, no. Come on!*

Michael hissed, and a pulse resonated as his Glory erupted, coating his uniform and melting my attack. "You think you can go up against an Archangel? You think your demonic powers have any sway over us?" he bellowed. "Who is your maker?"

"You wouldn't be able to handle the truth." Pain captured my voice, making it raspy and wet.

"You won't be able to handle the pain of your lies," he spat on my face. "See, I need to know. Because when I approached your mother about her miracle pregnancy and asked her if she used demon blood to create you, she said no. It was the truth. Yet the council still found dark energies on her, forcing her from the sanctuary in the clouds and away from *me*."

I'd roll in some dark energies to run away from him, too.

"When you were one, I sensed something was off. Years later, your Glory manifested. Each time it accidentally erupted, my senses heightened. A part of my power that usually only manifested around demons or threats." He placed the tip of his blade under my eyelashes.

I didn't dare move.

"Somehow, your mother was lying to me. But I had no proof. Did you know that my job as an Archangel is to eradicate impurity? Every year, I refrained from killing you because of your mother. I wouldn't have been allowed to without more proof of your sinful nature, anyway. But I received my proof when you froze me." The crinkle in the corner of his stormy eyes held my breath. "When I told the council, they disagreed with my demands for your immediate death and instead said I could be a part of their judgment ruling if I brought you into them. I agreed until you dream-walked to your past self and gave me the power to remember your dream-walk."

"I don't understand."

"Don't you remember what I said? Dream-walk to the memory, and you give it power, essentially making it real. Because of what you did, you not only allowed me to remember you in my memory but as a result, you changed your future. Originally, I was going to bring you into the council, but after I learned you could dream-walk, I knew I had to take it into my own hands." His vile smile widened. "The last thing I need from you to finish this and restore your mother's wings is your maker's name."

He wanted the name of my biological father. But if I told Michael, he'd kill me on the spot. The only leverage I had left was my father's name—one I now remembered.

"Why would I confess anything when you just admitted to killing me for it?"

He leaned back and puffed up his chest. "Well, I missed a few birthdays. I can always carve out your answer. Or..." He walked the few feet to my mom's padded table, setting the knife against her cheek. "I can carve your mother up a little instead."

I slammed against my chains. "You wouldn't!" My wounds pulsed and gushed, making me grind back a sob. "You claim to love her. You want to restore her wings. Why would you carve her up?"

But even if some part of him did love her, it never stopped his abuse. He may not want her dead, but he was all for punishment.

Michael circled to her hand, lifted the dagger, and said, "Because you tainted her." Then he plunged the knife through her palm. The tip punctured through the pad and the metal table.

I screamed, cursing him with every word, attempting to slam my body against my restraints with everything I had left, which wasn't much. My Infernus didn't even bat an eye.

He pushed a single finger back and forth on the hilt, watching as he inadvertently moved her fingers. She didn't wake. She didn't jerk. Her unconscious body just took his bloody abuse.

"Stop with the ungodly noise, and I'll remove it." He did, but then he returned to me and drove it into my own hand. "I hate when you scream. It's so childish and weak."

I banged my head against the metal table, hiding whimpered cries in the noise, and held the rest of my wails in with my teeth. I thought I could take it. After each slice, the pain lessened a bit, and adrenaline took over, making me think I had the strength to go round after round with him. I thought I could defeat him with my Infernus. But I was wrong.

"Better." He removed the knife. I begged myself to stay quiet. "But because you attacked me, I think a Reversal Rune will be great as your punishment. It's my favorite to use on the sinful and vile creatures of this world," he said, taking out a white feather tipped in black ink. He placed it against my wrist. "Do you know what it does?"

"No."

Excited, he smiled, talking as he carved. "It gives you access to all your powers but binds it in your body, so there's no way to expel it. Essentially eating itself from the inside out. My favorite part is that it allows you to heal just enough to endure the torture again until you die—or, in some cases, I've seen creatures explode."

I thought I knew pain. I thought I knew suffering.

But the gashes were nothing—absolutely nothing compared to the pressure that hit me after he removed the feather from my wrist.

From searing agony to bone-chilling cold, the sensation battered at my insides, as if striving to make room for Hell itself.

The sound that escaped my mouth was ear-splitting. I writhed on the table, tensing against my restraints, seeking release, help, or anything.

"Stop," I sobbed, not caring if it earned me another slice. "Stop it, please," I begged him. I never wanted to demean myself by pleading with him. But my body attacked my insides, bursting cell after cell until it felt like I was nothing but a mushy sack of skin.

"Too bad there wasn't a rune for a magical gag. But I suppose if I must hear such pitiful noises for my answers, I will."

"Stop it. Please!"

"Stop crying," he snapped, slashing my arm.

I could no longer feel the pain of his cuts. Nor could I tell if blood or sweat soaked my clothes and slid down my skin. My body convulsed between a searing heat that scorched my insides, causing my eyes to roll back, and an icy cold that froze and burned simultaneously, shattering and sending jagged, freezing shards through every nerve.

"You will—" I could hardly speak. "Never—get—his name," I stuttered.

The satisfaction on his face kept me from continued slashes from all my whimpers and tears.

He walked over to my mother with his feather. "Should we see if a Reversal Rune will force her from her slumber?"

Air existed in a place far out of reach, taunting my lungs. "No," I gasped.

I burned, blistered, melted, froze, and shattered.

After everything my mom did for me, she didn't deserve this pain. I wouldn't let him do that to her. No matter what she'd done to me or how misguided, she just wanted me safe. And I wanted her safe. I was never supposed to be born, and if I gave him the answer, he'd kill me. But if it kept her from this pain, that was okay.

"I'll—" I clenched my teeth, holding back a wail at the pain, breathing forcefully through my nose. When my Glory sprung to my skin, it didn't feel hot—more energy than fire. But now, I understood how I incinerated a tree in seconds and how the ice from my purple flames blistered Oliver's skin. "Tell you. If you make a runed deal with me."

That seemed to intrigue him.

"A three-way bind," I gasped out. Because if I died, I didn't want it to be nullified. "I'll tell you, if you make a binding promise never to hurt, touch, or abuse Saraqael, my mom, again."

He grimaced but agreed. I didn't expect him to yield so readily. My maker was essential to him, or he knew a way out of the binding. Since I had the memories of my past back, I knew what rune he needed to carve, and I watched as he carved the correct one on each of our shoulders.

"Tell me," he demanded once the feather left my skin.

I could die happy now, knowing my mom was safe from his fists. But I'd also die happy expressing my following answer. Michael was in for one hell of a treat.

With enough breath to whisper out my words, I explained. "My maker, my father, is the corrupted and uncorrupted. He is death and sin. Life and redemption. He is the ruler of the Seven Circles. A king. He is the Seraphim cast from your clouds to bring balance to the world."

That's how my mom found her loophole.

"You know him?" I smiled at his gaping mouth and pale face. It brought me a sickening bout of joy as his rune destroyed my body. If I wasn't on my deathbed, I might've laughed. But the shock on his face was enough to distract us both, especially as a blue fireball came beelining for Michael's head.

CHAPTER THIRTY-SEVEN

A pulse resonated as Michael flung up a flaming white arm, blocking his face. He roared in agony as the fireball struck, engulfing and blistering his skin. Astonished, he fixated on his arm, seething gasps escaping him as he processed the unexpected burn. Michael jerked his attention toward the figure covered in a dark cloak, staring down my fake father with murder in their glowing gaze.

But why didn't Michael attack back?

"A Seraphim shouldn't be in Elora. Why are you here? Who are you?" Michael asked with a shaky voice—a sound I enjoyed.

The figure bounced two fireballs in his hands. "Who I am is irrelevant, but I'd very much like to know who you are so I can send you a card when you arrive in Hell for your sins."

I let out a pitiful whimper at his voice.

Aspen found me.

My father's words made a lot of sense, matching my memories of the texts I read, and Miriam and my mom's words. *The cobalt rings.* They signified Seraphim.

Michael sputtered, clearly confused by Aspen's flames and proclamation. "I'm doing my duty. I'm eradicating impurity and sin as you all tell us to!" He slammed the ebony knife into my other hand to emphasize his words.

The pain of the slice hardly penetrated the pain of the rune, but it was yet another cut for my broken body to attempt to heal as my internal organs fought against the deadly temperatures of my power.

"That was the wrong choice, Michael." The deadly calm overtaking Aspen's voice spread goosebumps down my spine. He stepped forward until he stood a few feet from my bloody table. The heat of his fireballs brushed my skin.

"You can't kill me. It's against our laws. You need two more to cast judgment."

Aspen hid underneath the hood of his cloak. "And what of the female, Archangel Michael? Did she receive all three votes from the council before you cast judgment?"

"She—" He swallowed. "She's a Dream-Walker! I figured you would be pleased by my actions. She's born of pure sin! Her maker is—"

Aspen cut off his eager stuttering, holding a ball of flaming blue fire inches from Michael's face. "I do not care who or what she is. You speak of our laws and then go against them like you're above them. Now, she is mine to deal with. Take your wings and leave before I raze them from your back, Archangel Michael."

"But— but—" Michael looked between me and my mom. "You can't do this! We made a deal. They're mine!" he finally spat out.

Aspen pressed his hand into the white metal of Michael's chest. The surface heated to a fiery red and yielded to his touch, melting away. "You have seconds before I obliterate you from existence."

Michael stumbled back. "Which Seraphim are you? Who sent you?"

"Leave us!" Aspen bellowed. His entire body erupted in blue flame.

Michael luscelered out, and any relief I would've felt evaded me. Aspen was too late.

I was dying.

"Lucille?" Aspen flung back the hood of his cloak and let go of his power, the rune under his chin a flickering light red. I'd take that. Warm hands pressed into my face. I gasped, and he snapped his hands back.

"You found me," I said with rolling tears.

"Always."

"How'd you escape? Why did he listen to you?" Each word I forced out was like dragging heated, barbed wire up my raw throat. *Why didn't he just kill him?*

Lines pinched his face. His gaze raked up and down my body. His blue irises glinted with an inner light before becoming consumed by fire.

"Hold still," he demanded.

"What happened?"

"Don't speak, Lucille." He gripped his sword in a shaking, cuffless hand. I glanced at his ankles, finding them free as well.

"What happened?" I rasped out again.

"You did."

My brows pulled together as he raised his sword, hands still shaking. They never shook. Aspen's sword worked like an additional limb. Anyone with a brain could tell Aspen had unparalleled skill with a sword. Yet, as it hovered behind his shoulder, ready to cleave through the air and into my chains, and I felt his overwhelming fear, it wobbled.

"You're scared," I whispered.

"Our tether is weakening. I sensed it through the Nephilim's fear visions—it jolted me awake. I found the Nephilim locked in a struggle with the witch, and you were gone. I snapped. Somehow, I burned through the cuffs, and once I did, it was game over for the fucking witch."

He swung down. The sword did nothing to the thick links.

"She'd never witnessed my power before. When she did, she begged for mercy. She spilled everything about that bastard, Michael—where he took you and his fear of Seraphim. They outrank him; their word is law, and I wield the flames of one."

His flames sprung to his sword, licking up the edges. This close, the raging fire curled the hairs on my arms. He brought the sword over his shoulder and swung it into the largest chain across my chest. The clanking noise I expected didn't sound a second time—instead, tangy metallic infused the air, and liquid steel oozed off the edge. The heat blistered my skin, and as my body temperature plummeted, the liquid metal steamed.

"No, you are one. Your mom was one." I whispered. He was at least half of one. The other half must've been another angel paired with demon blood.

He was the first-born angel.

Aspen gave a sharp nod, but the rune under his chin didn't like the reminder of his mom. It flared, and he cursed.

Unimaginable pain wrecked my body. My flesh remained exposed to the air, bleeding freely, stinging, throbbing, and jiggling when I squirmed. My insides boiled, then froze. I didn't need any more agony, and yet... I would endure the searing heat of his rune if it could only free him from its influence.

I glared at Aspen's chin. "I'm sorry I can't touch you," I said.

"Don't apologize," he forced out on an air of breath. "I've known agony for a long time, sweetheart." Ever so gently, he smoothed away my trailing tears, the rune losing its battle and fading back into his skin. "But it's nothing compared to feeling our tether shrink."

I swallowed. "You should go." He shouldn't be here. I didn't want him to watch me die. "Go and take my mom somewhere safe."

The heaviness of my eyes eased as my Glory built.

Aspen ignored me and swung quicker.

Comfortable warmth turned hot, then hot turned to blistering heat. Toward its peak, needles shoved against my skin, begging to pop out. But release wasn't an option, so my insides battled against the searing pressure. Whimpers tore from my clenched lips as my thoughts prayed for the end. Then piles of snow dumped on the heat, shocking my system, and bringing me down to frigid temperatures. The cycle repeated again and again. I could almost handle the cold, the slowing of my thoughts, and the numbing of my pain. But it lasted for seconds before climbing back to a raging inferno. I didn't even feel Aspen's pain anymore.

There would be a point when my body would give up.

"Leave me and take her!" I sobbed, slamming against the rest of my chains. Blood oozed out of my gashes, sliding down my limbs to collect in the growing puddle. "Please."

He increased the force of his slamming sword.

"Aspen," I begged.

"No!" he snapped. His jaw throbbed as he attacked my ankle restraints with a force that sliced through the table.

Only one chain left, and it came. Billions of molten needles shoved their way into every cell of my body. An agonized scream spilled from my bloody lips. My Glory hit its first significant peak.

"Lucille!"

My hoarse cries died as the cold hit the warmth. A moment of reprieve before I descended into the beginnings of hypothermia.

"Leave."

He met my gaze. Unwavering determination seeped through our bond and flickered in his miserable eyes.

"I can't. I won't."

I nodded at his lightless rune. "It looks like you can."

He swung, melting my last chain, and released me.

"What happens when it lights back up, Aspen? Will you take me to your queen like this?" I rasped, struggling to string together sentences. "Will I die in your arms, or will I die in hers?"

He brushed my sweat-soaked hair back from my face, shaking his head vehemently. "You're not going to die. Do you hear me? I won't let you."

I wanted to laugh since I was all cried out, but I didn't want to move. "You're not a good liar. I can feel your emotions. Remember?" My finger twitched, yearning to trace his tense jaw and smooth away the worry etched between his brows, though I knew it wouldn't alleviate his inner turmoil. "Get my mom out." If he did this one thing for me, I'd be okay with my outcome. "For me," I begged.

He didn't respond, staring at me like I tore out his heart. I could feel the fissure cracking inside his soul. But there was nothing I could do about it. Elora stole all my reassuring words, and kind smiles the moment I stepped through the Earth portal. He didn't have a way to remove my Reversal Rune, even if he was a Seraphim. Michael took the feather with him.

"Aspen?"

"Only if you fight it. You have to survive."

"I am fighting it."

He shook his head, eyes glassy. "It doesn't fucking feel like it. You do not get to give up."

"I'm not." But I was. "Take her someplace safe, and I'll fight."

Lips pressed in a thin line, he nodded, but I felt his fear. He didn't believe me. It made sense. My words probably didn't match the tether he could feel between us. I wouldn't believe me either.

The sweat on my skin crystallized, a layer of frost coating my body. My eyelashes blanketed in my tears, froze together in the corner of my eyes. The beads of ice made it difficult to blink. Each drastic change in my power neared a new extreme. I didn't have much time left. The frost was a new development, but I knew it wouldn't be the power to take me out. One, maybe two hits of my Glory at peak, and it'd be enough to eradicate me like Michael wanted.

Aspen scanned my body with lowered brows, taking in the frost. When he lingered on my torn flesh, the muscle in his jaw throbbed, and fire leaped in his eyes.

"I'm going to take out the knife and pick you up. Ready?"

Sleep weighed on my lids, and my limbs became numb. Unable to feel Michael's presents, I almost sighed.

"No."

I couldn't let him touch me anymore. Not that I'd have much say in the matter if my eyes closed. *Wouldn't that be wonderful?* I would much rather die that way. But in my core, I knew how I'd die, which was why Aspen couldn't pick me up. Michael said he'd seen demons explode with the Reversal Rune. If my skin frosted over when the cold took hold, I didn't want to know what would happen when I transitioned to my Glory. It wasn't safe. For him or me.

My eyes fluttered.

"Sweetheart? Stay here. Stay with me. Please, just hang on a little longer. I'll take you to a healer first. I promise." I wished I could give him a smile for his sweet admission. But I didn't have the hours it would require for him to find a healer. Nor did I have the energy to dissect the word *first* as his rune flickered.

I wished I could've saved him like his mother wanted. That was my one regret. That and... I glanced over at my mom, noticing her hand was healed. She'd be okay. I made sure of it. But I wish I could've said goodbye.

"Stay with me, sweetheart." He grabbed the knife in my hand. I cringed. Carefully, he slid it from my cut.

"Put it in my waistband," I whispered on a whim. I'd die today, but at least I could say I tried for him.

He removed a dagger and sheath from his belt, exchanged it with my knife, and carefully tucked the humming, protected blade into my waistband.

The heaviness subsided, and I gave a weak smile—a lie of my own. I focused on the handsome male gazing down at me with that damned broken expression and something tender and raw. My eyes lifted to his deep brown locks, unable to hold his gaze, and I noticed a flickering shadow behind his ear.

The ache in my shattered heart paused. A figure cloaked in shadows spun a sphere of darkness and hurled it toward Aspen's back.

"Aspen! Behind you!"

It didn't matter I was seconds away from an agony that would kill me. It didn't matter only part of him was here for me. I knew one thing. Aspen would live.

I reacted when I saw the ball, anticipating his turn but knowing he'd keep himself between me and the threat. I rolled and pushed myself off the table, throwing myself in front of his body and screaming as the gashes in my thighs split further.

"No!" a voice yelled from the shadows as the ball hit me in the chest—a deep tenor filled with angry desperation.

I jolted, and Aspen caught me around the waist.

It was him. The one that woke me from my shadow prison.

I stared into horror-stricken golden eyes, and my pain ceased. A familiar, tantalizing blackness enveloped me and whisked me away.

CHAPTER THIRTY-EIGHT

BLOODHOUND AND RUNE

A day ago.

"Sir, Rune lost eyes on them... again." I stood in front of his desk. The mahogany wood stretched half the length of his chambers, centered with the fireplace. The king faced the fire, only the top of his ice-blonde head exposed above his cushioned chair.

"What do you mean, general?" The room dropped to an uncomfortable temperature. Usually, I didn't fear him, but tomorrow was the day, and we still didn't have a location.

After I let the king drain the last of my power to help out the female, we didn't have enough to connect to either her or the Nephilim again. So, Rune was our last resort. A fickle beast still in training. One we couldn't wholly trust at her age. Not when so much was riding on this mission.

"Sir, Rune chased off some Hellhounds and lost their trail."

The temperature plummeted. Fuck.

My skin burned from the frigid air, but I ignored it. I'd been through a lot worse in my three hundred years.

"We have five hours, general. We need to figure out where she is. You'll only have so much time to retrieve her."

My concern wasn't whether I could retrieve her but the matter of our imprisonment. It's been nine years since the gates shut.

"Sir, the gates—"

The king's fist slammed into this desk, spreading a thin layer of ice over the dark wood. "They will open." He removed his hand, standing to walk closer to the fire. "She passed the test. She's who I've been looking for," he muttered.

What test?

"And they all want her. The Ethereal Military, my damned wife, and whoever the pathetic demon works for." Ice spread across the floor as he toed the line of his restraint.

"They will open," I said, keeping the awkwardness from my tone. Comforting someone didn't come naturally to me, but the ice creeping up my leg pushed me to it. "And if they don't, I'll try the portal again."

"We'll have more luck with the gates. There is no use getting your wings wet again. The Dreads may demand I appoint a new general if you do." The ice crusting my pant leg receded. He turned around, drilling me with an icy gaze. "Go, Bloodhound, figure out where she is. I don't want to see your face again until you do."

"Yes, Sir." I left to connect with Rune.

Two Hours Ago.

I knocked on his door.

"If you're General Ronen, then enter. If you're anyone else, leave." The King's voice hinted at a slow death. Ice crystallized underneath the crack of the door. We were minutes away from our schedule.

I took a deep breath, gathering myself for this potential shitstorm, and confidently pushed into his office.

Fractured ice covered the wood-polished floor.

"Cutting it close, Bloodhound. Tell me." He stood from his chair. Leather, in black and red of our kingdom's colors, embraced the cords of his muscles. He dressed for battle. Yet he wouldn't be the one going out there. He was as much a prisoner to his kingdom as his wife was.

"Rune is outside an abandoned house at the edge of The Divide."

"How do you know it's the edge of The Divide?"

"They're next to the killing fields."

His dark gray eyes nearly vanished behind his two thickening white rings. Ever since he sensed her power months ago, his control had been on a relentless rampage.

I knew her name. I knew she was important, so much so that I had been threatened with my life if I didn't retrieve her. Not that I was worried. He called me Bloodhound for a reason. However, the lack of additional intel irritated me. If only bridging two separate minds allowed me to join the connection. But my powers had limits. Plus, he wasn't one to share unless it was absolutely necessary.

I squared my shoulders. The next part would prove challenging to convey, and there was no time to waste thawing me if I upset the king. "Marcus is with her. Which means Saraqael may be there too."

The rings swallowed the rest of his irises. "And?" He knew there was more. We'd been searching for Marcus's new employer, trying to find Saraqael.

"Rune didn't lay eyes on the face. But she did see white armor. Your old armor." I almost said our, but I never received the white, as my position decreed. No, I received black—not that it mattered anymore.

But what I said did.

I luscelered to the doorframe, feeling the change in the air before the ceiling and floor erupted in sharp spears of ice.

"Go stand by the gates, general. Wait until they open and bring them to me. Kill anyone who stands in your way and drag back their rotten souls. And if the gates don't open,"—the whites of his eyes glowed—"pray that they do."

The air pulsed, and my ebony wings manifested. I stretched them out, enjoying the relief of having them free.

"Oh, general, if the Nephilim is with them, bring him too. Put him on Rune if you have to."

"Yes, Sir." I left just as crashing ice erupted behind me.

Five Minutes Ago

The gates opened. How he knew they would, I didn't need to know. But they did, and I flew to Rune. Our connection made it easy to find her, even after years of separation. I popped my wings out of existence and crouched beside her in the tall grass. My shadows helped to blend us into the shade of a large oak. The dusk sky also helped.

She pushed her black body into me, craving attention after being away from me for so long. I didn't have the time. But as I was about to stand, Marcus came out, and two figures luscelered to the house's front porch. One of them tackled Marcus to the ground.

It was the Nephilim.

The other figure stormed past, leaving them to fight.

My shadows darkened as I drilled my gaze into the back of the cloaked figure. The king ordered me to kill anyone who stood in my way. Fortunately for the Nephilim, the king wanted him back, but the cloaked figure may be the first on my list.

Moments later, the front door slammed open, and an Archangel raced out of the house and into the skies. I eyed him for a second, knowing my king wouldn't be pleased, but brushing away the thought of chasing after him. His day would come. For now, I was here for the female and Saraqael.

"Stay here, pup. Keep an eye out. I'll be watching."

Rune butted her muzzle into my hand, a silent confirmation that she understood but wasn't happy about it.

I wrapped my shadows around myself, left the Nephilim and Marcus to fight it out, and entered the rickety old house.

Scanning each room, I strategically placed my steps to stay silent. Candy wrappers and chip bags, food only found on Earth, littered the living room. Encroaching upon the kitchen, my lip curled at the wretched smell of rot, blood, and rat piss. The surrounding rooms had the added benefit of peeled paint, glass, and more feces.

This place was a shit-hole. An empty shit-hole.

No one occupied the first floor. I was about to go to the second when a scream pierced the air. Diving deeper into my well, I pulled at the darkness, swathing more layers around myself to stay hidden and luscelered to the scream.

I stopped at the threshold of the basement.

The rancid, rotten blood overwhelmed my senses. *What kind of sick bastard would make their basement a butcher shop?* But the smell wasn't what stopped me.

Saraqael lay unconscious on a table next to the female, and from all the blood that covered the female's table, the butchering already started.

Her breaths stuttered in and out, clearly in a lot of pain, with the queen's *pet* hunched over her.

"Sweetheart? Stay here. Stay with me. Please, just hang on a little longer. I'll take you to a healer first. I promise," the pet said, not noticing me behind him.

He pulled a knife from her hand, the sound of suctioning blood getting lost in her whimpers.

"Put it in my waistband," she whispered with no strength.

He listened, tucking the sheathed knife beneath her bloody pants. Afterward, he sheathed his sword, freeing his hands to pick her up. That was a mistake, along with touching her.

I willed a shadowball to coalesce in my palm. It wouldn't kill him; I'd need his blood for that. But it'd knock him out long enough for me to slit his throat. I wound up and threw it. The female peered at me as I did, like she could pierce through my shadows.

But that wasn't possible. To her and the pet, I should look like a cloud of black. Only... Her eyes...

They drilled into me. Agony screamed in their star-flecked depths. I didn't even think. Pulling at the deepest parts of my power, the shadowball darkened as it flew toward the pet's back with enough force to knock him out for months. For the first time in a century, I allowed my rage to overpower my abilities.

A loss of control, first the king, now me.

"Aspen! Behind you!"

The pet turned, and the female rolled, pushing off the table and diving in front of him. My shadowball sank into her chest.

"No!"

Dammit! I didn't mean to say that aloud. But fuck!

I hoped she had a high power level, or I'd have to tell the king I knocked the female out for half a year.

She stared at me as my shadows swarmed her body and mind. I couldn't look away. And my shadows... *What were they doing?*

They... It almost felt like they were savoring her. Like they found something they liked and weren't quite ready to shut her down. When they eventually did, it was gentle, like tucking her into a dreamless sleep.

"Lucille!"

Her body went slack in the pet's arms, and before I knew it, a fireball flashed toward my face.

"What the fuck did you do to her!" he roared.

"It was meant for you, not her. She's alive." But I needed him to move out of my way so I could check on her wounds.

He laid her down on the ground, placing his feet in front of her, white knuckling his sword. "Who the fuck are you? Show yourself!" His power erupted in his eyes and transferred to the blade in his hands. The muscles in his legs and arms shook as he held his defensive stance.

This was the renowned Prince of the Mother of Demons?

The color of his power intrigued and confused me. Seraphim flames were almost as rare as my shadows. And on a bonded sword, no less. But those were the only two impressive things about him, especially since he couldn't be a Seraphim.

"Did you do that to her?" Blood pooled on the table, dripping to the discolored cement. I couldn't shake off the amount. If he caused this, I knew without a doubt the king would want me to make him beg before I broke his mind. And I didn't mind that thought at all. My shadows whirled around me, excited for their next fix.

His eyes flashed to a deeper blue. "No."

"The Archangel?"

"Michael," he spat as flames heightened on his sword.

Fuck. I should've chased him down.

He glared at me and my silence. "Who the hell are you? Are you just going to hide behind your shadows like a coward?"

Oh, the queen's pet had an attitude. "Don't bait me, pet."

"What did you call me?" He lifted his sword in a shaky hand and stepped toward me. I snorted. I needed two openings. One to knock the prince out and slit his throat, and one to retrieve the female.

"A pet. That's what you are," I stated. It may be an insult, but it was the truth. There were many stories about the prince back home.

He took another step, flames flickering on his blade, and then fell to both knees, sword clattering to the ground. "Lucille," he cried, voice breaking.

Again, this was the formidable Prince of the Tenebrous Kingdom?

I walked closer to him, still hidden from view.

"No, no. Please, no," he repeated, gathering the female in his arms. "Lucille." He rocked her limp body. "Lucille, stay with me." He bowed his head into her neck, murmuring into her skin. "Please. Stay with me. Let me give you the moon. You need to live. For your mom."

The tears in his voice stayed my hand for a moment. The Prince of the Mother of Demons cared for her.

"For me," he whispered.

"The shadows won't kill her." *Why was I consoling him?* Maybe it was the fact that this supposedly deadly male was reduced to a pile of tears just because I knocked out the female he cared for. My shadows could sense her heartbeat. Although it was slow, she lived.

The pet leaned his face close to her ear, foolishly ignoring my proximity. "It's fading, Lucille. I can feel it fading. Please fight. Please."

I tilted my head, staring at the two of them. There was something I was missing. But I didn't have the time to figure it out. Pulling at my shadows, I formed another ball, throwing it at his back. The pet fell backward, bringing the unconscious female with him. My lip curled in disgust. I reached behind my head for the hilt of one of my short swords, craving to spill his blood when the female convulsed.

First the female, then the pet.

I crouched on the floor, gently rolling her off him. I removed the sheathed knife from her waistband and froze at the sight of the dark blade. Tsal-mawet. The blade used to saw off the king's wings. The dark blade had been lost for centuries. *Where did she find it?*

Sliding it between my belt and waist, I scanned the gashes on her arms and legs. They steadily bled, but nothing looked life-threatening. Her healing must've helped with that. *But why was she convulsing?* I placed my fingers on her pulse and jerked back. Her skin was unbearably hot, yet she didn't sweat.

A shot of alarm that wasn't my own overpowered my concerns. Rune.

Someone was coming.

I expanded my shadows, covering up the female before I picked up her jerking body. Her heat penetrated the thick fabric of my fighting leathers. I shot a glance at the pet with clenched teeth, then strode for the door. Only to be blocked by the Nephilim.

Huh. He lived.

He panned from the pet to my shadows. "What the hell happened to him, and where is Lucy?" he demanded, emeralds turning to green fire.

"The female is in my arms, Nephilim. Consider your deal complete. He has requested your return."

His reaching hand paused. Lucky for him. "You work for that male?"

"I'm his general. I've come to collect you. We—" The female whimpered in my arms. My shadows swarmed toward her cuts, absorbing her blood. I didn't command them to; they just did it. But my surprise was short-lived. In our cloud of darkness, red seeped out of her nose, and pain creased her eyes, pink tears squeezing through her closed lids.

"What the hell are you doing to her?" The Nephilim took a step forward. My shadows whipped out in threat while still covering us.

"Nothing." Yet. As she writhed in my arms in agony, bleeding from her nose, eyes, and limbs, I made a decision. If he ever found out, I'd most likely be a dead male, but if I didn't... I'd probably still be a dead male.

This was the only way if he wanted her to live.

Pushing the rest of my doubts away, I brought my shadows to my mouth, tasting the blood they absorbed. Straight sunshine and sin tingled my tongue, weakening my knees. I'd never tasted anything like her. The addictive spice that lingered at the back of my throat spoke of power.

What the hell was she? The tangy, warm sunshine flavor I knew, but the rest—

She convulsed harder, taking me out of my thoughts of her blood. Instantly, I dove into her mind, berating myself for getting distracted. I never got distracted.

The moment I entered her mind, I knew two things.

One, they lied to me. And two, she was seconds away from death.

Her mind felt like the heat of a thousand suns. If her body became any hotter, no matter what kind of power she had, she'd die.

I sent a shot of shadows into her brain, using them to nullify some of her pain receptors and bring down her internal temperature, hoping that'd help long enough to get her to a healer.

"Hey! I'm speaking to you, Shadow-boy!" the Nephilim yelled.

"What!" I snapped. We needed to move.

"What are we going to do about the prince and…?" He pointed at Saraqael.

I wished I could taste his blood and tear his mind apart before I ran a blade across his neck, removing one more pet from her arsenal. But the female in my arms was my top priority. The king would want me to save her before killing him.

"He gets to live another day. Lucky him." I moved, then snapped. "Grab Saraqael."

"Hey, where are you going? She's unconscious! What makes you think I can pick her up? Wait!"

I didn't wait.

My nerves were tickling the fabric of reality near my wings. They itched to pop back into existence. I signaled to Rune, waiting for her bounding black form. She came a minute later, running at a full sprint.

A flash of silver flew by my head. I couldn't stop the dagger; my hands were full, and my shadows were busy protecting the female in my arms. Not that a little dagger would do much damage to a hound nearly the size of a horse. Rune snapped her head to the side, grabbing the dagger before it hit her.

"That's your ride," I growled back at the Nephilim, happy to see he brought up Saraqael. "Don't hurt my hound, or I'll let her devour you."

"You own a Hellhound?" the Nephilim panted, sounding both intrigued and hesitant.

"She's a Soulhound." I dropped my shadows and brought forth my wings.

"They're extinct..." he trailed off, eyeing my wings like he eyed my hound. Then, he caught sight of the female. "Holy shit. Is she going to live?"

"I don't know," I said, really hating that answer, feeling a seed of fear. She had to survive. The king needed her. The Nephilim needed her to survive his Ligamen Rune. And now... I needed her, too, which surprised me most of all.

They fucking lied to me.

"Get on the Soulhound. She'll take you to the gates. We don't have long before they close. Hold on tight, and don't you dare let Saraqael fall."

Rune dropped to the ground, giving the Nephilim permission to climb on. He was tall, so he wouldn't have to climb much. I grimaced at the way he wiggled and dragged up Saraqael's body. But at least we got them both, and she would never remember.

Before I took flight, I had one more question. "Did you kill Marcus?"

He met my gaze. "No, he ran away." The bitterness that laced his words matched the regret in his eyes.

I'd have to hunt him down and kill him later, just like the Archangel. I smiled at the thought.

"Rune, run fast. Stop for nothing. I'll see you at the gates." I pushed off the ground, spreading my ebony wings, and raced against time.

The wind battered our faces. Tapping into my dark well, I let my shadows form a small barrier between us and the wind, still allowing me to see ahead.

The female pressed closer into my body, freezing. Initially, I thought it was the wind and the high altitude. But when the pink in her cheeks bled away and blue tinged her lips, I dove back into her mind and put on a burst of speed. My shadows played with her neurons, returning her to a stable temperature. Still, I couldn't hold it for long, especially when half my shadows acted against my will, deciding to cover each one of her gashes to protect them from the forceful air and soak up her blood like wispy bandages.

The landscape changed, becoming more jagged and white. We were close.

Pushing myself harder, we barreled through the twenty-foot iron gates, Rune right on our tail. The moment they slammed through, I left them and flew to the castle, landing on the balcony of the king's office.

"Sir!" I yelled, not wanting to kick in his door. But I would.

Fortunately, he was there swinging the curtained glass open.

"You got her," he whispered.

I held back my burning question about who she was to him. The female didn't have the time. "Sir, something's wrong with her." My shadows covered most of her wounds for now. It'd only distract him, and they hardly bled because of my shadows and her healing.

"What do you mean?" His gaze raked up and down, narrowing on the dark wisps that slid across her skin.

I ignored his displeasure. "She's been fluctuating in temperature. Burning hot, then frigid. And it's getting worse." I wasn't about to tell him how I knew that. The shadows touching her were as much as he'd accept right now.

He lowered his brows, then thrust out his hand. "Her wrists. Give me her wrists."

I did, pulling my shadows off her arms but still covering the gashes.

The king's fingers lightly grabbed her hands, twisting. Her right wrist displayed inactive Binding Runes. I grimaced. Then he twisted her other wrist. Ice crackled against the stone balcony, and my shadows snaked around my palm and pressed into my eyes.

"Put her on my desk. Now."

I rushed her over as the king threw everything to the ground.

"Release her from your shadows," he demanded.

That was easier said than done. My shadows enjoyed protecting her before, but now... Now, they didn't want to leave.

A fucking Reversal Rune.

"General Ronen! Your shadows!" Ice encased my boots, traveling to my knees.

I whipped my head up to the king and pulled at my defiant wisps, pulling harder than I should have to. They swarmed back to me, slamming into my core.

At the site of the female, the king's pupils vanished into white. "Go to my vault. You know the code. Get my feather." Icicles grew from the ceiling, and I knew he was using the rest of his control to keep them from erupting from the ground.

I luscelered there, grabbed it, and came back within seconds. The feather was pure white up until the very tip, unlike my ebony feather, which was stolen when they left me for dead. Heavenly feathers with the gift to give runes.

"Hold her down," he commanded. "Counteracting a Reversal Rune will hurt."

I placed my hands against her shoulders, and the king held her wrist steady. The moment the feather touched her skin, the female wrenched awake. With my shadows in her system, that shouldn't be possible, but between her extreme pain and power level, this situation was anything but normal.

She wailed and shoved against my hold, nothing but skin and bones thrashing with little strength.

I avoided her strange eyes and glanced at the king. I understood the fear and rage in his expression, but there was also a calculating look—one that threatened my shadows to come back out and attack the king I swore fealty to. I made sure to keep them locked away. He was saving her life, nothing else.

Her screams died down after he removed the Reversal, and she passed out.

But she lived.

The king called for a cot and a healer. She'd be sleeping near him tonight. I didn't like that either.

Fuck. This female was already messing with my head.

My question burned through me once more. It wasn't my place, but I no longer cared after all this.

"Sir, who is she?"

The king sank into his cushy chair, eyeing his work and all the wounds slowly mending themselves on her skin. She'd still need stitches. My shadows surged, eager to seep through my skin and mend her wounds, yet I hesitated, bound by his command. His fear of my shadows was shared by all and with good reason.

He nodded to the female. "Put pressure on her wounds until the healers come, general."

My shadows burst forth, startling me with their force. They immediately covered every injury, both absorbing her delicious blood and keeping it inside.

The immortal king, perpetually appearing no older than thirty-five, now appeared as though he had aged a thousand years—his actual age catching up with him.

"I believe she's my offspring, general. My—" he paused, like he was tasting the word. "Daughter."

I don't think I had enough curse words in the book for what he just said. "Your daughter?"

"Yes."

"The test?" I asked, stunned. Now I understood what those words meant.

"She jumped into the Corruptible River and survived."

Of course. Only the offspring of Hell could survive that river. And Seraphims, but they were too powerful to leave their sanctuary in the clouds.

I stared at the unconscious female in the cot.

The Princess of Hell was my cordistella.

The king could never know.

CONTENT WARNINGS

-Sexual Violence

-Graphic Violence/Gore

-Verbal Abuse

-Child Abuse

-Physical Abuse

-Swearing

-Explicit Sexual Situations

ACKNOWLEDGEMENTS

First and foremost, I want to express my deepest gratitude to all my readers. Your choice to pick up my book and invest your time in Lucille's story means the world to me.

This story began as something entirely different when I first dreamed of writing it at nineteen. Reflecting on the early drafts, with ideas that were abandoned, characters that were removed, and scenes that were cut, I'm proud of how it has evolved into what it is today.

Over the years, I worked on it intermittently, but it wasn't until recent years that I committed myself to becoming an author and pursuing writing as a career. Through countless hours of effort, research, and dedication, this book has become something I'm truly proud of. Your support in picking up this book is helping me achieve my dreams.

Second, to my fiancé for believing in my dream and supporting me throughout this journey. You've been incredibly accommodating with my long writing hours during our busy life, and your reminders to eat and take breaks when I push myself too hard mean so much to me. I love your unwavering faith, especially when imposter syndrome kicks in and I second guess everything I'm doing. You are my best friend, and I couldn't have done this without you.

Third, to my hardworking parents, thank you for instilling in me the drive to work tirelessly on this story. Balancing life, a full-time job, and working on my book from morning till night on weekends has been a relentless journey. Your dedication and work ethic have been a profound inspiration, and I'm grateful for the qualities you've passed down to me.

Lastly, to all the amazing people I've met along this journey who have helped me and who I've built relationships with. I don't think I would've ended up where I am without you. It all started when I joined a writing critique group called New Authors Unite. I have met so many wonderful individuals who have been incredible sounding boards and sources of support. I remember being nervous about joining the group, but I'm immensely grateful that I did. Thank you to each and every one of you for being a part of this journey!

About the Author

Makayla Sagami grew up in a little town near Madison, Wisconsin, reading Twilight, City of Bones, Vampire Academy, and many other fantasy romance novels. She graduated college with an art and elementary education degree, which she enjoyed but not as much as storytelling. When not writing, she's most likely reading, spending time with her family and friends, or finding a new restaurant to try with her fiancé. Wings of Lies is her first fantasy romance novel. Find out more by following her on Instagram at M.S.Quinn or scanning the QR code below to join her newsletter.

https://website.beacons.ai/authorm.s.quinn

Printed in the USA
CPSIA information can be obtained
at www.ICGtesting.com
LVHW090558150924
791034LV00001B/11